PI NG!

At last, the evil syndicate Team Galactic arrives on the scene! Did something happen in the past between Mitsumi and Team Galactic?! And now the Pokémon battles are even more intense. Let's all fight alongside Hareta and the others! I'll fight too!

– *Shigekatsu Ihara*

Shigekatsu Ihara's other manga titles include *Pokémon: Lucario and the Mystery of Mew*, *Pokémon Emerald Challenge!! Battle Frontier*, and *Dual Jack!!*.

Vol. 2
VIZ Kids Edition

Story & Art by SHIGEKATSU IHARA

Translation/Kaori Inoue
Touch-up Art & Lettering/Rina Mapa
Graphics & Cover Design/Hitomi Yokoyama Ross
Editor/Leyla Aker

Editor in Chief, Books/Alvin Lu
Editor in Chief, Magazines/Marc Weidenbaum
VP, Publishing Licensing/Rika Inouye
VP, Sales & Product Marketing/Gonzalo Ferreyra
VP, Creative/Linda Espinosa
Publisher/Hyoe Narita

ⓒ 2008 Pokémon.
ⓒ 1995-2008 Nintendo/Creatures Inc./GAME FREAK inc.
TM & ® are trademarks of Nintendo.
Pokémon D•P POCKET MONSTER DIAMOND PEARL MONOGATARI
ⓒ 2007 Shigekatsu IHARA
All rights reserved.
Original Japanese edition published in 2007 by Shogakukan Inc., Tokyo.

Printed in the U.S.A.

Published by VIZ Media, LLC
P.O. Box 77064
San Francisco, CA 94107

VIZ Kids Edition
10 9 8 7 6 5 4 3
First printing, September 2008
Third printing, November 2008

store.viz.com

VIZ
MEDIA
www.viz.com

PARENTAL ADVISORY
POKÉMON DIAMOND AND PEARL
ADVENTURE! is rated A and is
suitable for readers of all ages.
ratings.viz.com

RATED
Ⓐ FOR
ALL AGES

POKÉMON®

DIAMOND AND PEARL ADVENTURE!

Volume 2

Story & Art by
Shigekatsu Ihara

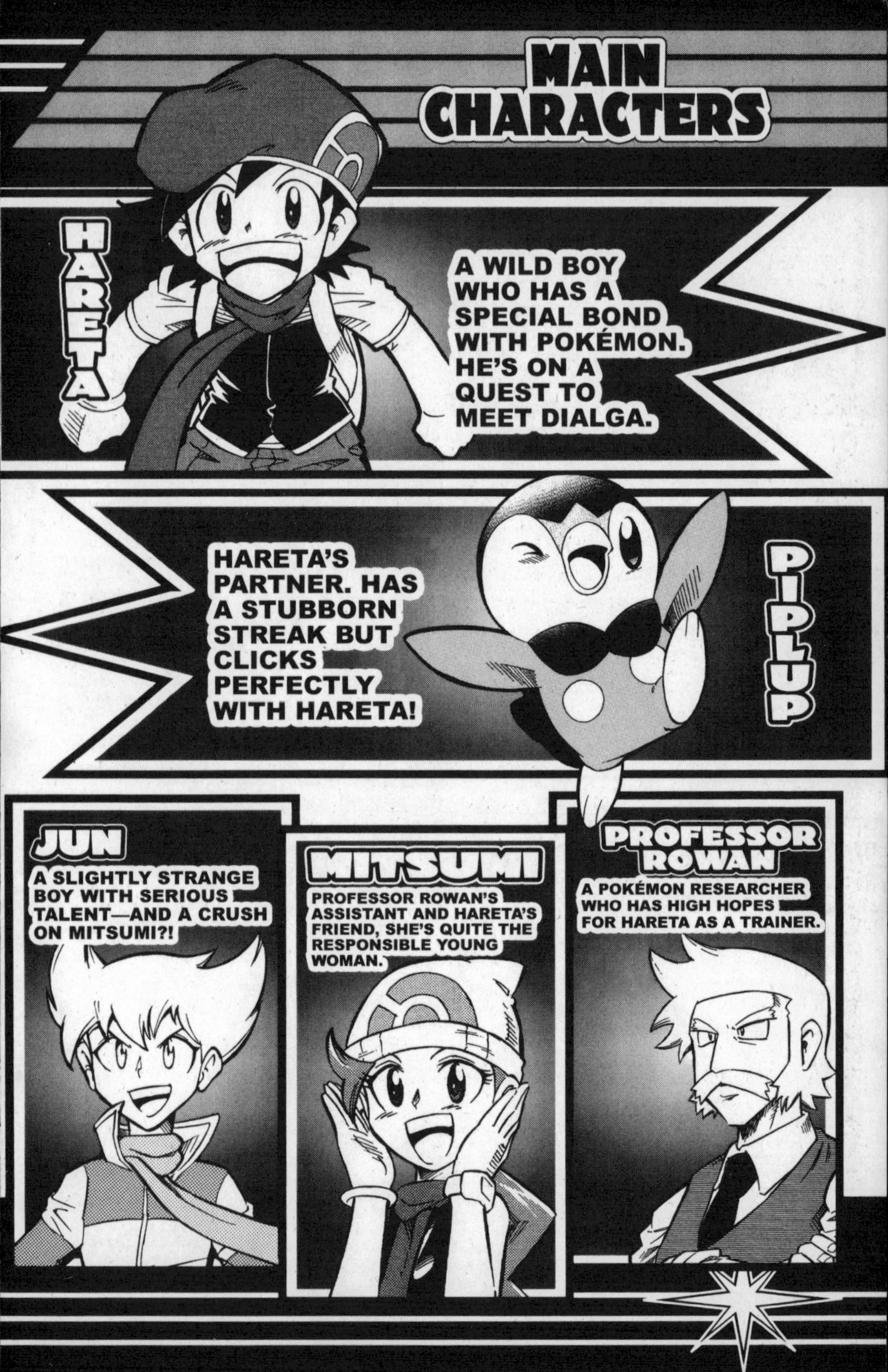
MAIN CHARACTERS
HARETA
A WILD BOY WHO HAS A SPECIAL BOND WITH POKÉMON. HE'S ON A QUEST TO MEET DIALGA.
PIPLUP
HARETA'S PARTNER. HAS A STUBBORN STREAK BUT CLICKS PERFECTLY WITH HARETA!
PROFESSOR ROWAN
A POKÉMON RESEARCHER WHO HAS HIGH HOPES FOR HARETA AS A TRAINER.
MITSUMI
PROFESSOR ROWAN'S ASSISTANT AND HARETA'S FRIEND, SHE'S QUITE THE RESPONSIBLE YOUNG WOMAN.
JUN
A SLIGHTLY STRANGE BOY WITH SERIOUS TALENT—AND A CRUSH ON MITSUMI?!

TEAM GALACTIC

AN EVIL ORGANIZATION THAT SEEKS TO EXPLOIT POKÉMON.

◀ JUPITER

▼ SATURN

CYRUS

A MAN WITH AN UNKNOWN PAST, HE SAYS HE'S MITSUMI'S FRIEND, BUT...

RILEY

A MYSTERIOUS YOUNG MAN WITH A LUCARIO.

BYRON

GYM LEADER OF CANALAVE CITY. DRIVES HIS TRAINERS VERY HARD.

THE STORY SO FAR

After Professor Rowan sees Hareta's innate ability to connect on a heart-to-heart level with Pokémon, he sends Hareta off with Mitsumi on a quest to find Dialga, the Pokémon that rules time. On their journey, Hareta and his partner Piplup become stronger every day—while ruining Team Galactic's schemes and getting into plenty of Pokémon battles on the way!!

CONTENTS

Chapter 1 Beauty Contest:

The Pokémon Super Contest!! 6

Chapter 2 Dialga's Secret Keys 43

Chapter 3 Team Galactic's Conspiracy, Revealed!! 79

Chapter 4 Challenge! The Fortress of Steel!! 116

Chapter 5 Serious Training on Iron Island!! 150

D·P Snapshots 185

CHAPTER 1

BEAUTY CONTEST:

THE POKÉMON SUPER CONTEST!!

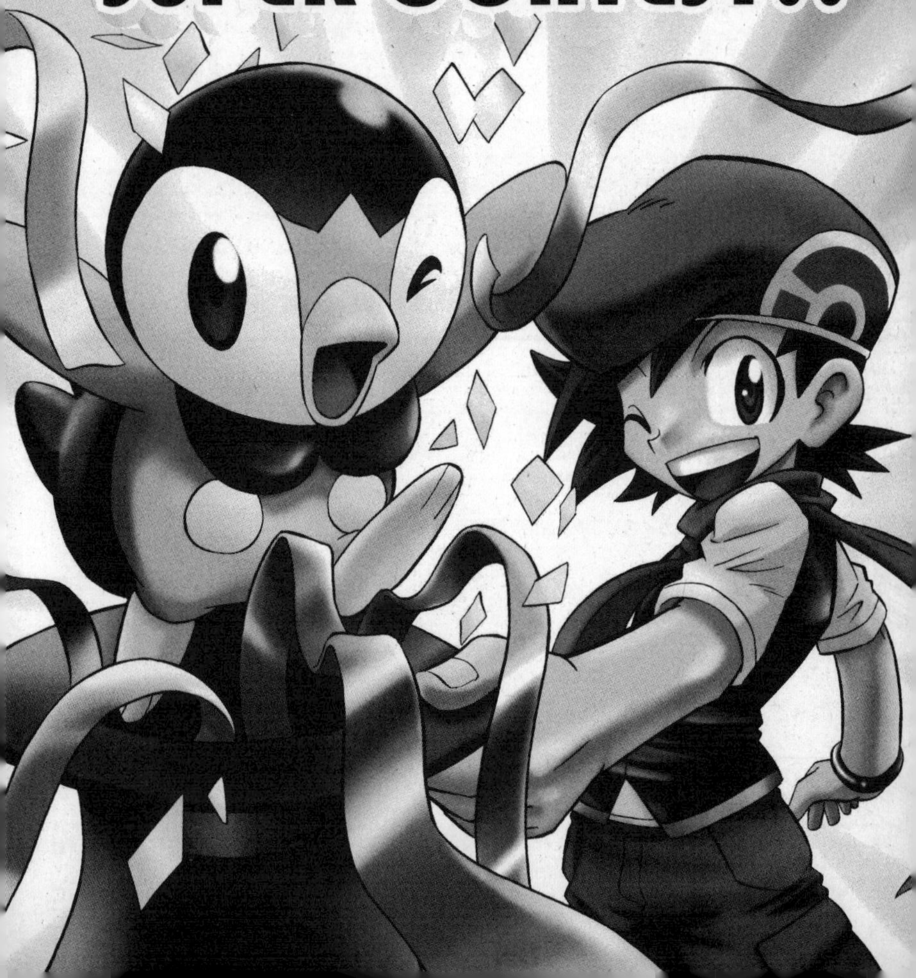

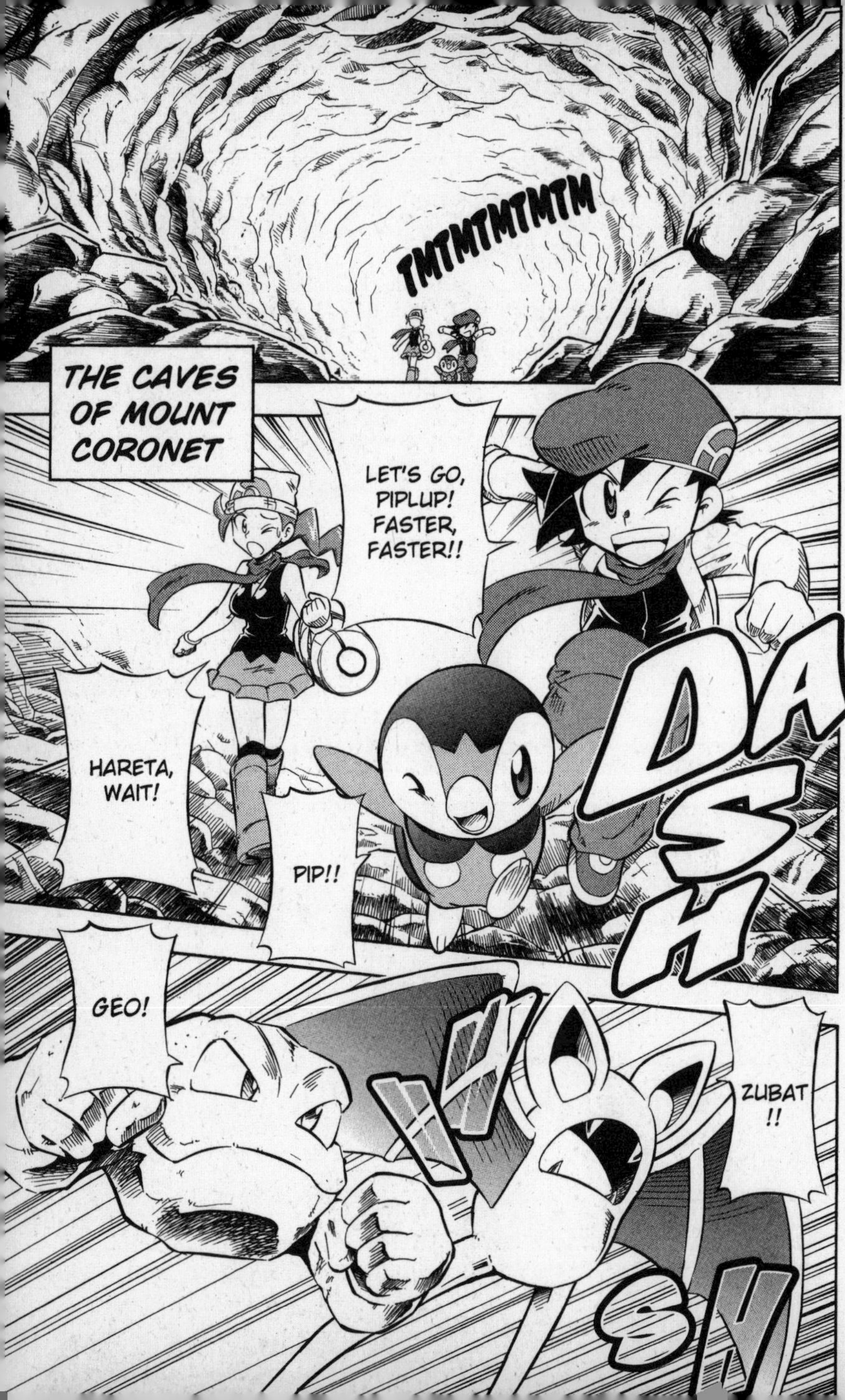

TMTMTMTMTM
THE CAVES OF MOUNT CORONET
LET'S GO, PIPLUP! FASTER, FASTER!!
DASH
HARETA, WAIT!
PIP!!
ZUBAT !!
GEO!

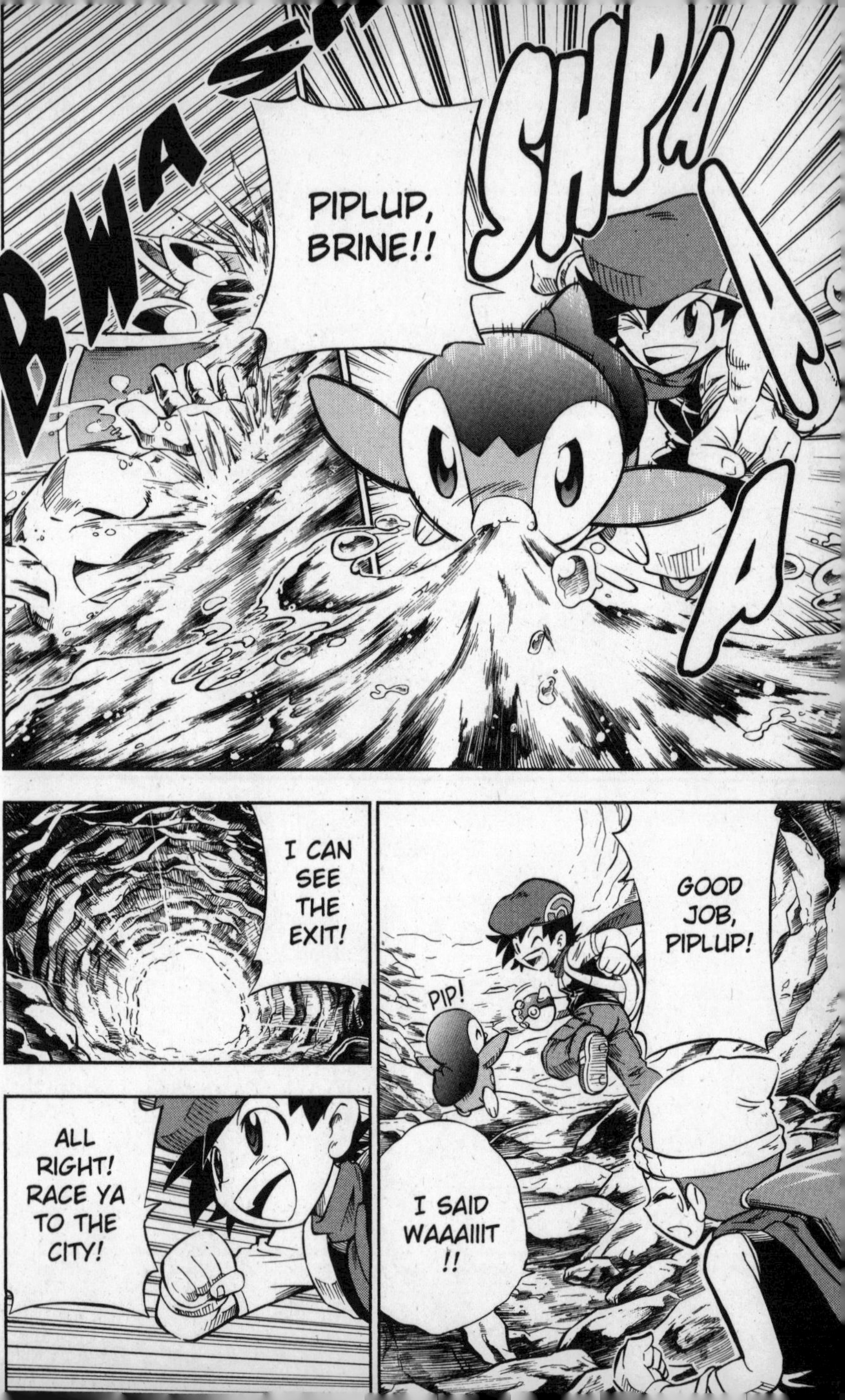
CHPA
PIPLUP, BRINE!!
BWA
GOOD JOB, PIPLUP!
PIP!
I SAID WAAAIIIT!!
I CAN SEE THE EXIT!
ALL RIGHT! RACE YA TO THE CITY!

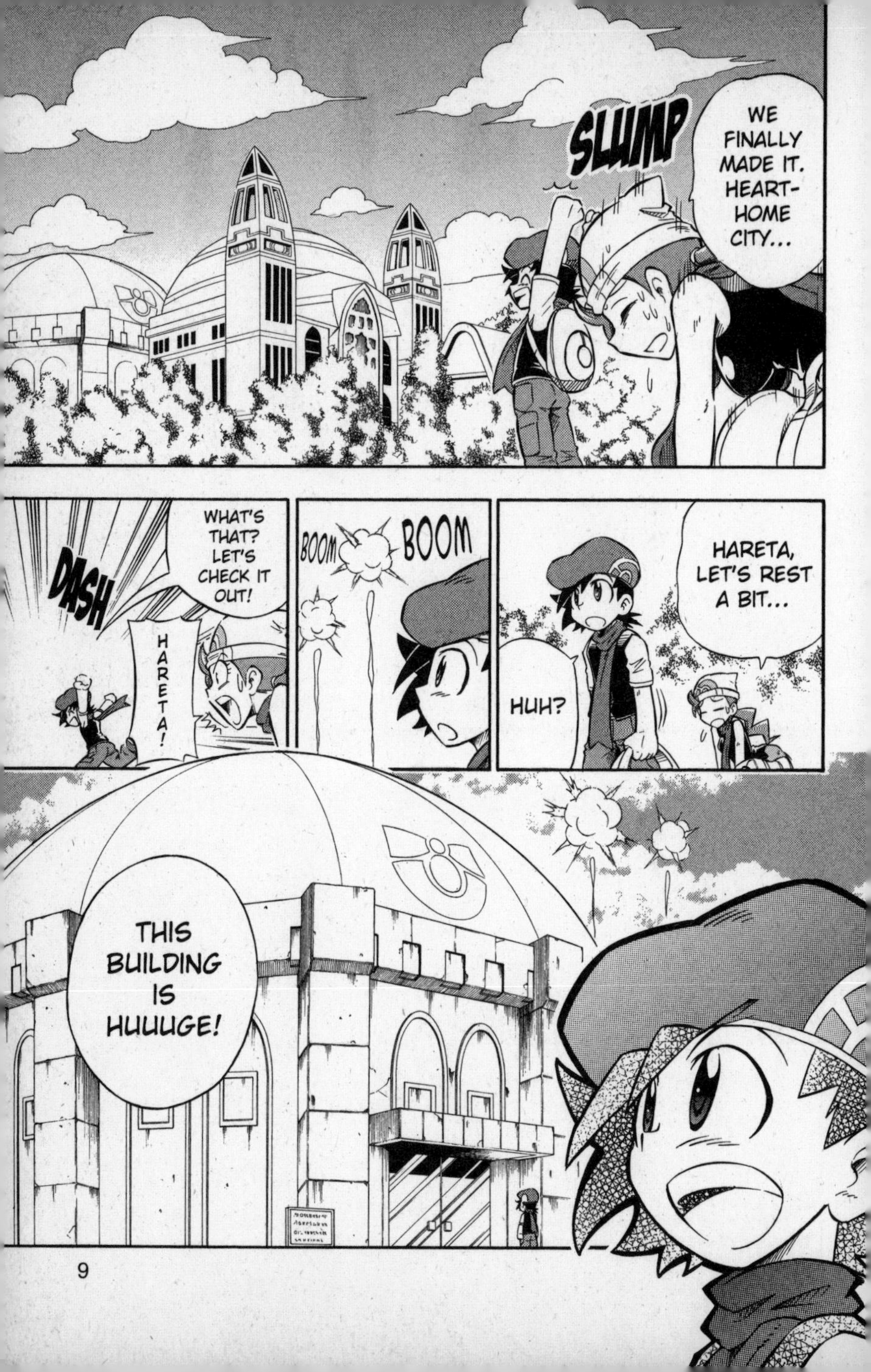
SLUMP
WE FINALLY MADE IT. HEART-HOME CITY...
HARETA, LET'S REST A BIT...
HUH?
BOOM BOOM
WHAT'S THAT? LET'S CHECK IT OUT!
DASH
HARETA!
THIS BUILDING IS HUUUGE!

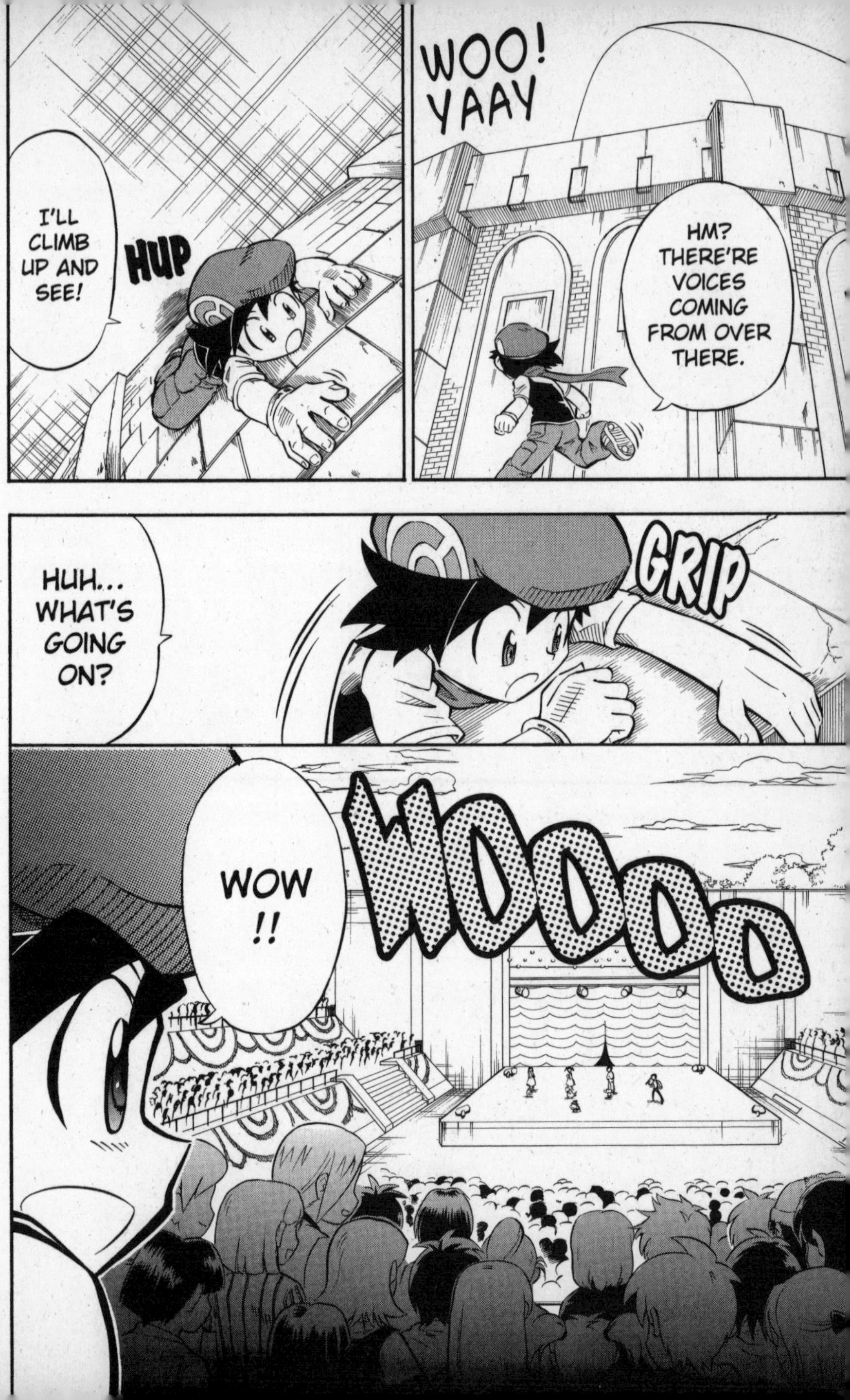
WOO! YAAY
HM? THERE'RE VOICES COMING FROM OVER THERE.
I'LL CLIMB UP AND SEE!
HUP
GRIP
HUH... WHAT'S GOING ON?
WOW !!
WOOOO

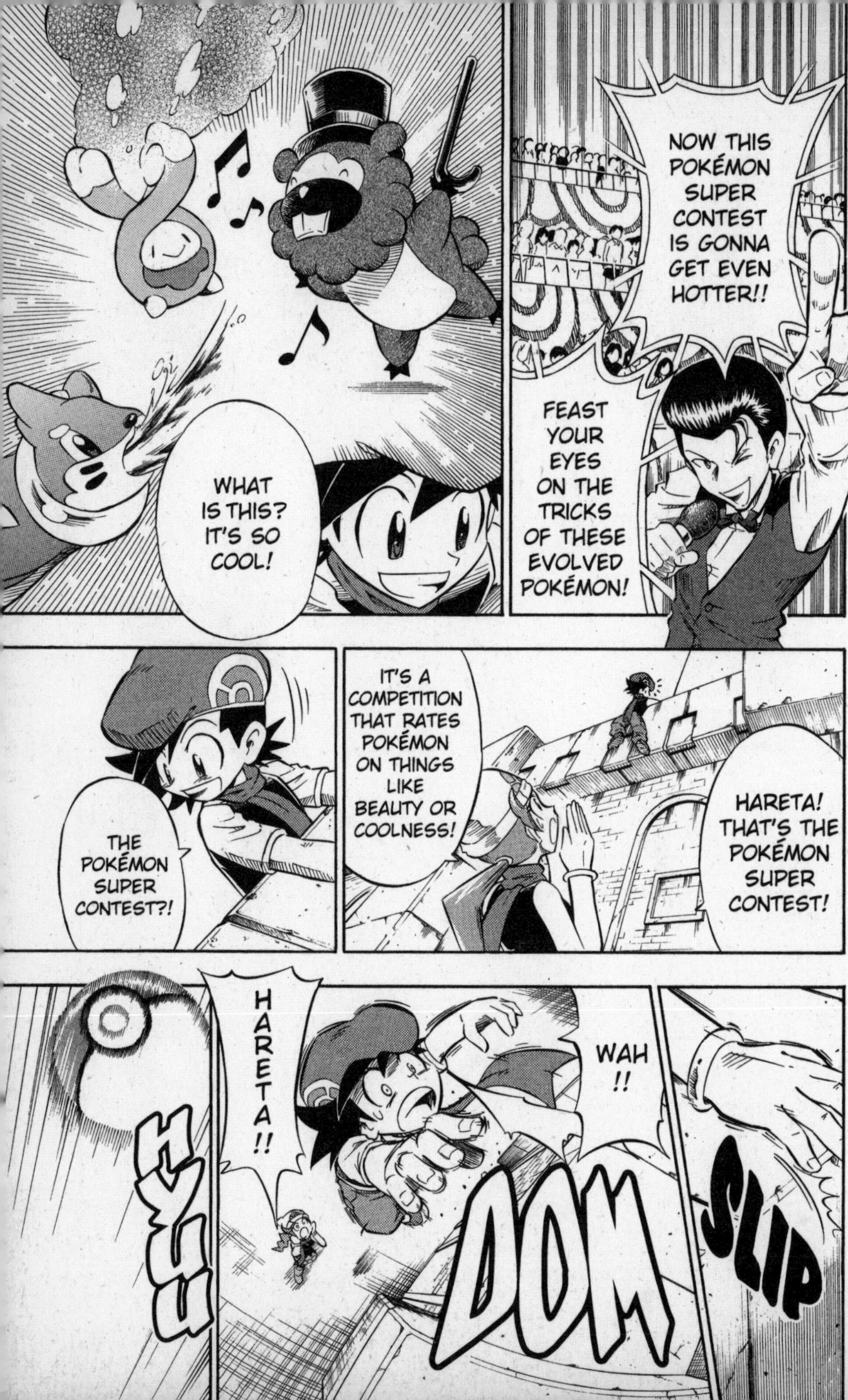
NOW THIS POKÉMON SUPER CONTEST IS GONNA GET EVEN HOTTER!!
FEAST YOUR EYES ON THE TRICKS OF THESE EVOLVED POKÉMON!
WHAT IS THIS? IT'S SO COOL!
HARETA! THAT'S THE POKÉMON SUPER CONTEST!
IT'S A COMPETITION THAT RATES POKÉMON ON THINGS LIKE BEAUTY OR COOLNESS!
THE POKÉMON SUPER CONTEST?!
SLIP
WAH!!
DOM
HARETA!!
HYUU

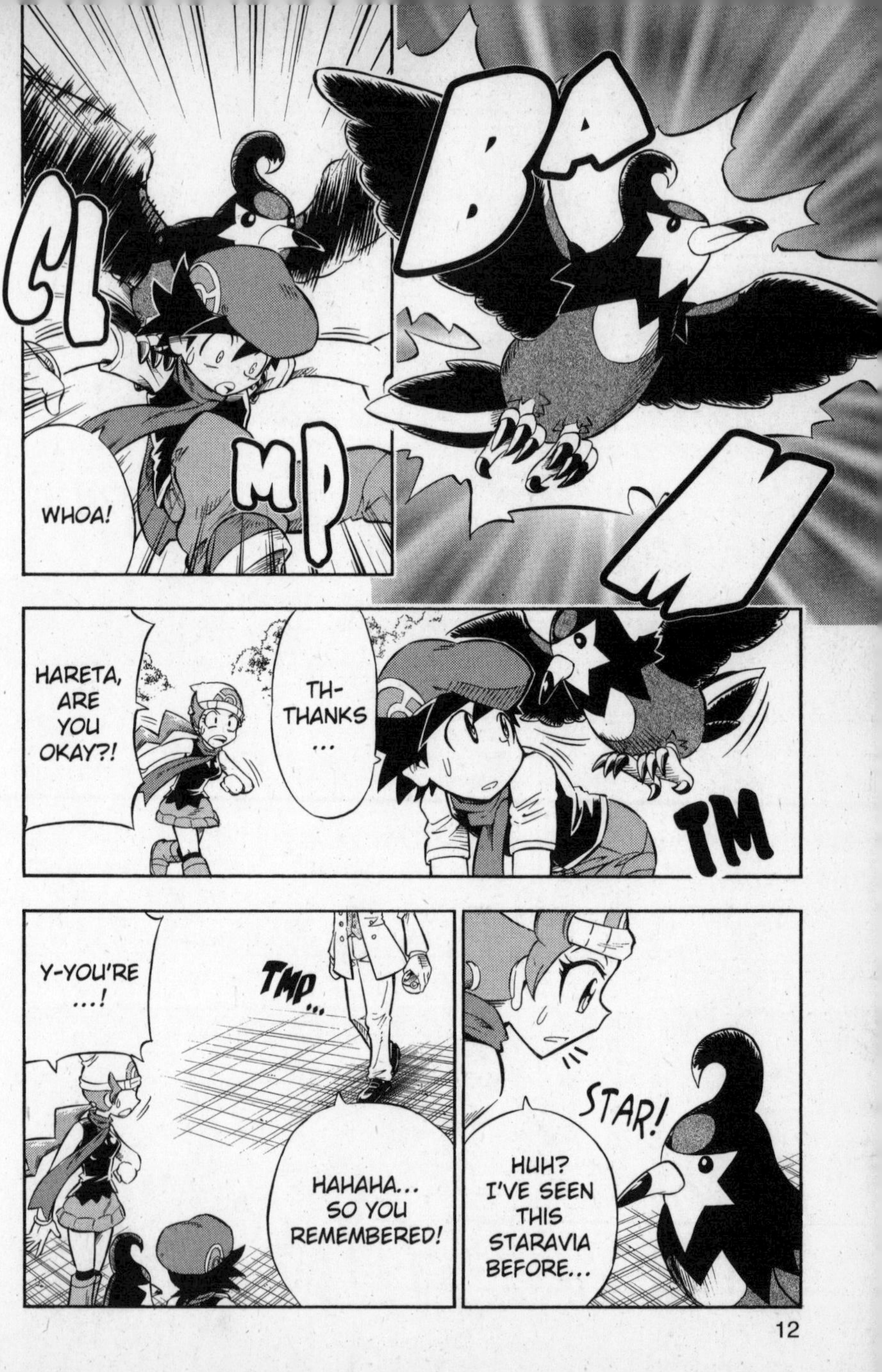
BAM
CLMP
WHOA!
TH-THANKS...
HARETA, ARE YOU OKAY?!
TM
STAR!
HUH? I'VE SEEN THIS STARAVIA BEFORE...
TMP...
Y-YOU'RE ...!
HAHAHA... SO YOU REMEMBERED!

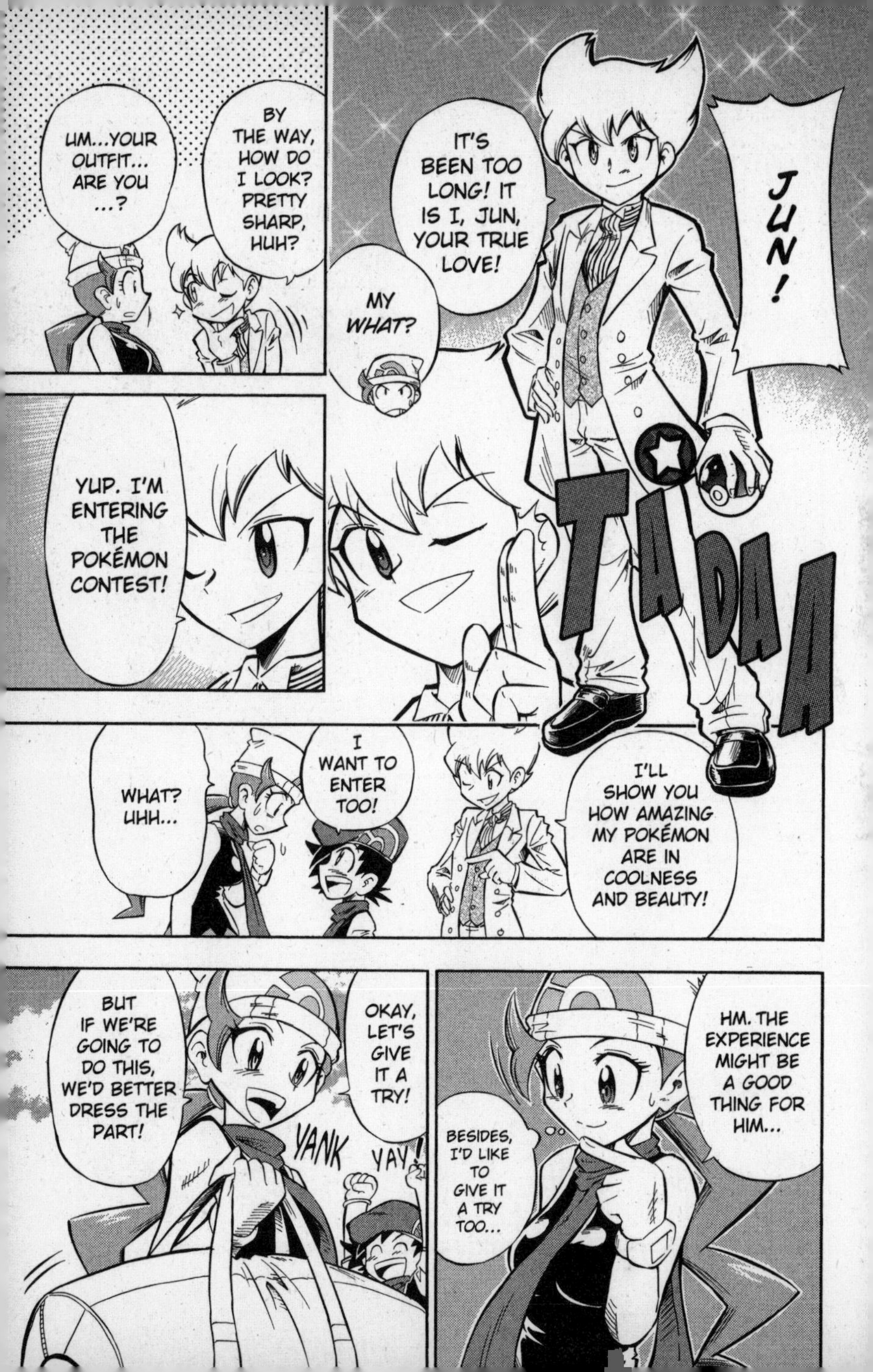
JUN!
IT'S BEEN TOO LONG! IT IS I, JUN, YOUR TRUE LOVE!
MY WHAT?
TA DA A
BY THE WAY, HOW DO I LOOK? PRETTY SHARP, HUH?
UM...YOUR OUTFIT... ARE YOU ...?
YUP. I'M ENTERING THE POKÉMON CONTEST!
I'LL SHOW YOU HOW AMAZING MY POKÉMON ARE IN COOLNESS AND BEAUTY!
I WANT TO ENTER TOO!
WHAT? UHH...
HM. THE EXPERIENCE MIGHT BE A GOOD THING FOR HIM...
BESIDES, I'D LIKE TO GIVE IT A TRY TOO...
OKAY, LET'S GIVE IT A TRY!
BUT IF WE'RE GOING TO DO THIS, WE'D BETTER DRESS THE PART!
YANK
YAY!

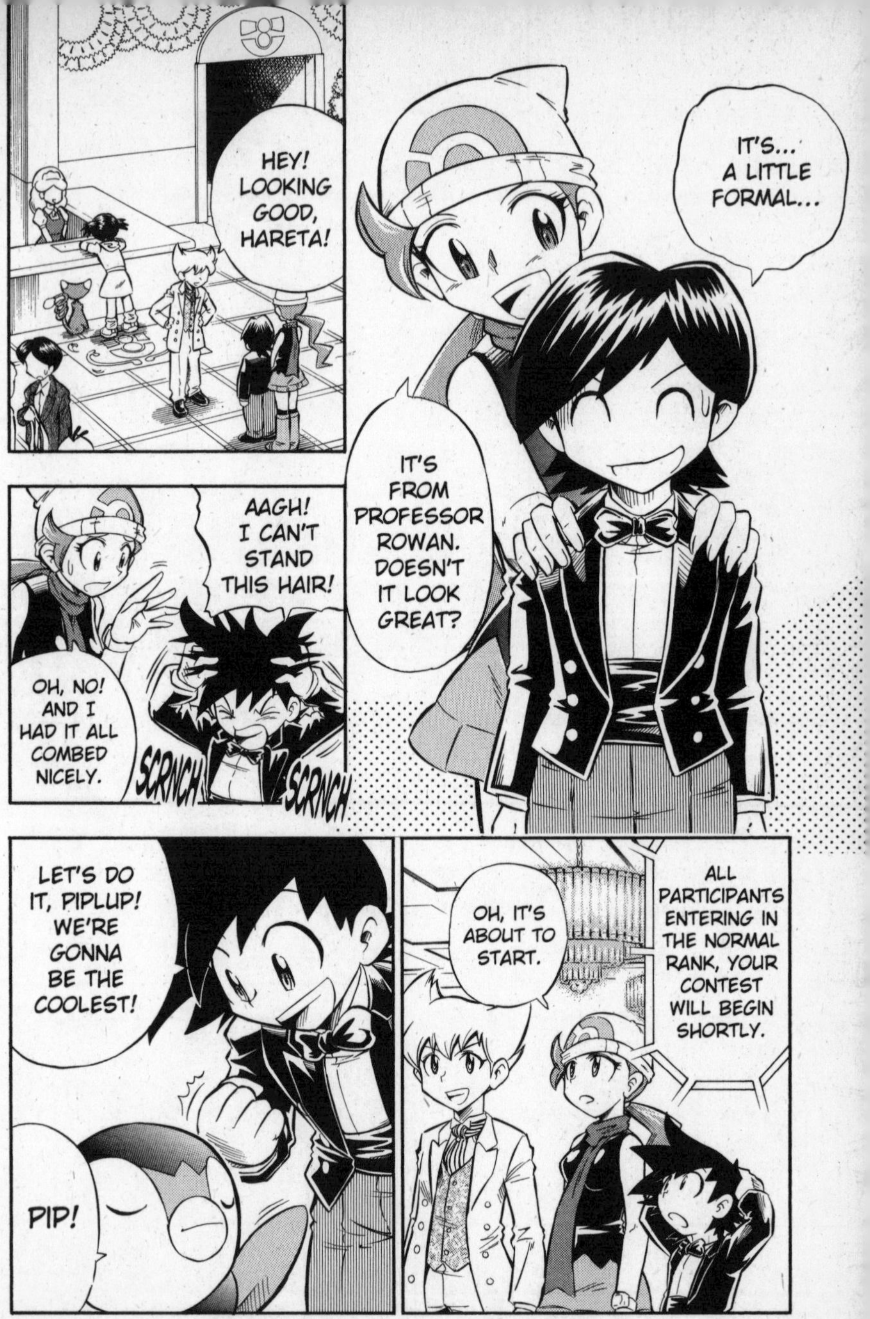
IT'S... A LITTLE FORMAL...
IT'S FROM PROFESSOR ROWAN. DOESN'T IT LOOK GREAT?
HEY! LOOKING GOOD, HARETA!
AAGH! I CAN'T STAND THIS HAIR!
OH, NO! AND I HAD IT ALL COMBED NICELY.
SCRNCH
SCRNCH
ALL PARTICIPANTS ENTERING IN THE NORMAL RANK, YOUR CONTEST WILL BEGIN SHORTLY.
OH, IT'S ABOUT TO START.
LET'S DO IT, PIPLUP! WE'RE GONNA BE THE COOLEST!
PIP!

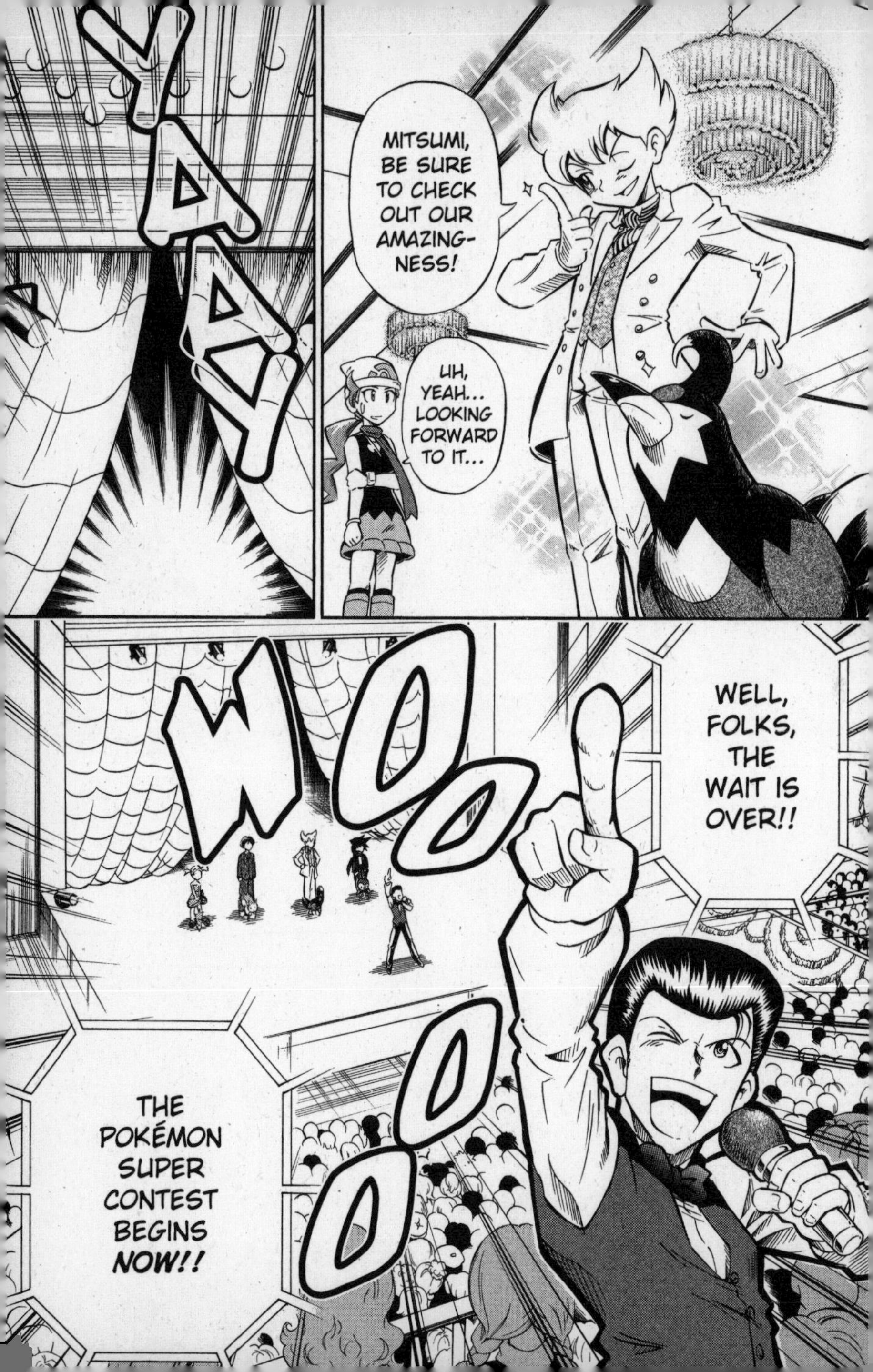
MITSUMI, BE SURE TO CHECK OUT OUR AMAZING-NESS!
UH, YEAH... LOOKING FORWARD TO IT...
YAAY
WELL, FOLKS, THE WAIT IS OVER!!
THE POKÉMON SUPER CONTEST BEGINS NOW!!
WOOOOO

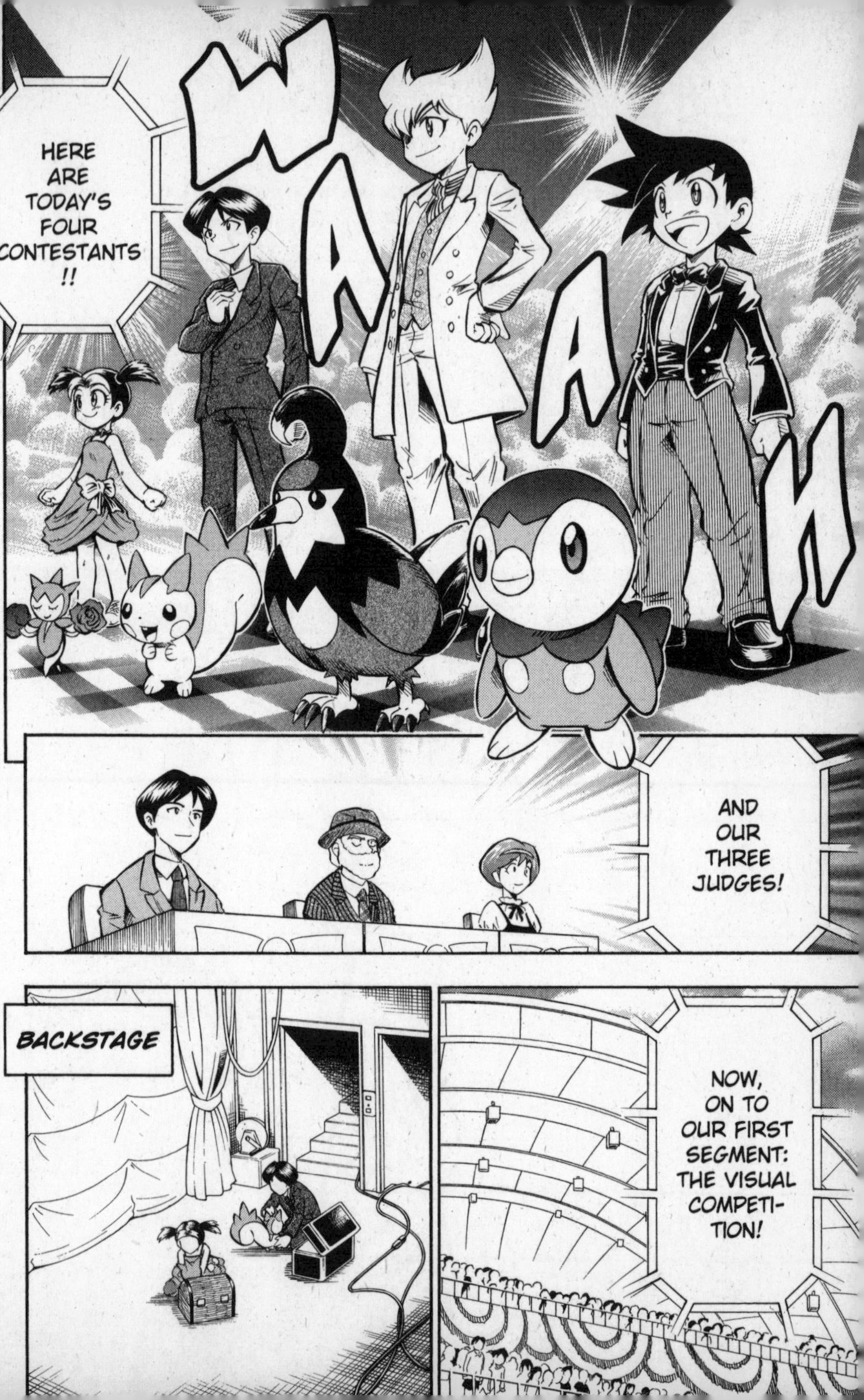
WAAH
HERE ARE TODAY'S FOUR CONTESTANTS!!
AND OUR THREE JUDGES!
NOW, ON TO OUR FIRST SEGMENT: THE VISUAL COMPETITION!
BACKSTAGE

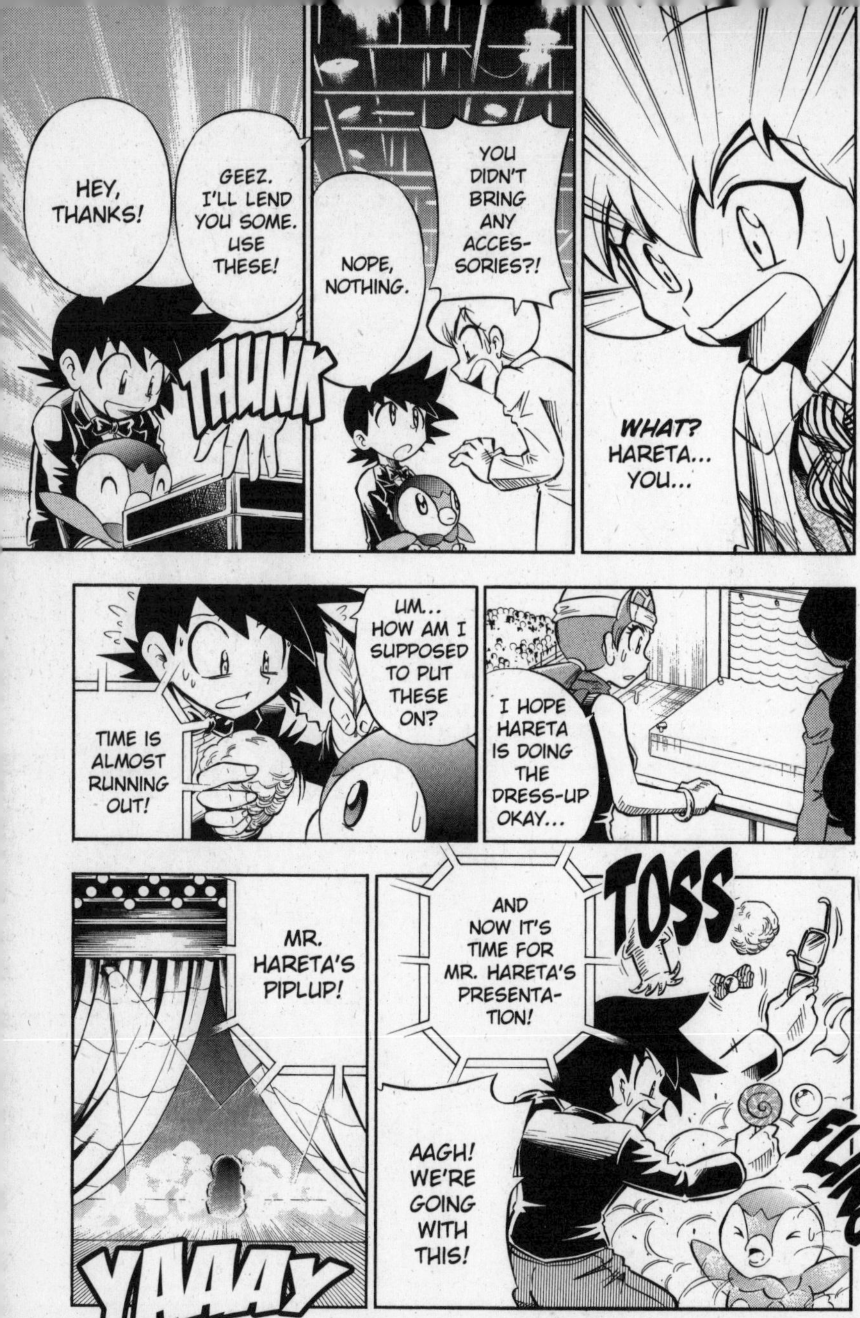
WHAT? HARETA... YOU...
YOU DIDN'T BRING ANY ACCES-SORIES?!
NOPE, NOTHING.
GEEZ. I'LL LEND YOU SOME. USE THESE!
HEY, THANKS!
THUNK
I HOPE HARETA IS DOING THE DRESS-UP OKAY...
UM... HOW AM I SUPPOSED TO PUT THESE ON?
TIME IS ALMOST RUNNING OUT!
TOSS
AND NOW IT'S TIME FOR MR. HARETA'S PRESENTA-TION!
FLING
AAGH! WE'RE GOING WITH THIS!
MR. HARETA'S PIPLUP!
YAAAY

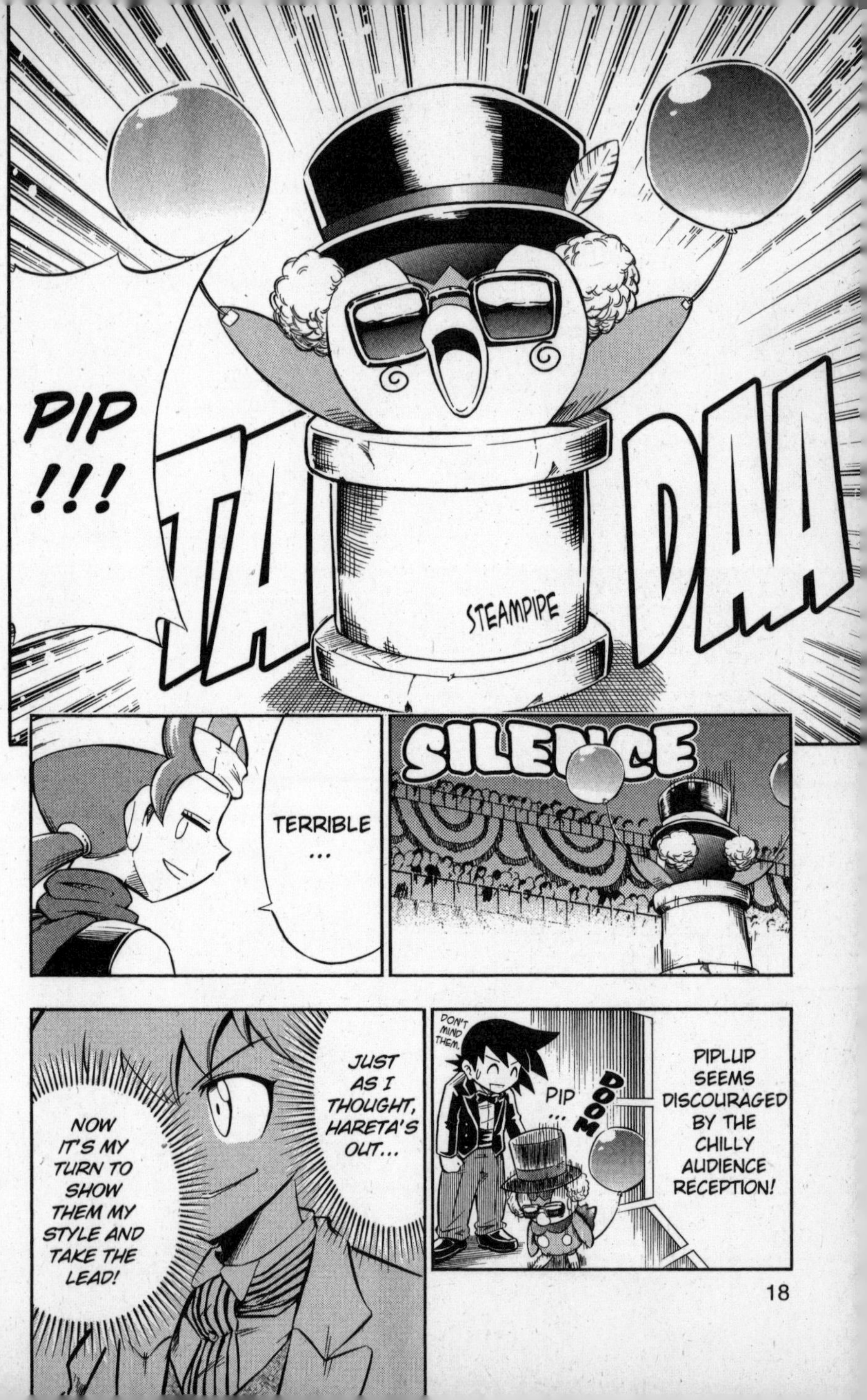
TA DAA
PIP !!!
STEAMPIPE
SILENCE
TERRIBLE ...
PIPLUP SEEMS DISCOURAGED BY THE CHILLY AUDIENCE RECEPTION!
DON'T MIND THEM.
PIP ...
DOOM
JUST AS I THOUGHT, HARETA'S OUT...
NOW IT'S MY TURN TO SHOW THEM MY STYLE AND TAKE THE LEAD!

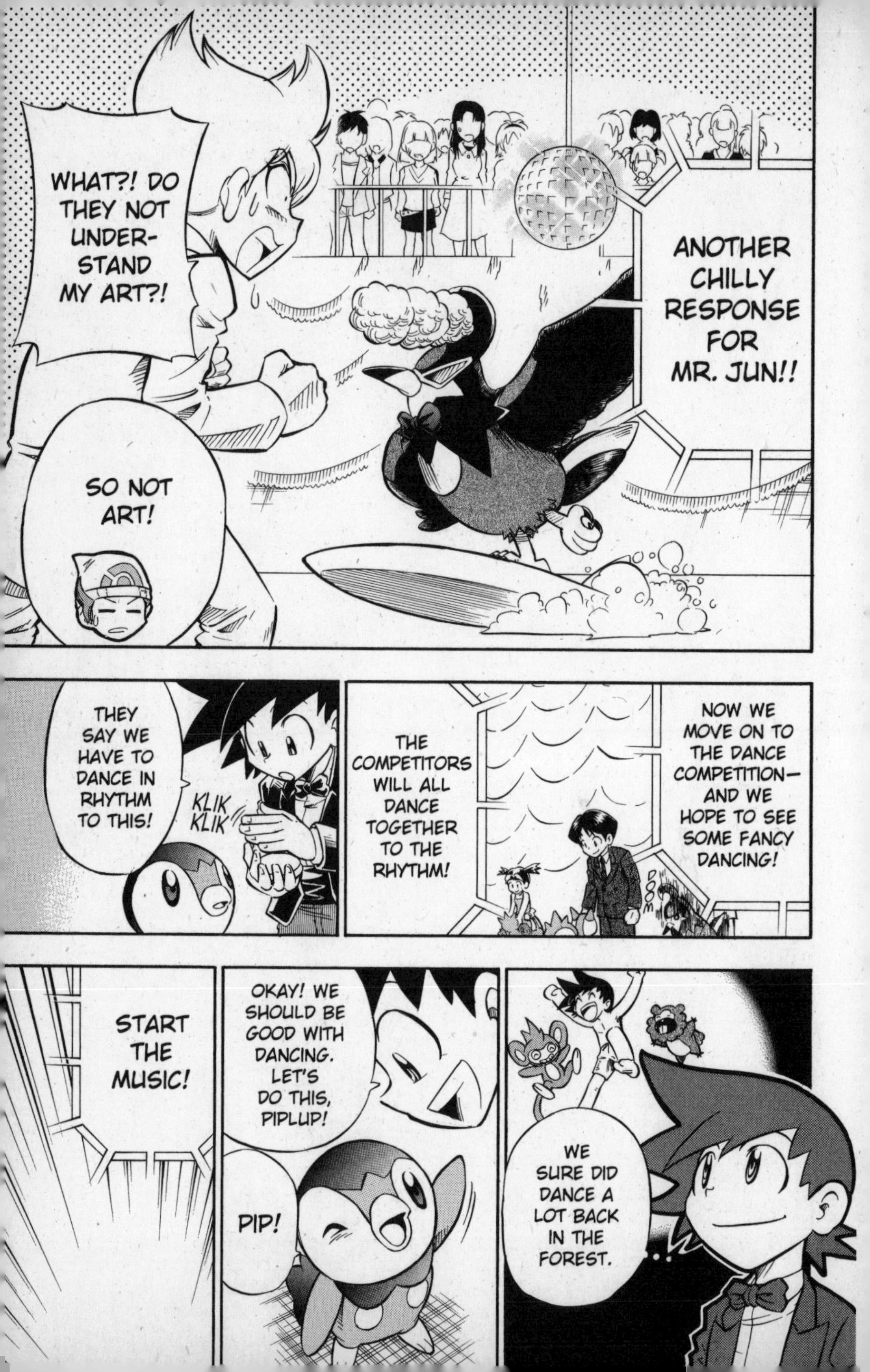
ANOTHER CHILLY RESPONSE FOR MR. JUN!!
WHAT?! DO THEY NOT UNDER-STAND MY ART?!
SO NOT ART!
NOW WE MOVE ON TO THE DANCE COMPETITION— AND WE HOPE TO SEE SOME FANCY DANCING!
THE COMPETITORS WILL ALL DANCE TOGETHER TO THE RHYTHM!
DOOM
THEY SAY WE HAVE TO DANCE IN RHYTHM TO THIS!
KLIK KLIK
WE SURE DID DANCE A LOT BACK IN THE FOREST.
...
OKAY! WE SHOULD BE GOOD WITH DANCING. LET'S DO THIS, PIPLUP!
PIP!
START THE MUSIC!

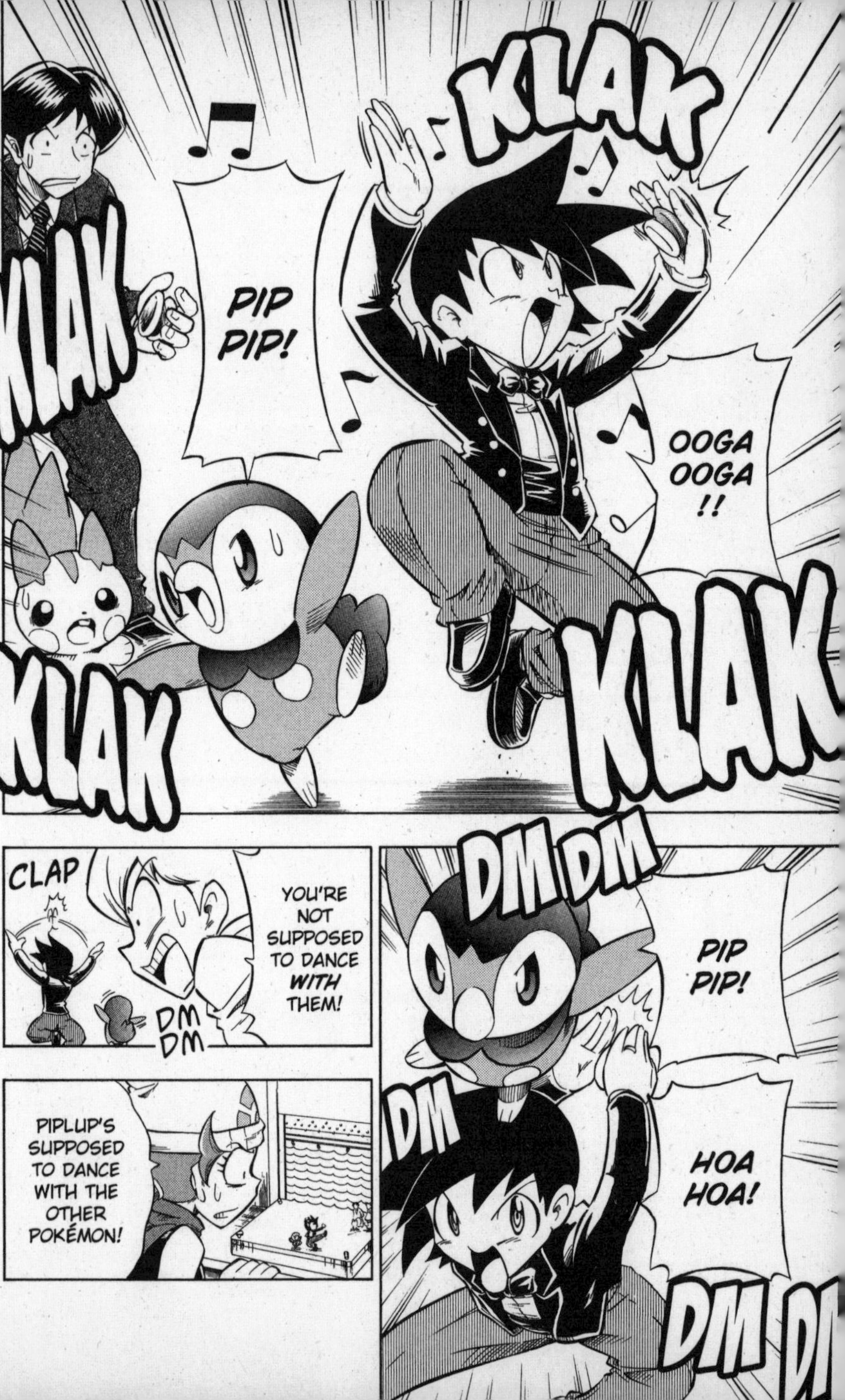
KLAK
OOGA OOGA !!
PIP PIP!
KLAK
KLAK
KLAK
DM DM
PIP PIP!
DM
HOA HOA!
DM DM
CLAP
YOU'RE NOT SUPPOSED TO DANCE WITH THEM!
DM DM
PIPLUP'S SUPPOSED TO DANCE WITH THE OTHER POKÉMON!

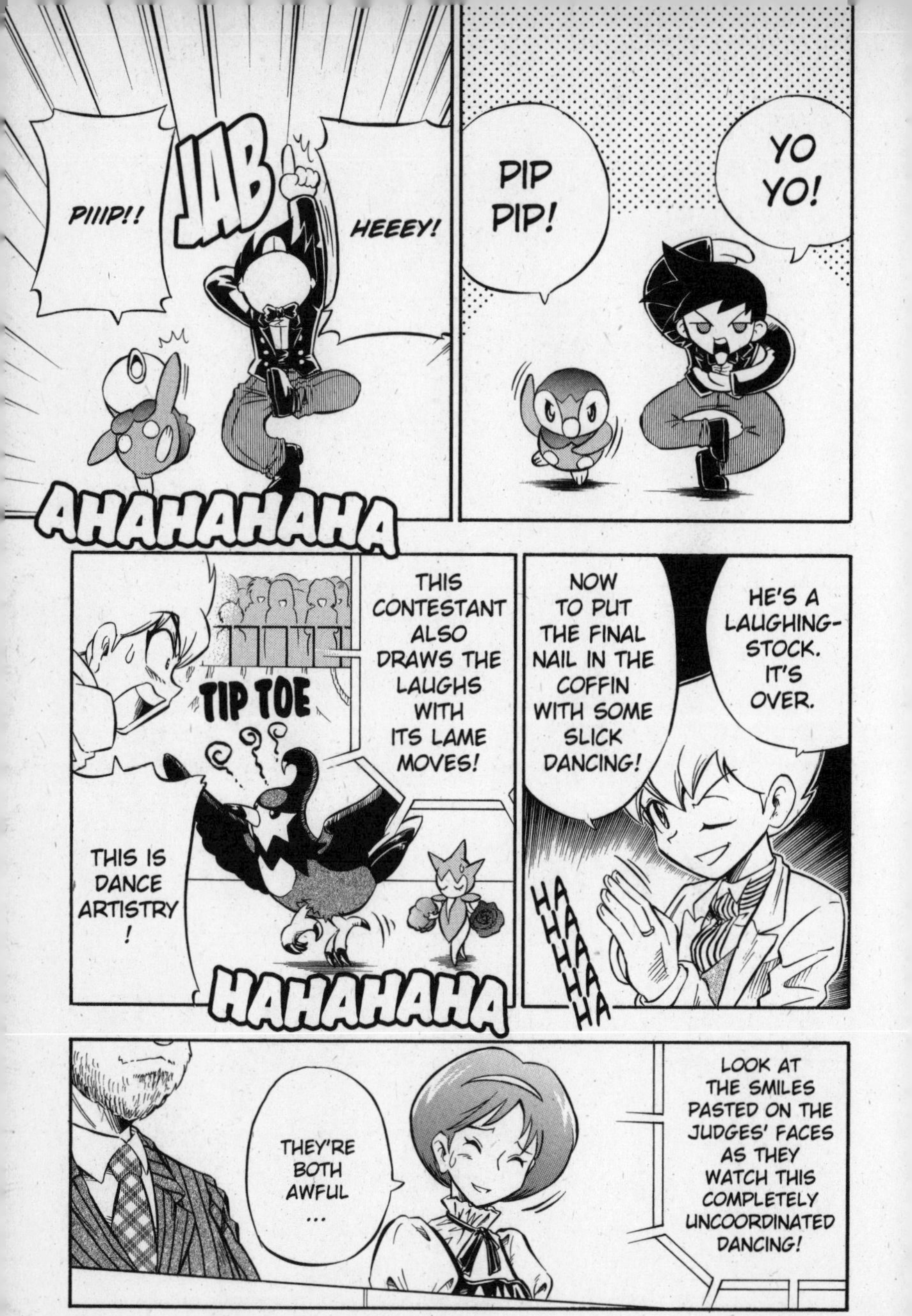
YO YO!
PIP PIP!
HEEEY!
JAB
PIIIP!!
AHAHAHAHA
HE'S A LAUGHING-STOCK. IT'S OVER.
NOW TO PUT THE FINAL NAIL IN THE COFFIN WITH SOME SLICK DANCING!
THIS CONTESTANT ALSO DRAWS THE LAUGHS WITH ITS LAME MOVES!
TIP TOE
THIS IS DANCE ARTISTRY!
HAHAHAHA
LOOK AT THE SMILES PASTED ON THE JUDGES' FACES AS THEY WATCH THIS COMPLETELY UNCOORDINATED DANCING!
THEY'RE BOTH AWFUL...

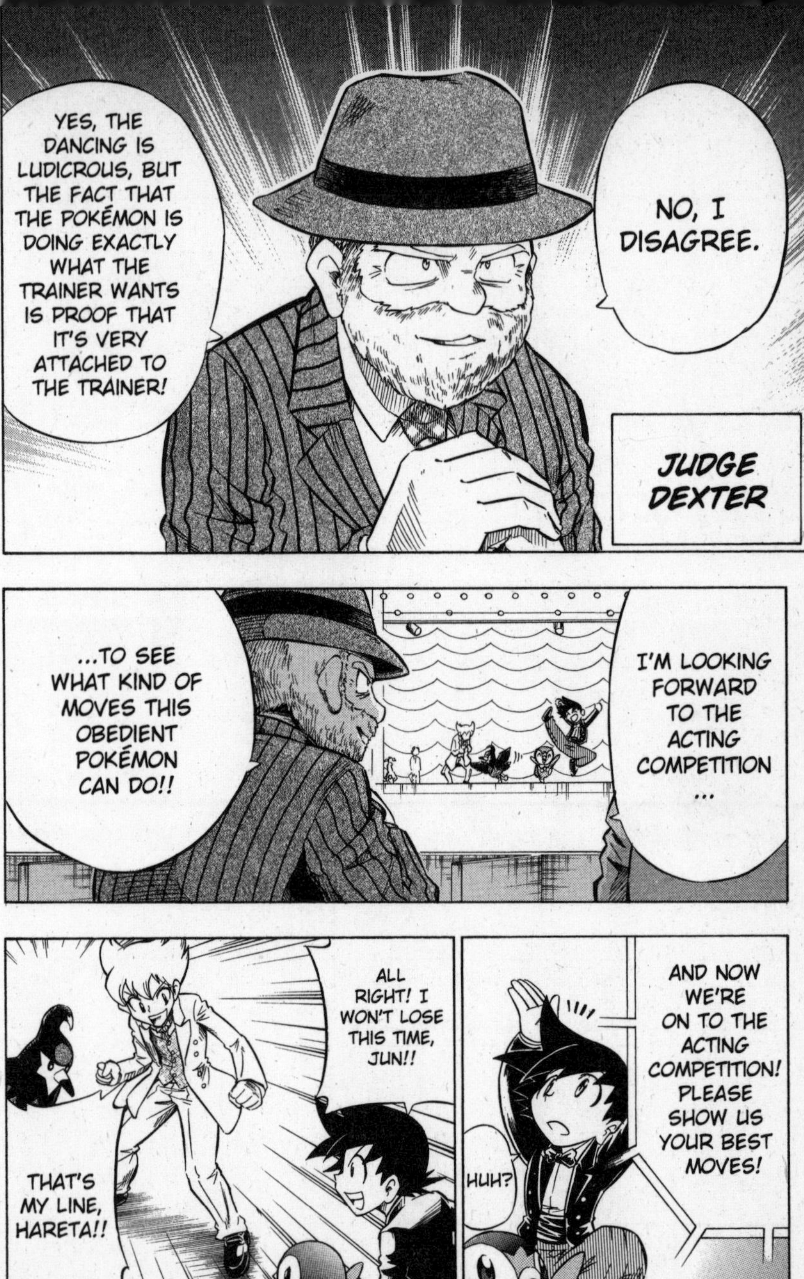
NO, I DISAGREE.
YES, THE DANCING IS LUDICROUS, BUT THE FACT THAT THE POKÉMON IS DOING EXACTLY WHAT THE TRAINER WANTS IS PROOF THAT IT'S VERY ATTACHED TO THE TRAINER!
JUDGE DEXTER
I'M LOOKING FORWARD TO THE ACTING COMPETITION ...
...TO SEE WHAT KIND OF MOVES THIS OBEDIENT POKÉMON CAN DO!!
AND NOW WE'RE ON TO THE ACTING COMPETITION! PLEASE SHOW US YOUR BEST MOVES!
HUH?
ALL RIGHT! I WON'T LOSE THIS TIME, JUN!!
THAT'S MY LINE, HARETA!!

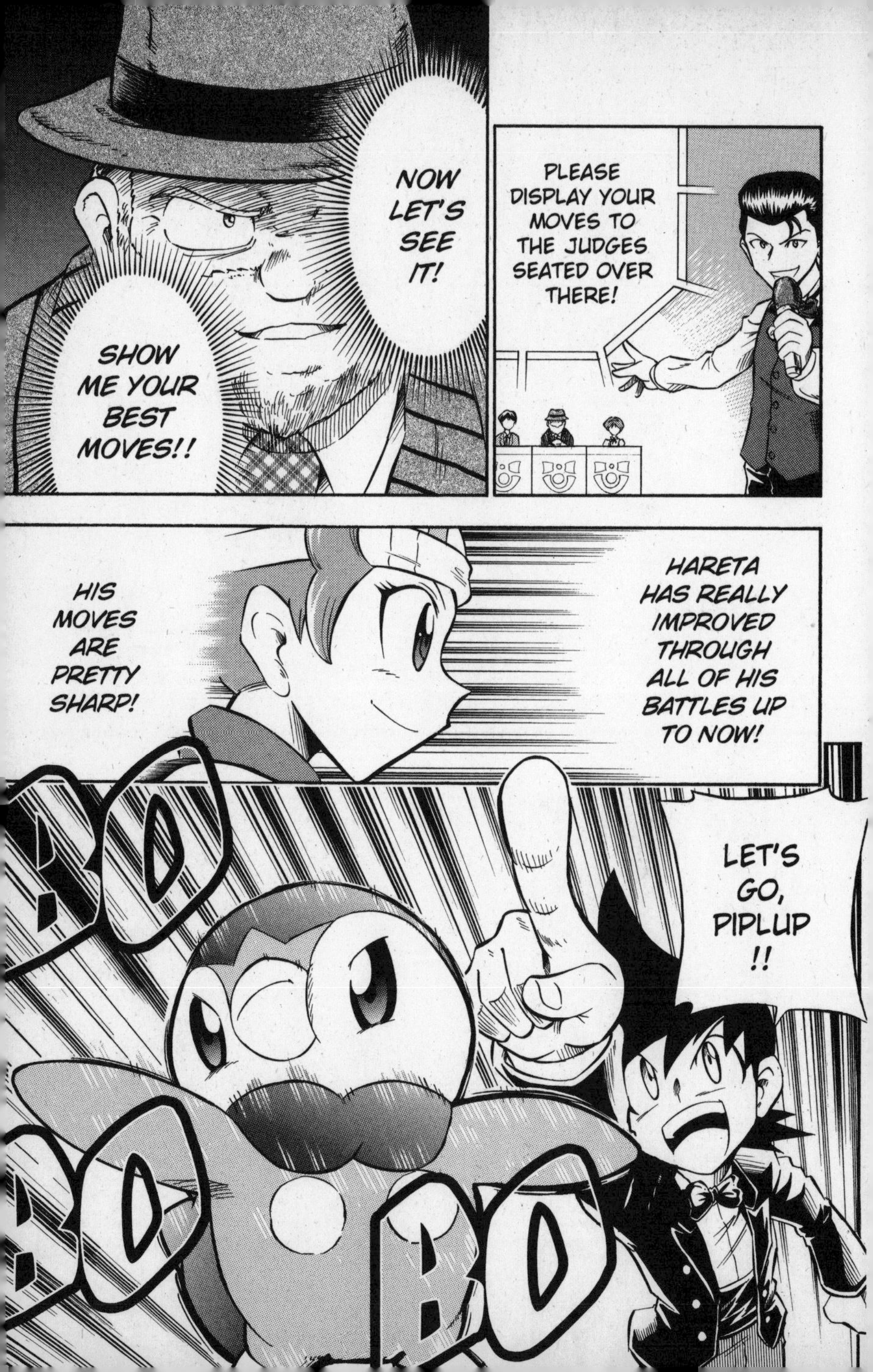
PLEASE DISPLAY YOUR MOVES TO THE JUDGES SEATED OVER THERE!
NOW LET'S SEE IT!
SHOW ME YOUR BEST MOVES!!
HARETA HAS REALLY IMPROVED THROUGH ALL OF HIS BATTLES UP TO NOW!
HIS MOVES ARE PRETTY SHARP!
LET'S GO, PIPLUP!!
BO
BO
BO
BO

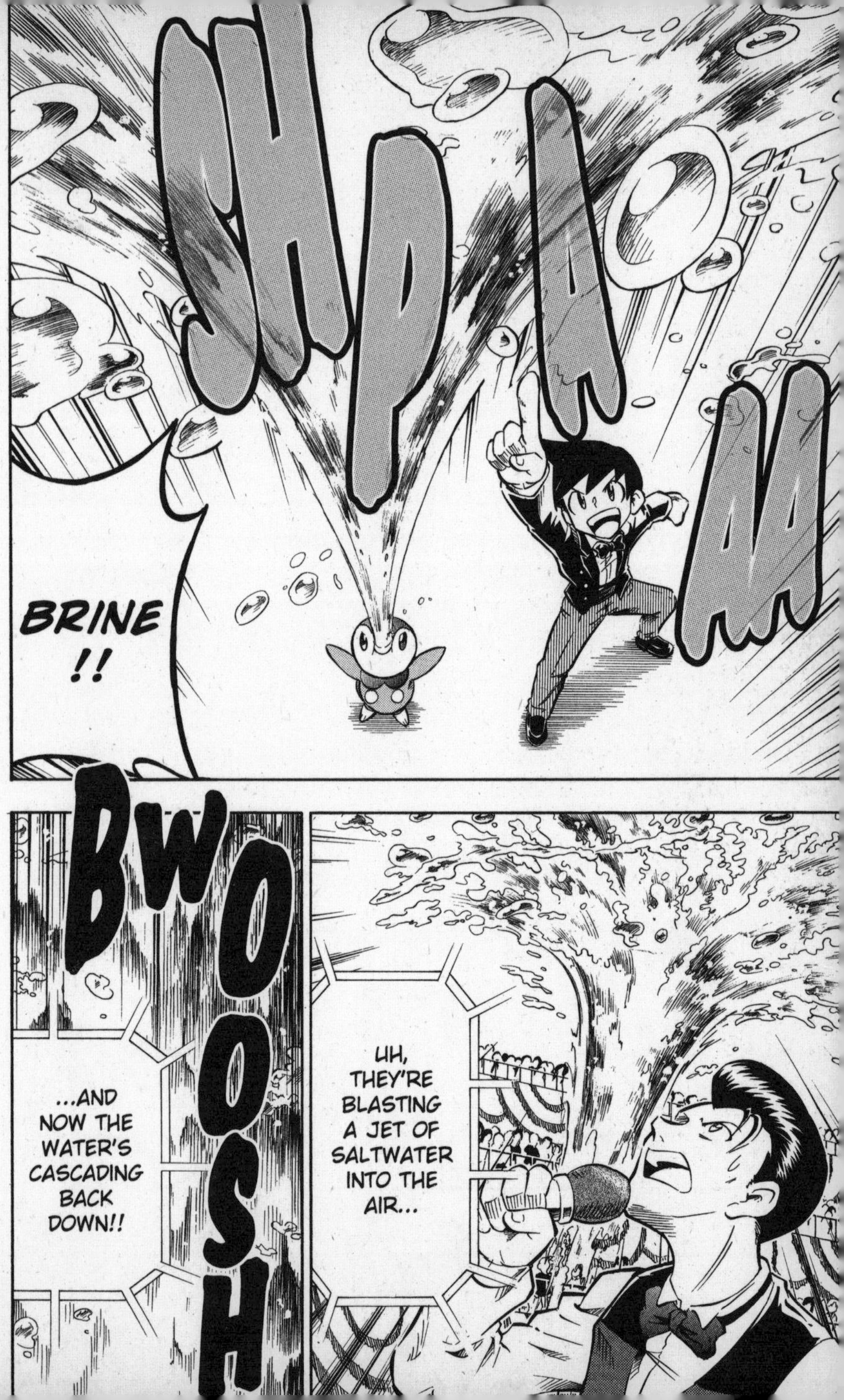
BRINE !!
UH, THEY'RE BLASTING A JET OF SALTWATER INTO THE AIR...
...AND NOW THE WATER'S CASCADING BACK DOWN!!
BWOOSH

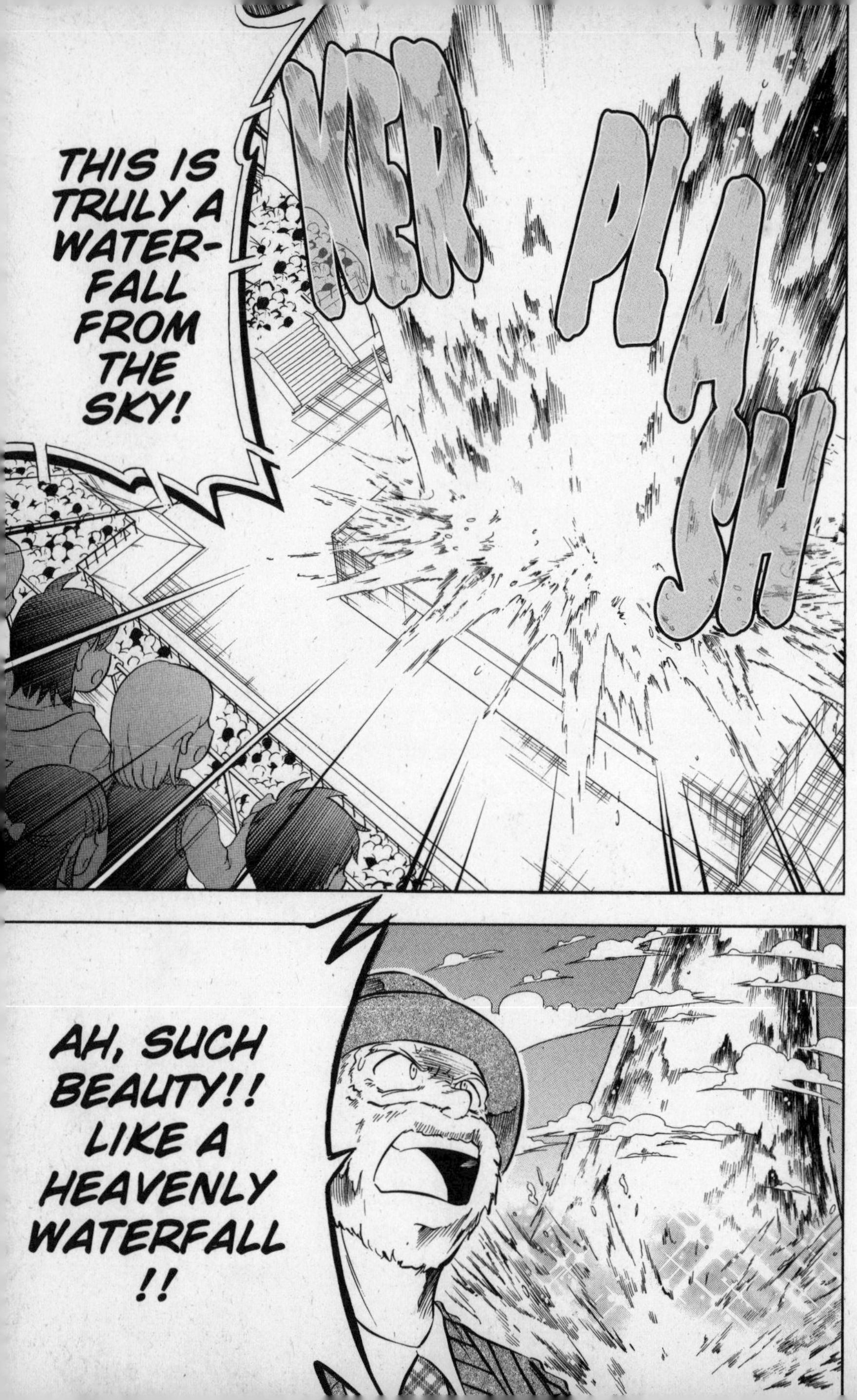
KER PLASH
THIS IS TRULY A WATER-FALL FROM THE SKY!
AH, SUCH BEAUTY!! LIKE A HEAVENLY WATERFALL!!

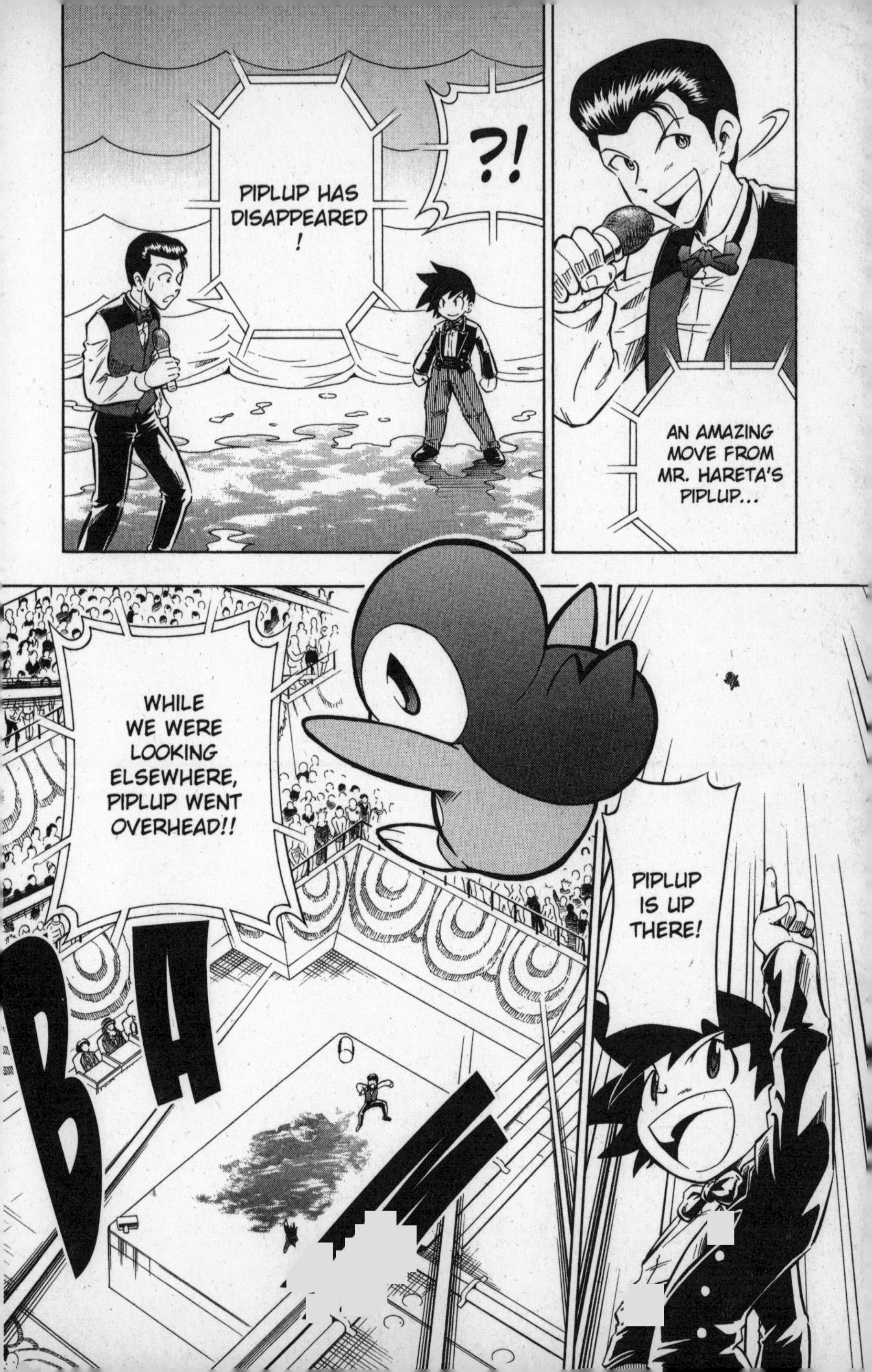
AN AMAZING MOVE FROM MR. HARETA'S PIPLUP...
?!
PIPLUP HAS DISAPPEARED!
PIPLUP IS UP THERE!
WHILE WE WERE LOOKING ELSEWHERE, PIPLUP WENT OVERHEAD!!
BA

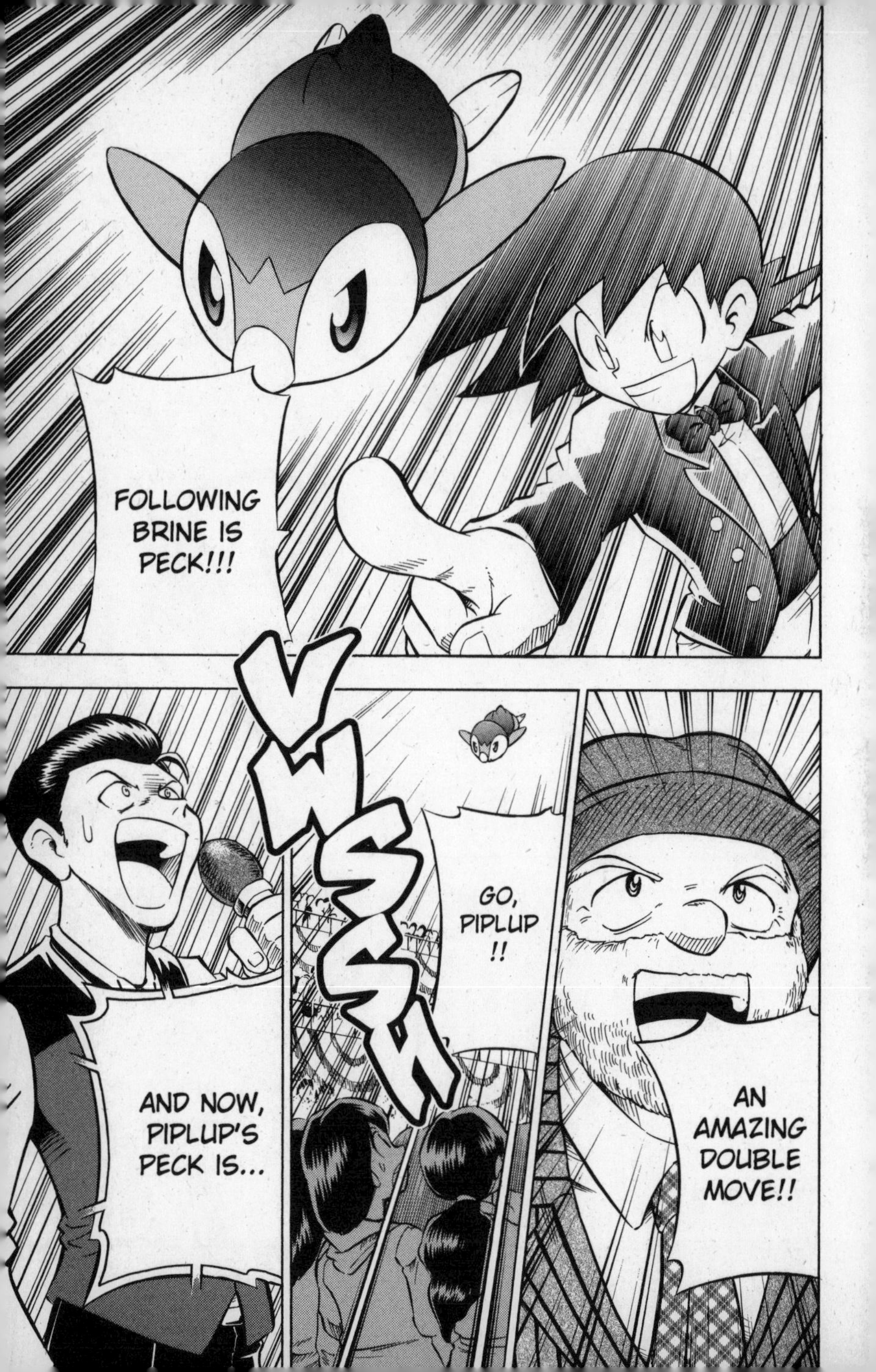
FOLLOWING BRINE IS PECK!!!
VWSSH
AND NOW, PIPLUP'S PECK IS...
GO, PIPLUP !!
AN AMAZING DOUBLE MOVE!!

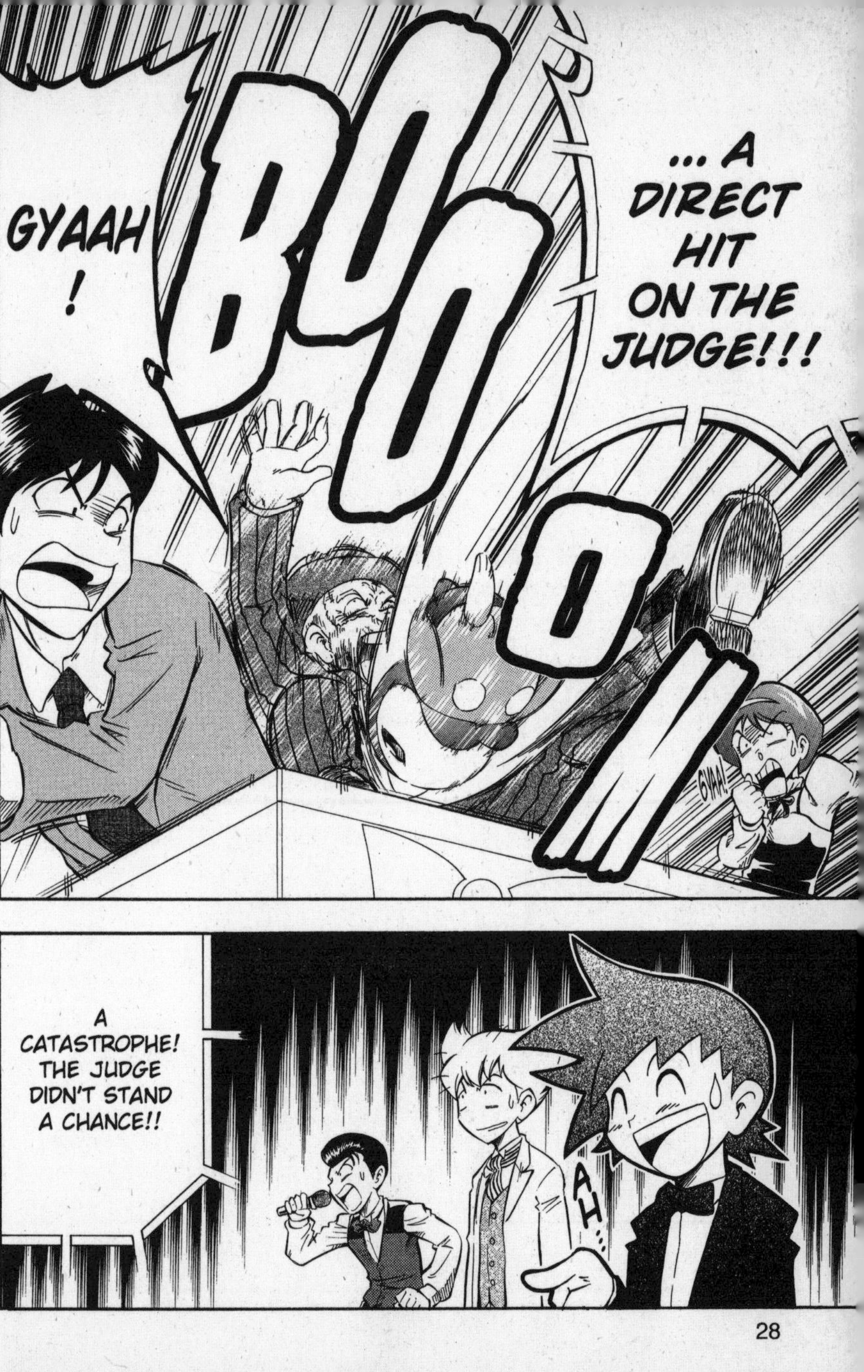
... A DIRECT HIT ON THE JUDGE!!!
BOOOM
GYAAH!
GYAA!
AH...
A CATASTROPHE! THE JUDGE DIDN'T STAND A CHANCE!!

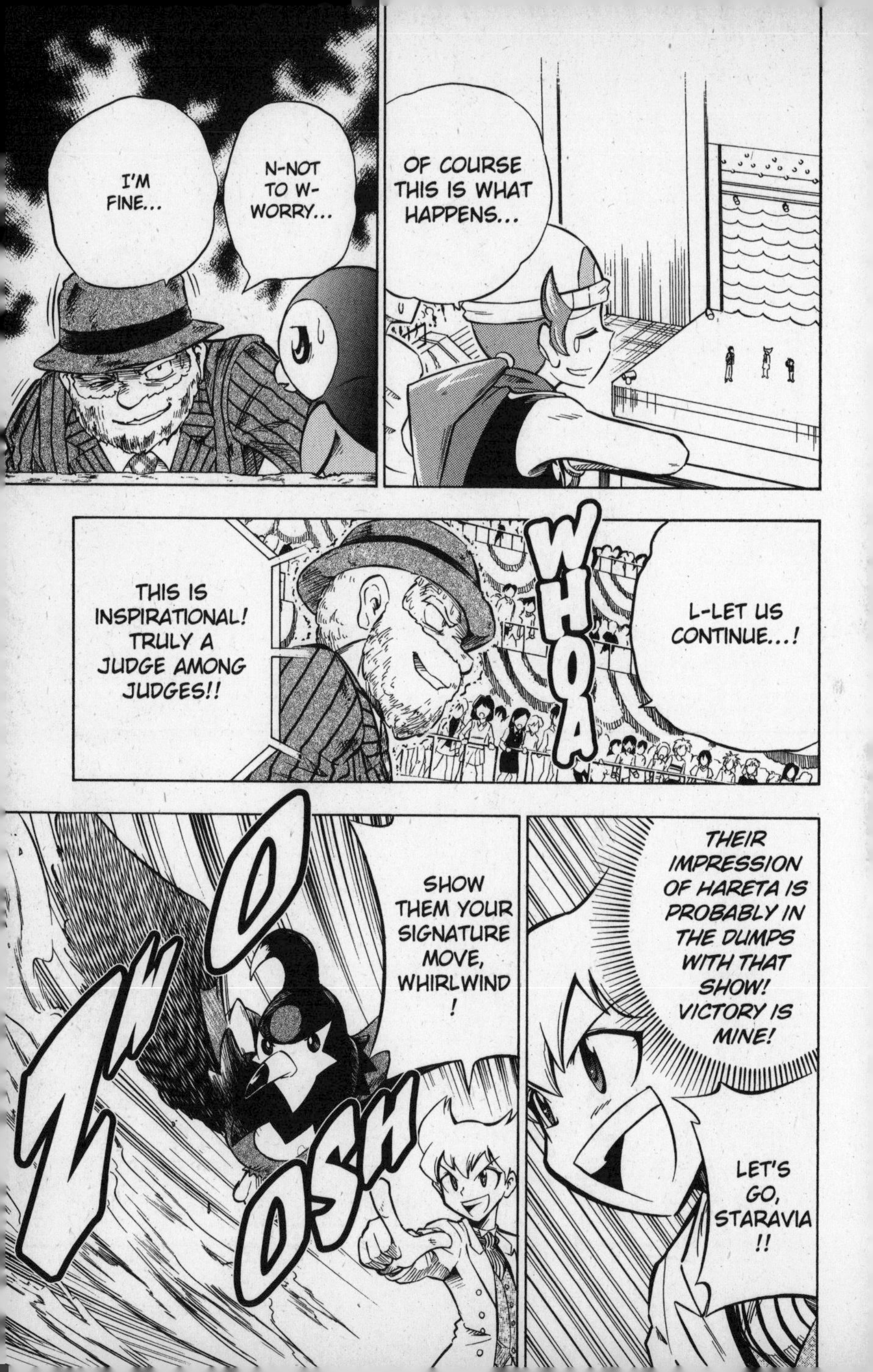
OF COURSE THIS IS WHAT HAPPENS...
N-NOT TO W-WORRY...
I'M FINE...
L-LET US CONTINUE...!
WHOA
THIS IS INSPIRATIONAL! TRULY A JUDGE AMONG JUDGES!!
THEIR IMPRESSION OF HARETA IS PROBABLY IN THE DUMPS WITH THAT SHOW! VICTORY IS MINE!
LET'S GO, STARAVIA!!
SHOW THEM YOUR SIGNATURE MOVE, WHIRLWIND!
WHOOSH

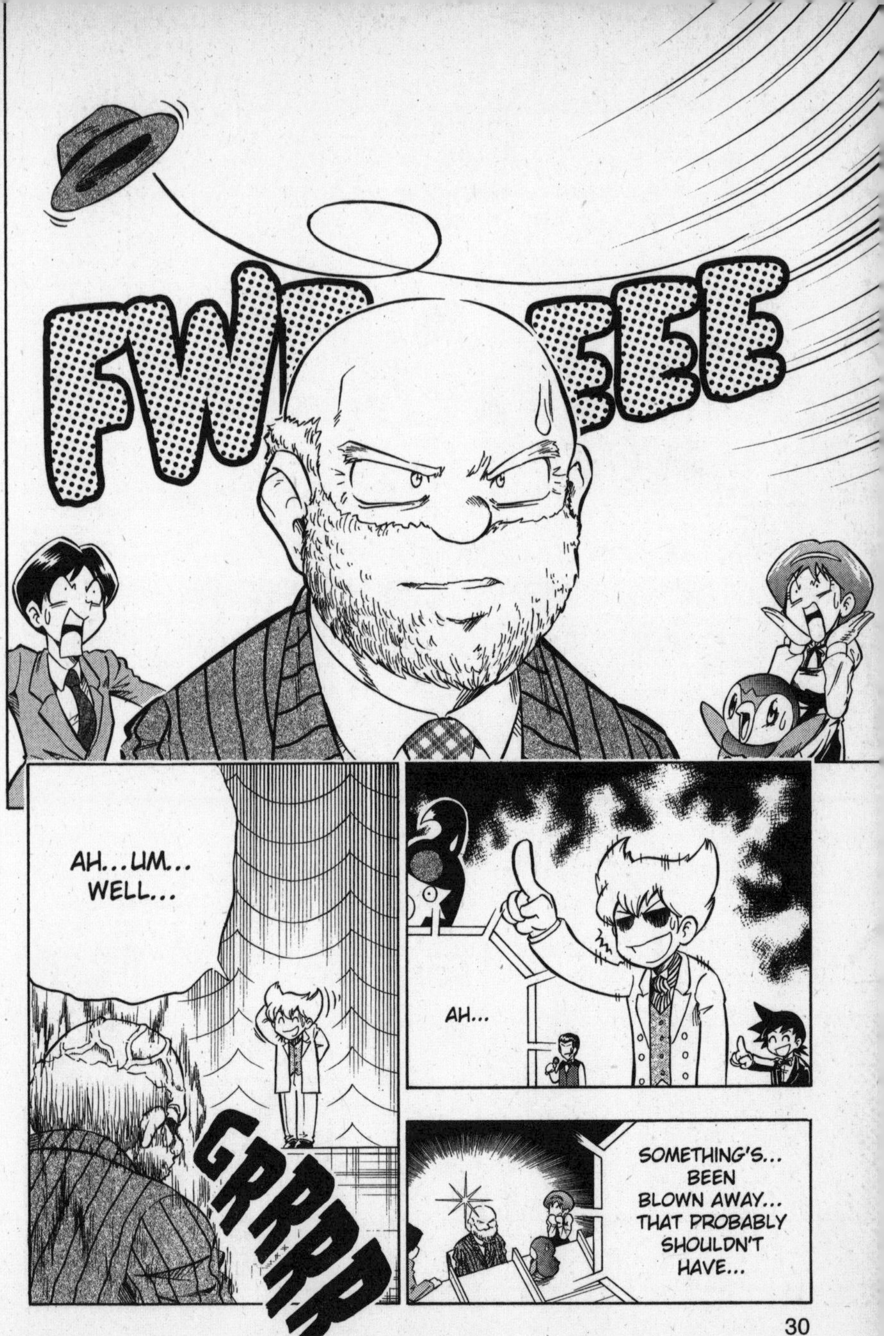
FWEEE
AH...
SOMETHING'S... BEEN BLOWN AWAY... THAT PROBABLY SHOULDN'T HAVE...
AH...UM... WELL...
GRRRR

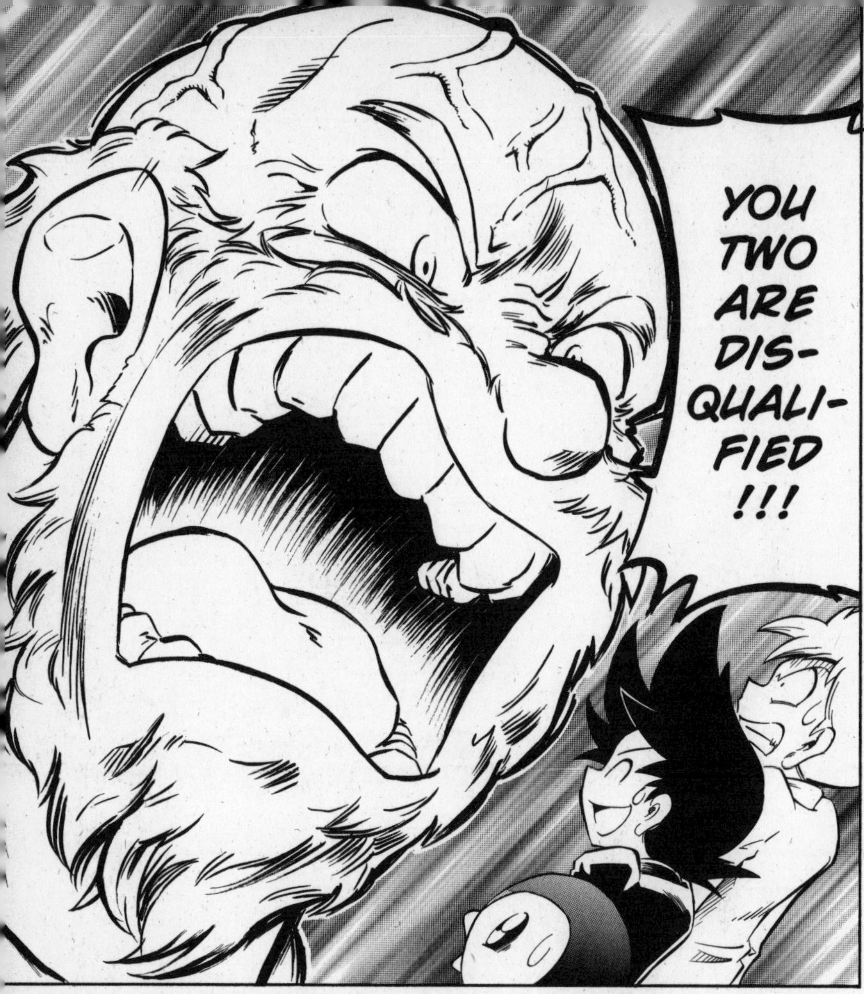
YOU TWO ARE DIS-QUALI-FIED!!!

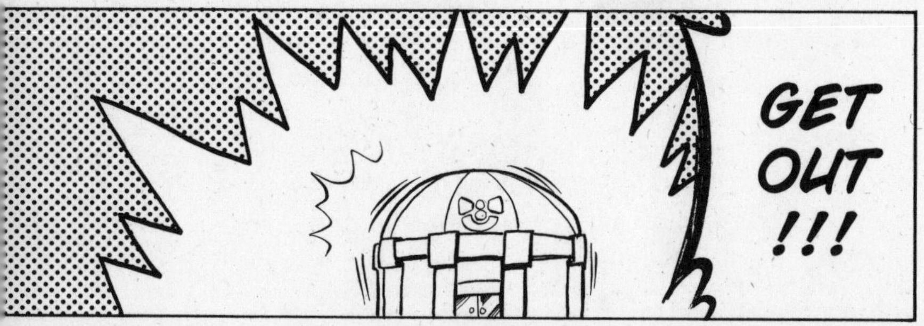
GET OUT!!!

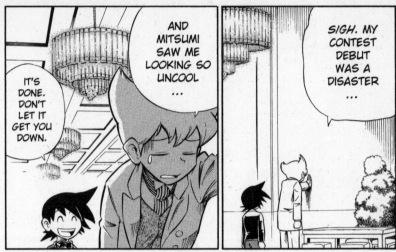

SIGH. MY CONTEST DEBUT WAS A DISASTER ...
AND MITSUMI SAW ME LOOKING SO UNCOOL ...
IT'S DONE. DON'T LET IT GET YOU DOWN.
IT'S BECAUSE YOU DID ALL THOSE STUPID THINGS!
YOU DID PLENTY TOO, JUN.
WE NOW MOVE ON TO THE MASTER CLASS ACTING COMPETITION.
HERE IS MISS MITSUMI WITH HER PERFORMANCE !!
HUH?
DASH
MITSUMI?! IN THE MASTER CLASS?!

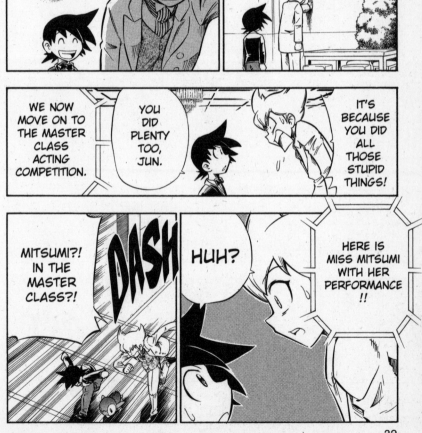

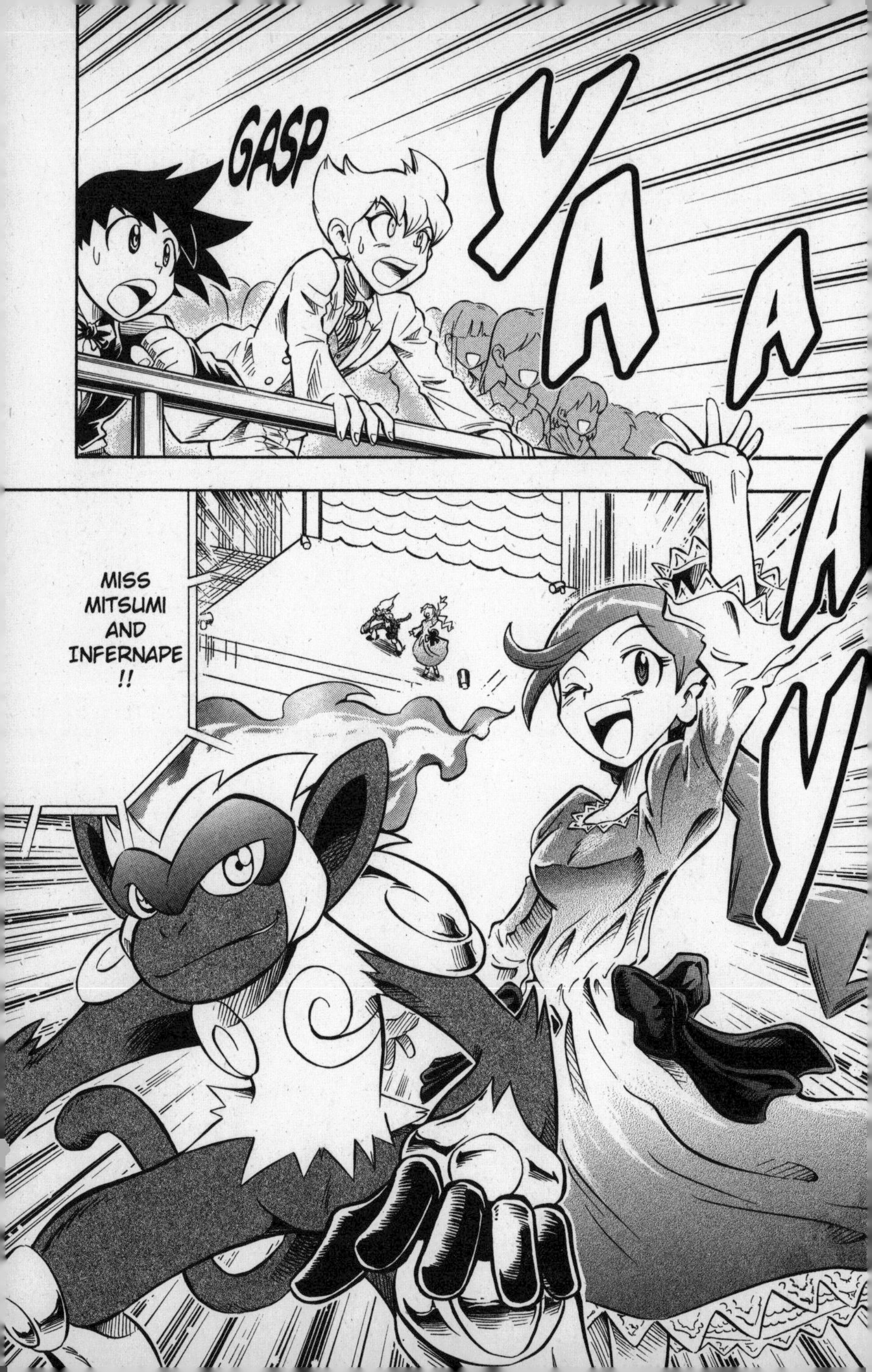
YAAAAY
GASP
MISS MITSUMI AND INFERNAPE !!

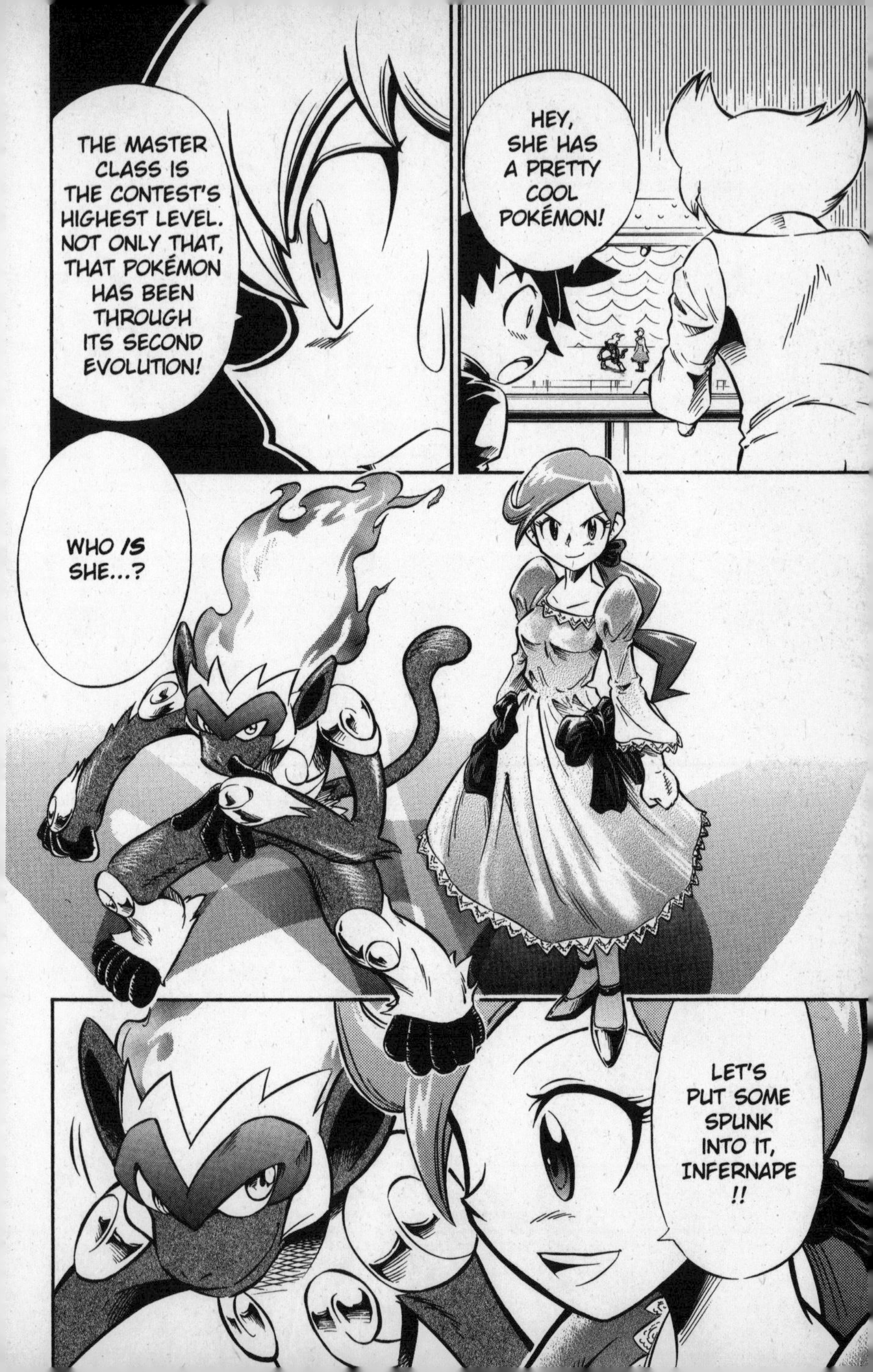
HEY, SHE HAS A PRETTY COOL POKÉMON!
THE MASTER CLASS IS THE CONTEST'S HIGHEST LEVEL. NOT ONLY THAT, THAT POKÉMON HAS BEEN THROUGH ITS SECOND EVOLUTION!
WHO *IS* SHE...?
LET'S PUT SOME SPUNK INTO IT, INFERNAPE!!

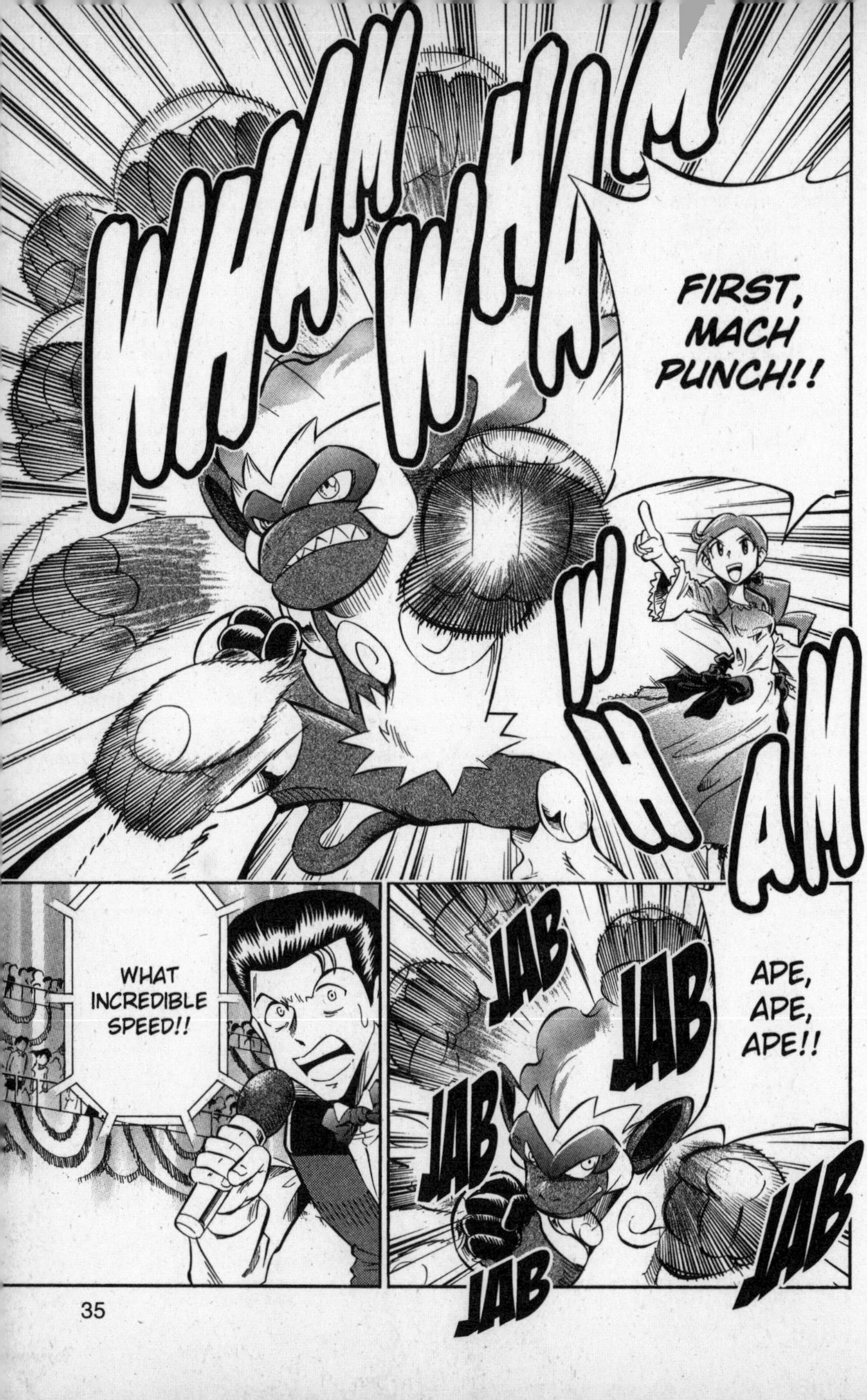
WHAM
WHAM
WHAM
FIRST, MACH PUNCH!!
APE, APE, APE!!
JAB
JAB
JAB
JAB
JAB
WHAT INCREDIBLE SPEED!!

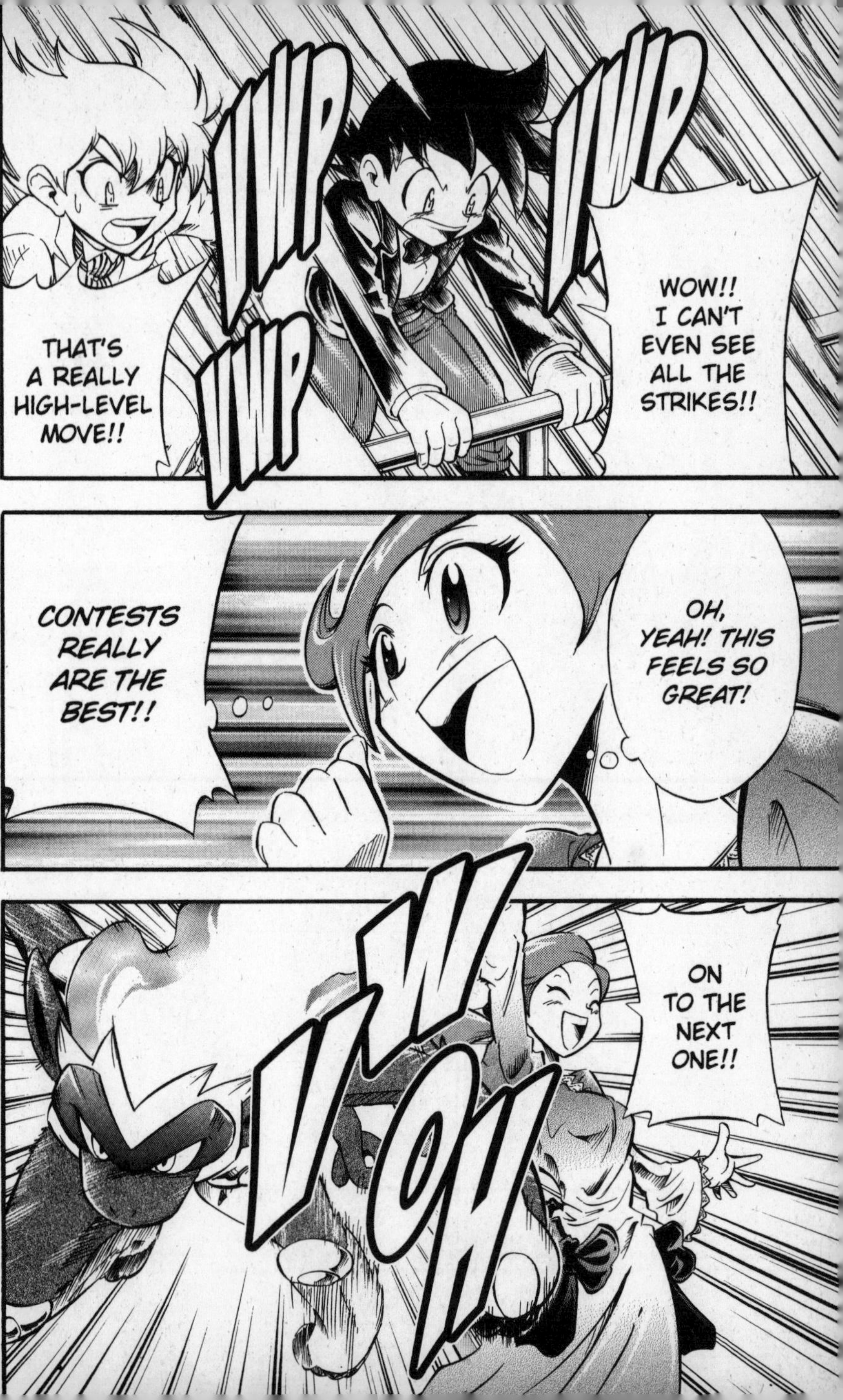
WOW!! I CAN'T EVEN SEE ALL THE STRIKES!!
THAT'S A REALLY HIGH-LEVEL MOVE!!
OH, YEAH! THIS FEELS SO GREAT!
CONTESTS REALLY ARE THE BEST!!
ON TO THE NEXT ONE!!

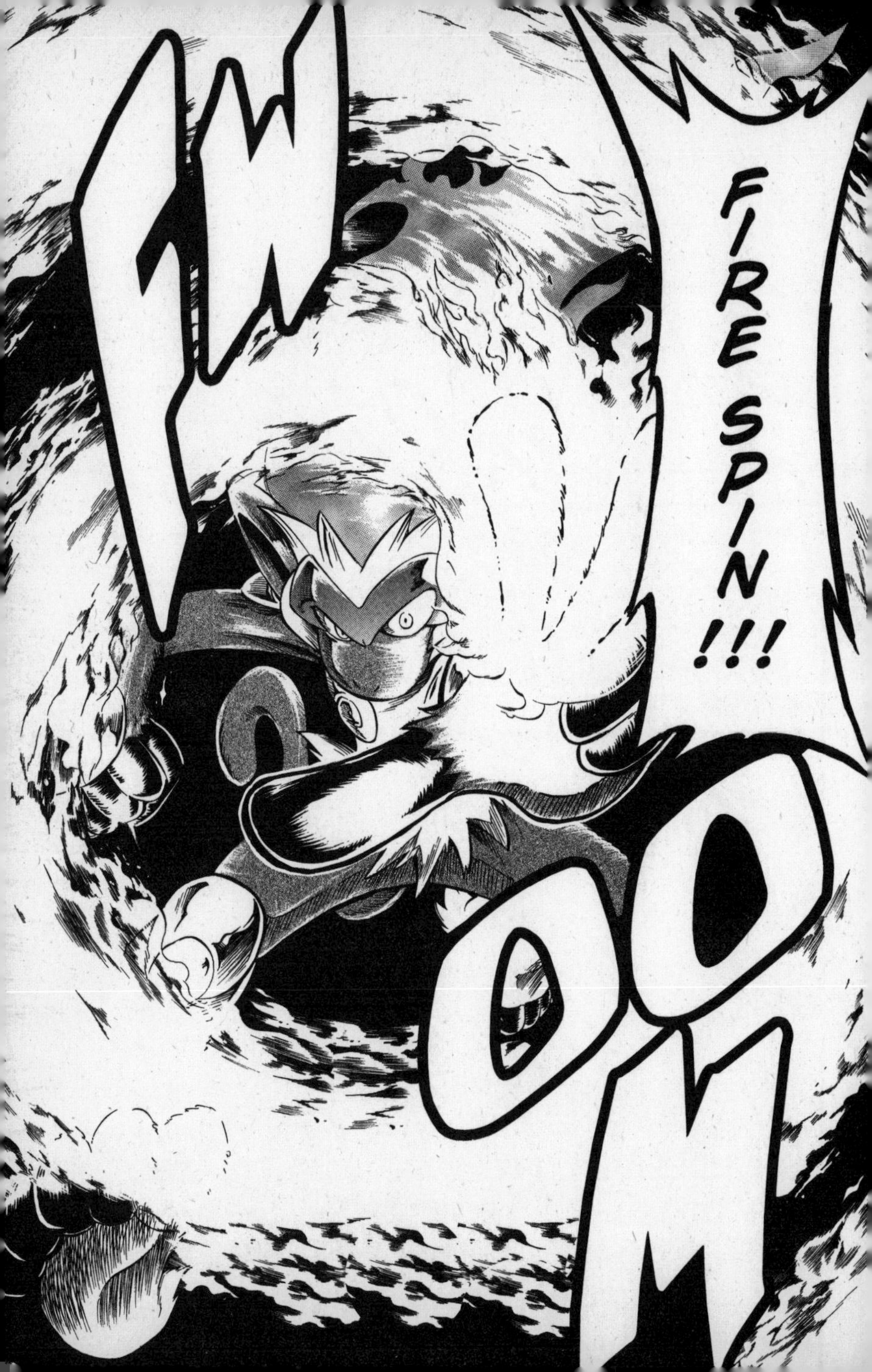
FIRE SPIN!!!

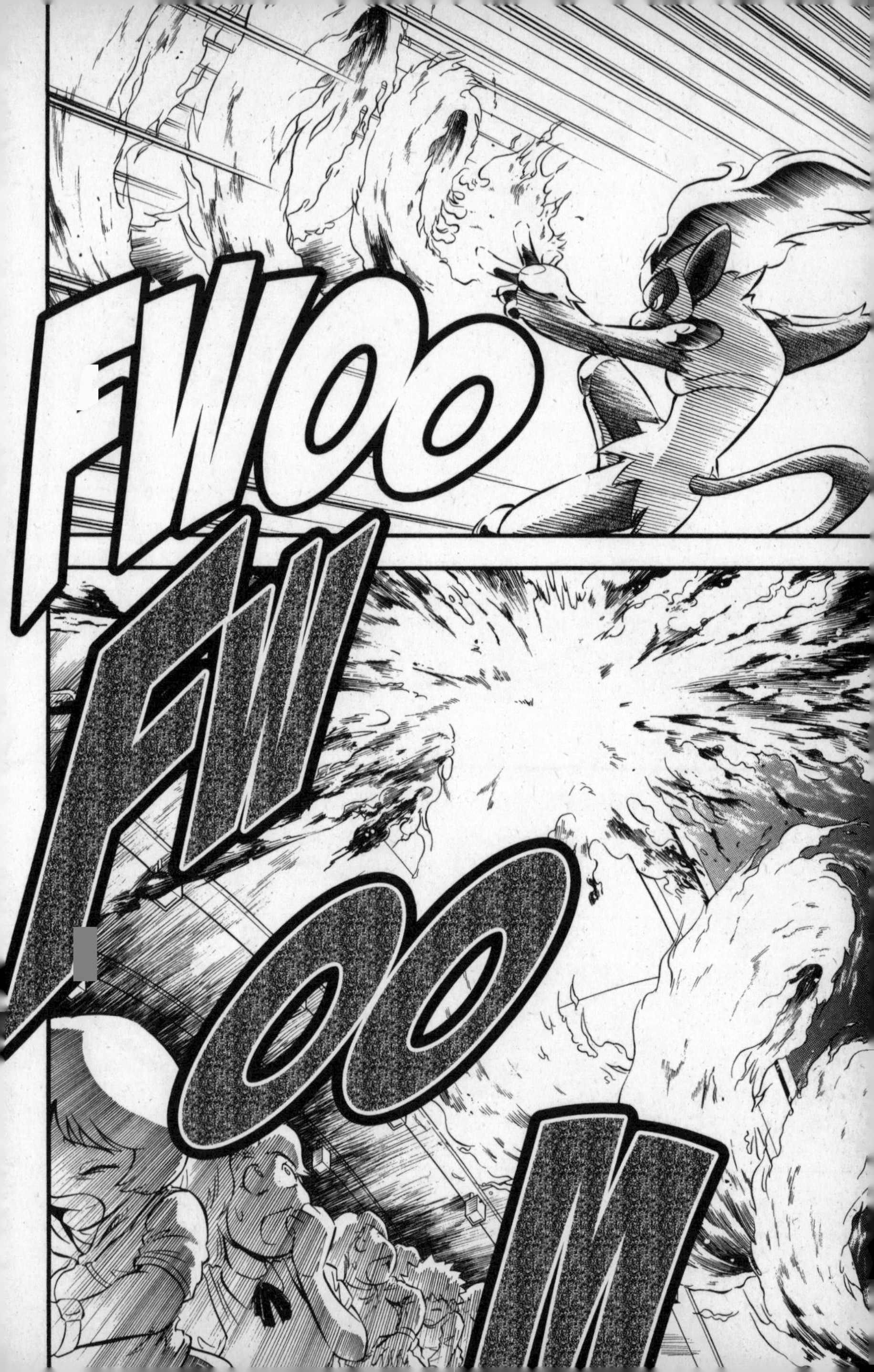
FWOO
FWOOM

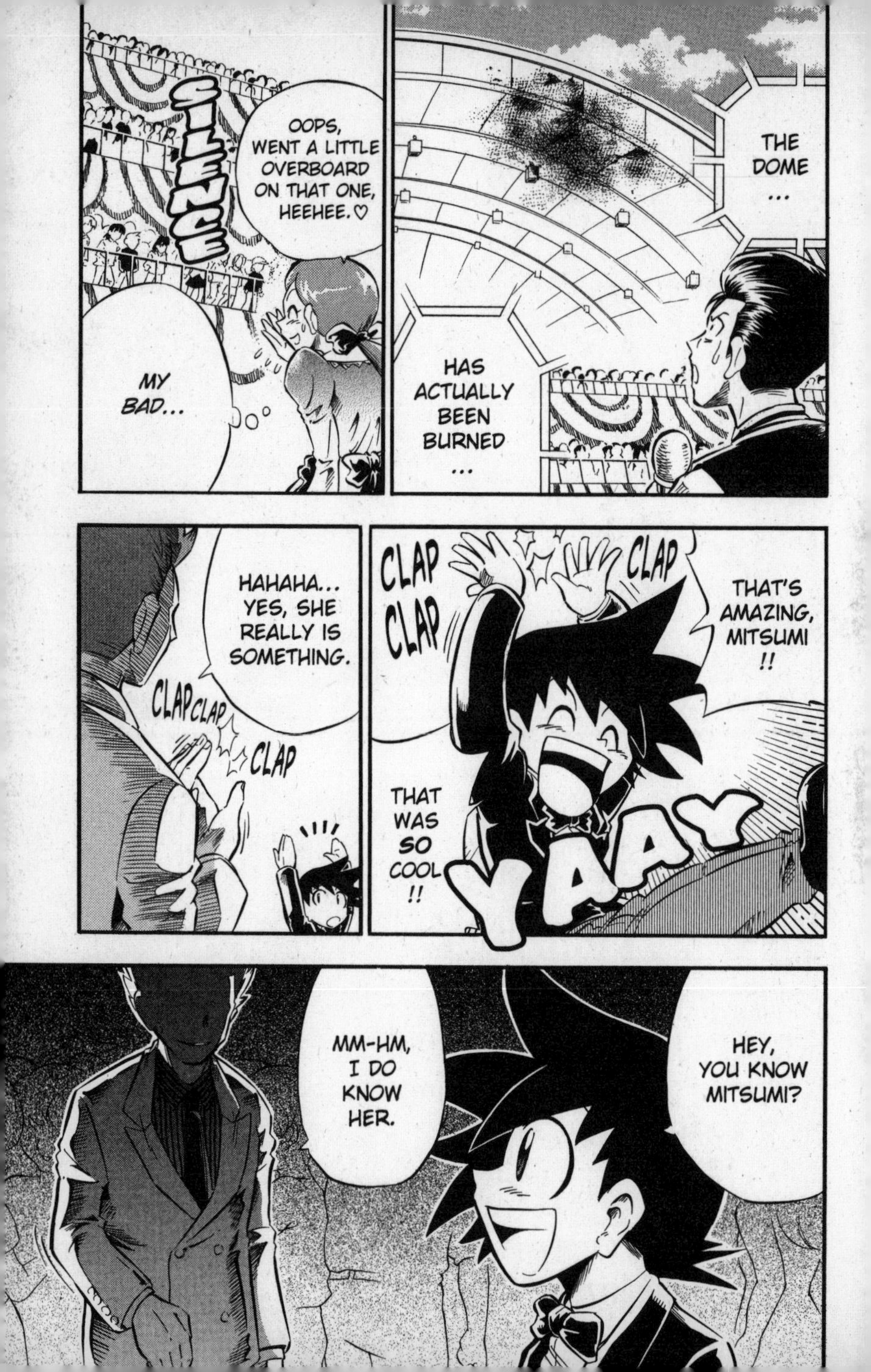
THE DOME ...
HAS ACTUALLY BEEN BURNED ...
SILENCE
OOPS, WENT A LITTLE OVERBOARD ON THAT ONE, HEEHEE.♡
MY BAD...
CLAP
CLAP CLAP
THAT'S AMAZING, MITSUMI !!
THAT WAS SO COOL !!
YAAY
HAHAHA... YES, SHE REALLY IS SOMETHING.
CLAP CLAP
CLAP
HEY, YOU KNOW MITSUMI?
MM-HM, I DO KNOW HER.

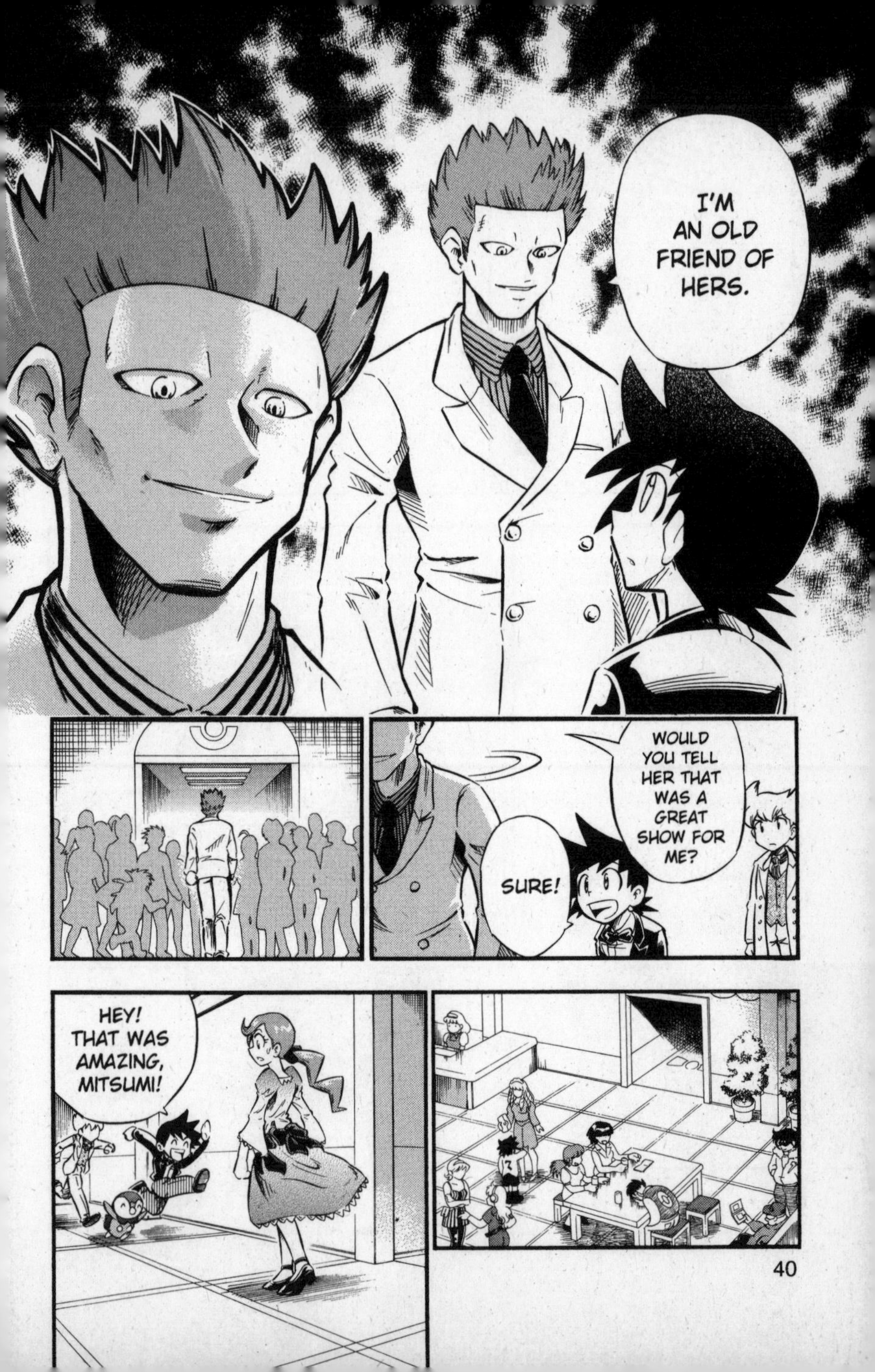
I'M AN OLD FRIEND OF HERS.
WOULD YOU TELL HER THAT WAS A GREAT SHOW FOR ME?
SURE!
HEY! THAT WAS AMAZING, MITSUMI!

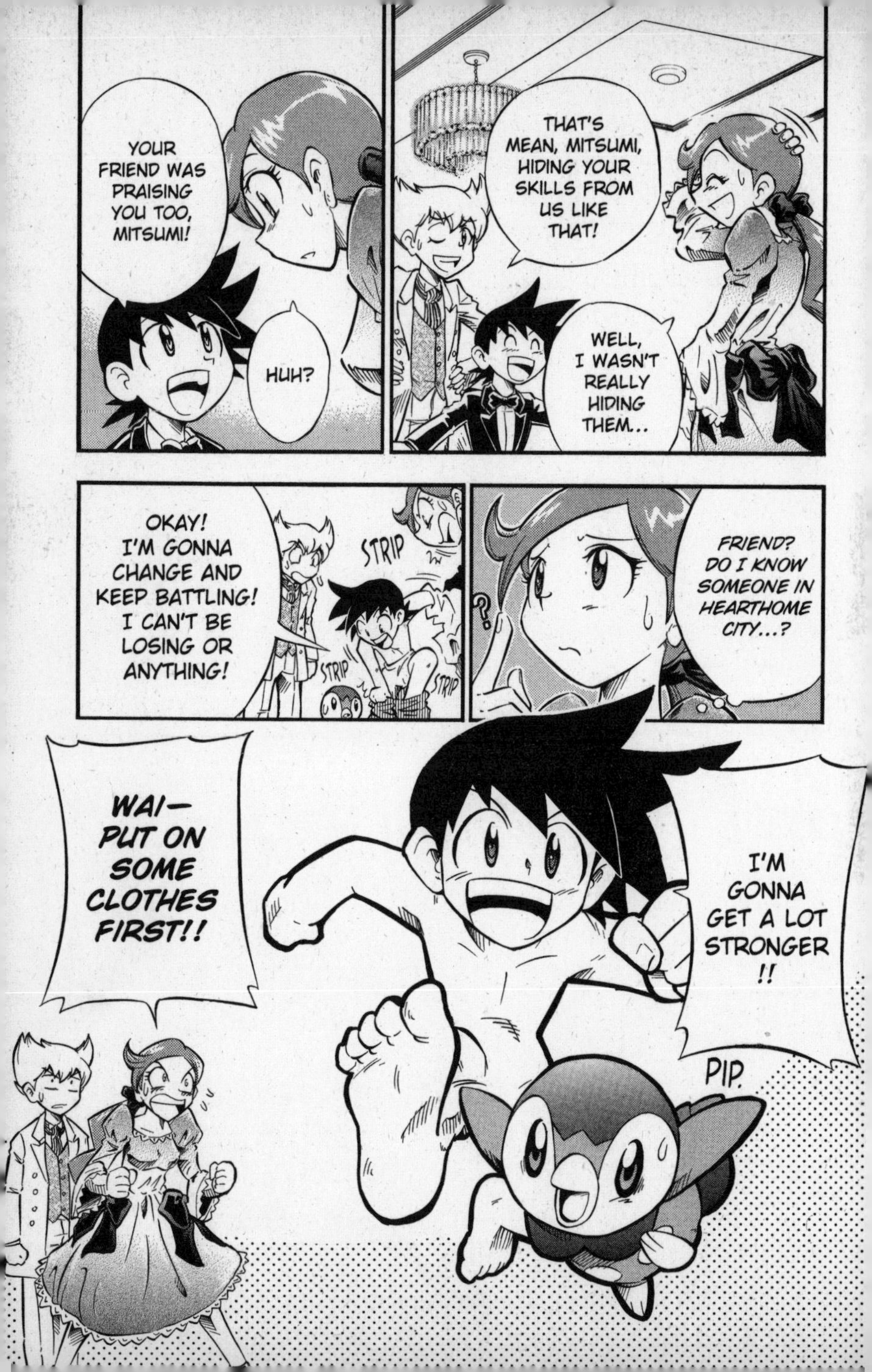
THAT'S MEAN, MITSUMI, HIDING YOUR SKILLS FROM US LIKE THAT!
WELL, I WASN'T REALLY HIDING THEM...
YOUR FRIEND WAS PRAISING YOU TOO, MITSUMI!
HUH?
FRIEND? DO I KNOW SOMEONE IN HEARTHOME CITY...?
?
STRIP
OKAY! I'M GONNA CHANGE AND KEEP BATTLING! I CAN'T BE LOSING OR ANYTHING!
STRIP
STRIP
I'M GONNA GET A LOT STRONGER!!
PIP.
WAI— PUT ON SOME CLOTHES FIRST!!

SNAP

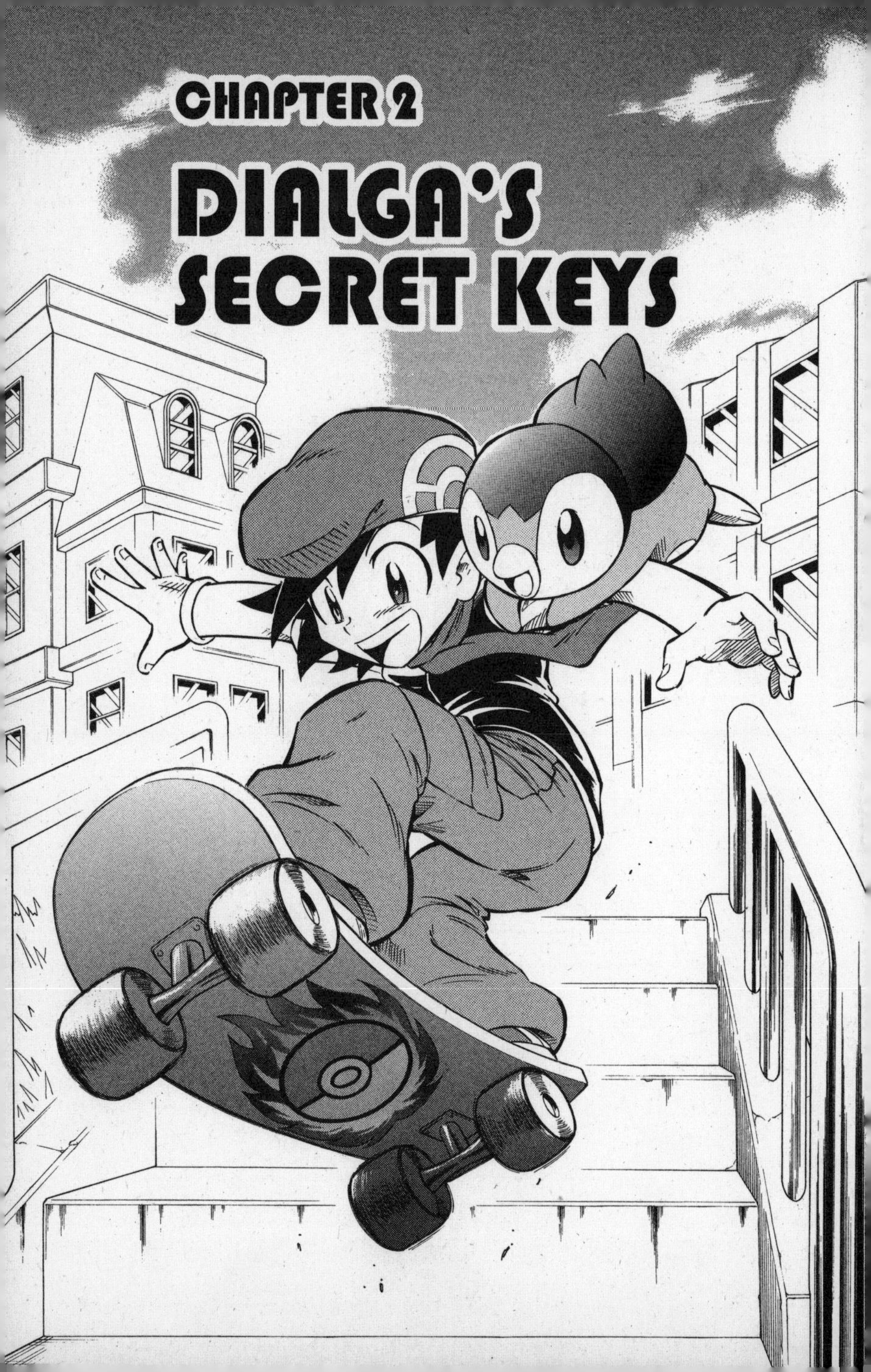
CHAPTER 2
DIALGA'S
SECRET KEYS

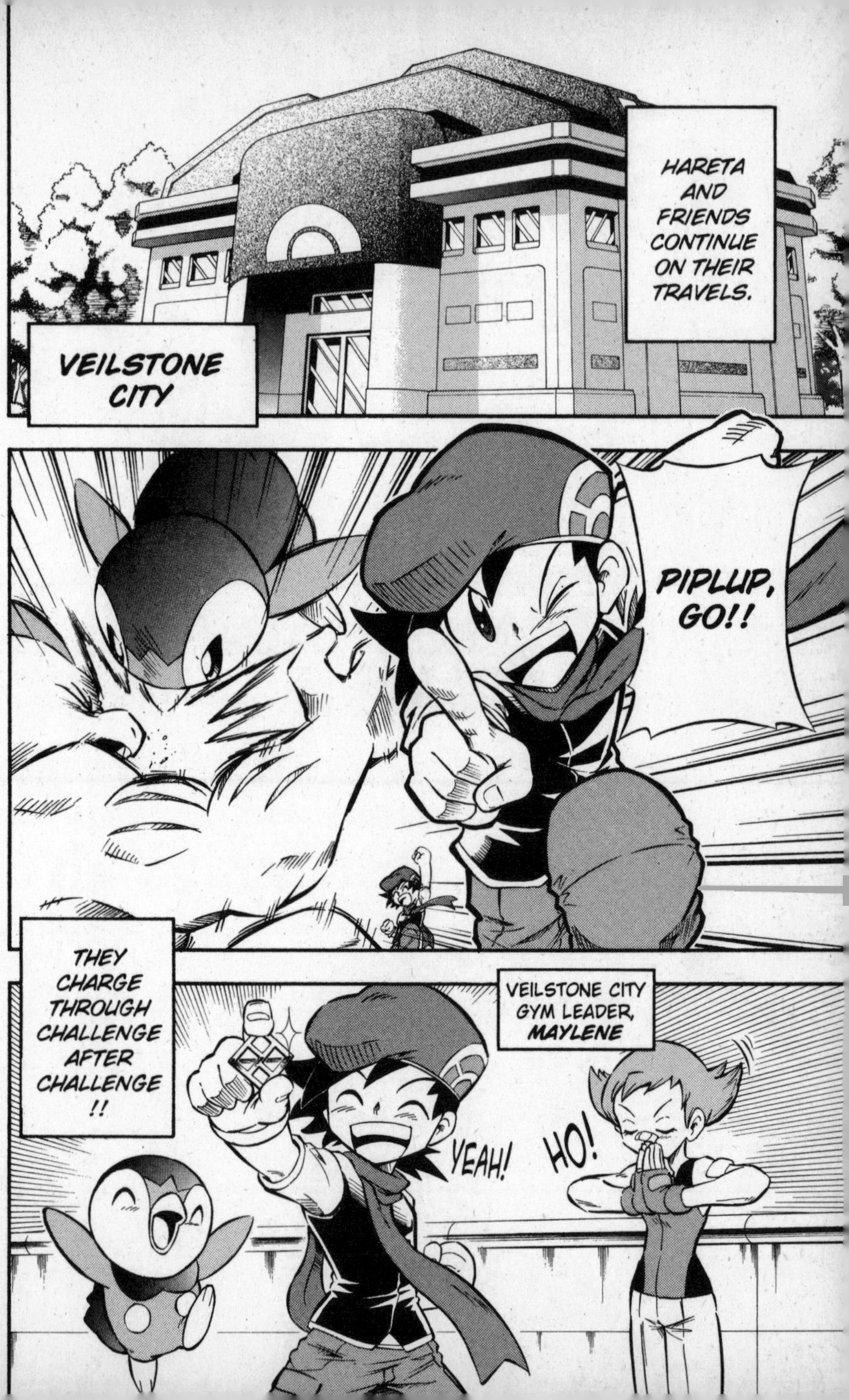
HARETA AND FRIENDS CONTINUE ON THEIR TRAVELS.
VEILSTONE CITY
PIPLUP, GO!!
VEILSTONE CITY GYM LEADER, MAYLENE
THEY CHARGE THROUGH CHALLENGE AFTER CHALLENGE!!
HO!
YEAH!

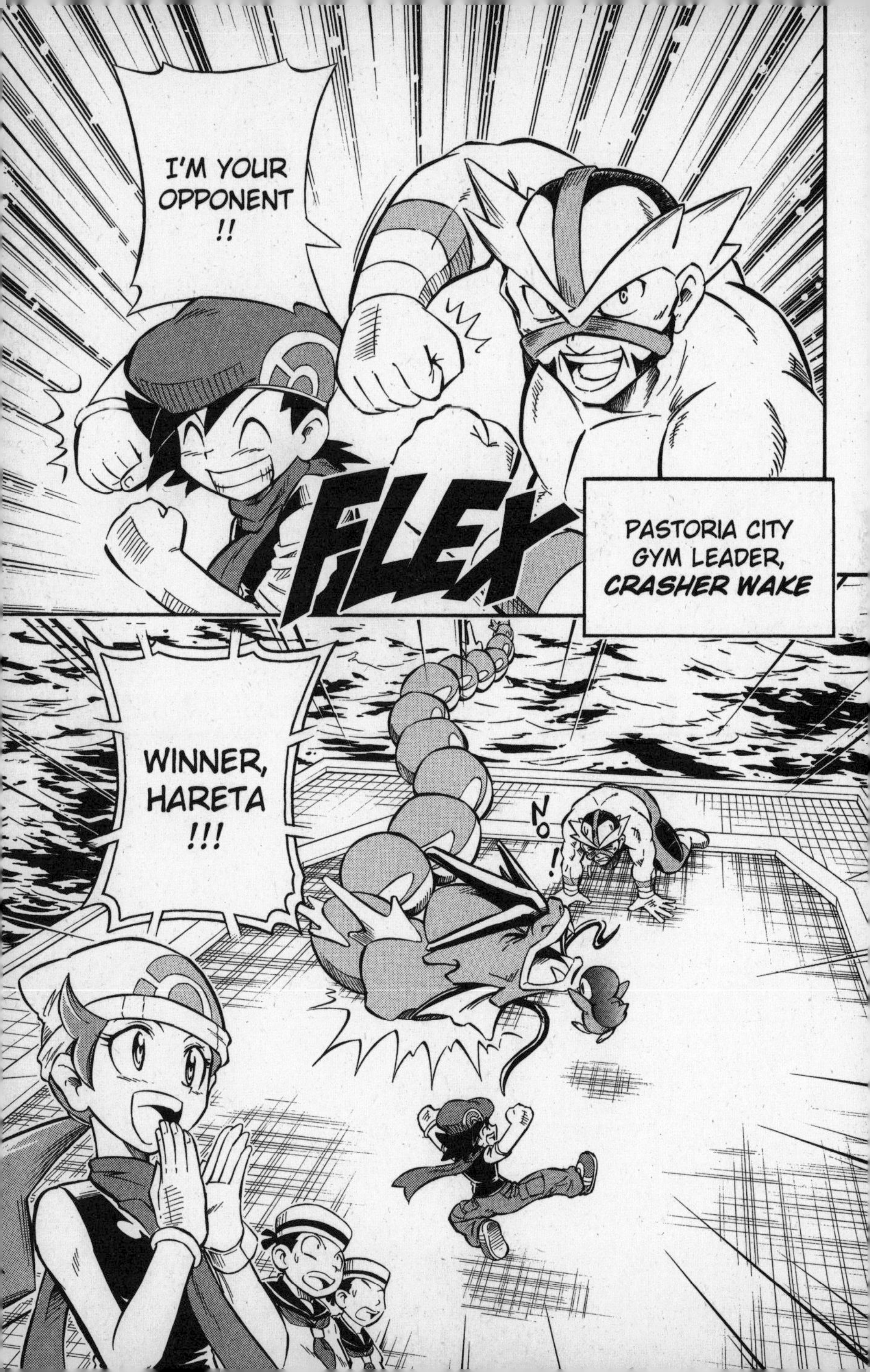
I'M YOUR OPPONENT !!
FLEX
PASTORIA CITY GYM LEADER, CRASHER WAKE
WINNER, HARETA !!!
NO !

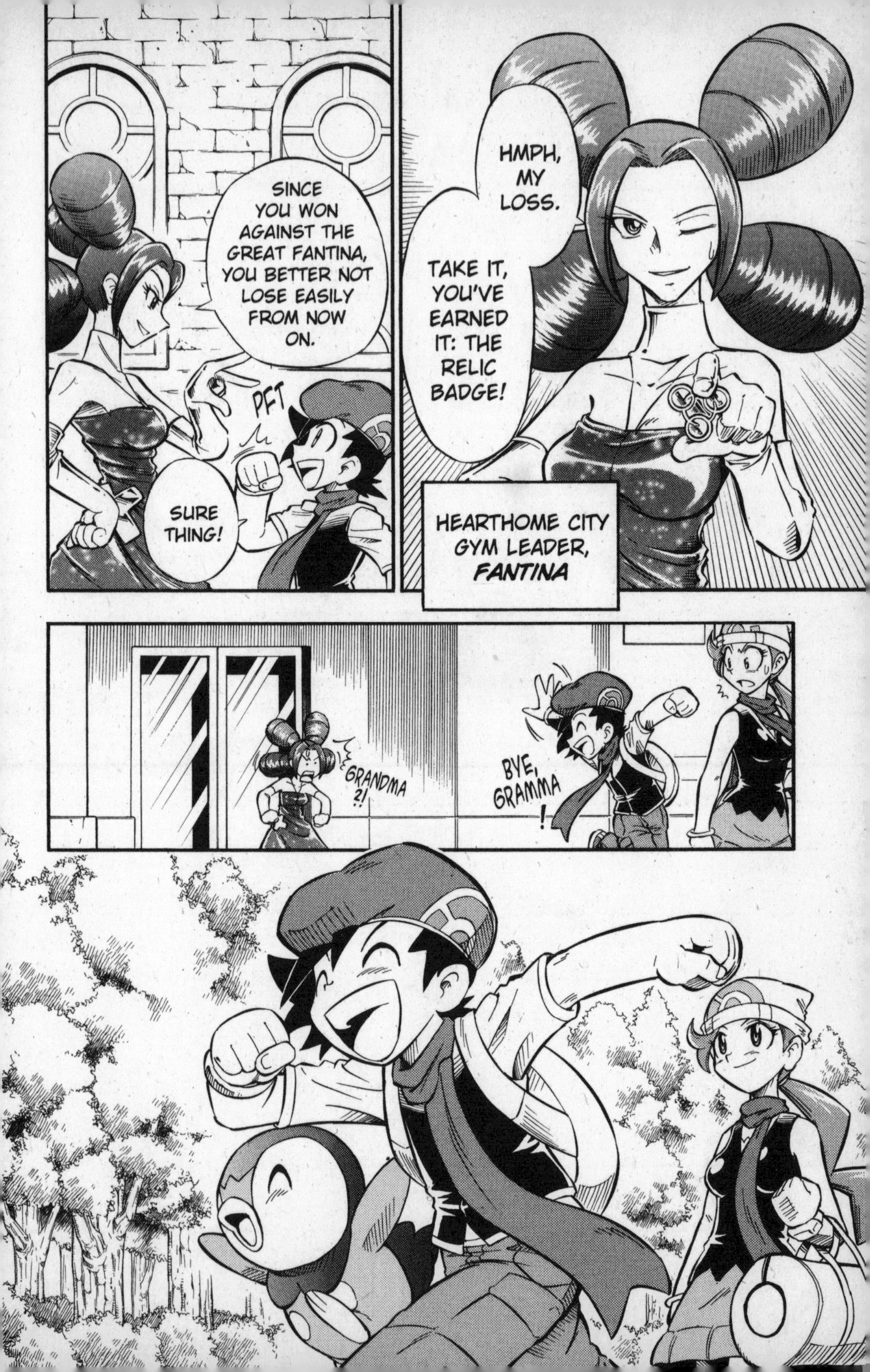
HMPH, MY LOSS.
TAKE IT, YOU'VE EARNED IT: THE RELIC BADGE!
HEARTHOME CITY GYM LEADER, *FANTINA*
SINCE YOU WON AGAINST THE GREAT FANTINA, YOU BETTER NOT LOSE EASILY FROM NOW ON.
PFT
SURE THING!
BYE, GRAMMA!
GRANDMA?!

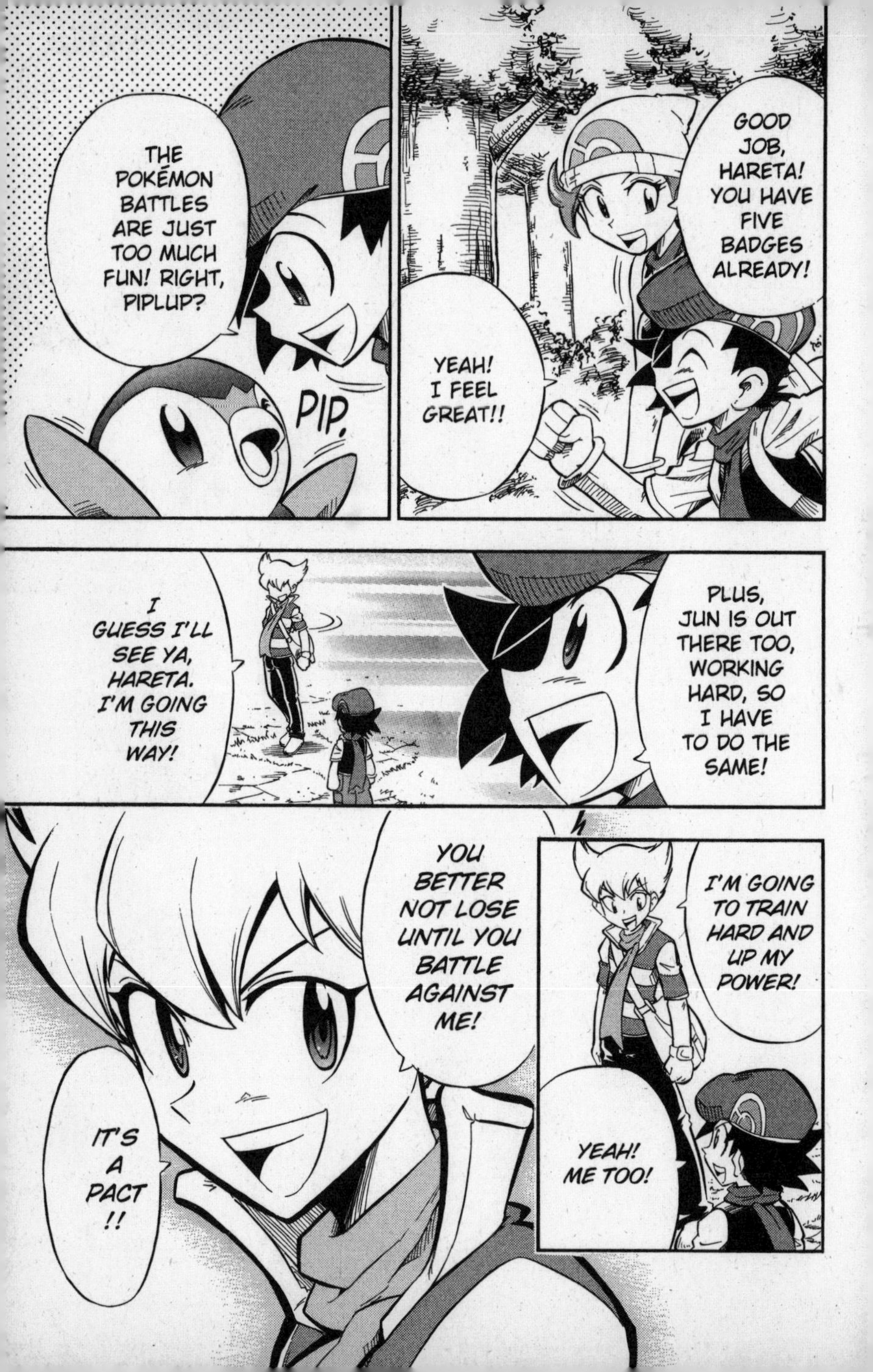
GOOD JOB, HARETA! YOU HAVE FIVE BADGES ALREADY!
YEAH! I FEEL GREAT!!
THE POKÉMON BATTLES ARE JUST TOO MUCH FUN! RIGHT, PIPLUP?
PIP.
PLUS, JUN IS OUT THERE TOO, WORKING HARD, SO I HAVE TO DO THE SAME!
I GUESS I'LL SEE YA, HARETA. I'M GOING THIS WAY!
I'M GOING TO TRAIN HARD AND UP MY POWER!
YEAH! ME TOO!
YOU BETTER NOT LOSE UNTIL YOU BATTLE AGAINST ME!
IT'S A PACT!!

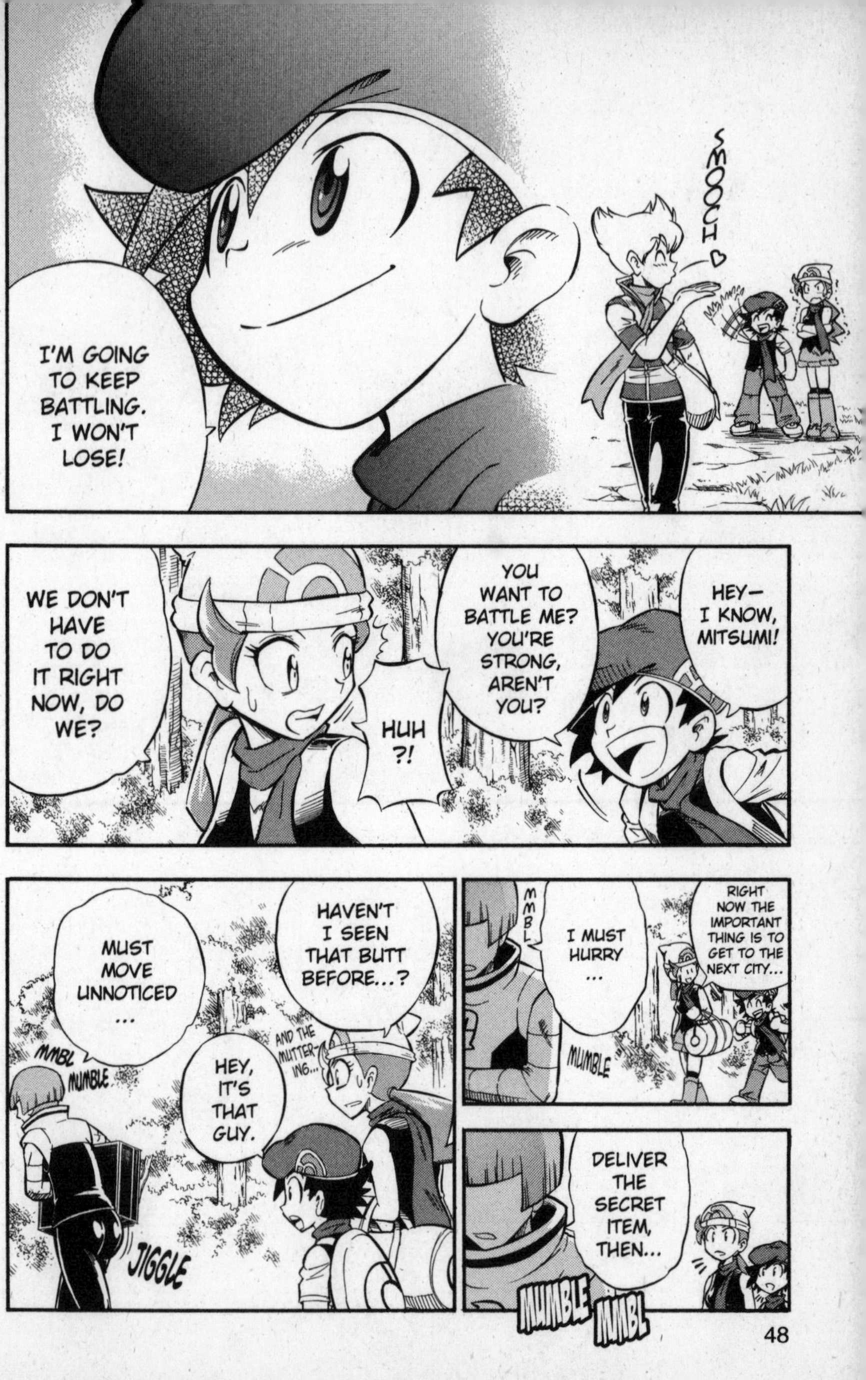
SMOOCH
I'M GOING TO KEEP BATTLING. I WON'T LOSE!
HEY— I KNOW, MITSUMI!
YOU WANT TO BATTLE ME? YOU'RE STRONG, AREN'T YOU?
HUH ?!
WE DON'T HAVE TO DO IT RIGHT NOW, DO WE?
RIGHT NOW THE IMPORTANT THING IS TO GET TO THE NEXT CITY...
MMBL
I MUST HURRY ...
MUMBLE
DELIVER THE SECRET ITEM, THEN...
MUMBLE MMBL
HAVEN'T I SEEN THAT BUTT BEFORE...?
AND THE MUTTERING...
MUST MOVE UNNOTICED ...
HEY, IT'S THAT GUY.
MMBL MUMBLE
JIGGLE

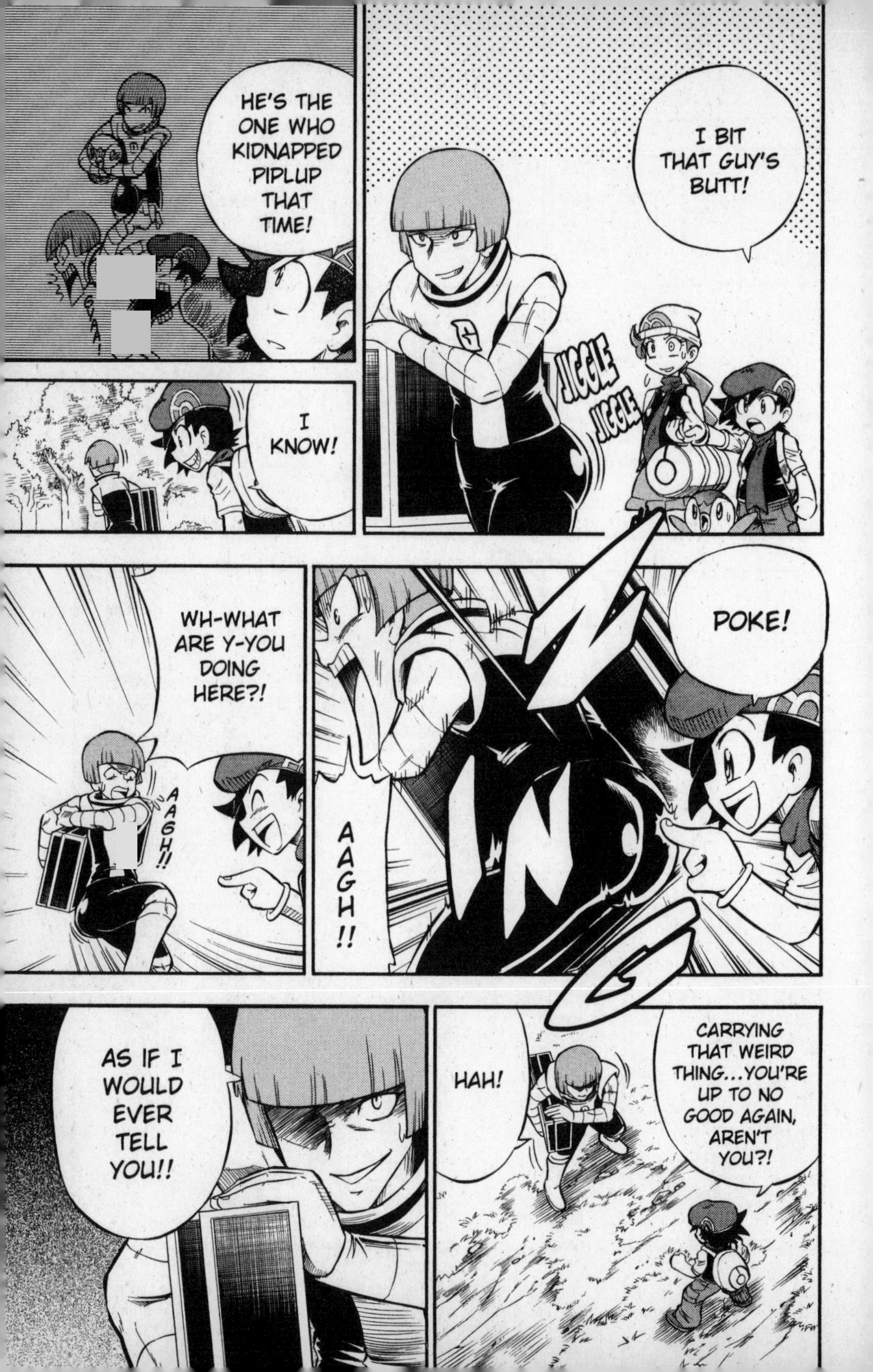
I BIT THAT GUY'S BUTT!
JIGGLE JIGGLE
HE'S THE ONE WHO KIDNAPPED PIPLUP THAT TIME!
GIAA!
I KNOW!
POKE!
ZING
AAGH!!
WH-WHAT ARE Y-YOU DOING HERE?!
AAGH!!
CARRYING THAT WEIRD THING...YOU'RE UP TO NO GOOD AGAIN, AREN'T YOU?!
HAH!
AS IF I WOULD EVER TELL YOU!!

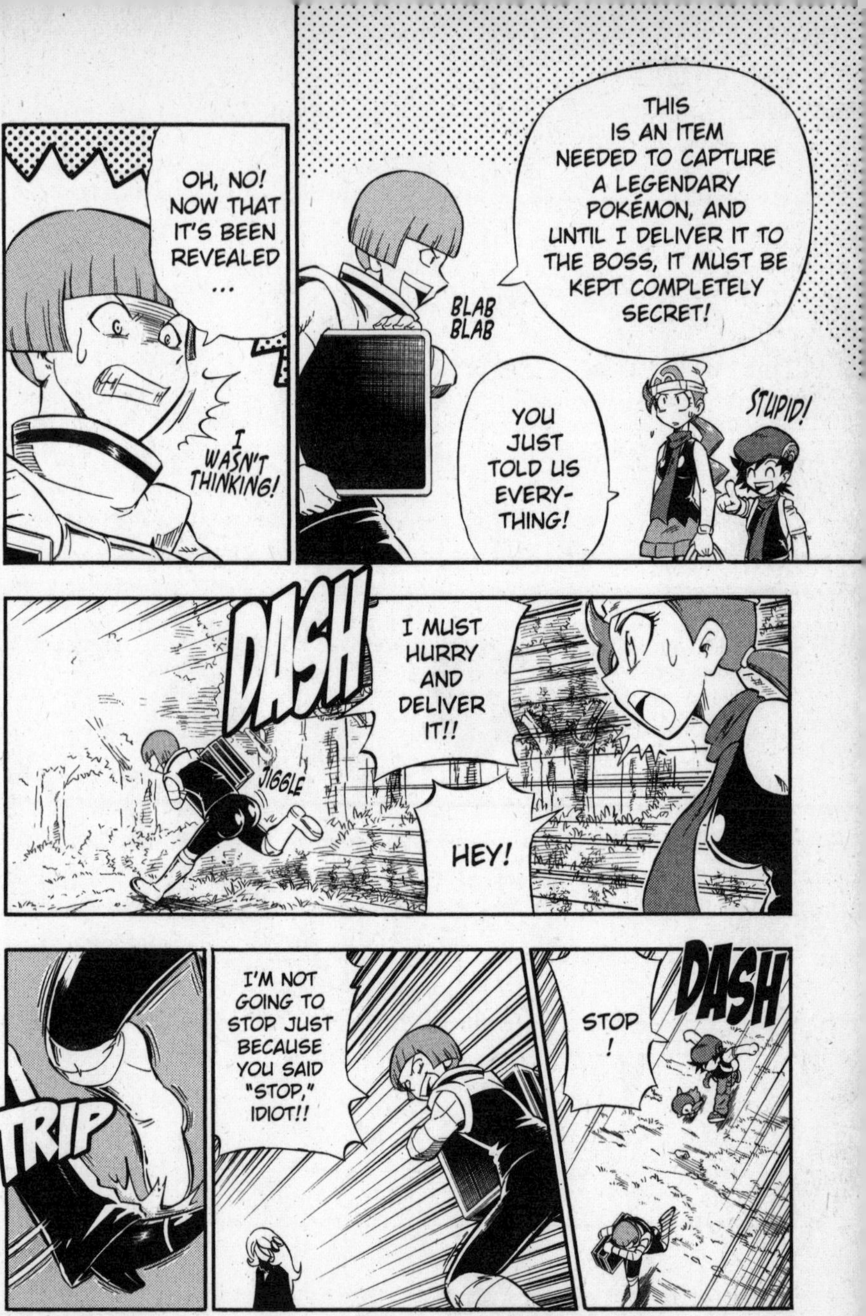
THIS IS AN ITEM NEEDED TO CAPTURE A LEGENDARY POKÉMON, AND UNTIL I DELIVER IT TO THE BOSS, IT MUST BE KEPT COMPLETELY SECRET!
BLAB BLAB
STUPID!
YOU JUST TOLD US EVERY-THING!
OH, NO! NOW THAT IT'S BEEN REVEALED ...
I WASN'T THINKING!
I MUST HURRY AND DELIVER IT!!
DASH
HEY!
JIGGLE
DASH
STOP!
I'M NOT GOING TO STOP JUST BECAUSE YOU SAID "STOP," IDIOT!!
TRIP

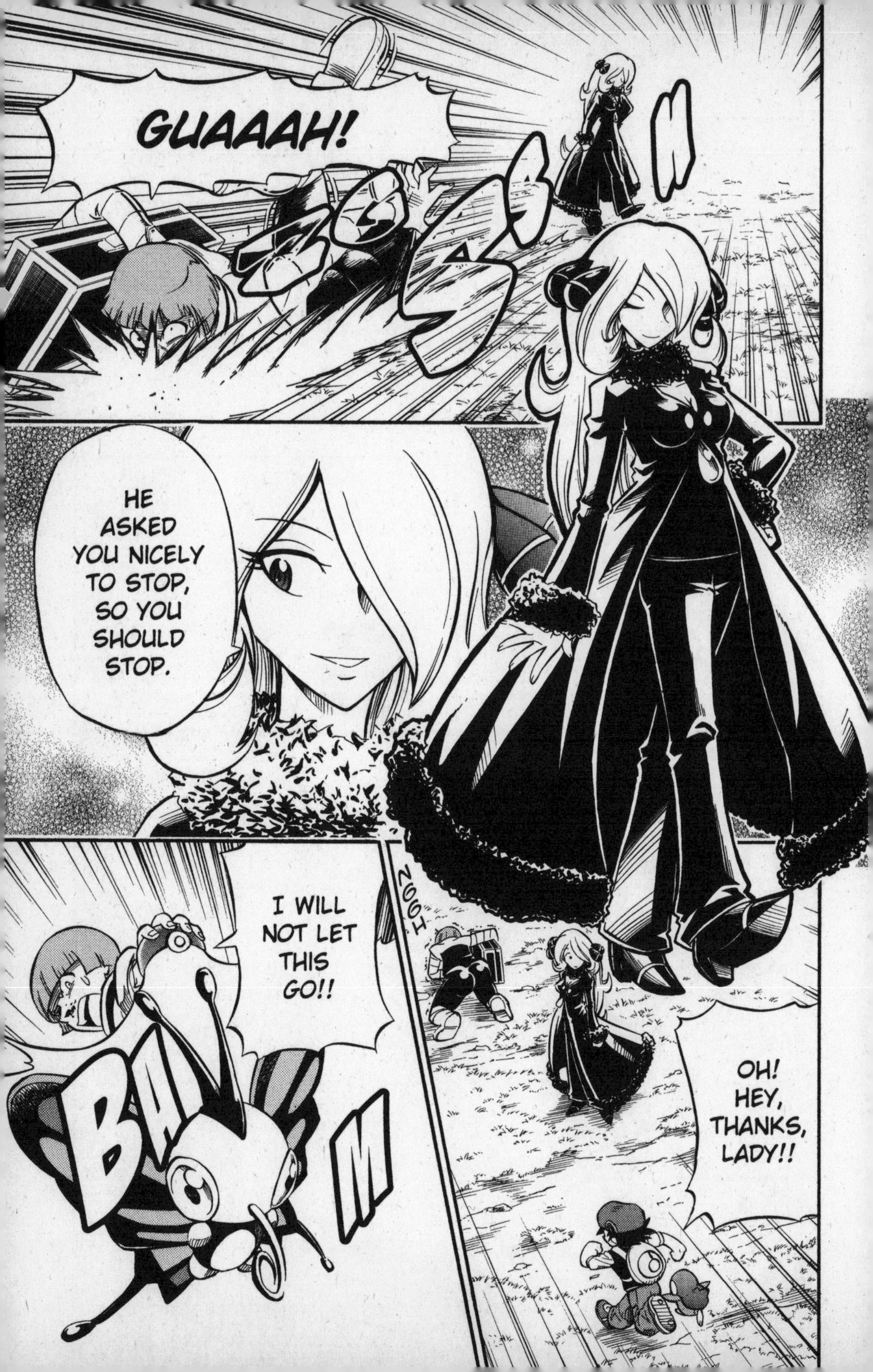
GUAAAH!
HE ASKED YOU NICELY TO STOP, SO YOU SHOULD STOP.
OH! HEY, THANKS, LADY!!
I WILL NOT LET THIS GO!!
BAM

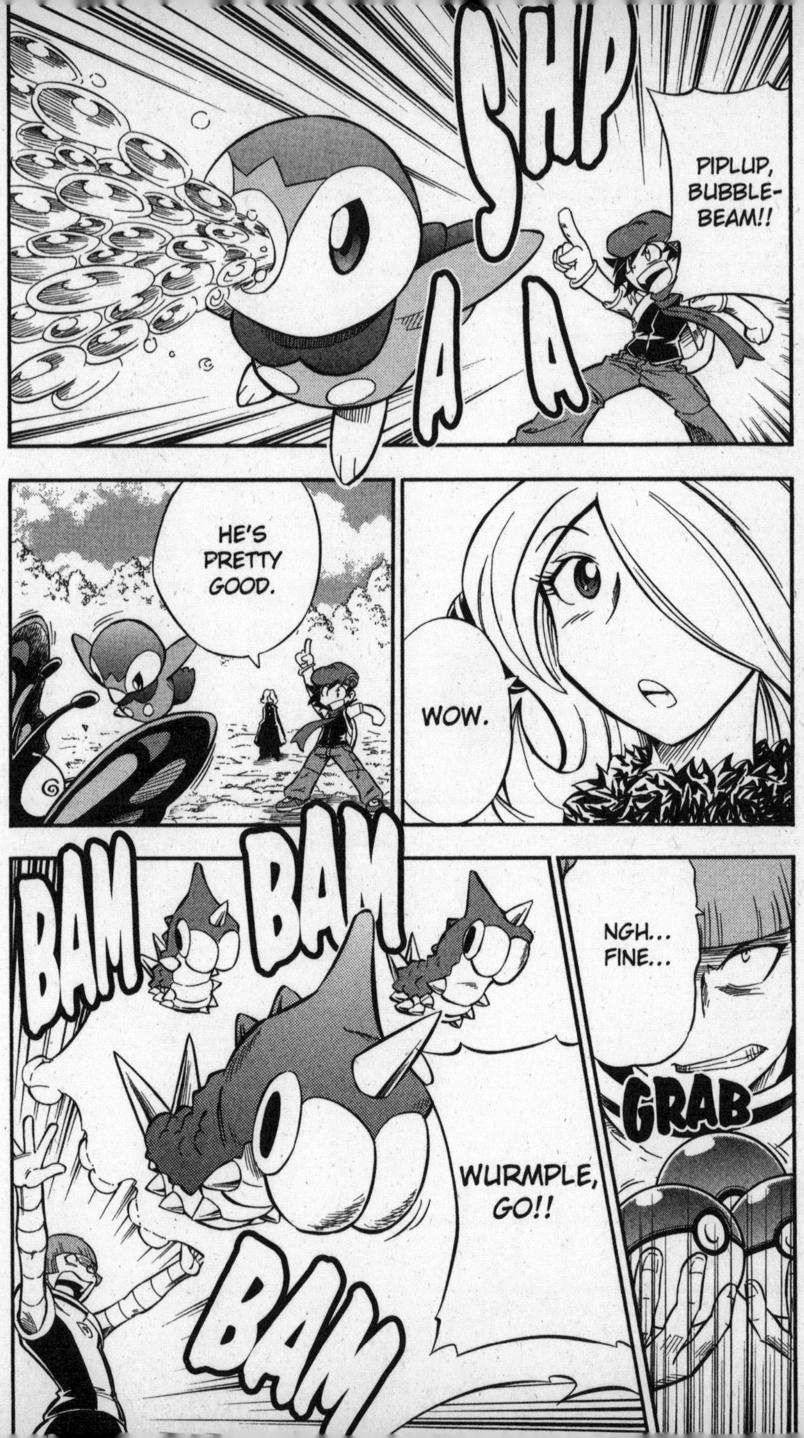
SHP
PIPLUP, BUBBLE-BEAM!!
A A
WOW.
HE'S PRETTY GOOD.
NGH... FINE...
GRAB
BAM BAM
WURMPLE, GO!!
BAM

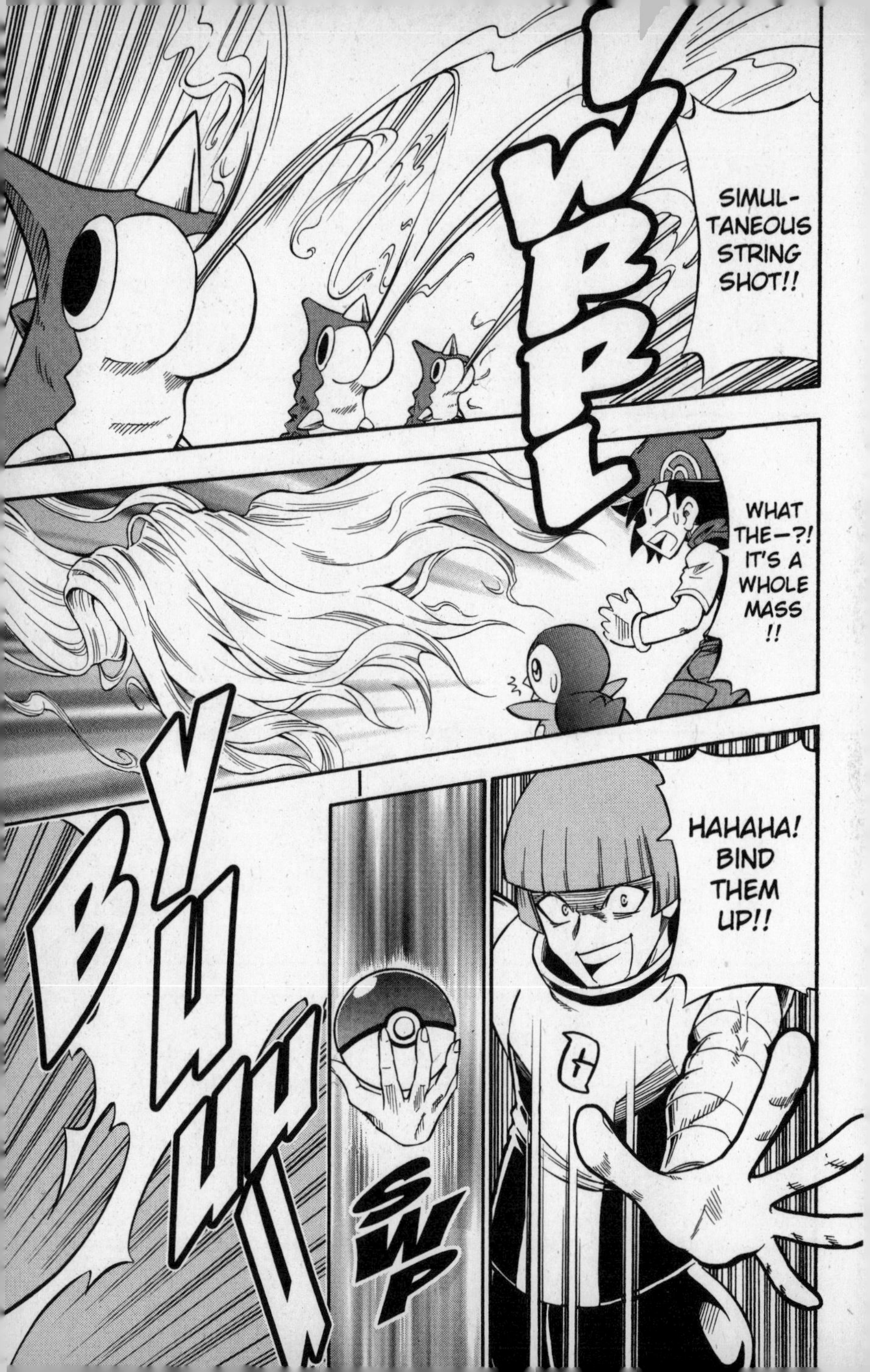
SIMUL-TANEOUS STRING SHOT!!
WHAT THE—?! IT'S A WHOLE MASS!!
HAHAHA! BIND THEM UP!!
SWP

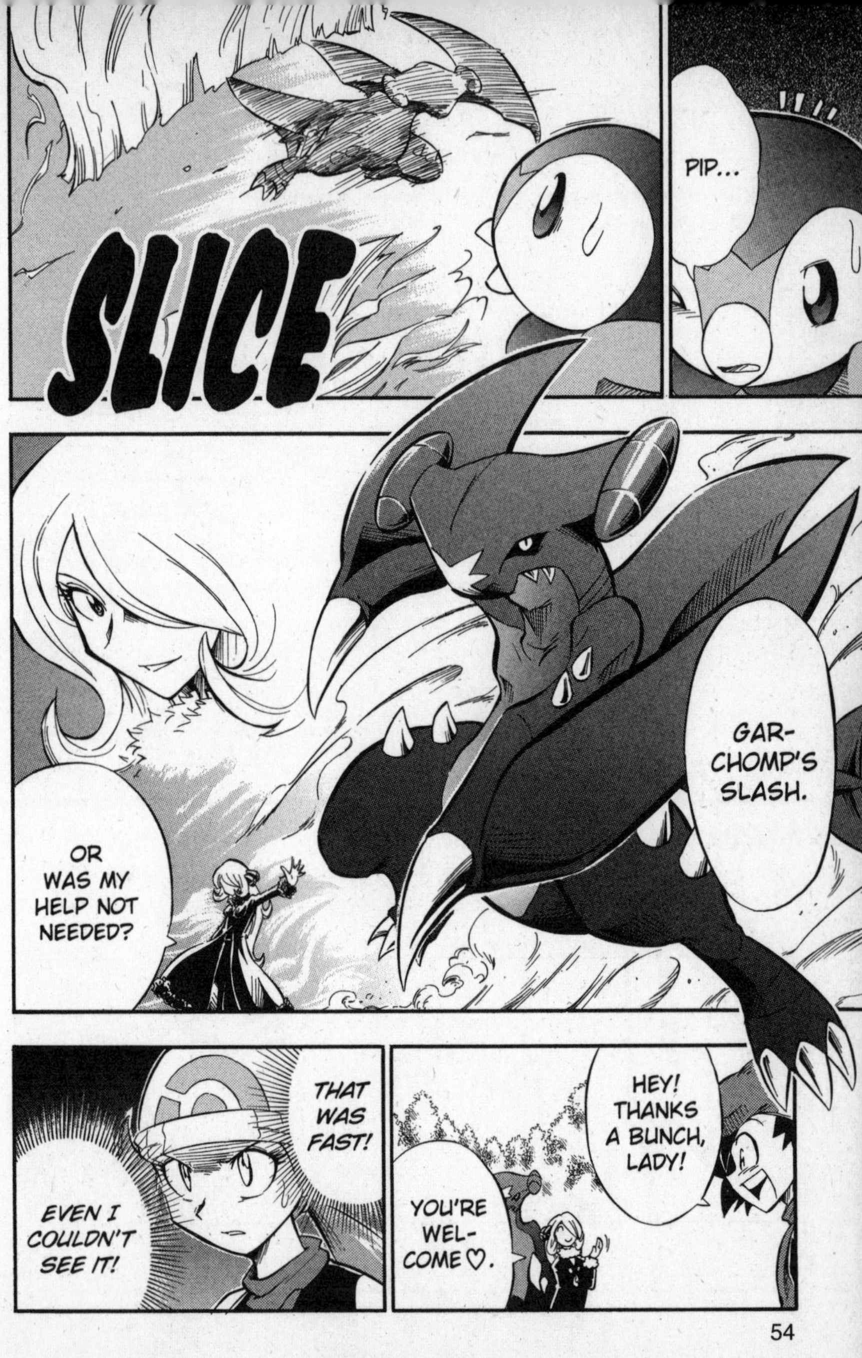
PIP...
SLICE
GAR-CHOMP'S SLASH.
OR WAS MY HELP NOT NEEDED?
HEY! THANKS A BUNCH, LADY!
YOU'RE WEL-COME♡.
THAT WAS FAST!
EVEN I COULDN'T SEE IT!

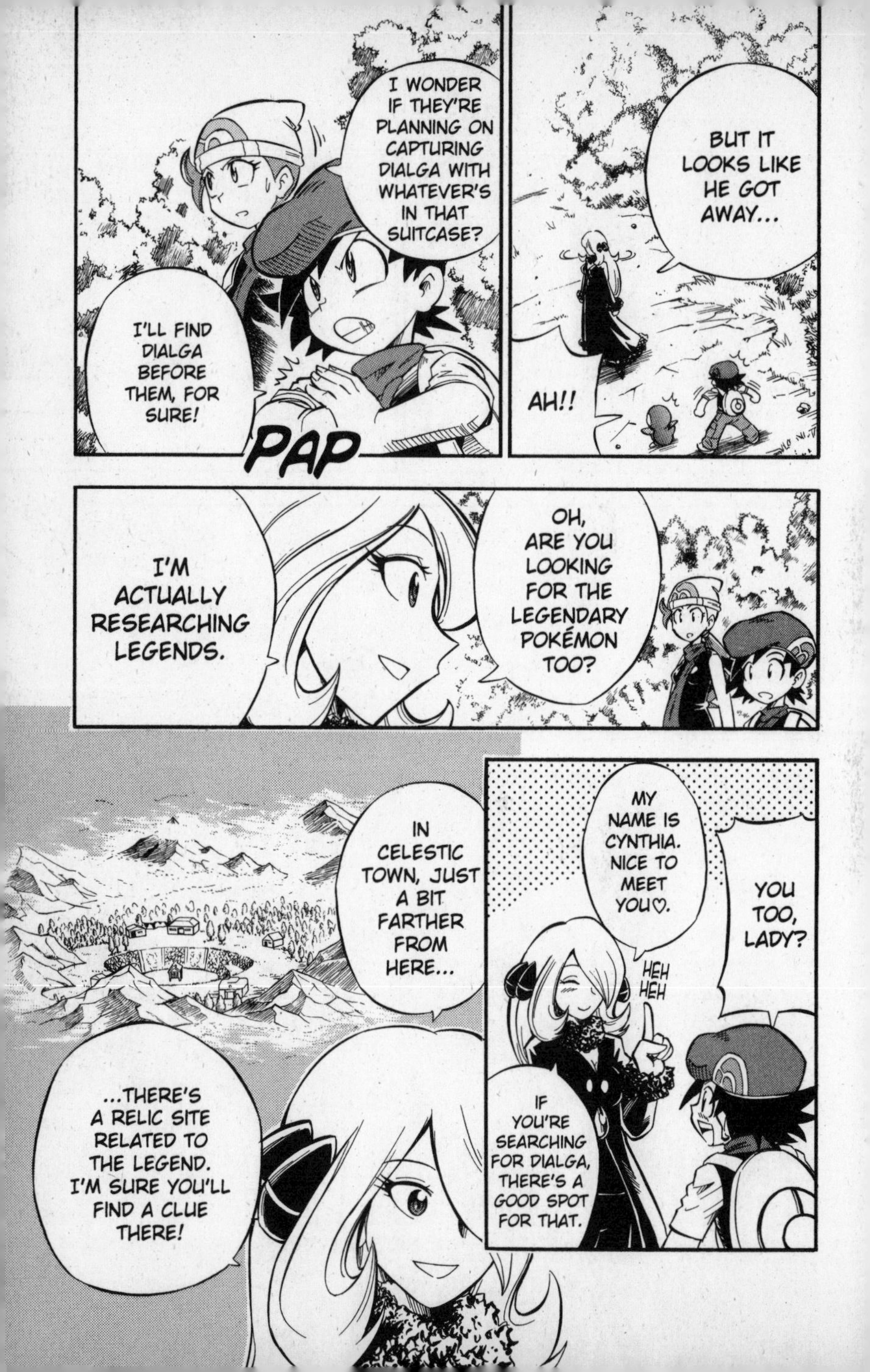
BUT IT LOOKS LIKE HE GOT AWAY...
AH!!
I WONDER IF THEY'RE PLANNING ON CAPTURING DIALGA WITH WHATEVER'S IN THAT SUITCASE?
I'LL FIND DIALGA BEFORE THEM, FOR SURE!
PAP
OH, ARE YOU LOOKING FOR THE LEGENDARY POKÉMON TOO?
I'M ACTUALLY RESEARCHING LEGENDS.
YOU TOO, LADY?
MY NAME IS CYNTHIA. NICE TO MEET YOU♡.
HEH HEH
IF YOU'RE SEARCHING FOR DIALGA, THERE'S A GOOD SPOT FOR THAT.
IN CELESTIC TOWN, JUST A BIT FARTHER FROM HERE...
...THERE'S A RELIC SITE RELATED TO THE LEGEND. I'M SURE YOU'LL FIND A CLUE THERE!

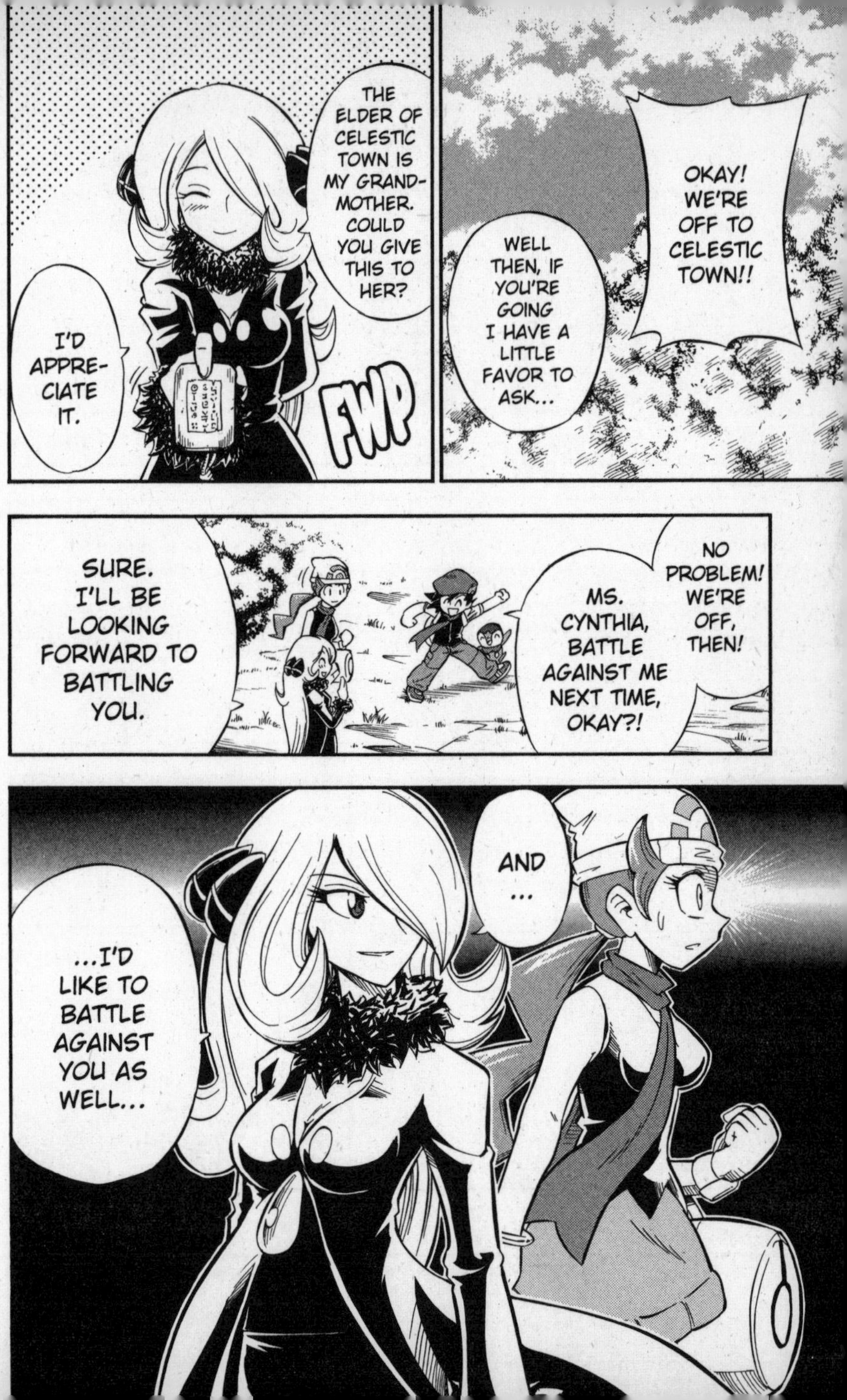
OKAY! WE'RE OFF TO CELESTIC TOWN!!
WELL THEN, IF YOU'RE GOING I HAVE A LITTLE FAVOR TO ASK...
THE ELDER OF CELESTIC TOWN IS MY GRAND-MOTHER. COULD YOU GIVE THIS TO HER?
FWP
I'D APPRE-CIATE IT.
NO PROBLEM! WE'RE OFF, THEN!
MS. CYNTHIA, BATTLE AGAINST ME NEXT TIME, OKAY?!
SURE. I'LL BE LOOKING FORWARD TO BATTLING YOU.
AND ...
...I'D LIKE TO BATTLE AGAINST YOU AS WELL...

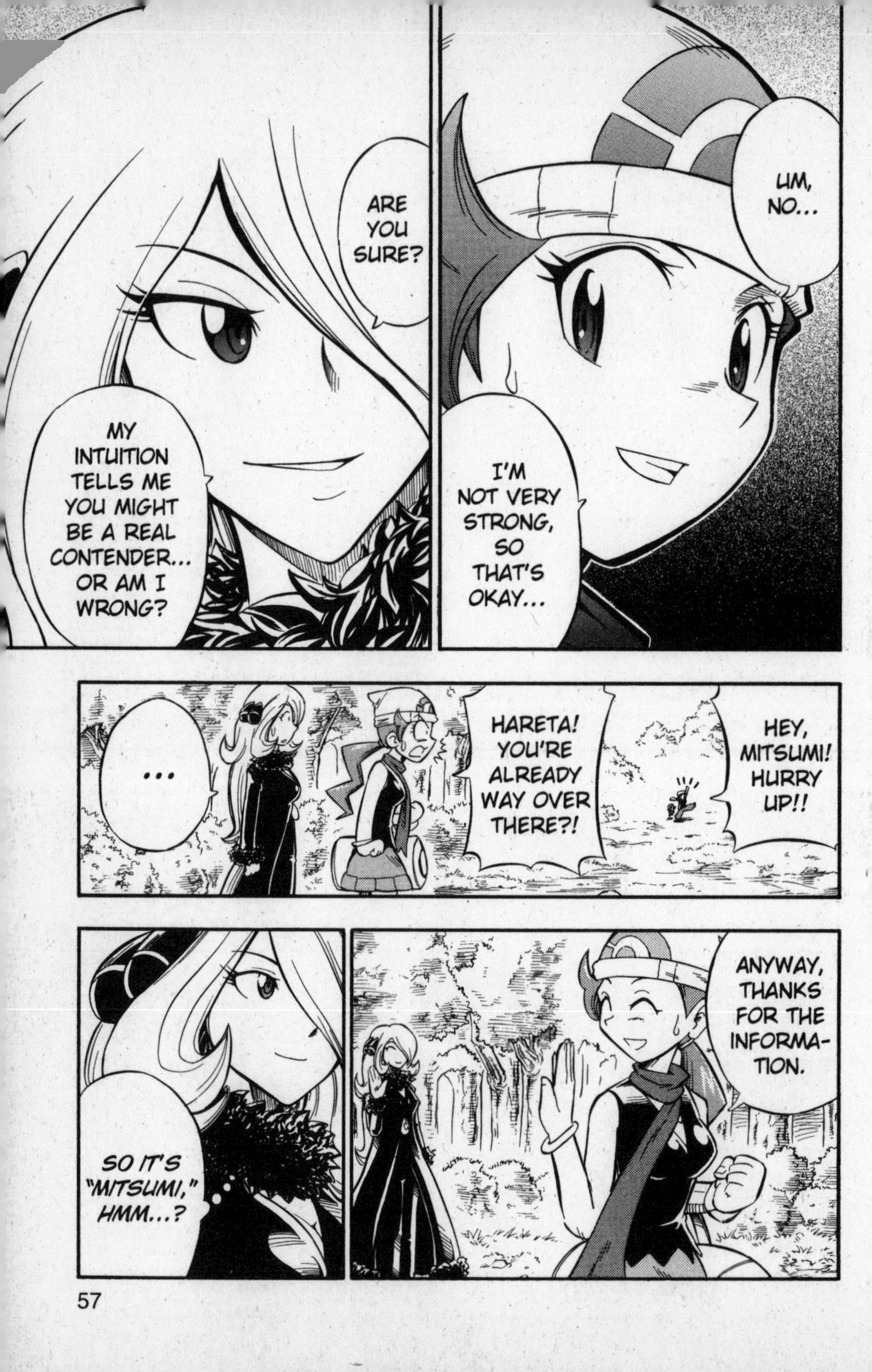
UM, NO...
I'M NOT VERY STRONG, SO THAT'S OKAY...
ARE YOU SURE?
MY INTUITION TELLS ME YOU MIGHT BE A REAL CONTENDER... OR AM I WRONG?
HEY, MITSUMI! HURRY UP!!
HARETA! YOU'RE ALREADY WAY OVER THERE?!
...
ANYWAY, THANKS FOR THE INFORMATION.
SO IT'S "MITSUMI," HMM...?

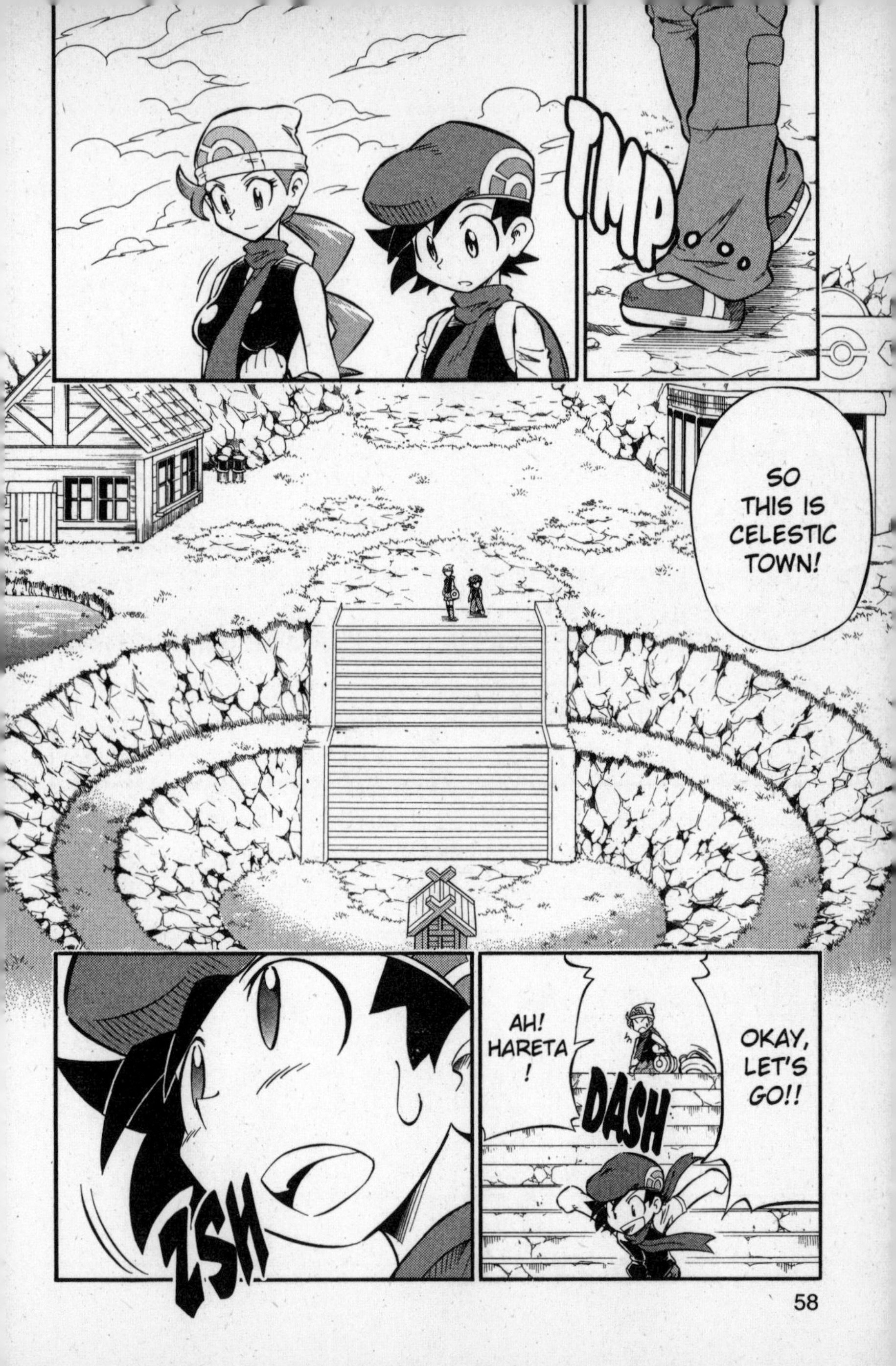
TMP
SO THIS IS CELESTIC TOWN!
OKAY, LET'S GO!!
AH! HARETA!
DASH
ZSH

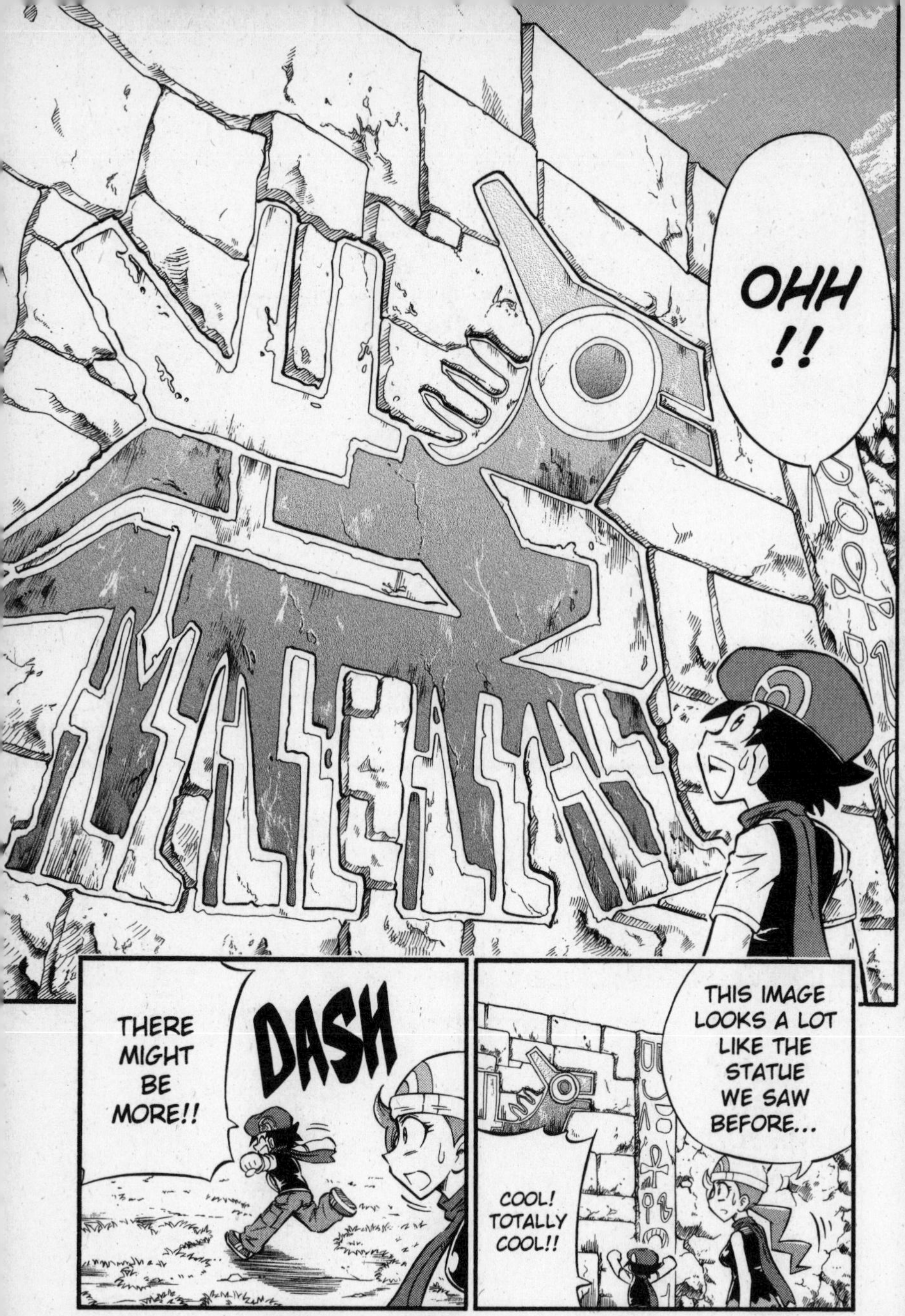
OHH !!
THIS IMAGE LOOKS A LOT LIKE THE STATUE WE SAW BEFORE...
COOL! TOTALLY COOL!!
DASH
THERE MIGHT BE MORE!!

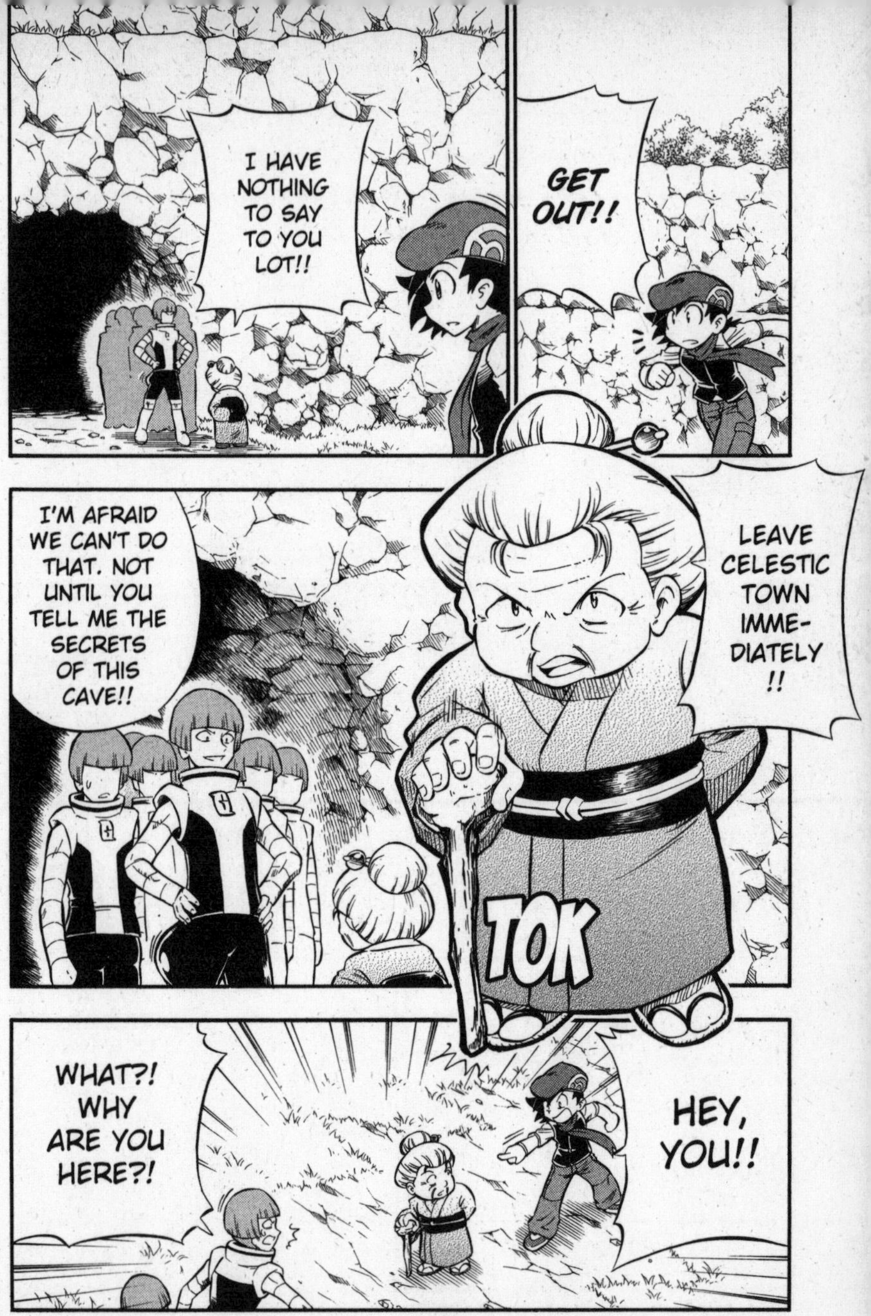
GET OUT!!
I HAVE NOTHING TO SAY TO YOU LOT!!
LEAVE CELESTIC TOWN IMME-DIATELY !!
I'M AFRAID WE CAN'T DO THAT. NOT UNTIL YOU TELL ME THE SECRETS OF THIS CAVE!!
TOK
HEY, YOU!!
WHAT?! WHY ARE YOU HERE?!

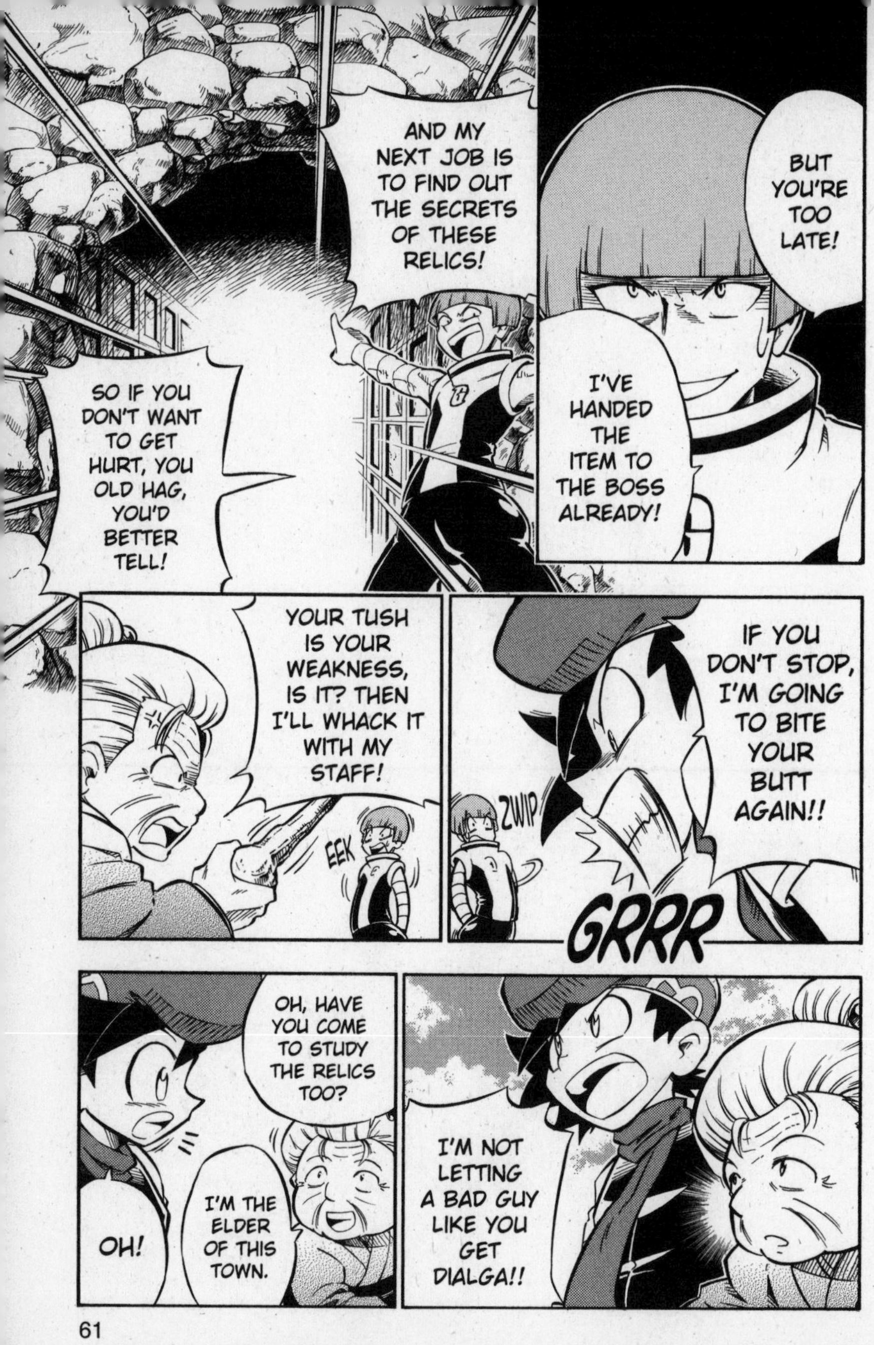
BUT YOU'RE TOO LATE!
I'VE HANDED THE ITEM TO THE BOSS ALREADY!
AND MY NEXT JOB IS TO FIND OUT THE SECRETS OF THESE RELICS!
SO IF YOU DON'T WANT TO GET HURT, YOU OLD HAG, YOU'D BETTER TELL!
IF YOU DON'T STOP, I'M GOING TO BITE YOUR BUTT AGAIN!!
ZWIP
GRRR
YOUR TUSH IS YOUR WEAKNESS, IS IT? THEN I'LL WHACK IT WITH MY STAFF!
EEK
I'M NOT LETTING A BAD GUY LIKE YOU GET DIALGA!!
OH, HAVE YOU COME TO STUDY THE RELICS TOO?
I'M THE ELDER OF THIS TOWN.
OH!

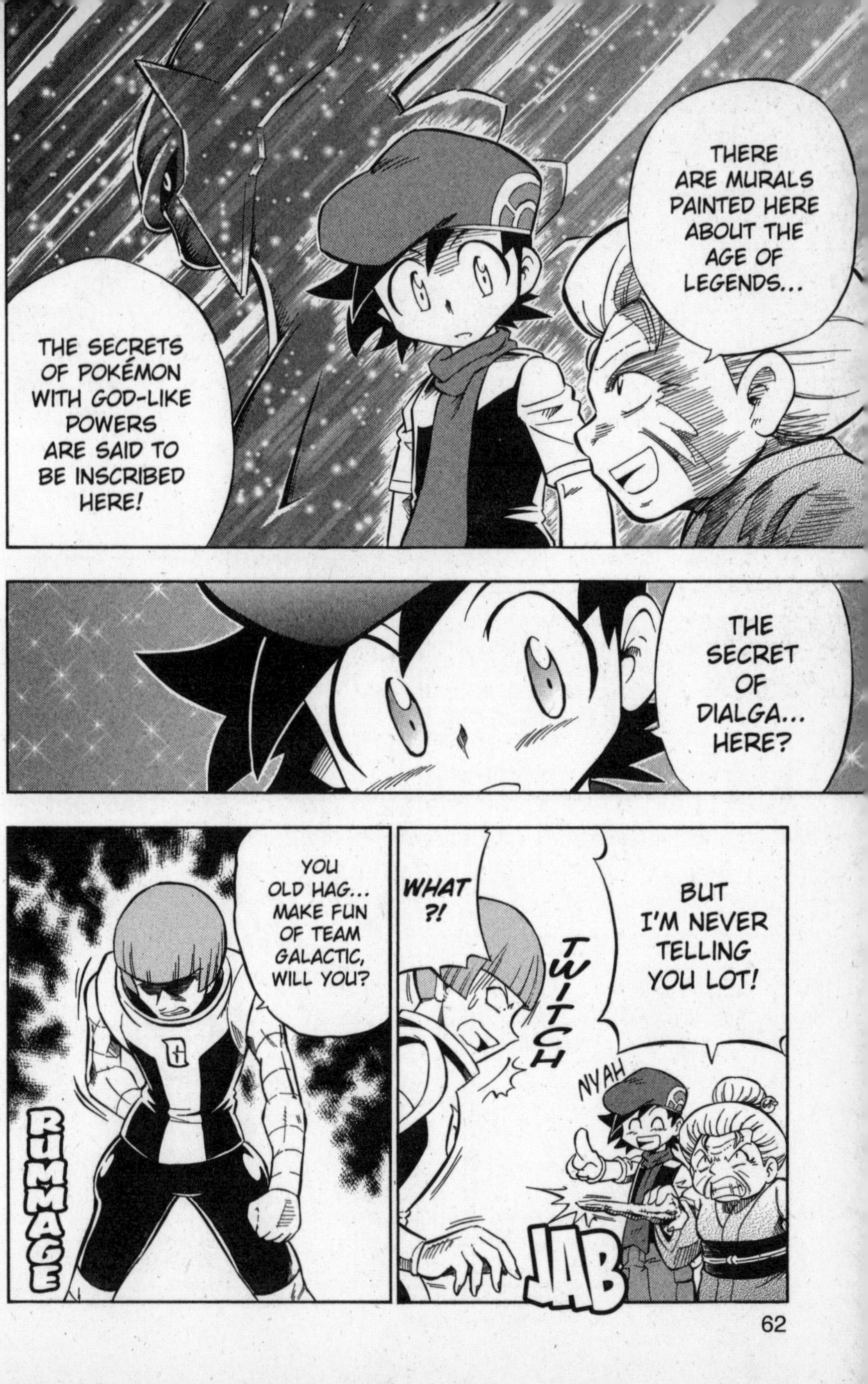
THERE ARE MURALS PAINTED HERE ABOUT THE AGE OF LEGENDS...
THE SECRETS OF POKÉMON WITH GOD-LIKE POWERS ARE SAID TO BE INSCRIBED HERE!
THE SECRET OF DIALGA... HERE?
BUT I'M NEVER TELLING YOU LOT!
NYAH
JAB
TWITCH
WHAT?!
YOU OLD HAG... MAKE FUN OF TEAM GALACTIC, WILL YOU?
RUMMAGE

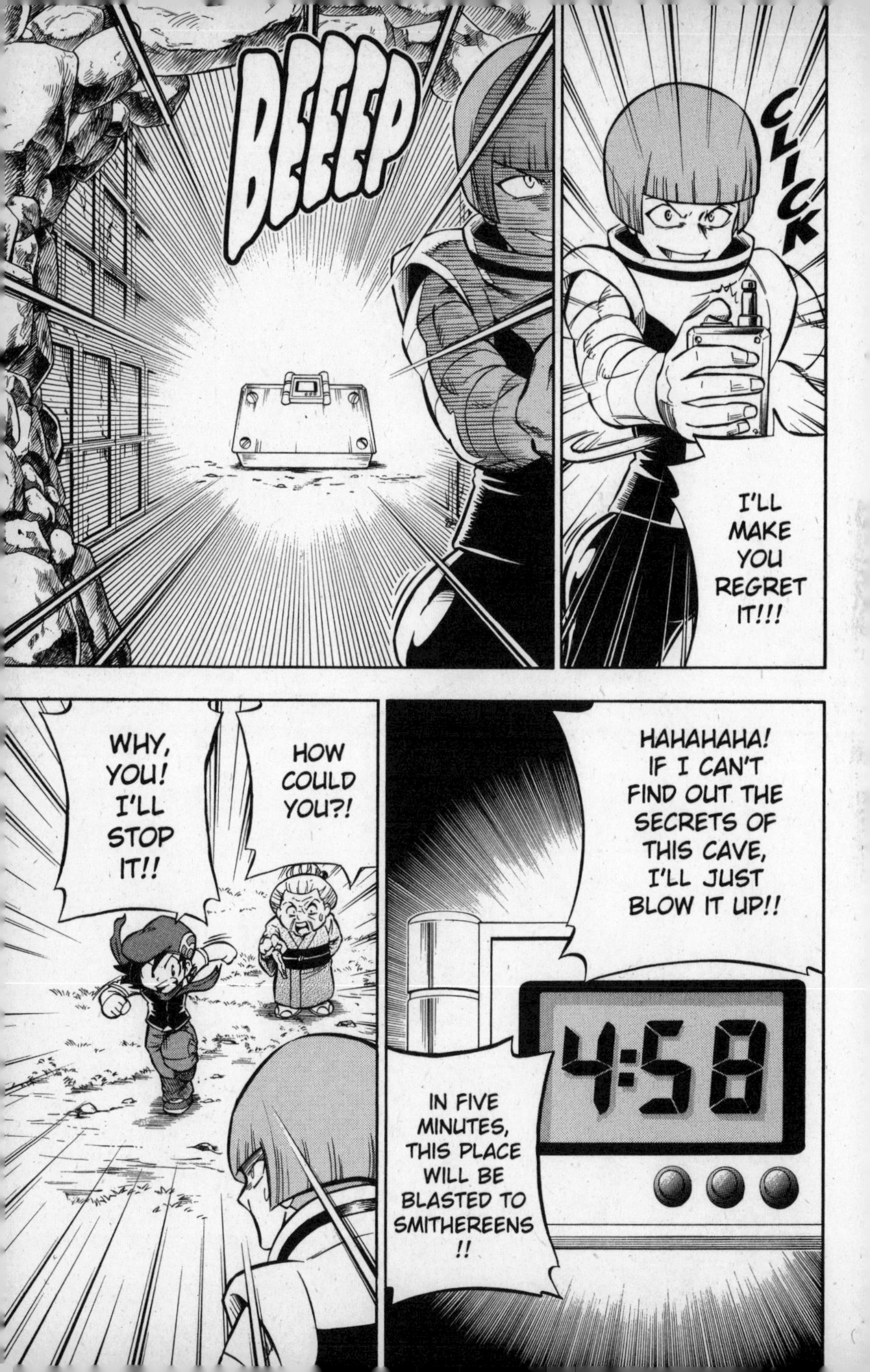
CLICK
I'LL MAKE YOU REGRET IT!!!
BEEEP
HAHAHAHA! IF I CAN'T FIND OUT THE SECRETS OF THIS CAVE, I'LL JUST BLOW IT UP!!
4:58
IN FIVE MINUTES, THIS PLACE WILL BE BLASTED TO SMITHEREENS!!
HOW COULD YOU?!
WHY, YOU! I'LL STOP IT!!

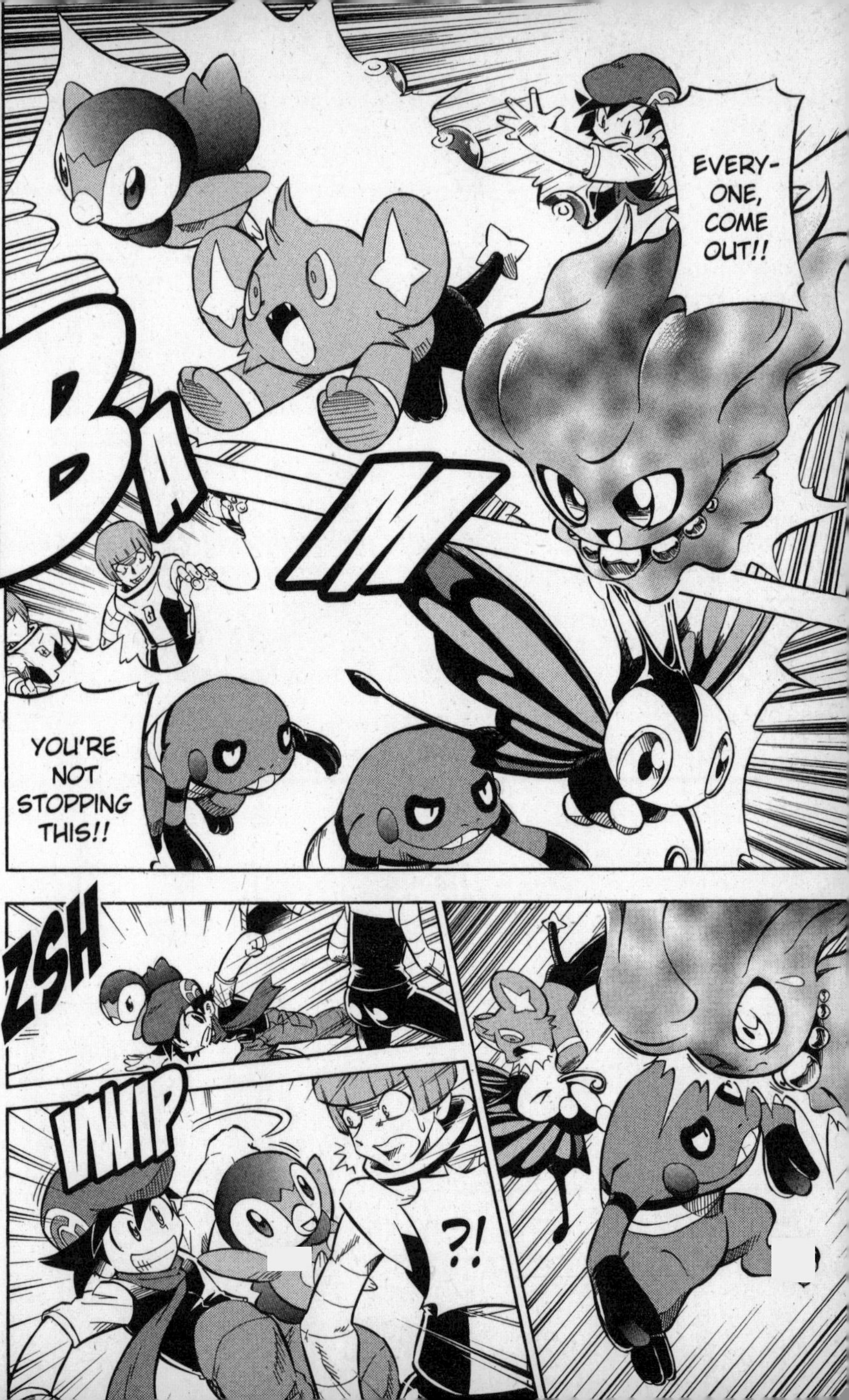
EVERY-ONE, COME OUT!!
BAM
YOU'RE NOT STOPPING THIS!!
ZSH
VWIP
?!

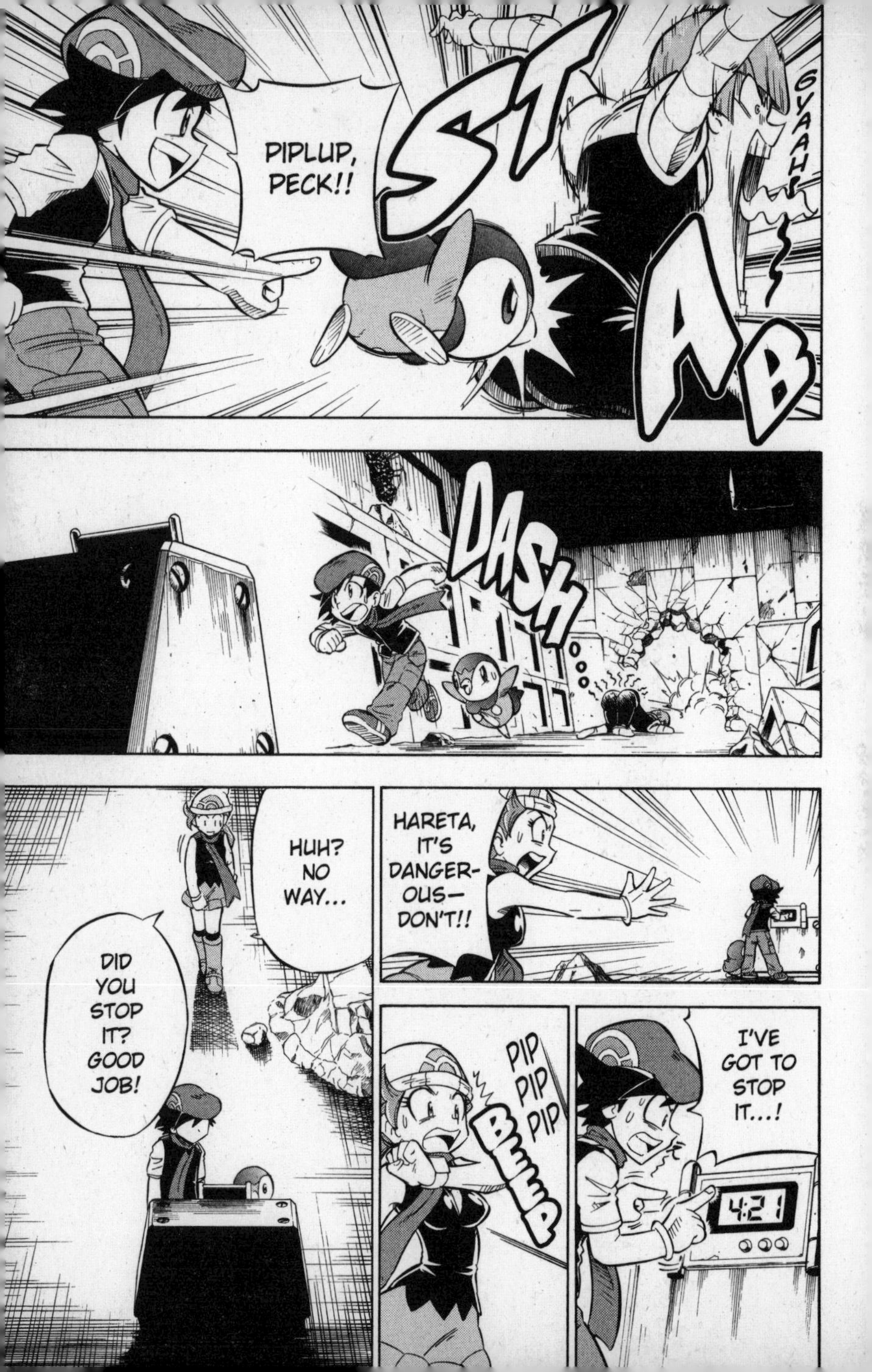
GYAAH!
STAB
PIPLUP, PECK!!
DASH
HARETA, IT'S DANGER-OUS—DON'T!!
I'VE GOT TO STOP IT...!
4:21
PIP PIP PIP
BEEP
HUH? NO WAY...
DID YOU STOP IT? GOOD JOB!

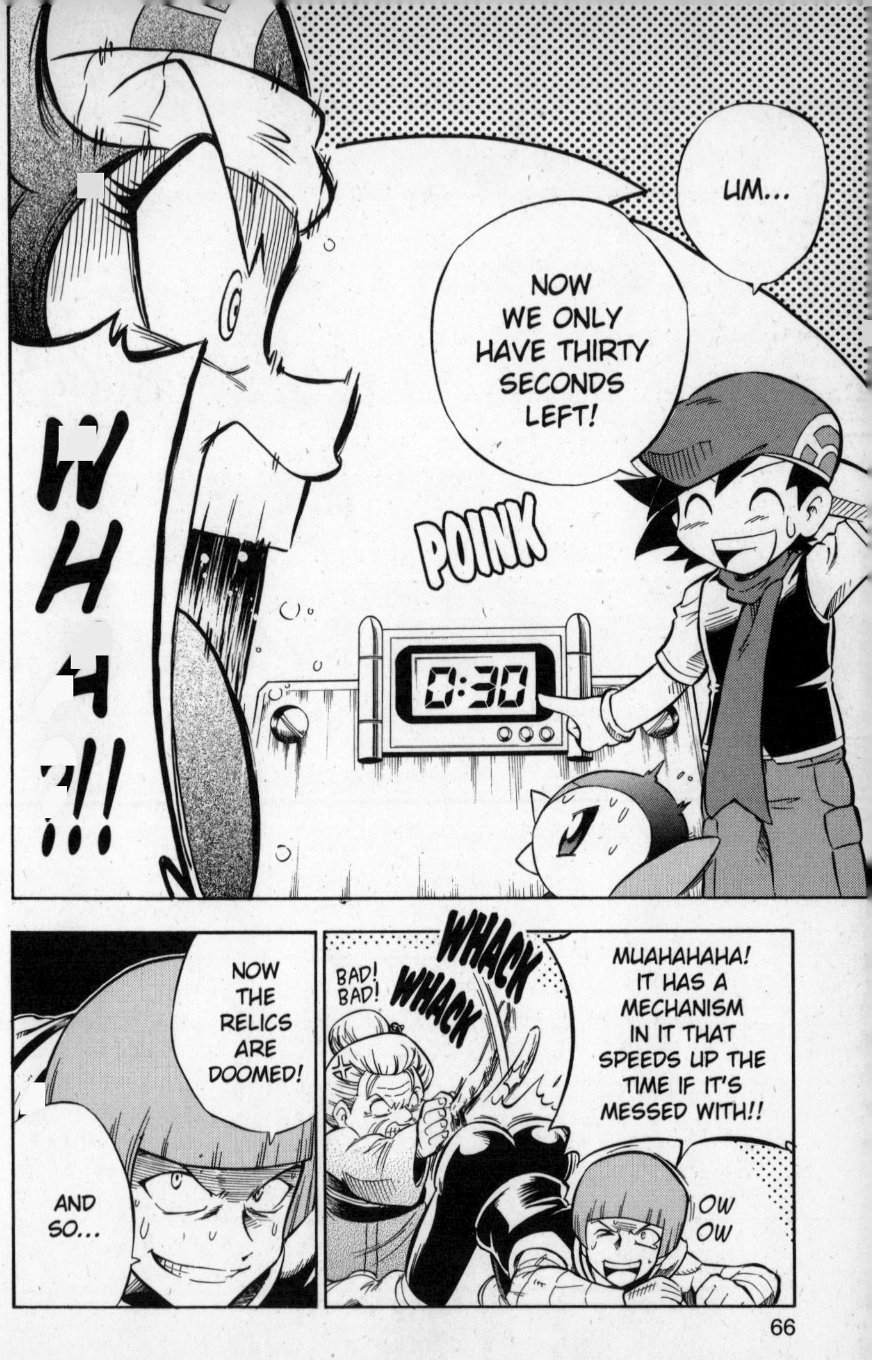
UM...
NOW WE ONLY HAVE THIRTY SECONDS LEFT!
POINK
0:30
MUAHAHAHA! IT HAS A MECHANISM IN IT THAT SPEEDS UP THE TIME IF IT'S MESSED WITH!!
WHACK
WHACK
BAD! BAD!
OW OW
NOW THE RELICS ARE DOOMED!
AND SO...

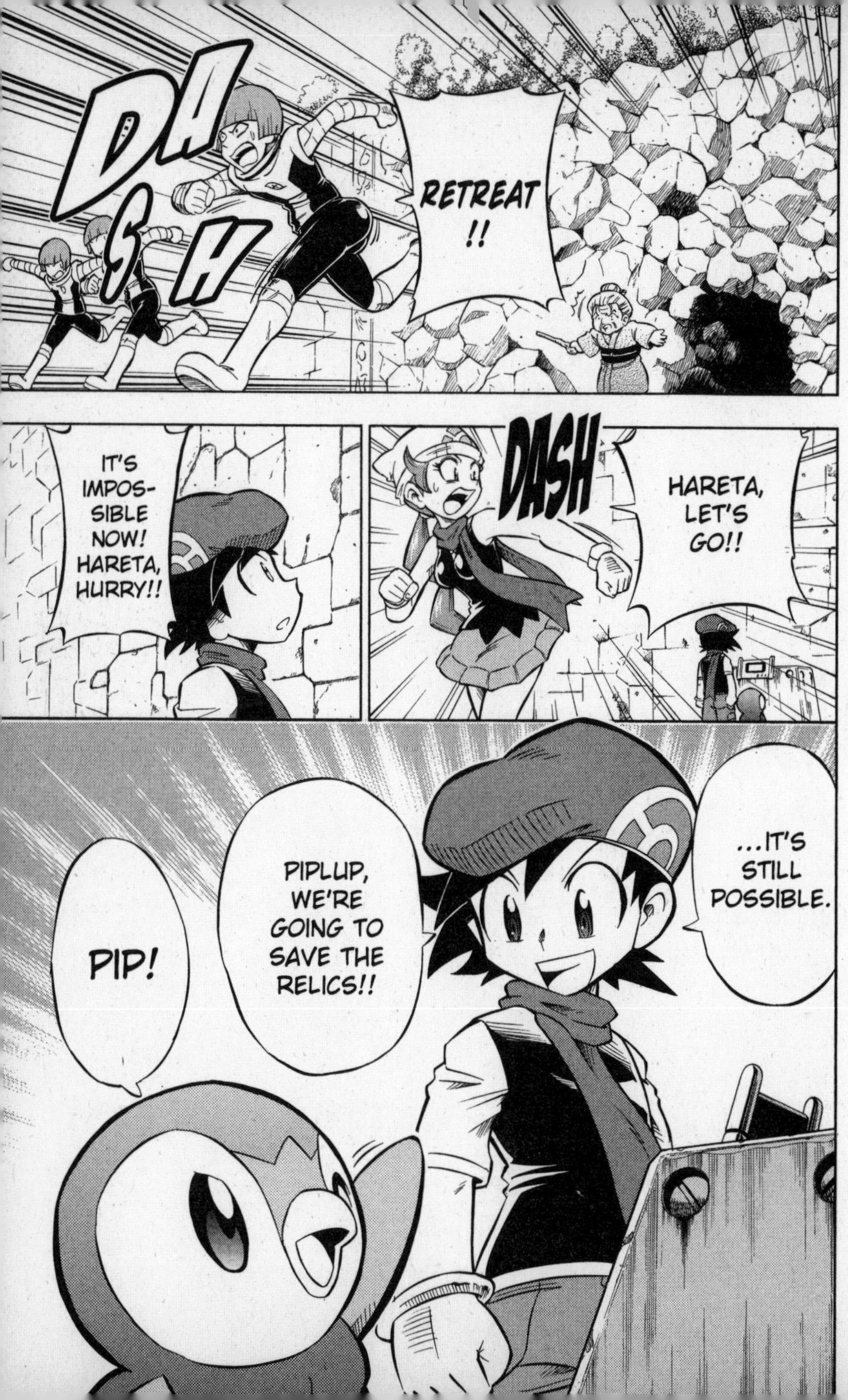
RETREAT!!
DASH
HARETA, LET'S GO!!
DASH
IT'S IMPOSSIBLE NOW! HARETA, HURRY!!
...IT'S STILL POSSIBLE.
PIPLUP, WE'RE GOING TO SAVE THE RELICS!!
PIP!

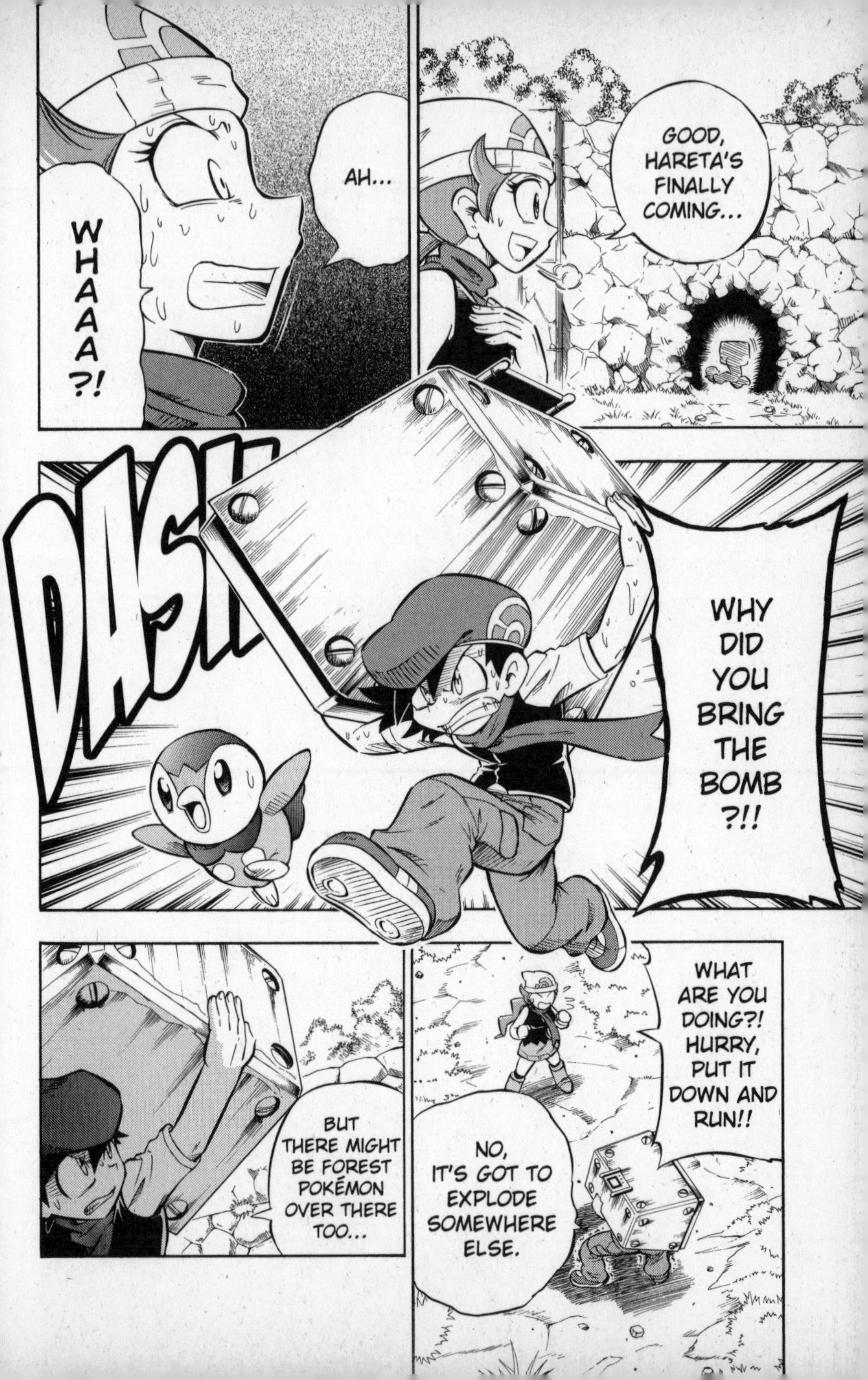
GOOD, HARETA'S FINALLY COMING...
AH...
WHAAAA?!
WHY DID YOU BRING THE BOMB?!!
DASH
WHAT ARE YOU DOING?! HURRY, PUT IT DOWN AND RUN!!
NO, IT'S GOT TO EXPLODE SOMEWHERE ELSE.
BUT THERE MIGHT BE FOREST POKÉMON OVER THERE TOO...

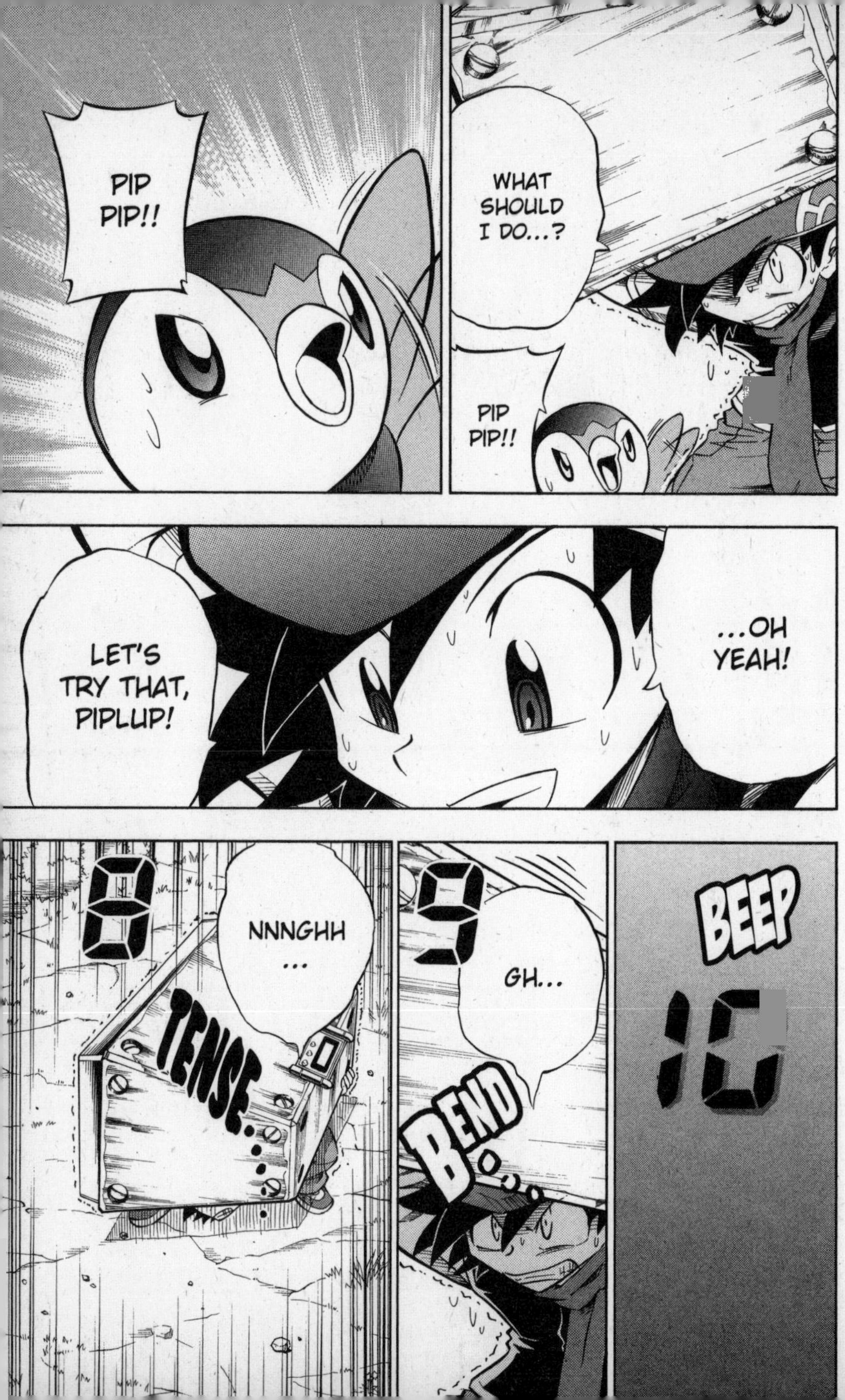
WHAT SHOULD I DO...?
PIP PIP!!
PIP PIP!!
...OH YEAH!
LET'S TRY THAT, PIPLUP!
BEEP
10
9
GH...
BEND...
8
NNNGHH...
TENSE...

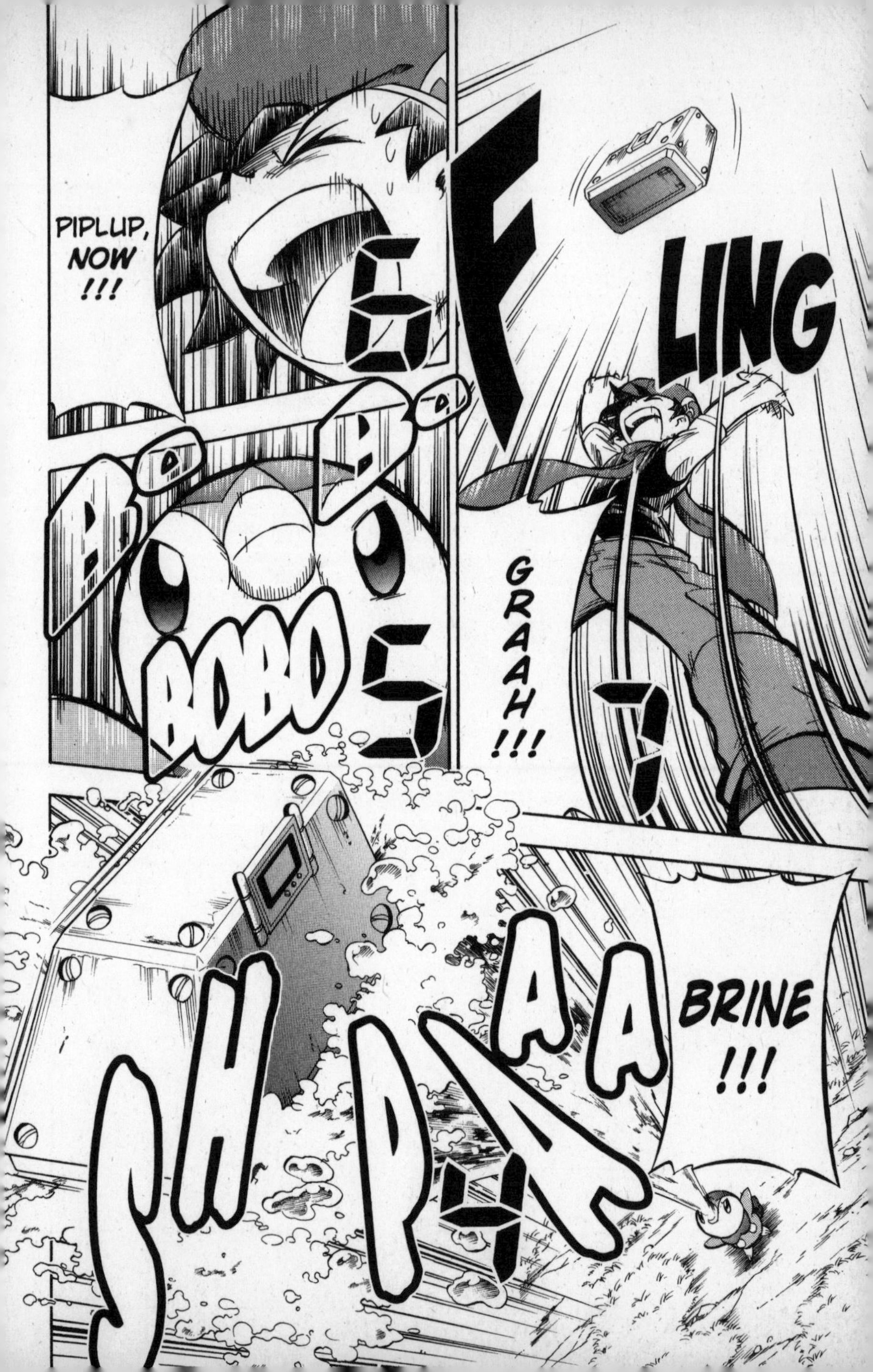
FLING
GRAAH!!!
PIPLUP, NOW!!!
BOBO
SHPAAA
BRINE!!!

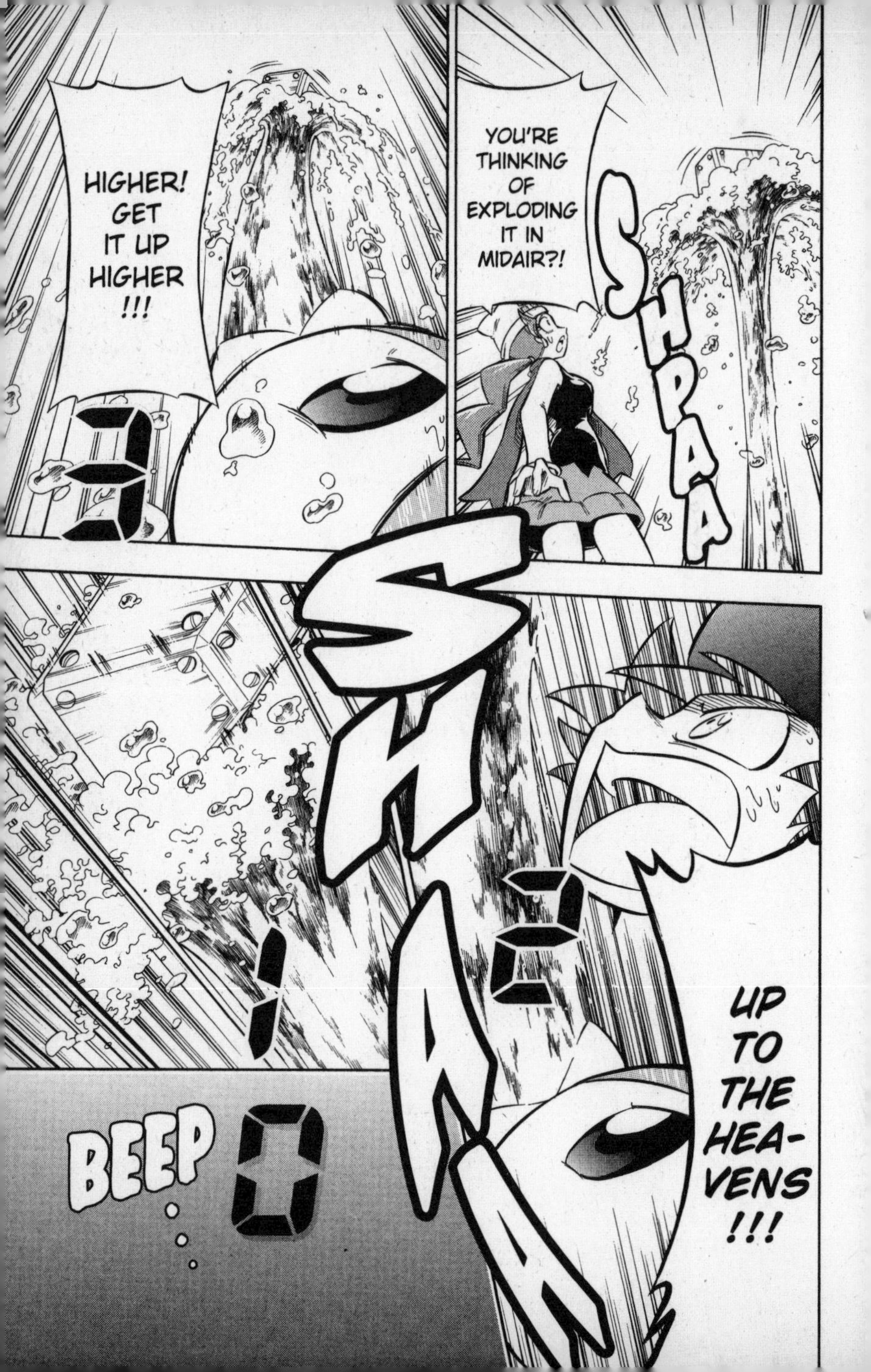
YOU'RE THINKING OF EXPLODING IT IN MIDAIR?!
SHPAA
HIGHER! GET IT UP HIGHER!!!
SHAAA
UP TO THE HEA-VENS!!!
BEEP
0

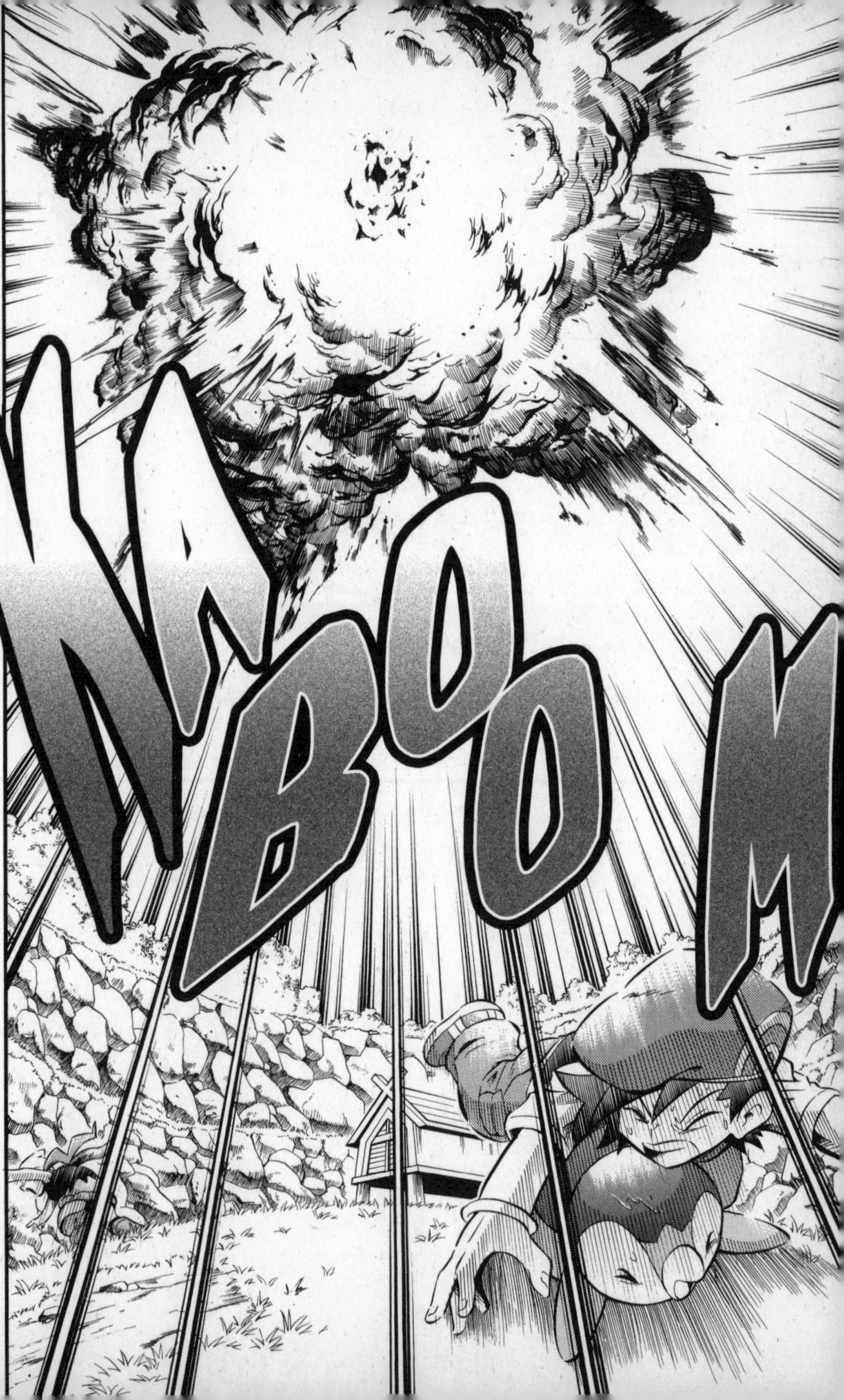
KABOOM

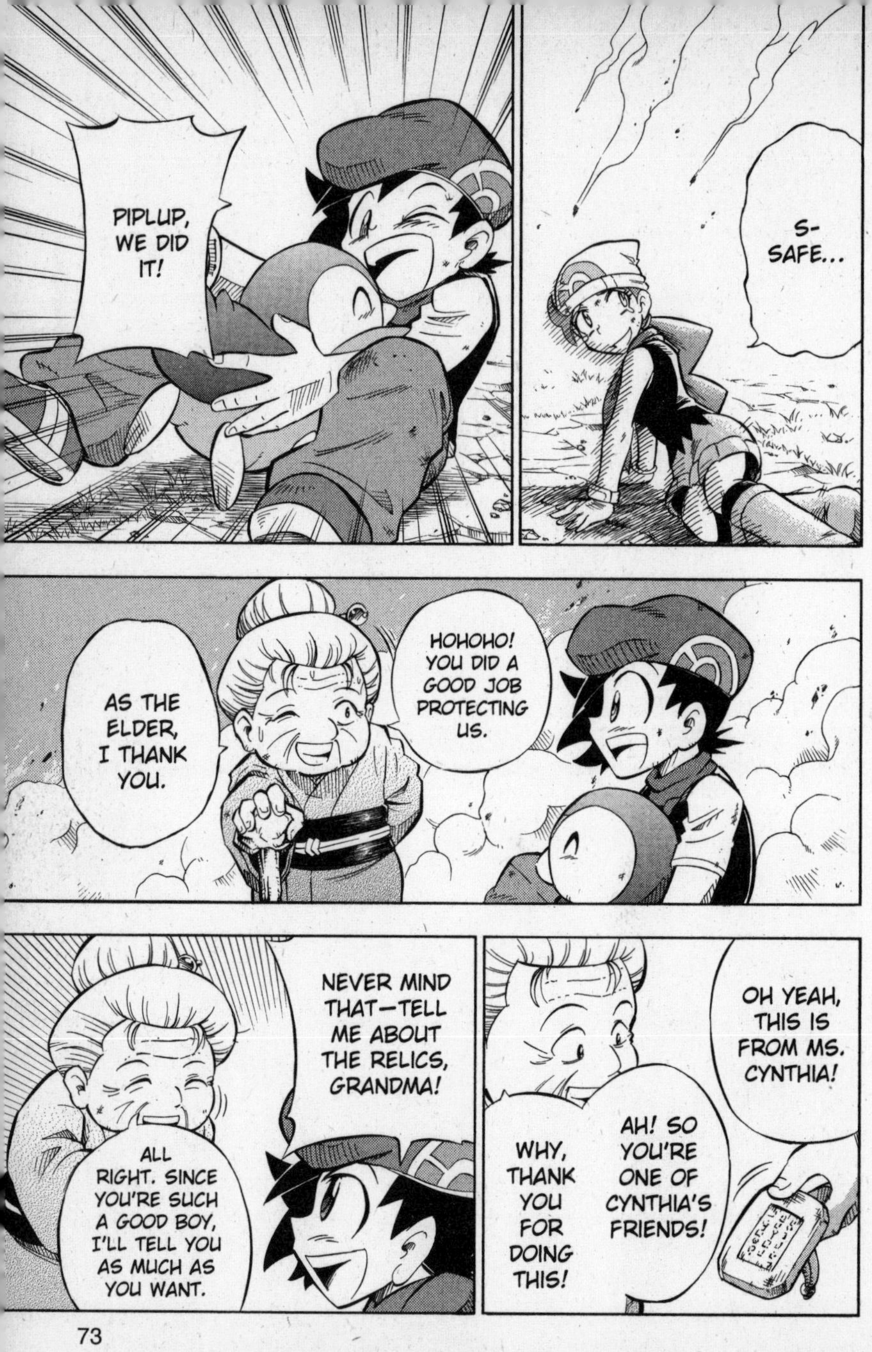
S- SAFE...
PIPLUP, WE DID IT!
HOHOHO! YOU DID A GOOD JOB PROTECTING US.
AS THE ELDER, I THANK YOU.
OH YEAH, THIS IS FROM MS. CYNTHIA!
AH! SO YOU'RE ONE OF CYNTHIA'S FRIENDS!
WHY, THANK YOU FOR DOING THIS!
NEVER MIND THAT—TELL ME ABOUT THE RELICS, GRANDMA!
ALL RIGHT. SINCE YOU'RE SUCH A GOOD BOY, I'LL TELL YOU AS MUCH AS YOU WANT.

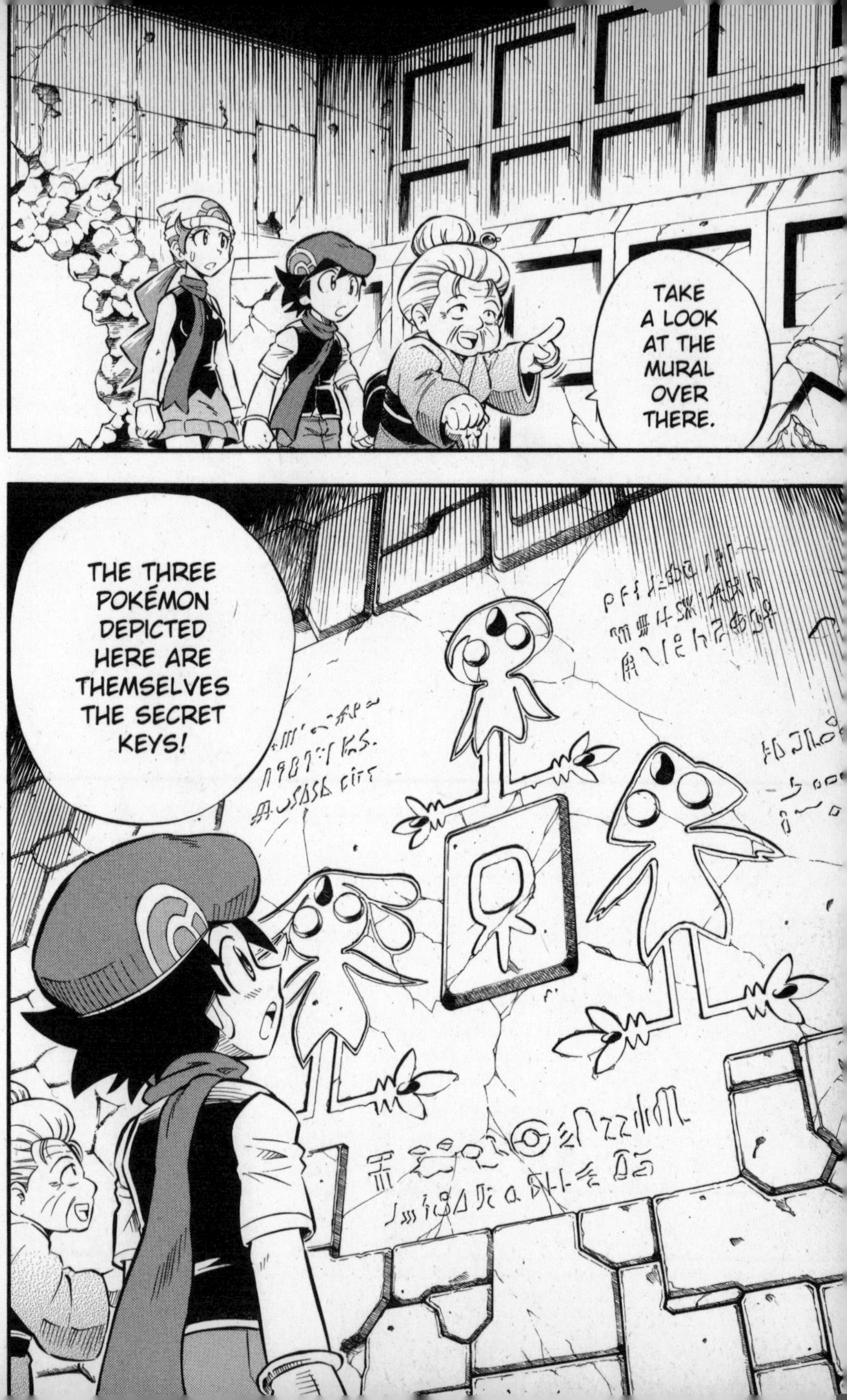
TAKE A LOOK AT THE MURAL OVER THERE.
THE THREE POKÉMON DEPICTED HERE ARE THEMSELVES THE SECRET KEYS!

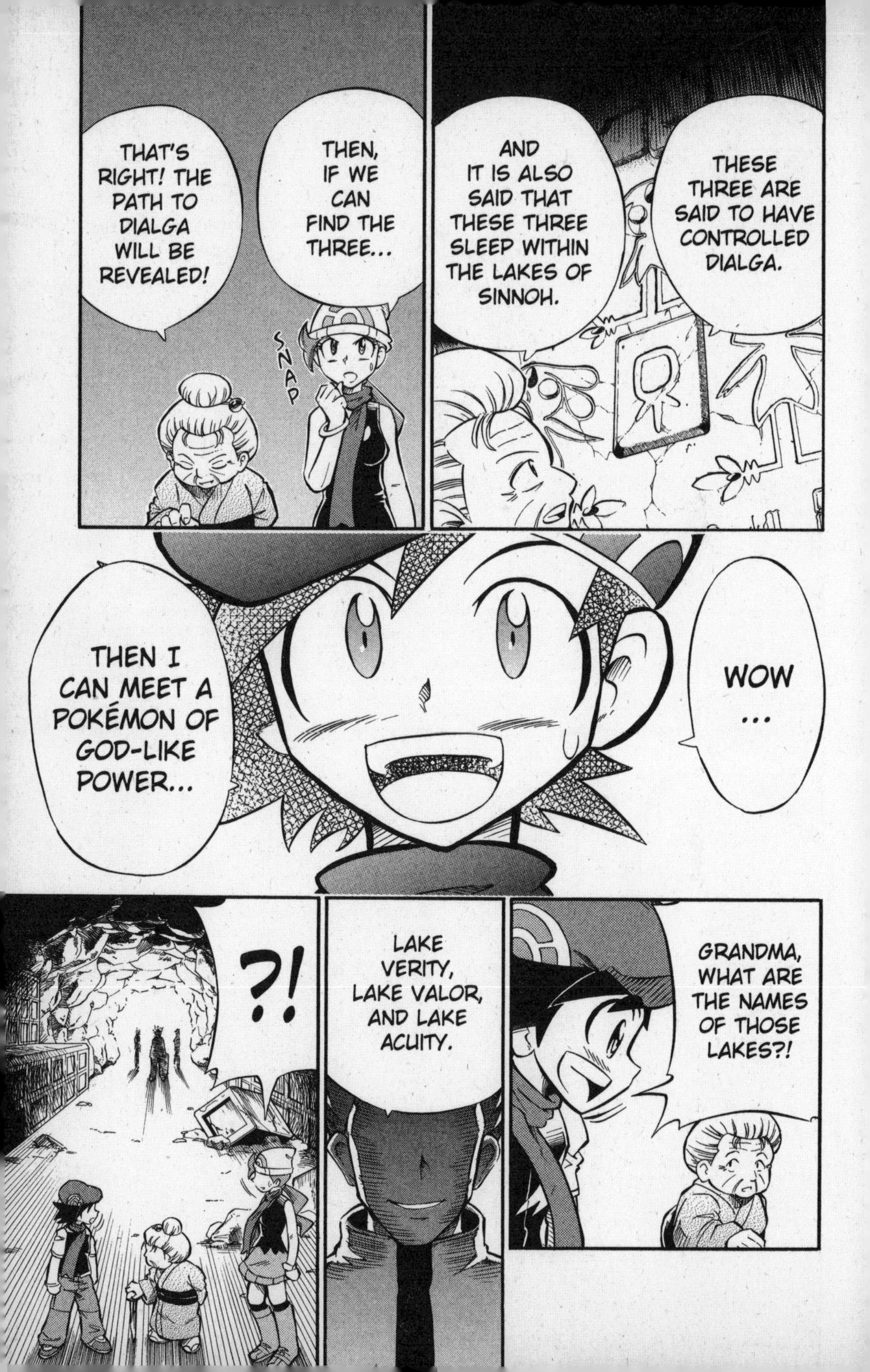
THESE THREE ARE SAID TO HAVE CONTROLLED DIALGA.
AND IT IS ALSO SAID THAT THESE THREE SLEEP WITHIN THE LAKES OF SINNOH.
THEN, IF WE CAN FIND THE THREE...
THAT'S RIGHT! THE PATH TO DIALGA WILL BE REVEALED!
SNAP
WOW ...
THEN I CAN MEET A POKÉMON OF GOD-LIKE POWER...
GRANDMA, WHAT ARE THE NAMES OF THOSE LAKES?!
LAKE VERITY, LAKE VALOR, AND LAKE ACUITY.
?!

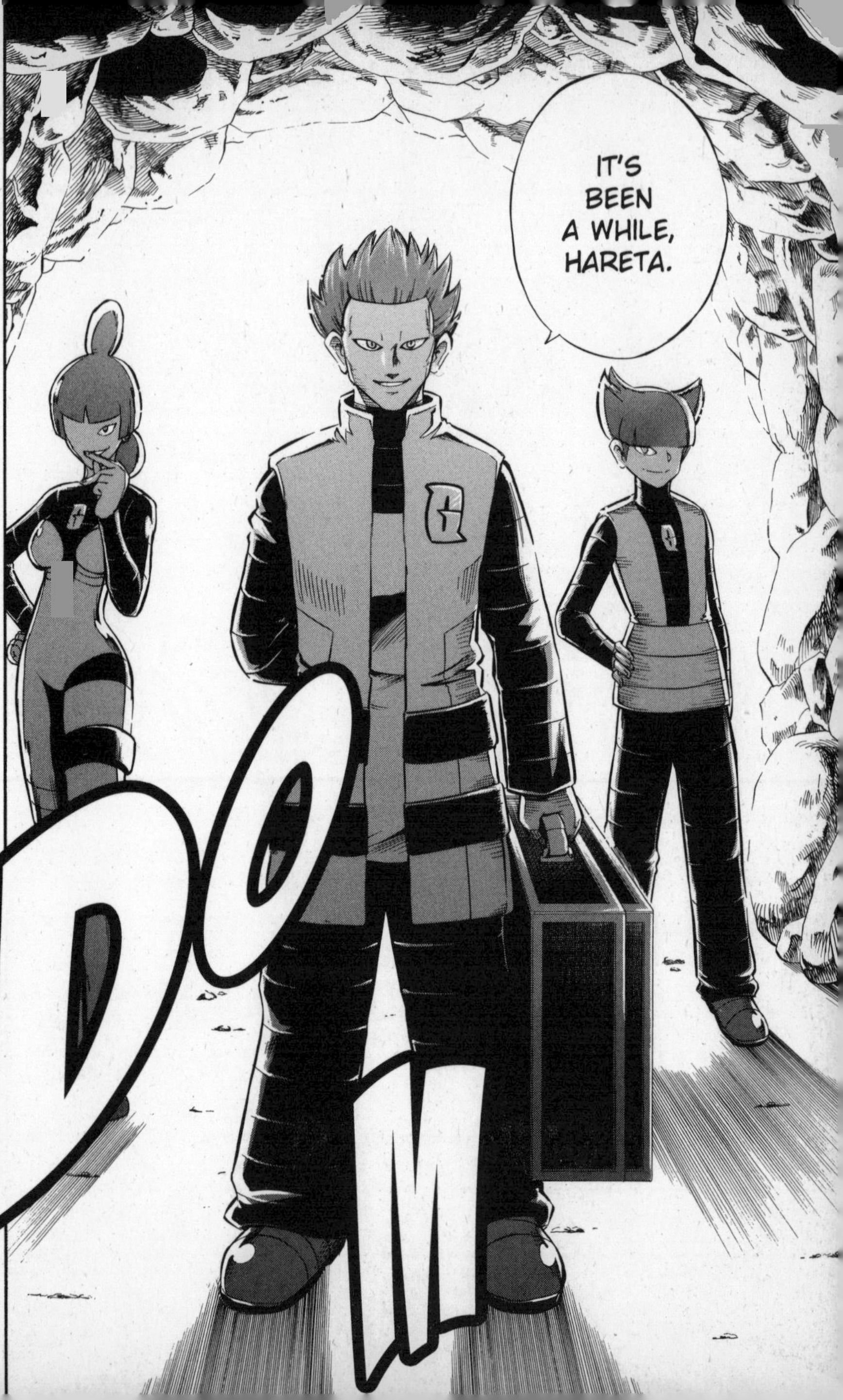
IT'S BEEN A WHILE, HARETA.
DOM

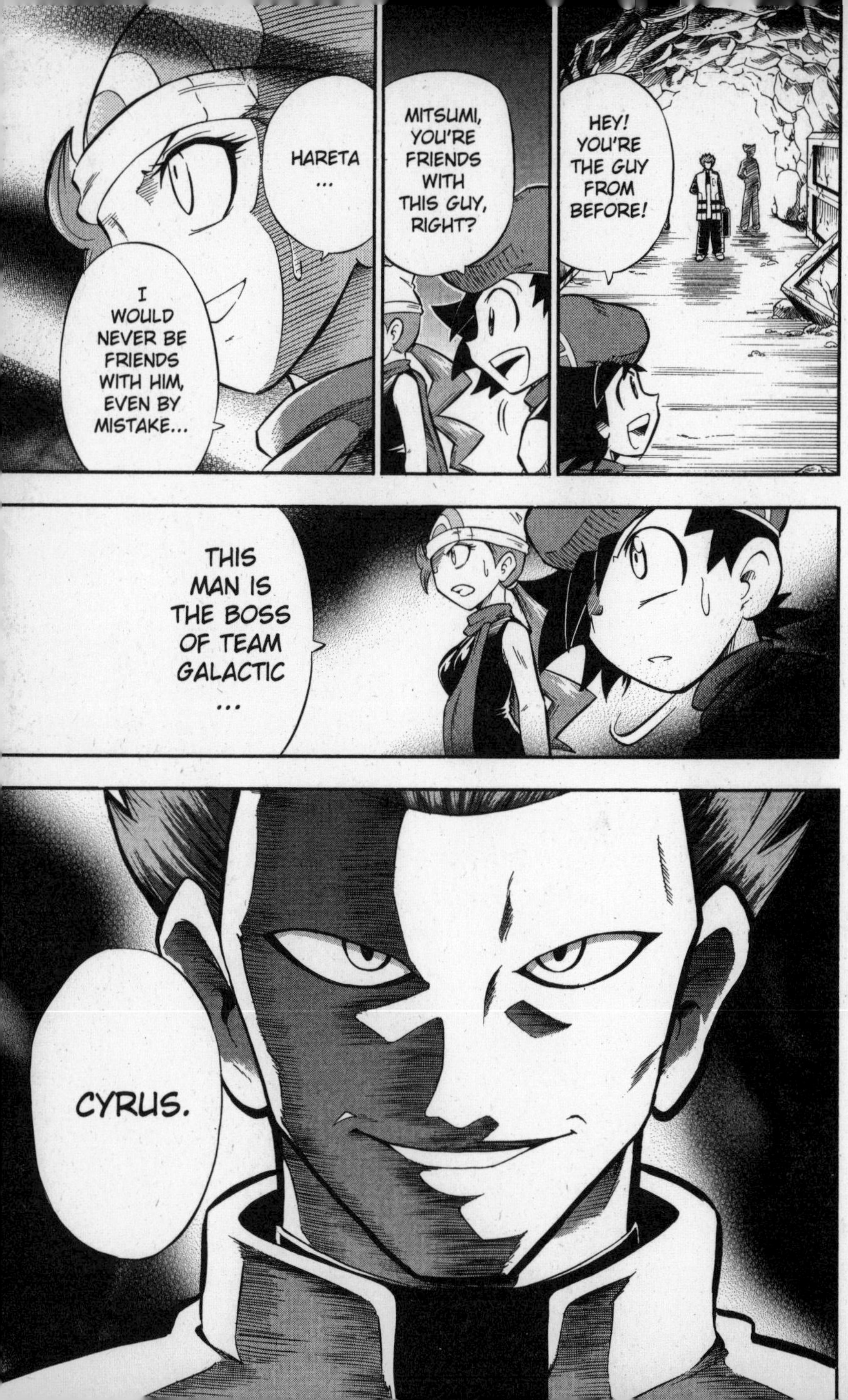
HEY! YOU'RE THE GUY FROM BEFORE!
MITSUMI, YOU'RE FRIENDS WITH THIS GUY, RIGHT?
HARETA ...
I WOULD NEVER BE FRIENDS WITH HIM, EVEN BY MISTAKE...
THIS MAN IS THE BOSS OF TEAM GALACTIC ...
CYRUS.

KINDA
SAD
THAT
I'M
ONLY
IN ONE
PANEL
...

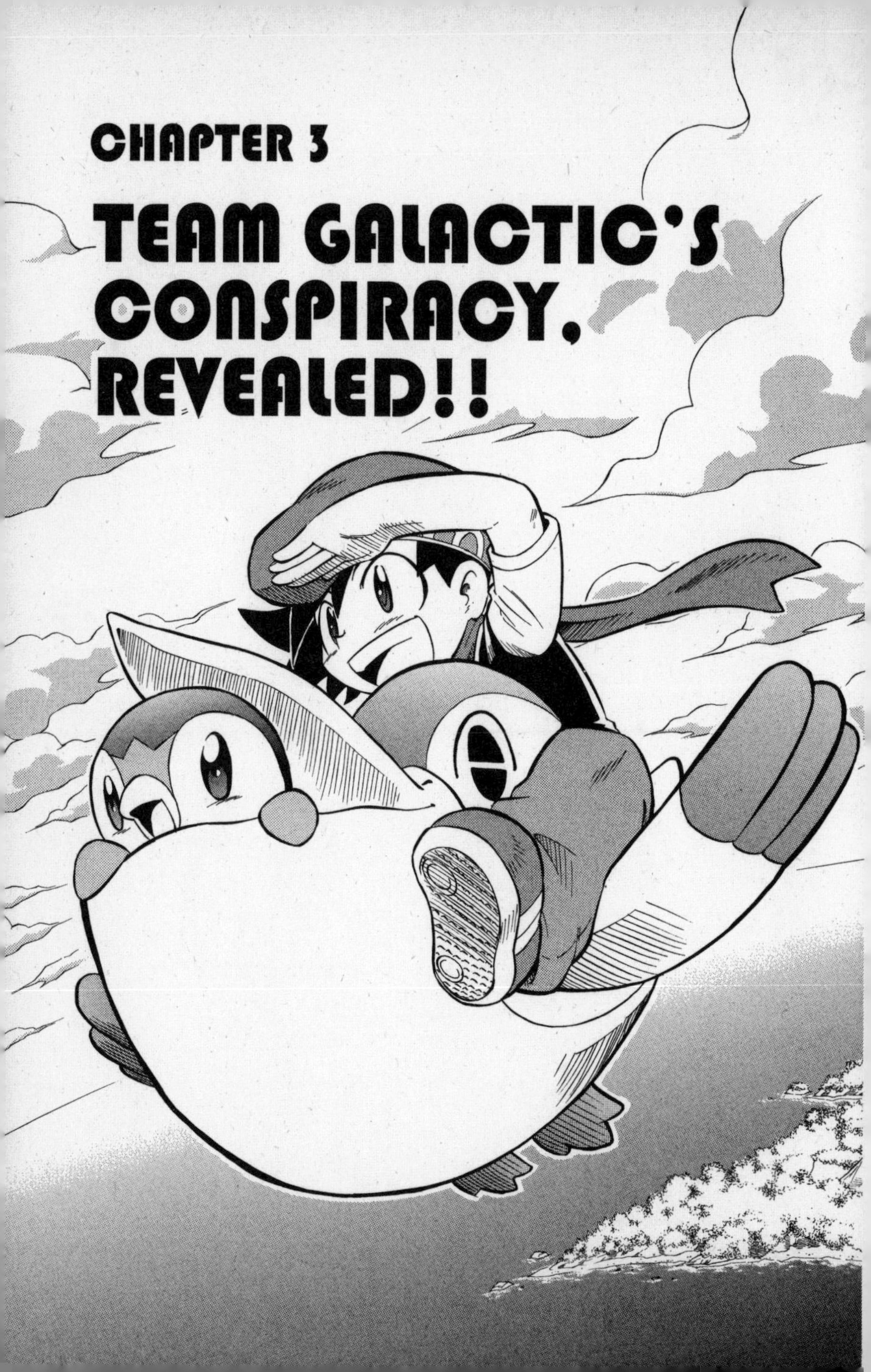
CHAPTER 3
TEAM GALACTIC'S CONSPIRACY, REVEALED!!

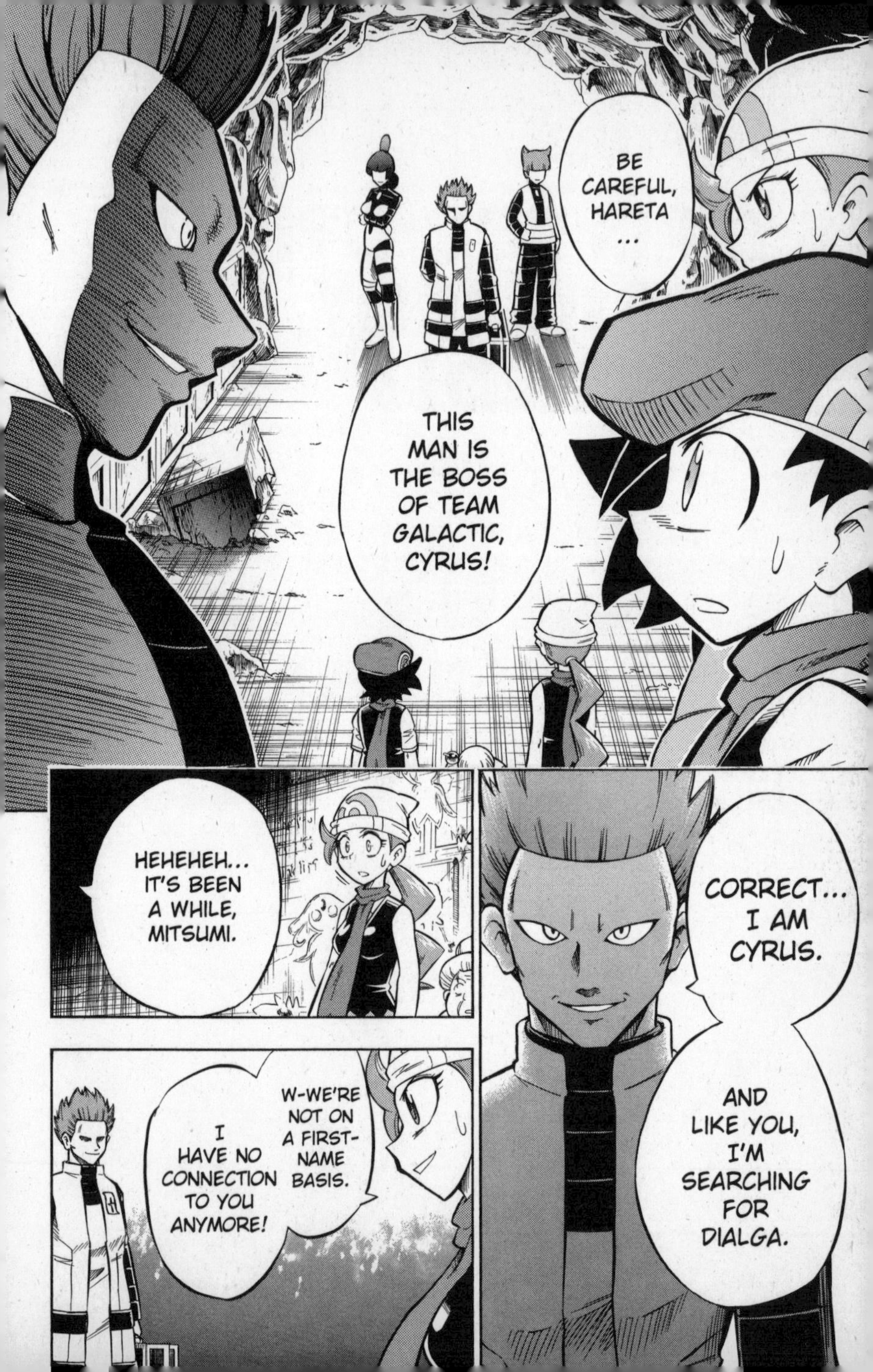
BE CAREFUL, HARETA...
THIS MAN IS THE BOSS OF TEAM GALACTIC, CYRUS!
CORRECT... I AM CYRUS.
AND LIKE YOU, I'M SEARCHING FOR DIALGA.
HEHEHEH... IT'S BEEN A WHILE, MITSUMI.
W-WE'RE NOT ON A FIRST-NAME BASIS.
I HAVE NO CONNECTION TO YOU ANYMORE!

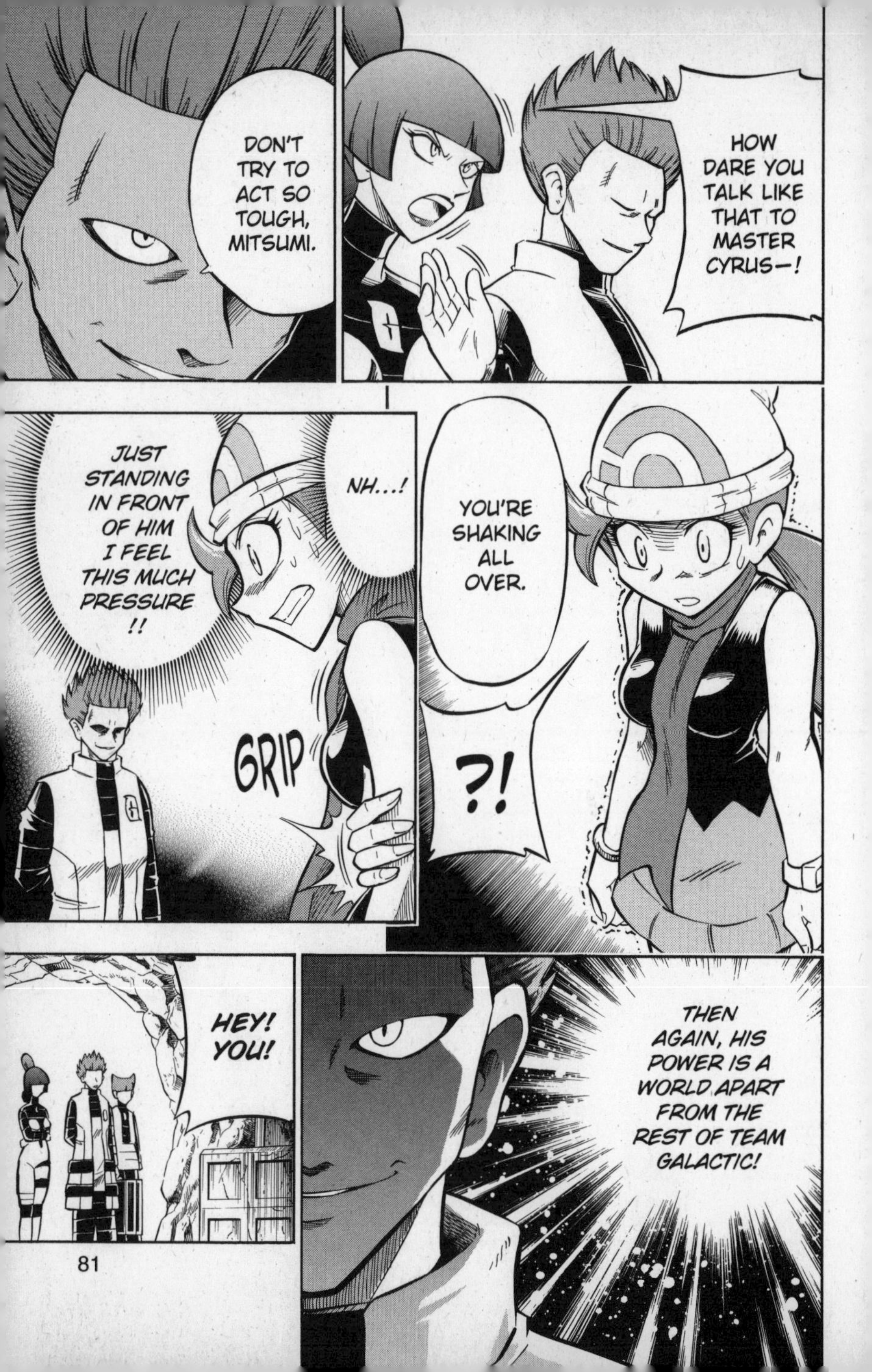
HOW DARE YOU TALK LIKE THAT TO MASTER CYRUS—!
DON'T TRY TO ACT SO TOUGH, MITSUMI.
YOU'RE SHAKING ALL OVER.
?!
NH...!
JUST STANDING IN FRONT OF HIM I FEEL THIS MUCH PRESSURE!!
GRIP
THEN AGAIN, HIS POWER IS A WORLD APART FROM THE REST OF TEAM GALACTIC!
HEY! YOU!

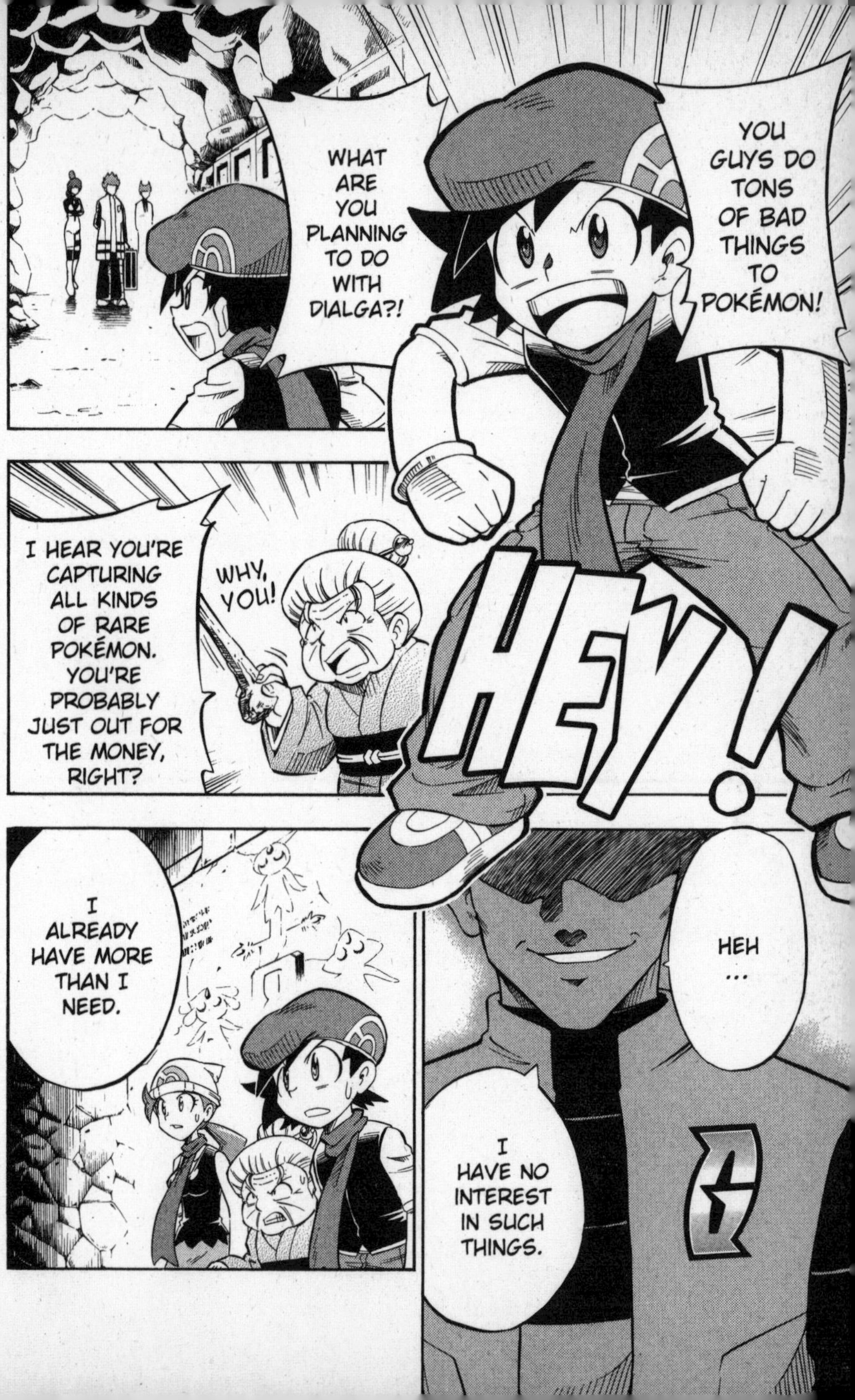
YOU GUYS DO TONS OF BAD THINGS TO POKÉMON!
HEY!
WHAT ARE YOU PLANNING TO DO WITH DIALGA?!
WHY, YOU!
I HEAR YOU'RE CAPTURING ALL KINDS OF RARE POKÉMON. YOU'RE PROBABLY JUST OUT FOR THE MONEY, RIGHT?
HEH ...
I HAVE NO INTEREST IN SUCH THINGS.
I ALREADY HAVE MORE THAN I NEED.

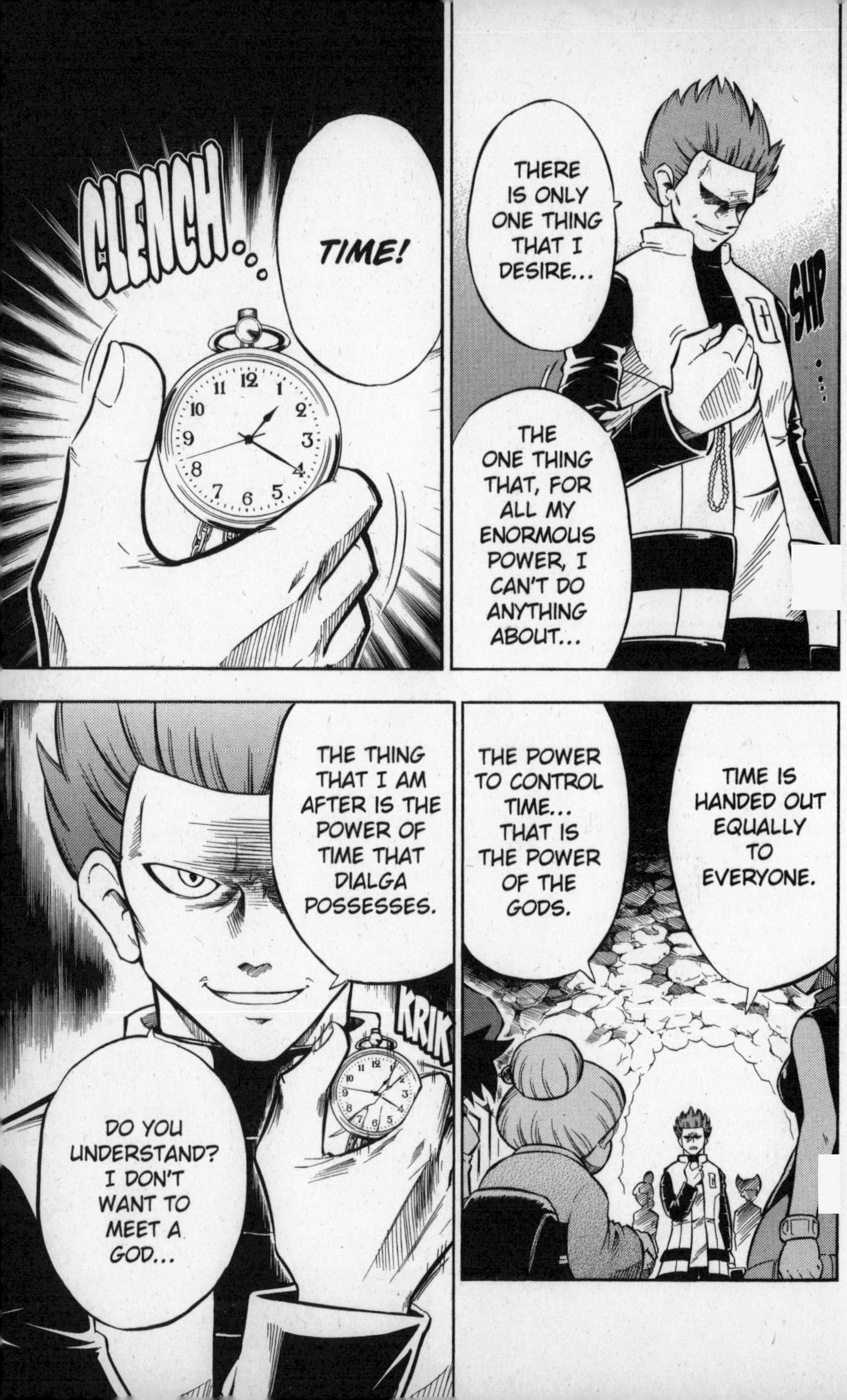
THERE IS ONLY ONE THING THAT I DESIRE...
SHP
THE ONE THING THAT, FOR ALL MY ENORMOUS POWER, I CAN'T DO ANYTHING ABOUT...
TIME!
CLENCH
TIME IS HANDED OUT EQUALLY TO EVERYONE.
THE POWER TO CONTROL TIME... THAT IS THE POWER OF THE GODS.
THE THING THAT I AM AFTER IS THE POWER OF TIME THAT DIALGA POSSESSES.
KRIK
DO YOU UNDERSTAND? I DON'T WANT TO MEET A GOD...

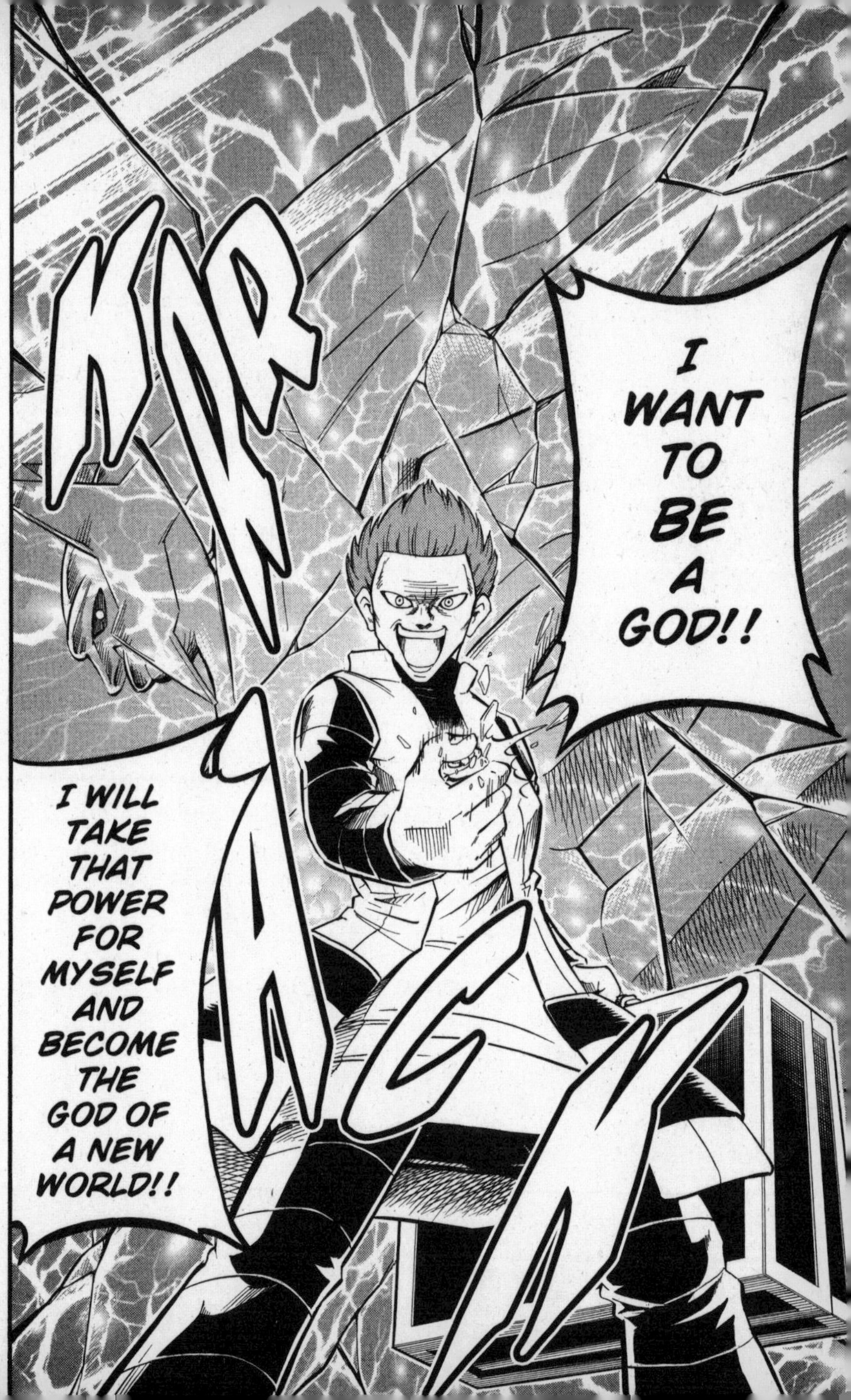
I WANT TO BE A GOD!!
KRACK
I WILL TAKE THAT POWER FOR MYSELF AND BECOME THE GOD OF A NEW WORLD!!

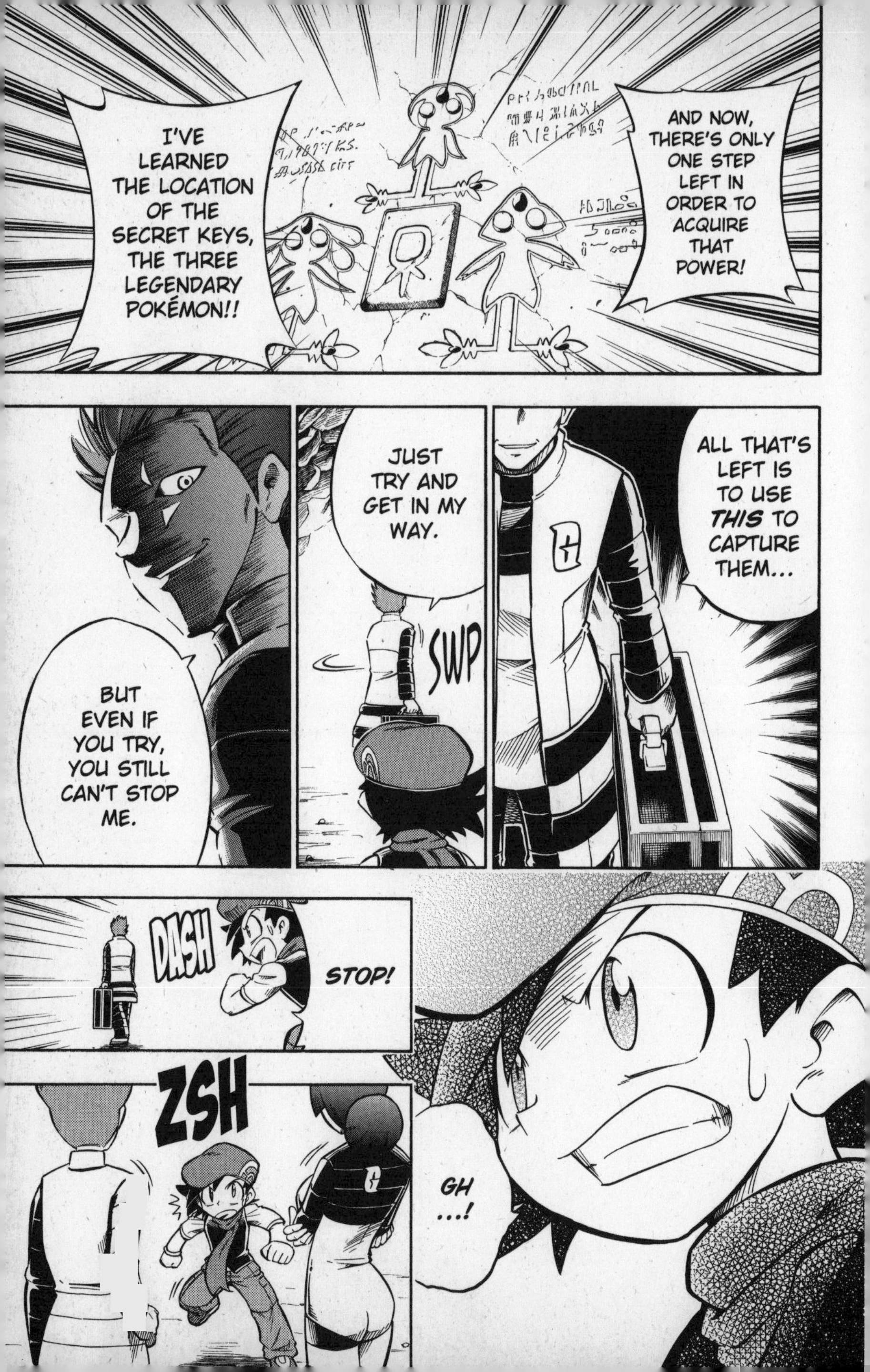
AND NOW, THERE'S ONLY ONE STEP LEFT IN ORDER TO ACQUIRE THAT POWER!
I'VE LEARNED THE LOCATION OF THE SECRET KEYS, THE THREE LEGENDARY POKÉMON!!
ALL THAT'S LEFT IS TO USE *THIS* TO CAPTURE THEM...
JUST TRY AND GET IN MY WAY.
SWP
BUT EVEN IF YOU TRY, YOU STILL CAN'T STOP ME.
DASH
STOP!
ZSH
GH ...!

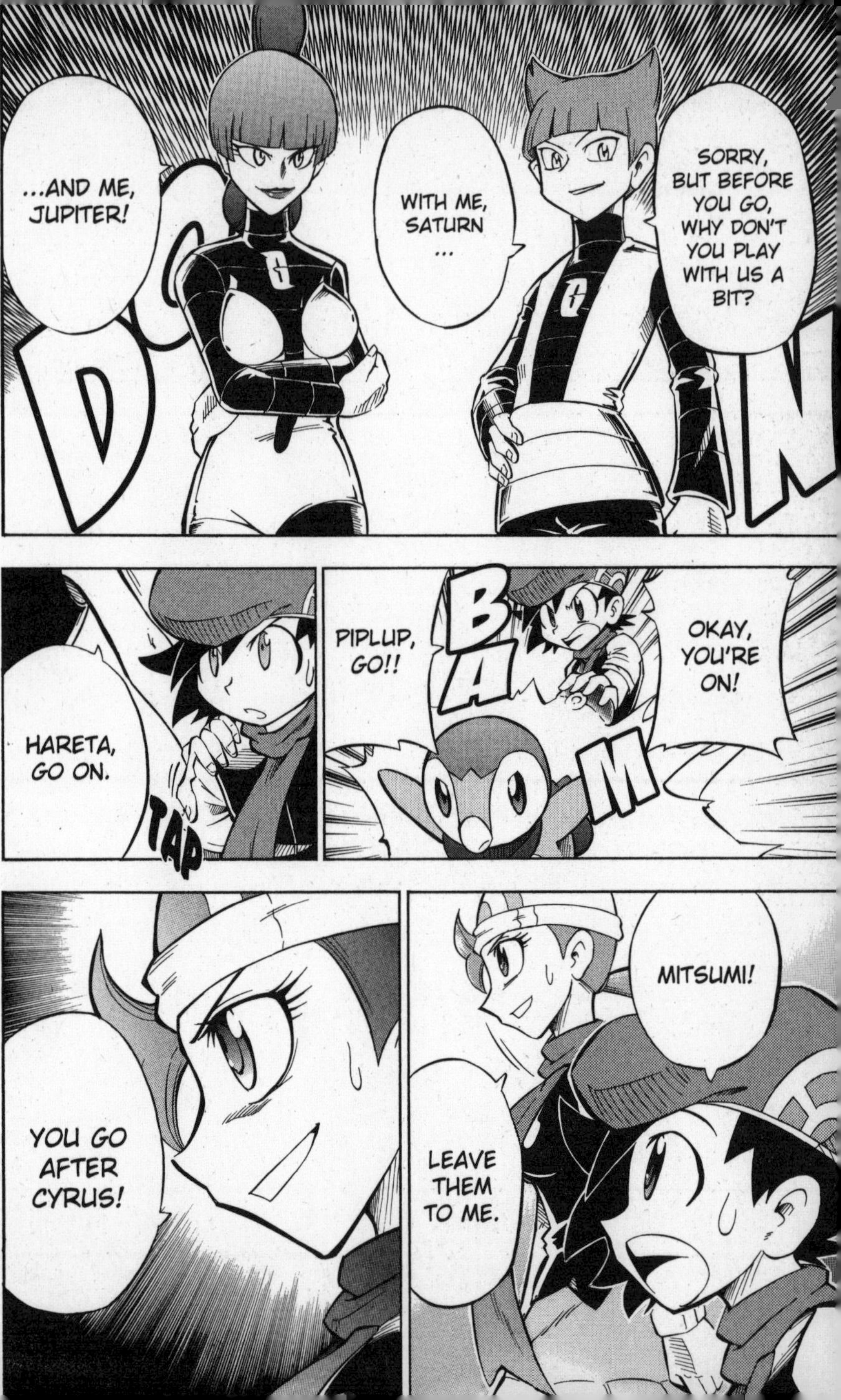
SORRY, BUT BEFORE YOU GO, WHY DON'T YOU PLAY WITH US A BIT?
WITH ME, SATURN ...
...AND ME, JUPITER!
OKAY, YOU'RE ON!
PIPLUP, GO!!
BAM
HARETA, GO ON.
TAP
MITSUMI!
LEAVE THEM TO ME.
YOU GO AFTER CYRUS!

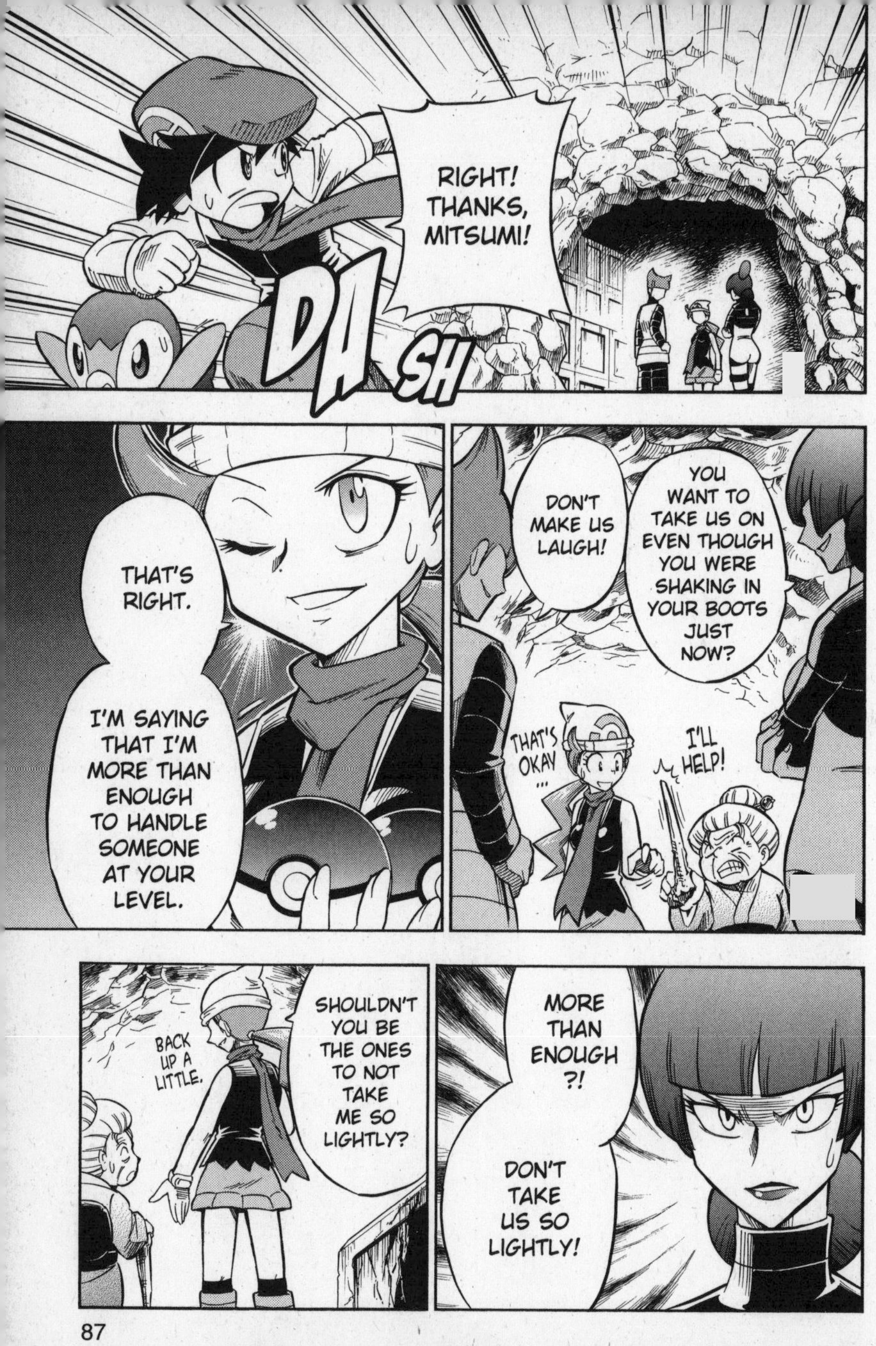
RIGHT! THANKS, MITSUMI!
DASH
YOU WANT TO TAKE US ON EVEN THOUGH YOU WERE SHAKING IN YOUR BOOTS JUST NOW?
DON'T MAKE US LAUGH!
I'LL HELP!
THAT'S OKAY...
THAT'S RIGHT.
I'M SAYING THAT I'M MORE THAN ENOUGH TO HANDLE SOMEONE AT YOUR LEVEL.
MORE THAN ENOUGH?!
DON'T TAKE US SO LIGHTLY!
SHOULDN'T YOU BE THE ONES TO NOT TAKE ME SO LIGHTLY?
BACK UP A LITTLE.

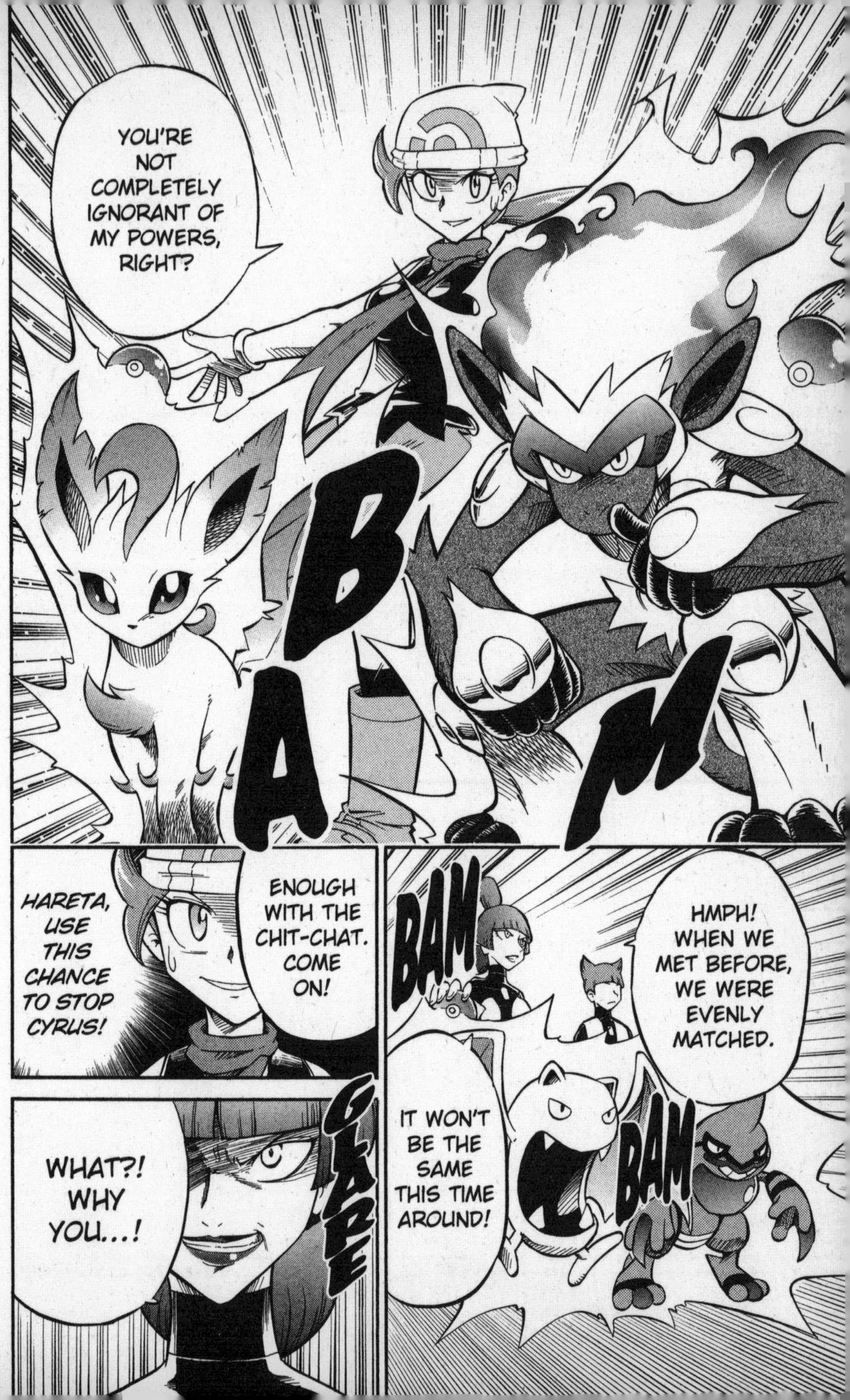
YOU'RE NOT COMPLETELY IGNORANT OF MY POWERS, RIGHT?
BAM
BAM
HMPH! WHEN WE MET BEFORE, WE WERE EVENLY MATCHED.
IT WON'T BE THE SAME THIS TIME AROUND!
BAM
ENOUGH WITH THE CHIT-CHAT. COME ON!
HARETA, USE THIS CHANCE TO STOP CYRUS!
GLARE
WHAT?! WHY YOU...!

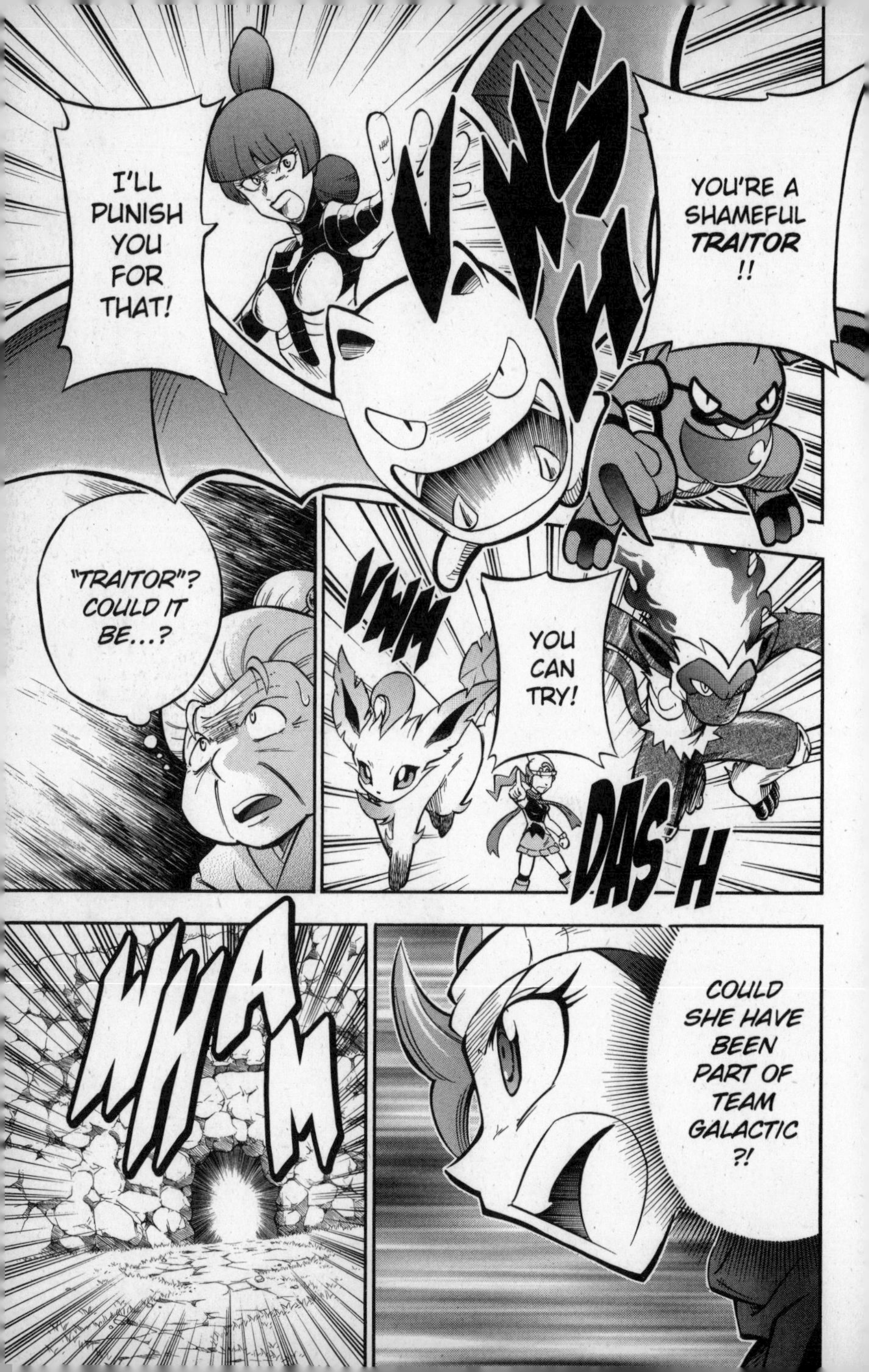
YOU'RE A SHAMEFUL TRAITOR !!
VWSH
I'LL PUNISH YOU FOR THAT!
VWM
YOU CAN TRY!
DASH
"TRAITOR"? COULD IT BE...?
COULD SHE HAVE BEEN PART OF TEAM GALACTIC ?!
WHAM

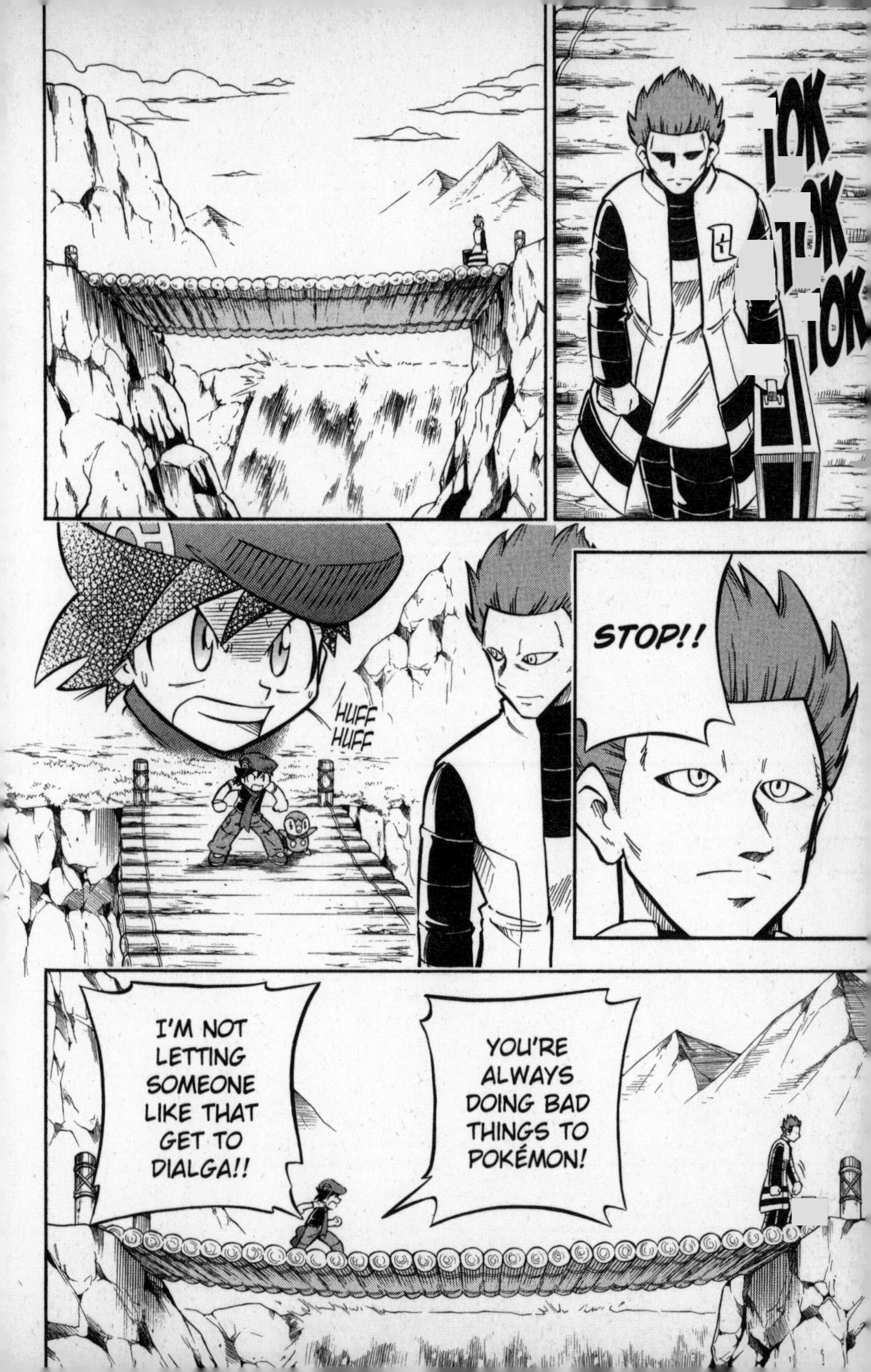
STOP!!
HUFF HUFF
YOU'RE ALWAYS DOING BAD THINGS TO POKÉMON!
I'M NOT LETTING SOMEONE LIKE THAT GET TO DIALGA!!

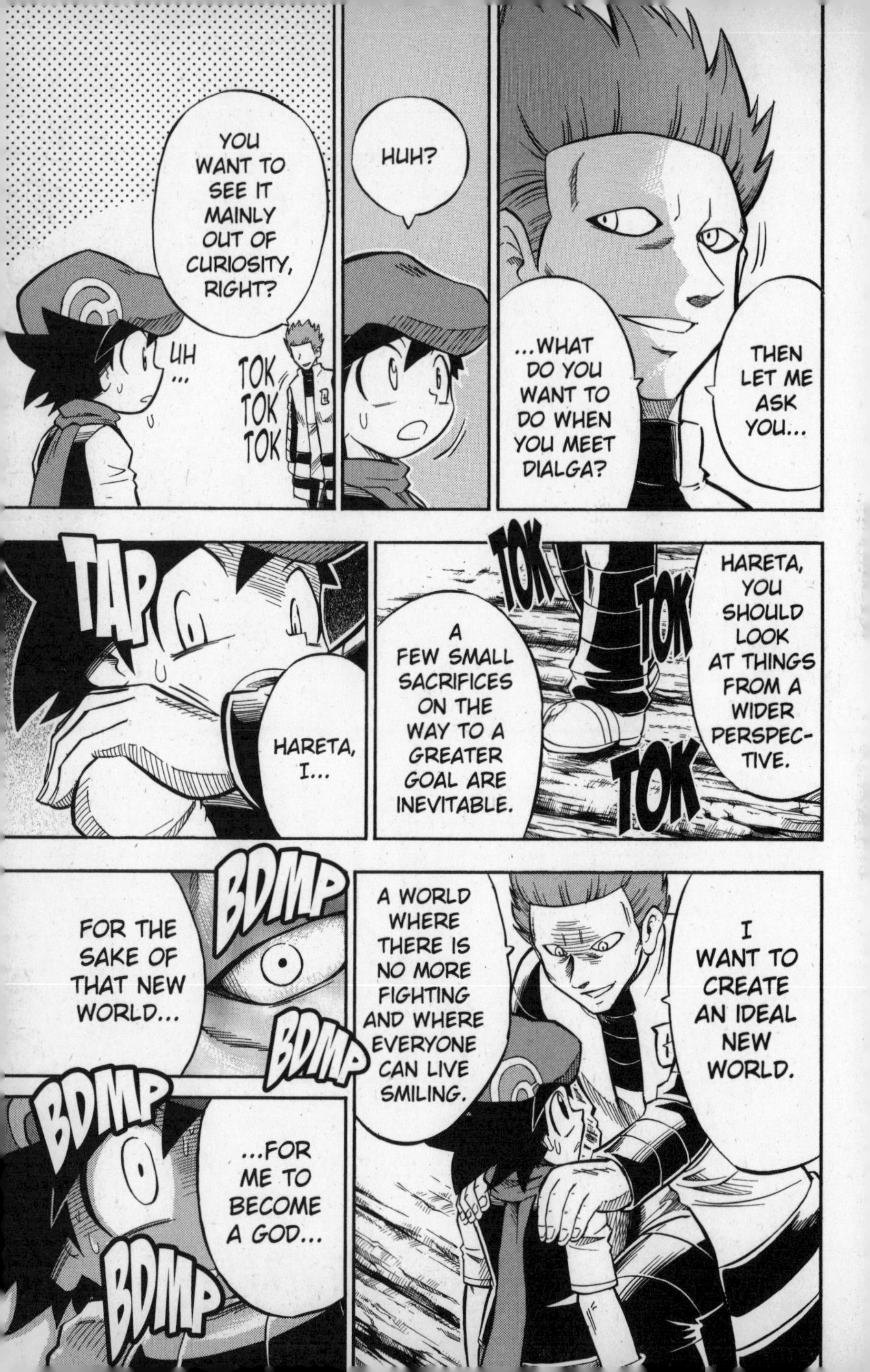

YOU WANT TO SEE IT MAINLY OUT OF CURIOSITY, RIGHT?
UH...
TOK TOK TOK
HUH?
THEN LET ME ASK YOU...
...WHAT DO YOU WANT TO DO WHEN YOU MEET DIALGA?
TAP
HARETA, I...
TOK
TOK
HARETA, YOU SHOULD LOOK AT THINGS FROM A WIDER PERSPEC-TIVE.
A FEW SMALL SACRIFICES ON THE WAY TO A GREATER GOAL ARE INEVITABLE.
TOK
I WANT TO CREATE AN IDEAL NEW WORLD.
A WORLD WHERE THERE IS NO MORE FIGHTING AND WHERE EVERYONE CAN LIVE SMILING.
BDMP
FOR THE SAKE OF THAT NEW WORLD...
BDMP
BDMP
...FOR ME TO BECOME A GOD...
BDMP

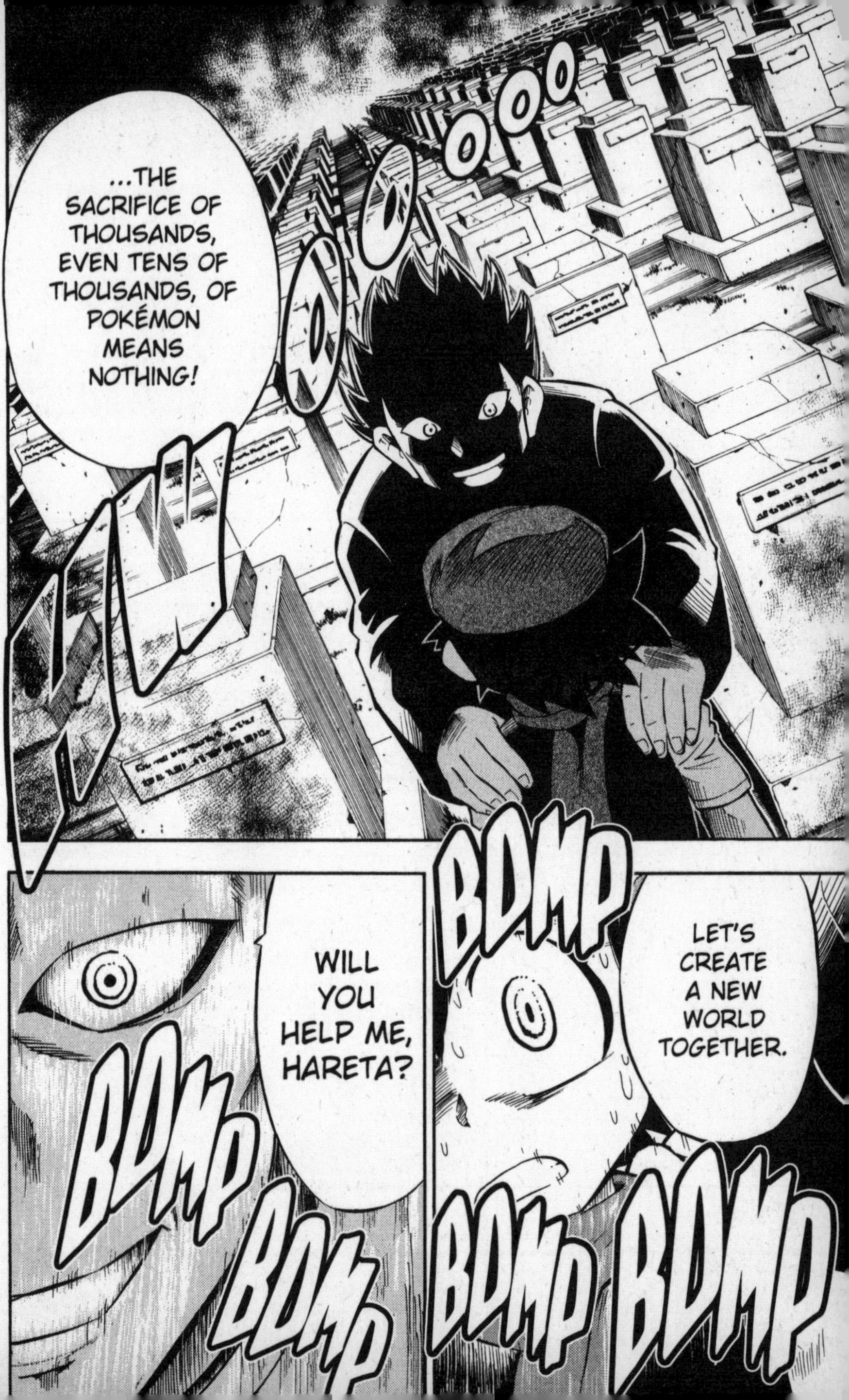
...THE SACRIFICE OF THOUSANDS, EVEN TENS OF THOUSANDS, OF POKÉMON MEANS NOTHING!
BDMP
LET'S CREATE A NEW WORLD TOGETHER.
BDMP
BDMP
WILL YOU HELP ME, HARETA?
BDMP
BDMP

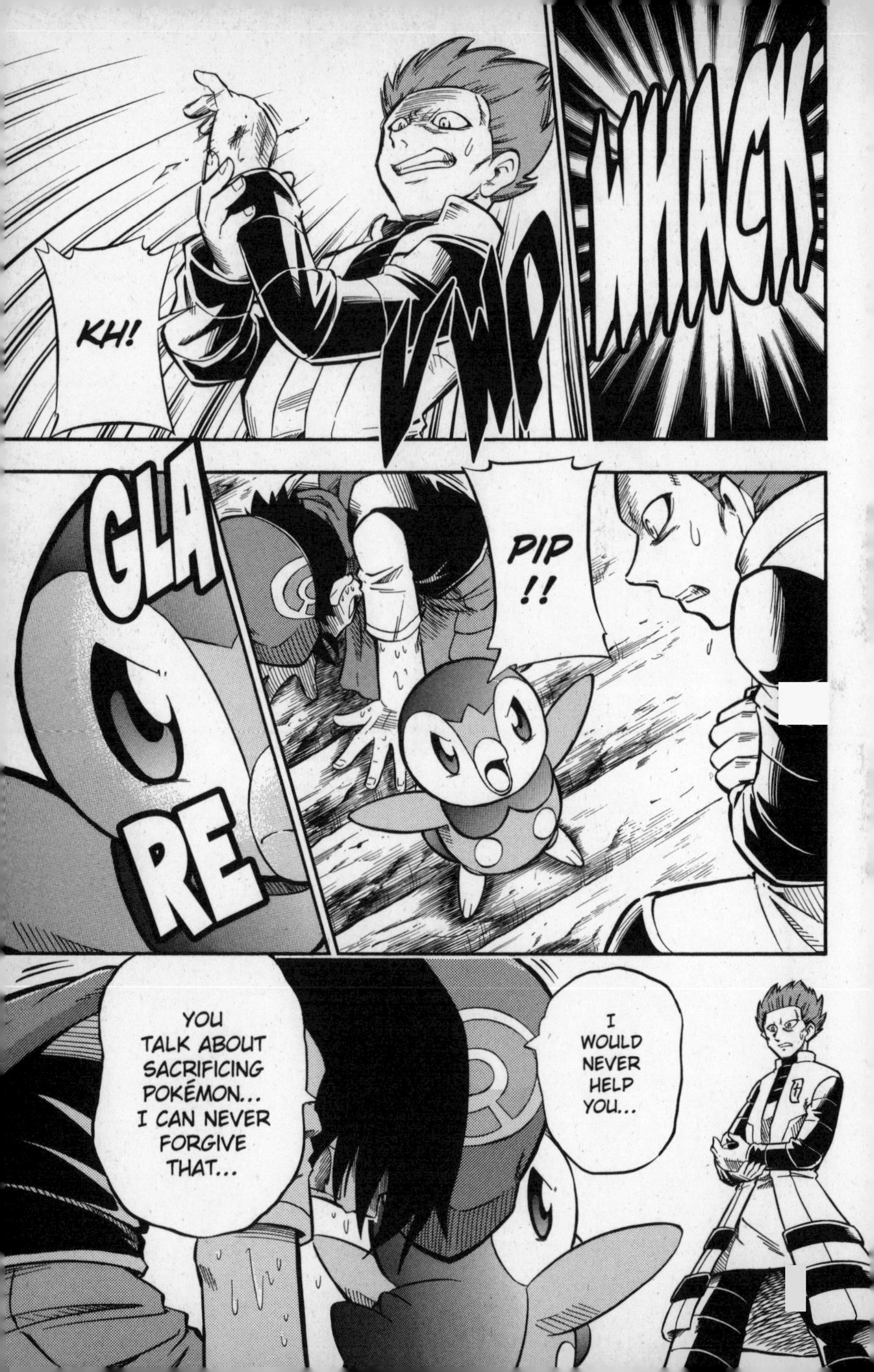
WHACK
KH!
PIP !!
GLARE
I WOULD NEVER HELP YOU...
YOU TALK ABOUT SACRIFICING POKÉMON... I CAN NEVER FORGIVE THAT...

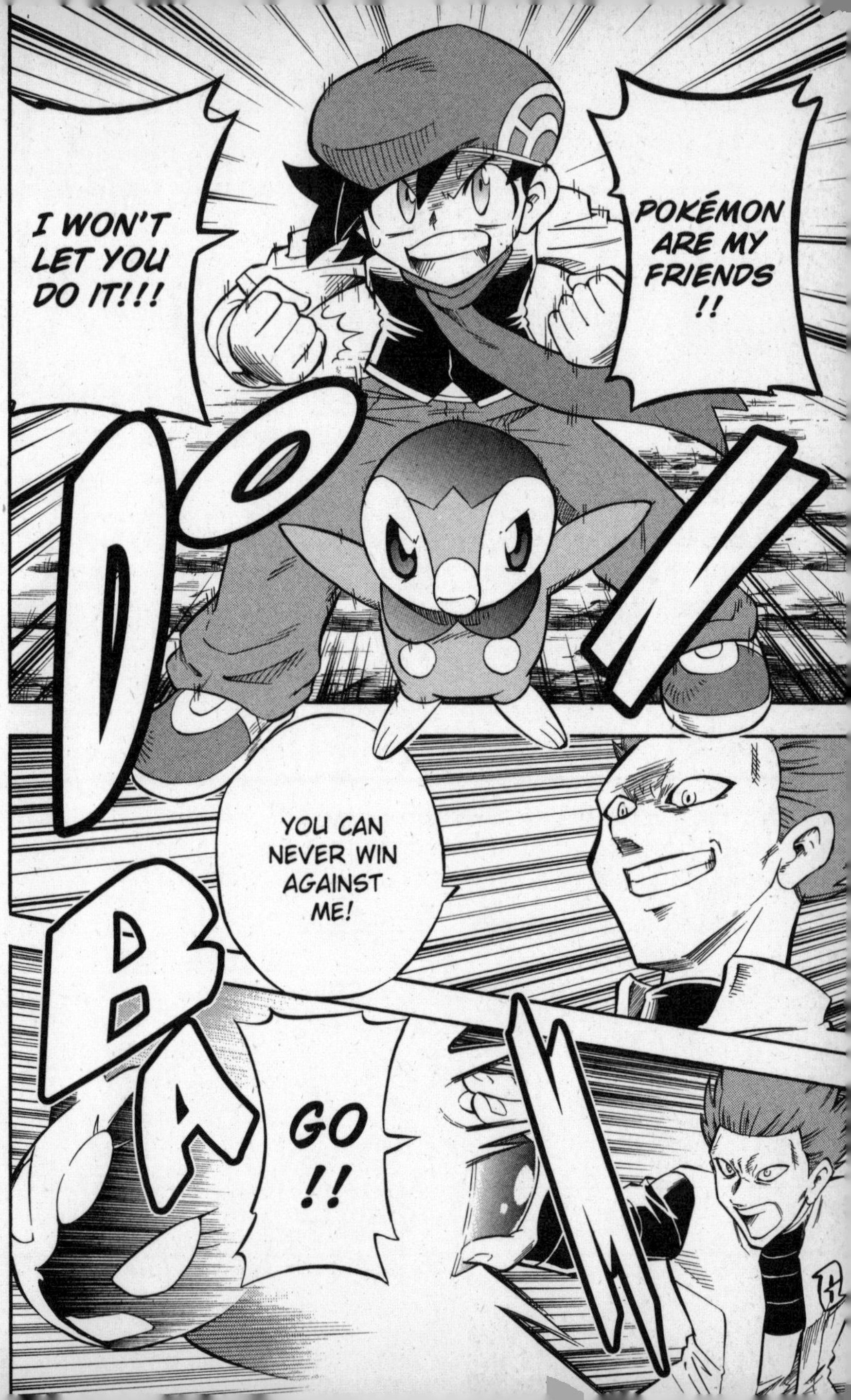
POKÉMON ARE MY FRIENDS !!
I WON'T LET YOU DO IT!!!
DON
YOU CAN NEVER WIN AGAINST ME!
GO !!
BAM

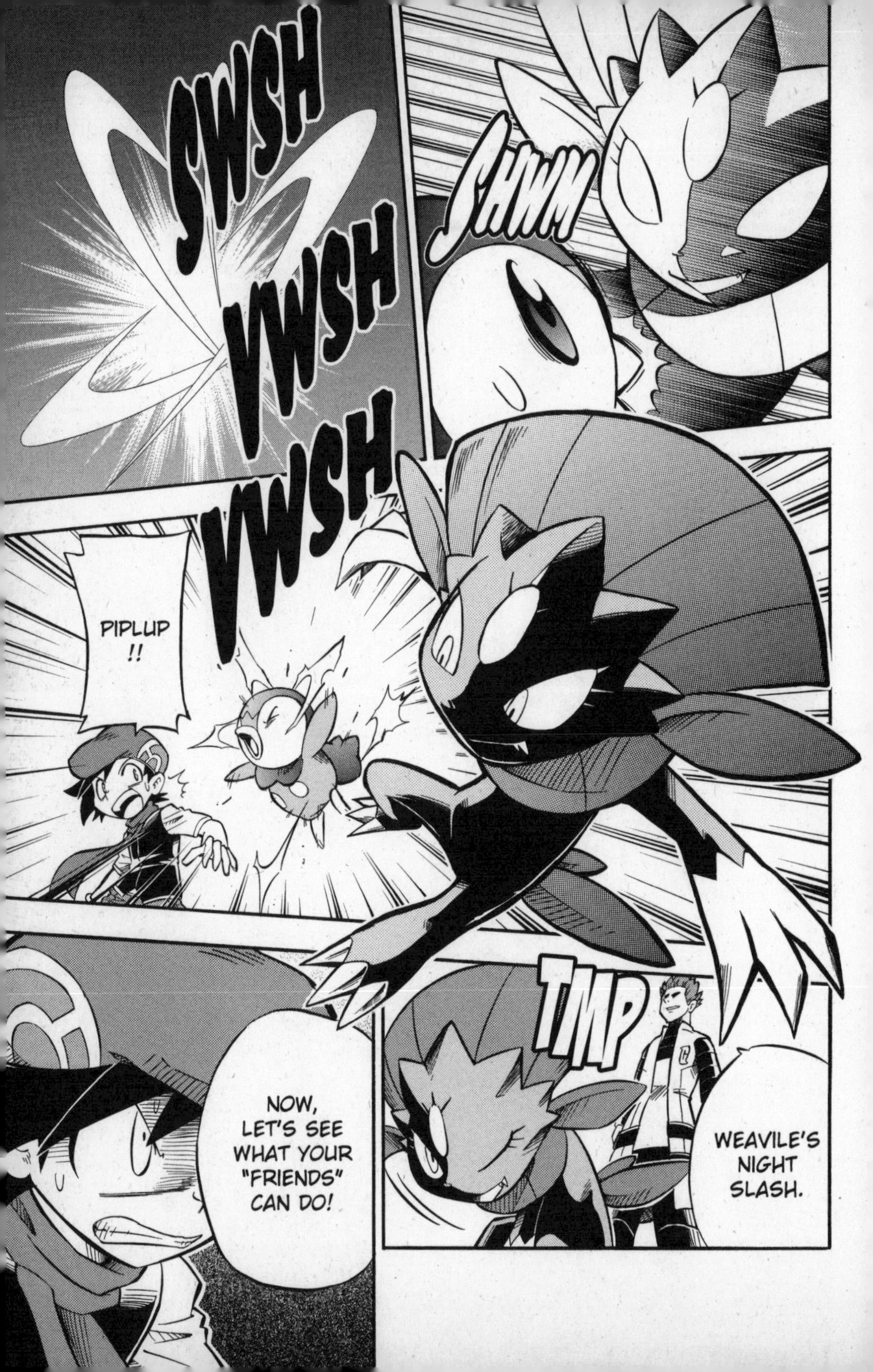
SHWM
SWSH
VWSH
VWSH
PIPLUP !!
TMP
WEAVILE'S NIGHT SLASH.
NOW, LET'S SEE WHAT YOUR "FRIENDS" CAN DO!

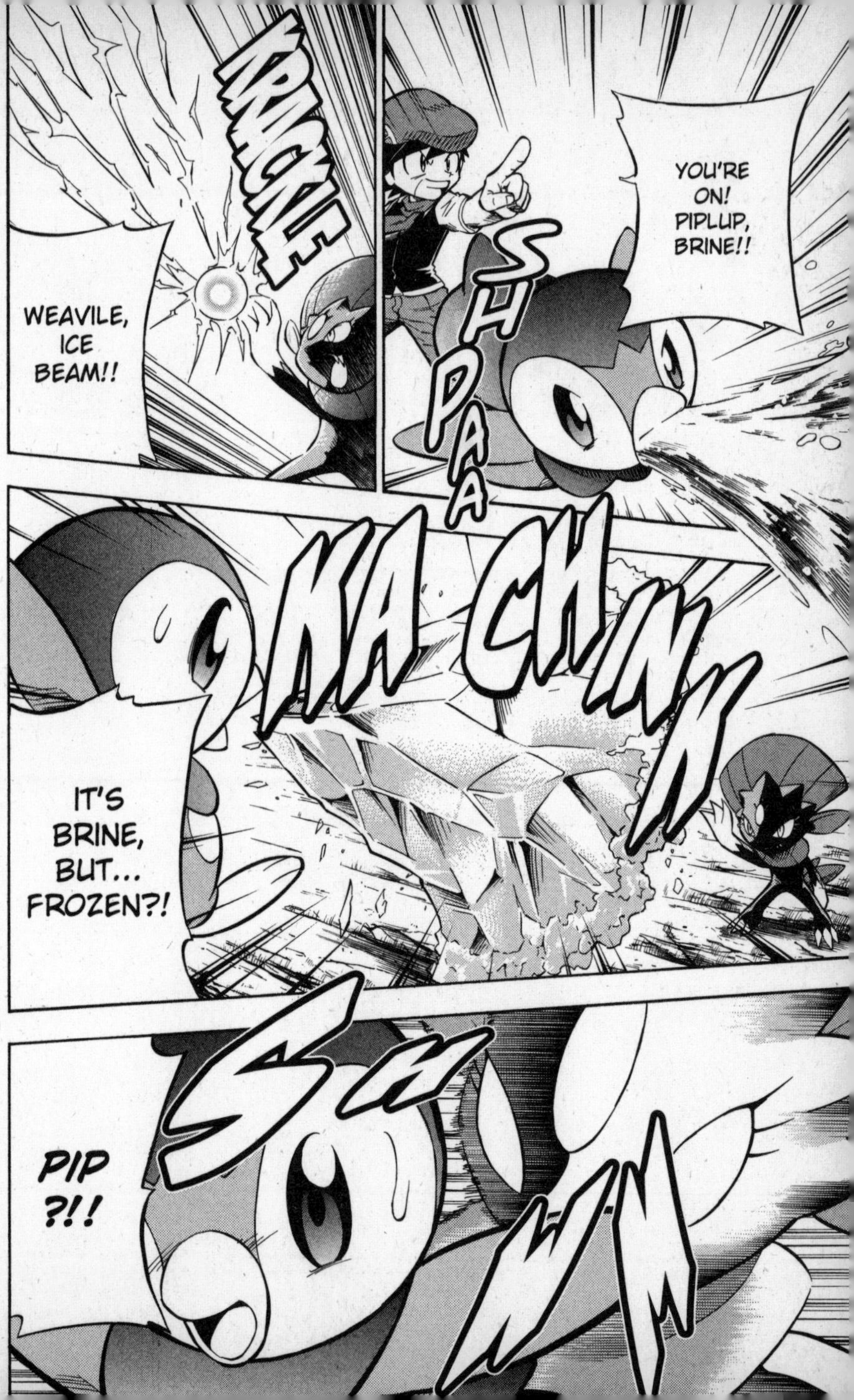
YOU'RE ON! PIPLUP, BRINE!!
SHPAAA
KRACKLE
WEAVILE, ICE BEAM!!
KA CHIN
IT'S BRINE, BUT... FROZEN?!
PIP ?!!

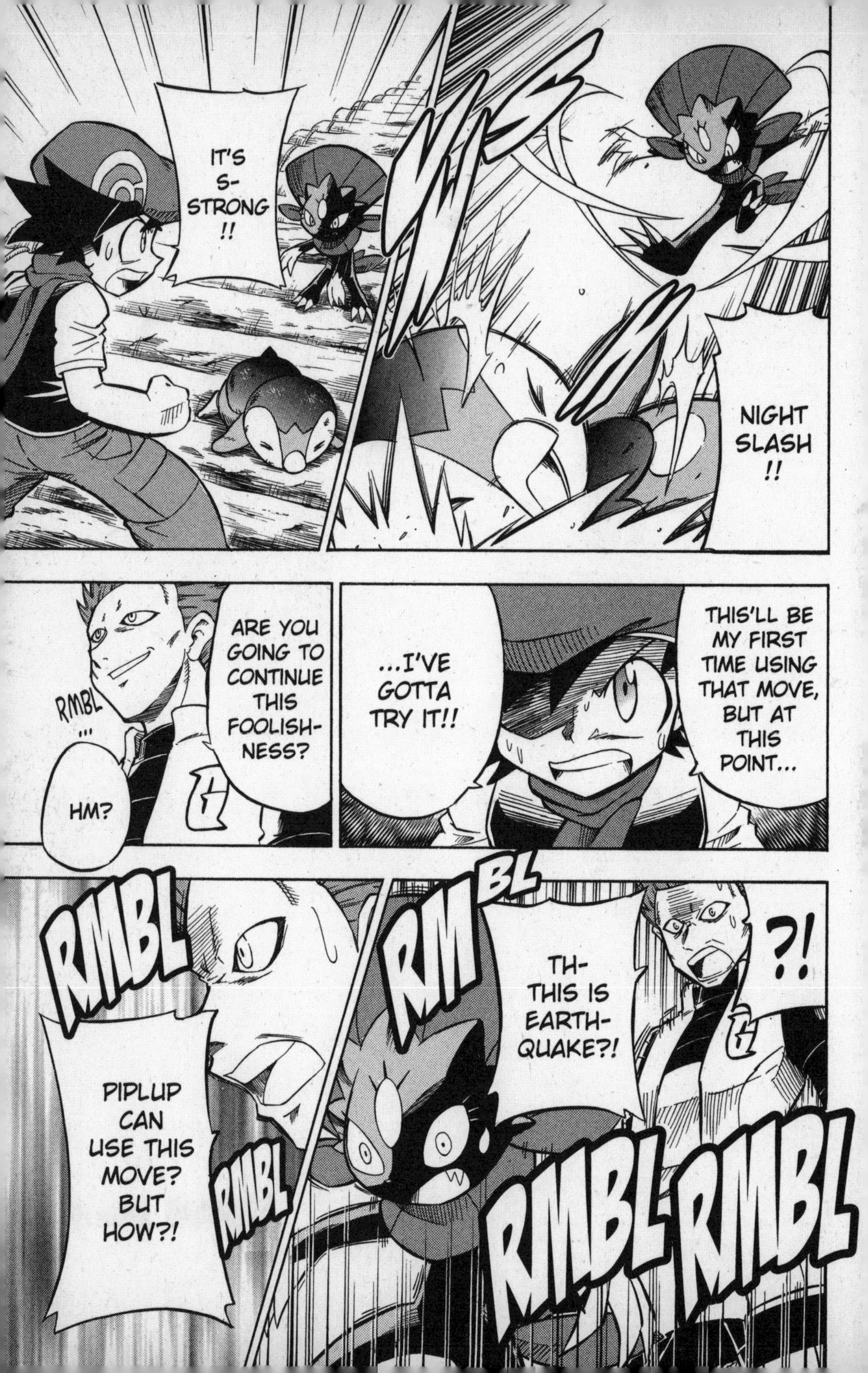
NIGHT SLASH !!
IT'S S-STRONG !!
THIS'LL BE MY FIRST TIME USING THAT MOVE, BUT AT THIS POINT...
...I'VE GOTTA TRY IT!!
ARE YOU GOING TO CONTINUE THIS FOOLISHNESS?
RMBL ...
HM?
?!
TH-THIS IS EARTHQUAKE?!
RMBL
RMBL-RMBL
RMBL
RMBL
PIPLUP CAN USE THIS MOVE? BUT HOW?!

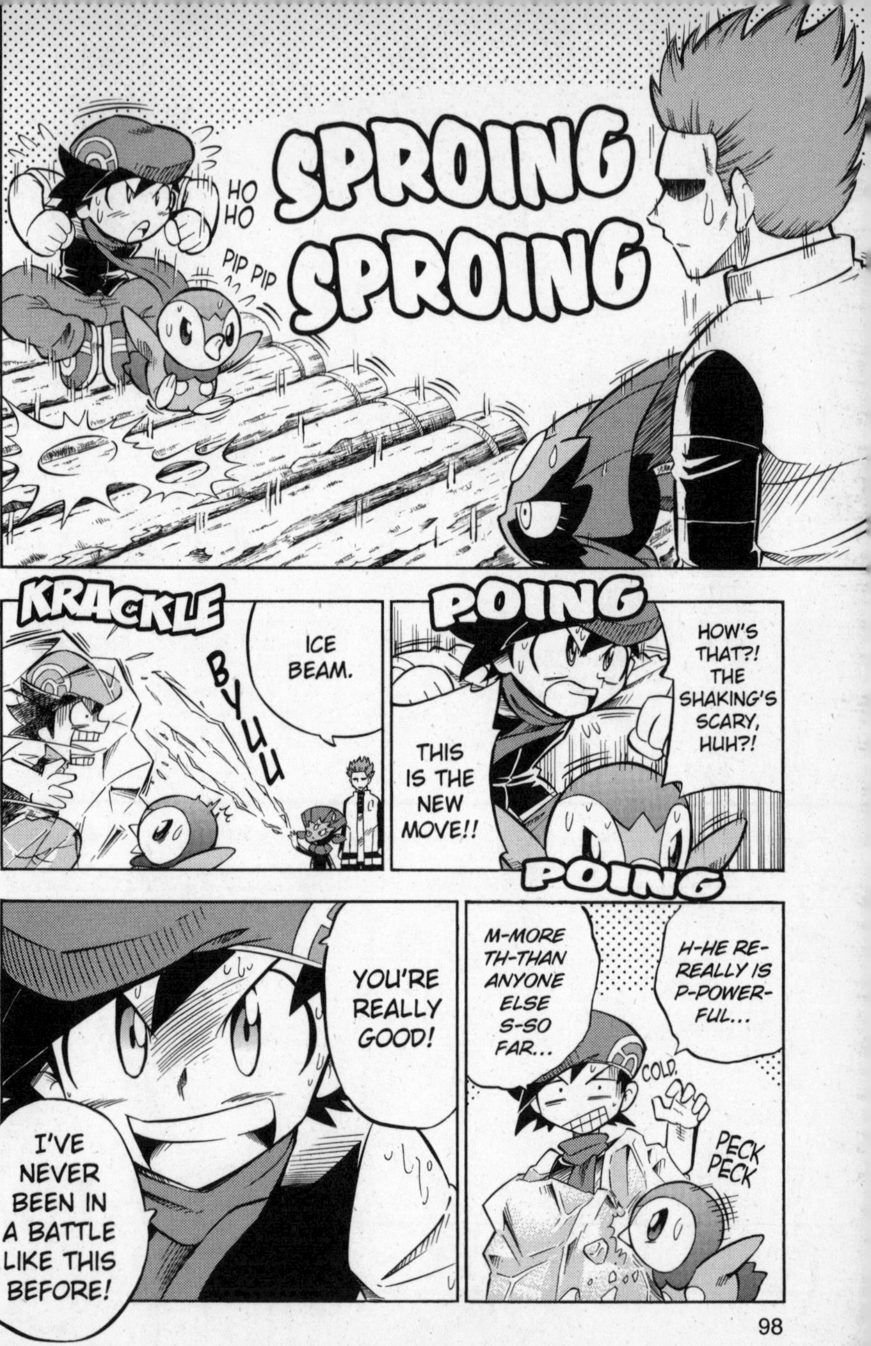

SPROING SPROING
HO HO
PIP PIP
POING
HOW'S THAT?! THE SHAKING'S SCARY, HUH?!
THIS IS THE NEW MOVE!!
POING
KRACKLE
ICE BEAM.
BYUUU
H-HE RE-REALLY IS P-POWER-FUL...
M-MORE TH-THAN ANYONE ELSE S-SO FAR...
COLD.
PECK PECK
YOU'RE REALLY GOOD!
I'VE NEVER BEEN IN A BATTLE LIKE THIS BEFORE!

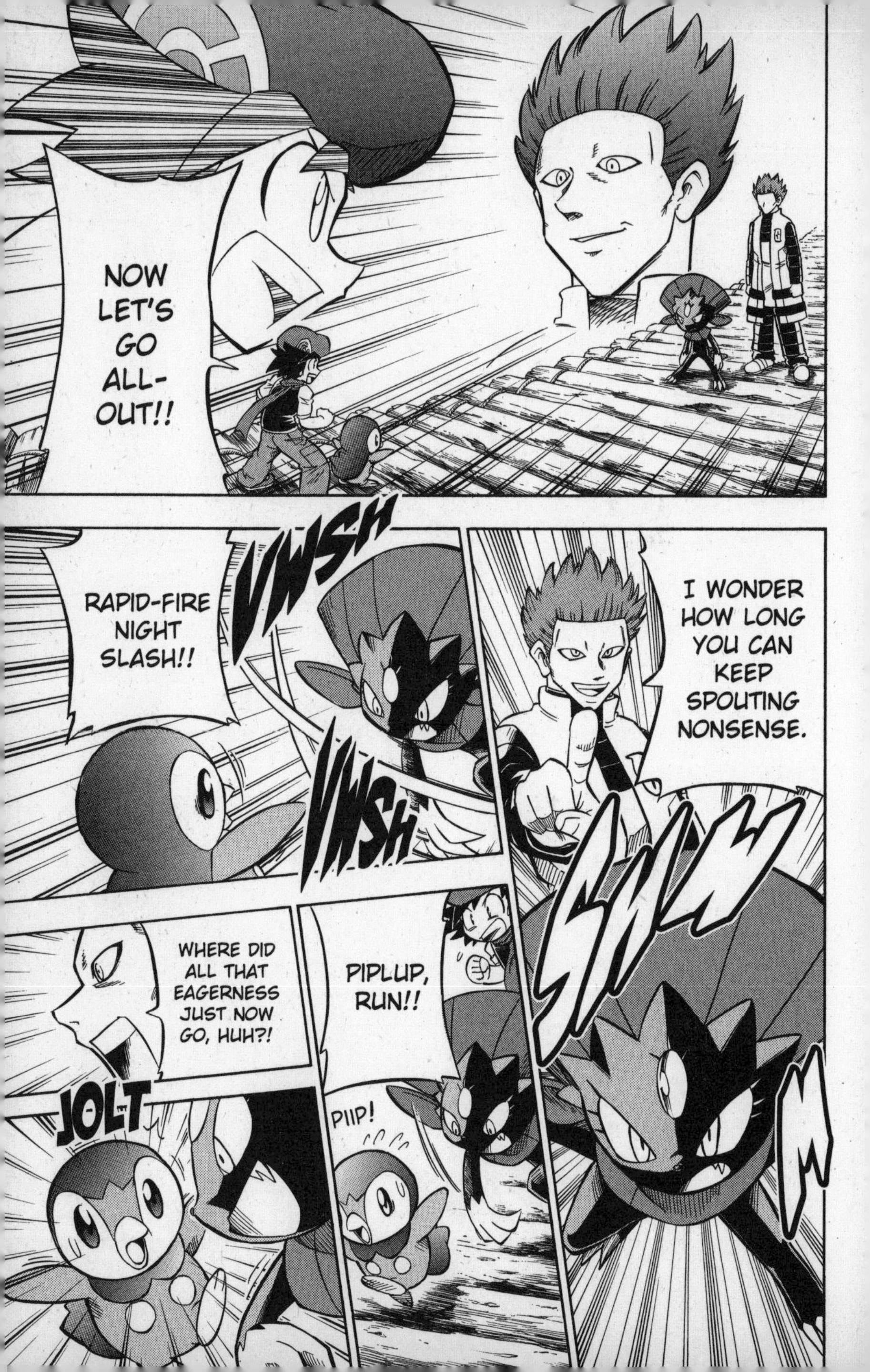
NOW LET'S GO ALL-OUT!!
I WONDER HOW LONG YOU CAN KEEP SPOUTING NONSENSE.
RAPID-FIRE NIGHT SLASH!!
VWSH
VWSH
PIPLUP, RUN!!
PIIP!
WHERE DID ALL THAT EAGERNESS JUST NOW GO, HUH?!
JOLT

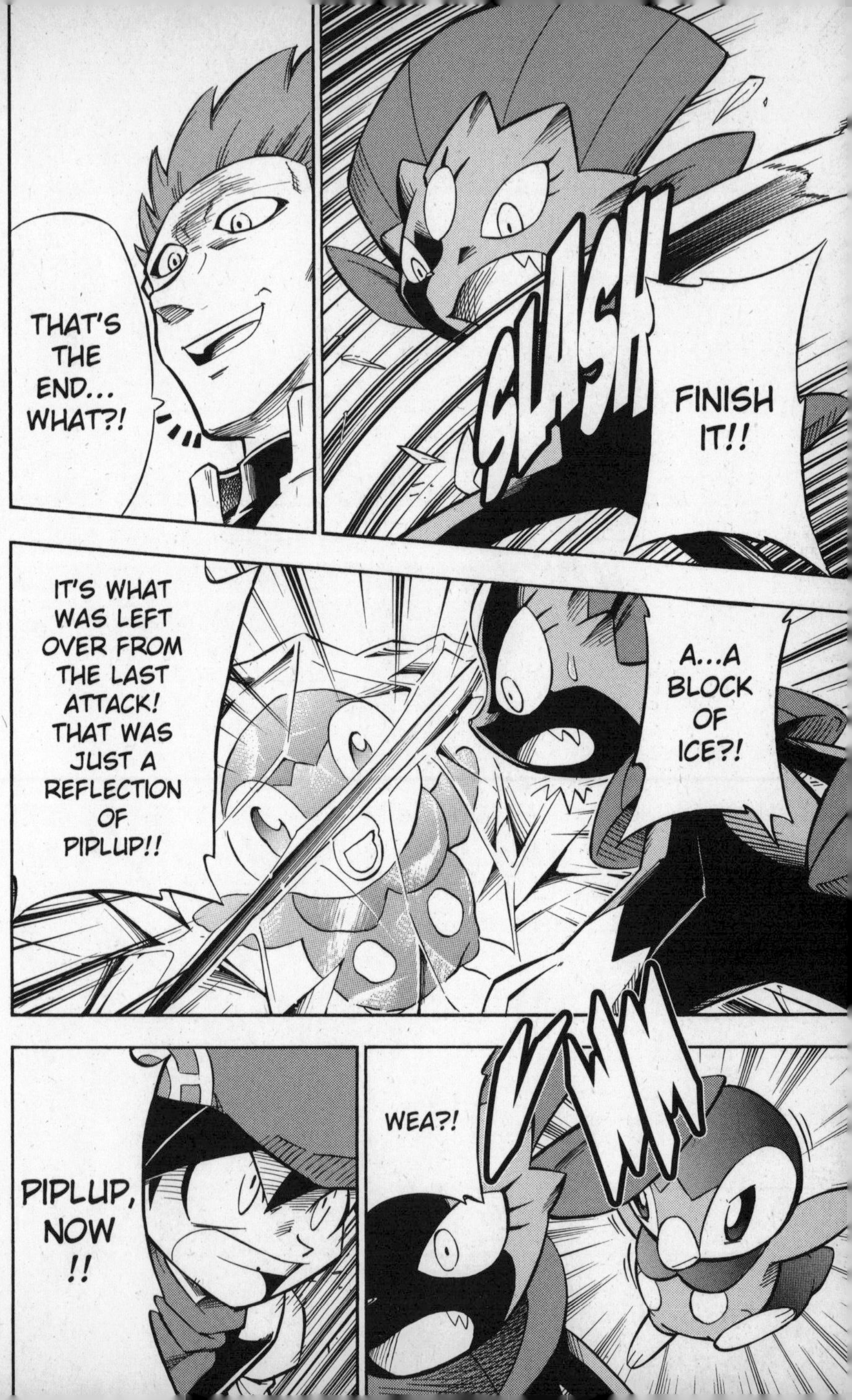
FINISH IT!!
CLASH
THAT'S THE END... WHAT?!
A...A BLOCK OF ICE?!
IT'S WHAT WAS LEFT OVER FROM THE LAST ATTACK! THAT WAS JUST A REFLECTION OF PIPLUP!!
WEA?!
PIPLUP, NOW!!

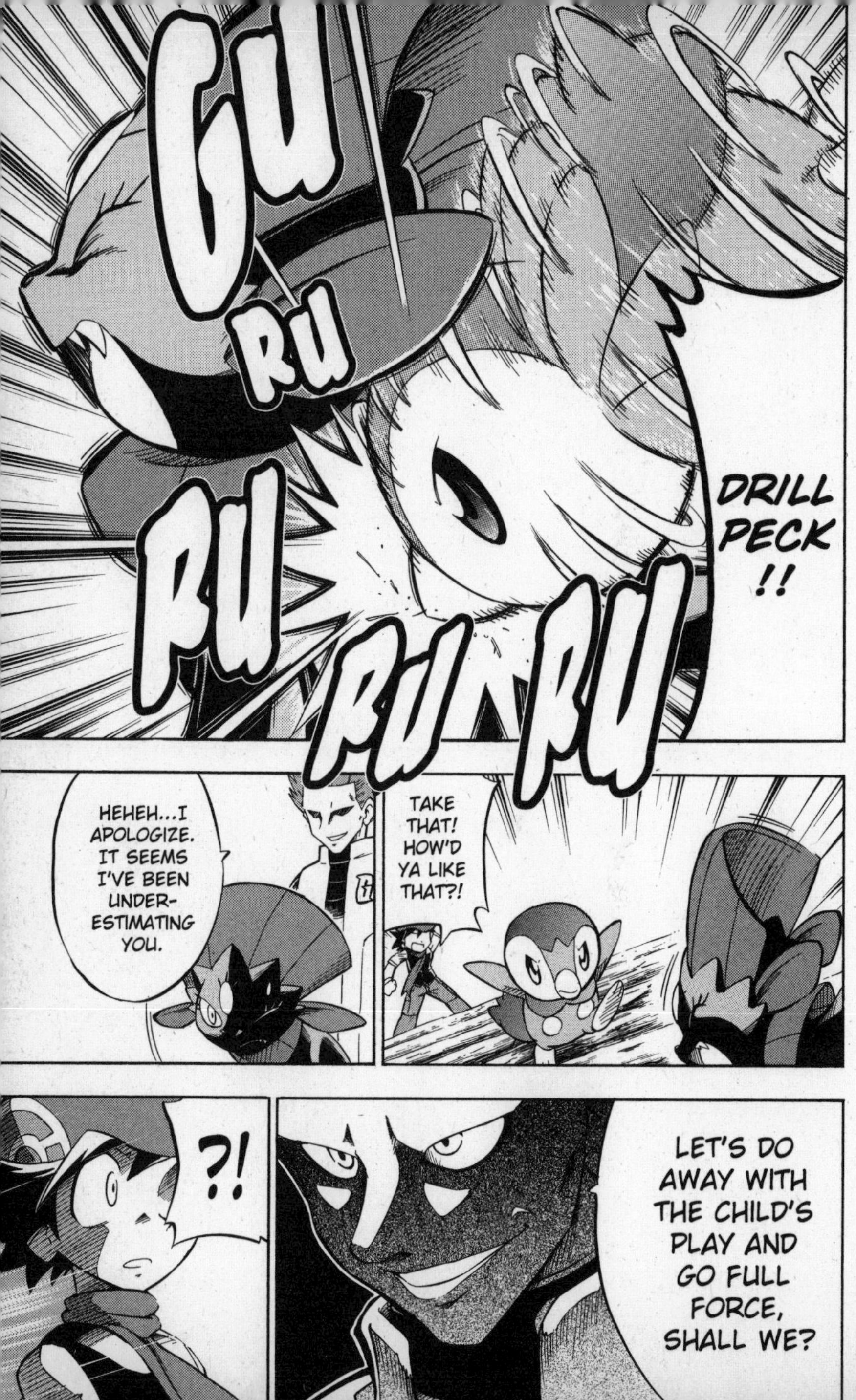
DRILL PECK !!
GURURURURU
TAKE THAT! HOW'D YA LIKE THAT?!
HEHEH...I APOLOGIZE. IT SEEMS I'VE BEEN UNDER-ESTIMATING YOU.
LET'S DO AWAY WITH THE CHILD'S PLAY AND GO FULL FORCE, SHALL WE?
?!

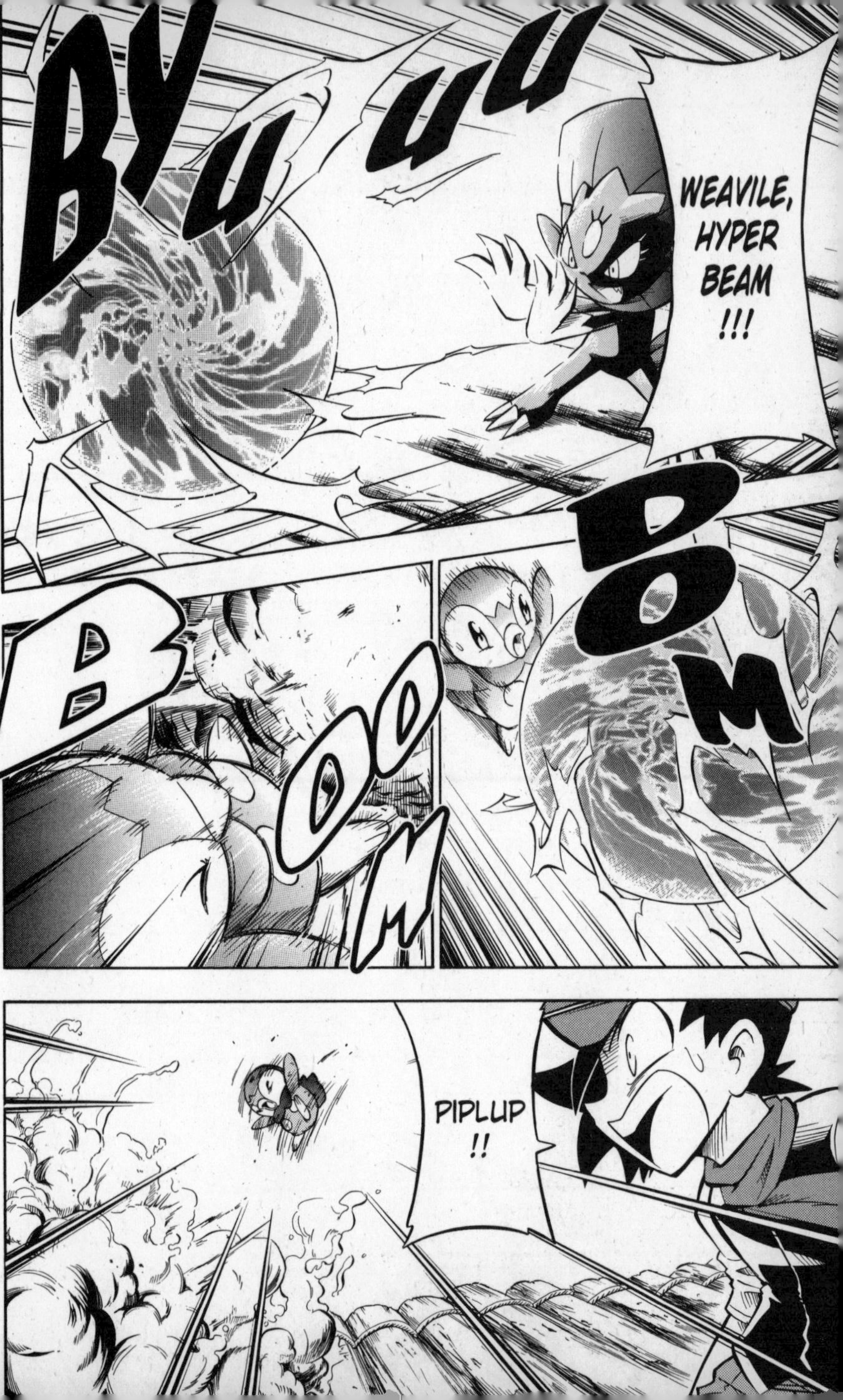
WEAVILE, HYPER BEAM !!!
BYUUUU
DOM
BOOM
PIPLUP !!

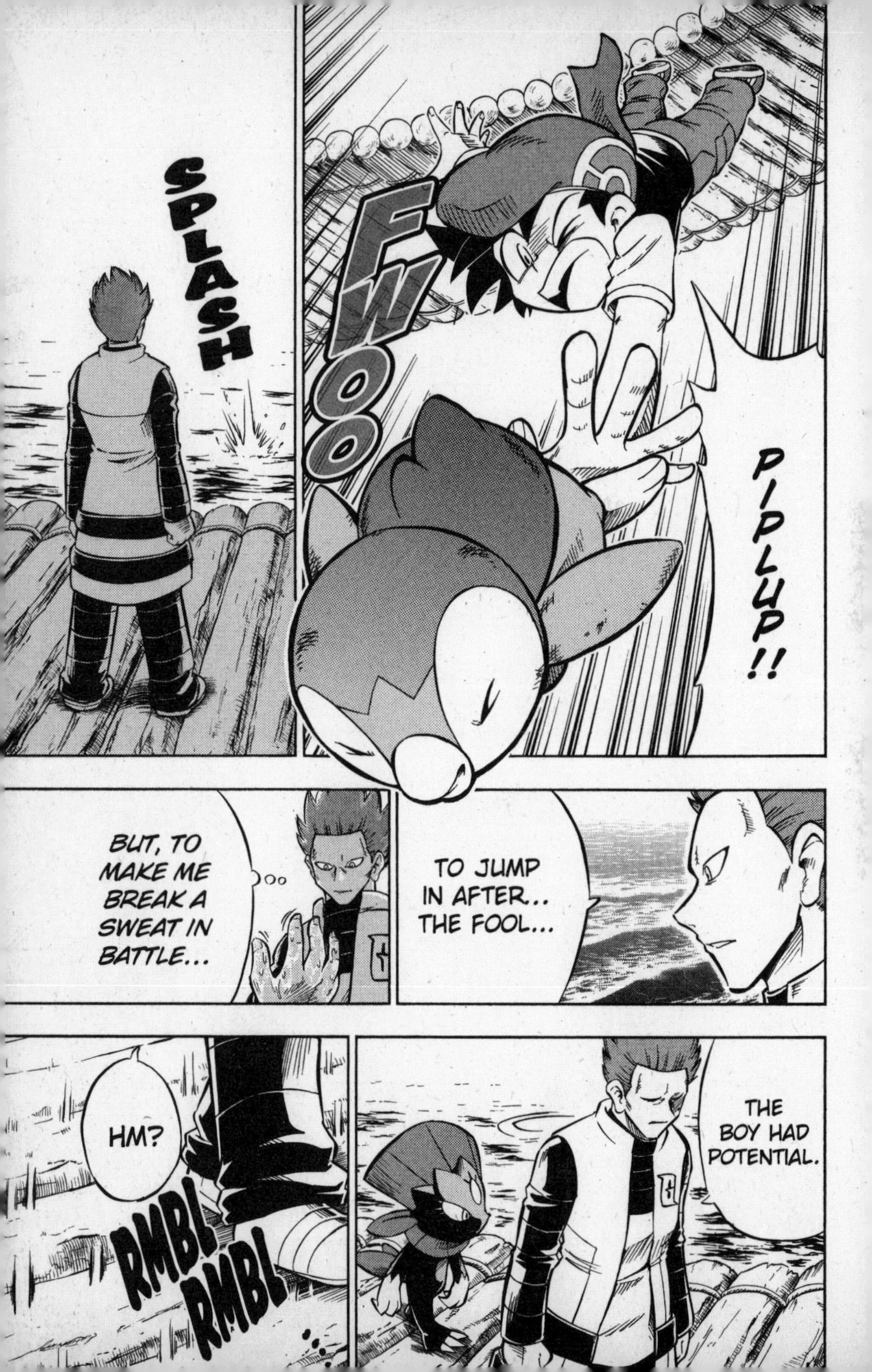
PIPLUP!!
FWOOO
SPLASH
TO JUMP IN AFTER... THE FOOL...
BUT, TO MAKE ME BREAK A SWEAT IN BATTLE...
THE BOY HAD POTENTIAL.
HM?
RMBL RMBL

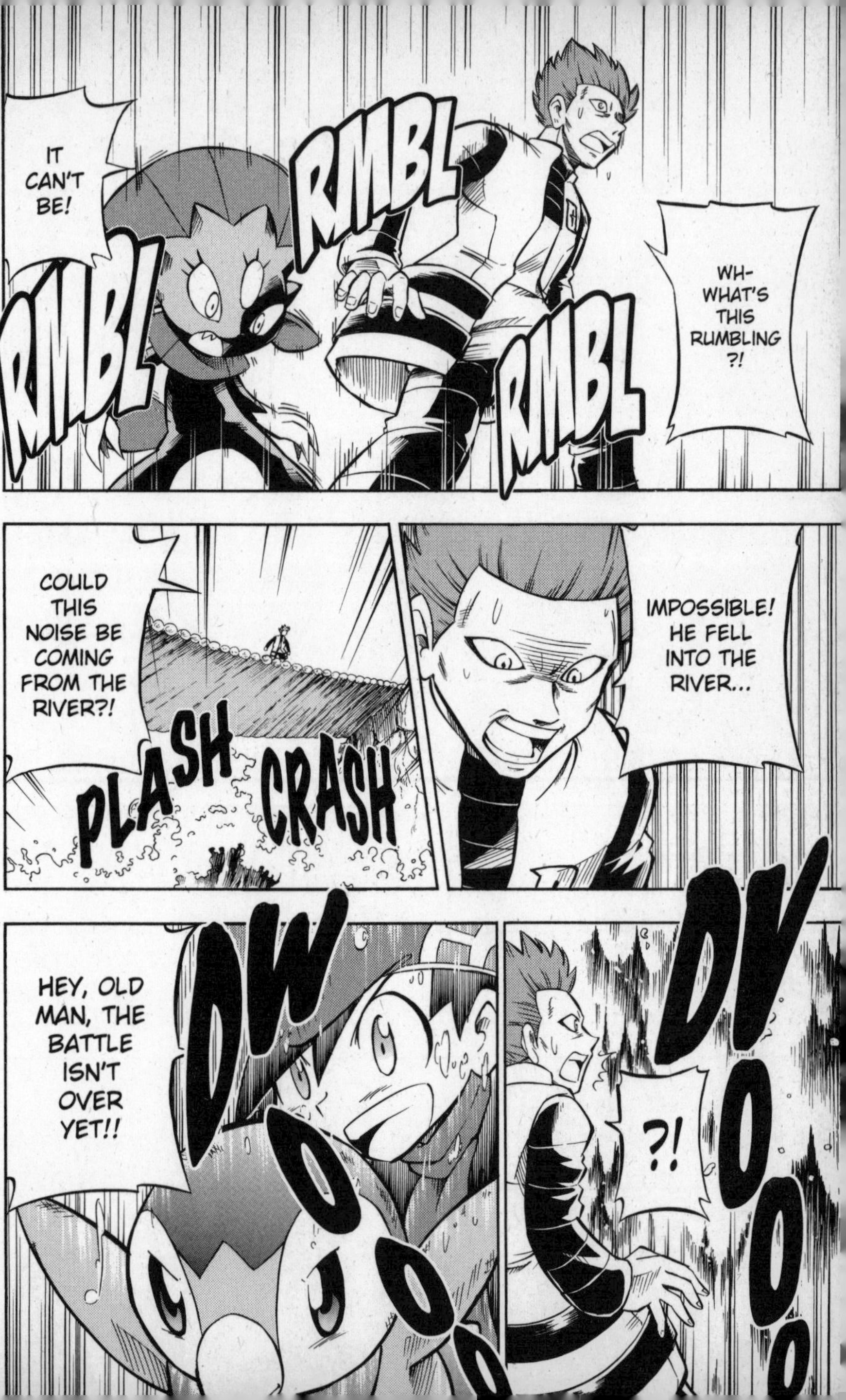
RMBL
WH-WHAT'S THIS RUMBLING?!
IT CAN'T BE!
RMBL
RMBL
IMPOSSIBLE! HE FELL INTO THE RIVER...
COULD THIS NOISE BE COMING FROM THE RIVER?!
CRASH
PLASH
DVOOOO
?!
HEY, OLD MAN, THE BATTLE ISN'T OVER YET!!
DWOOOO

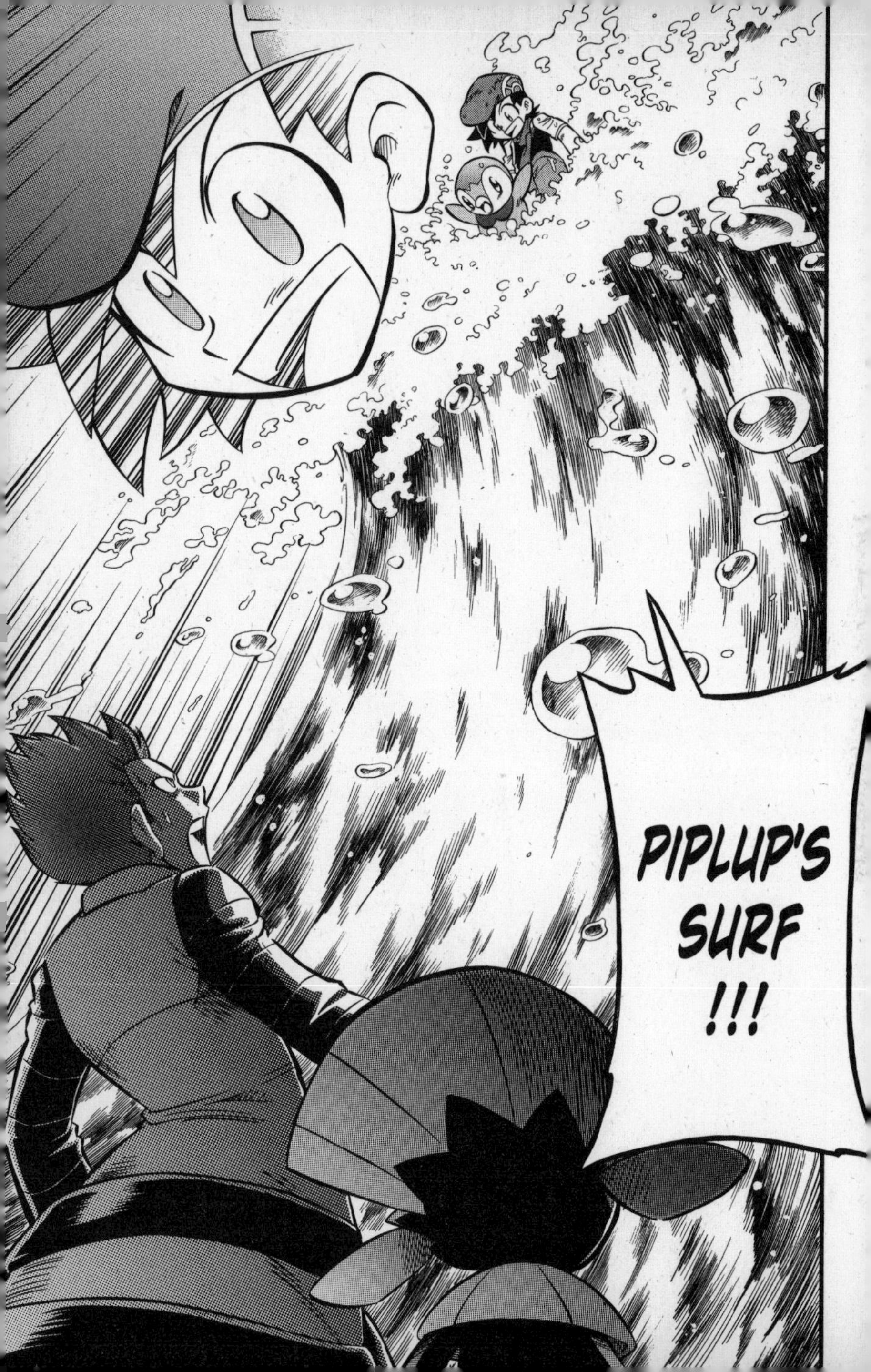
PIPLUP'S SURF !!!

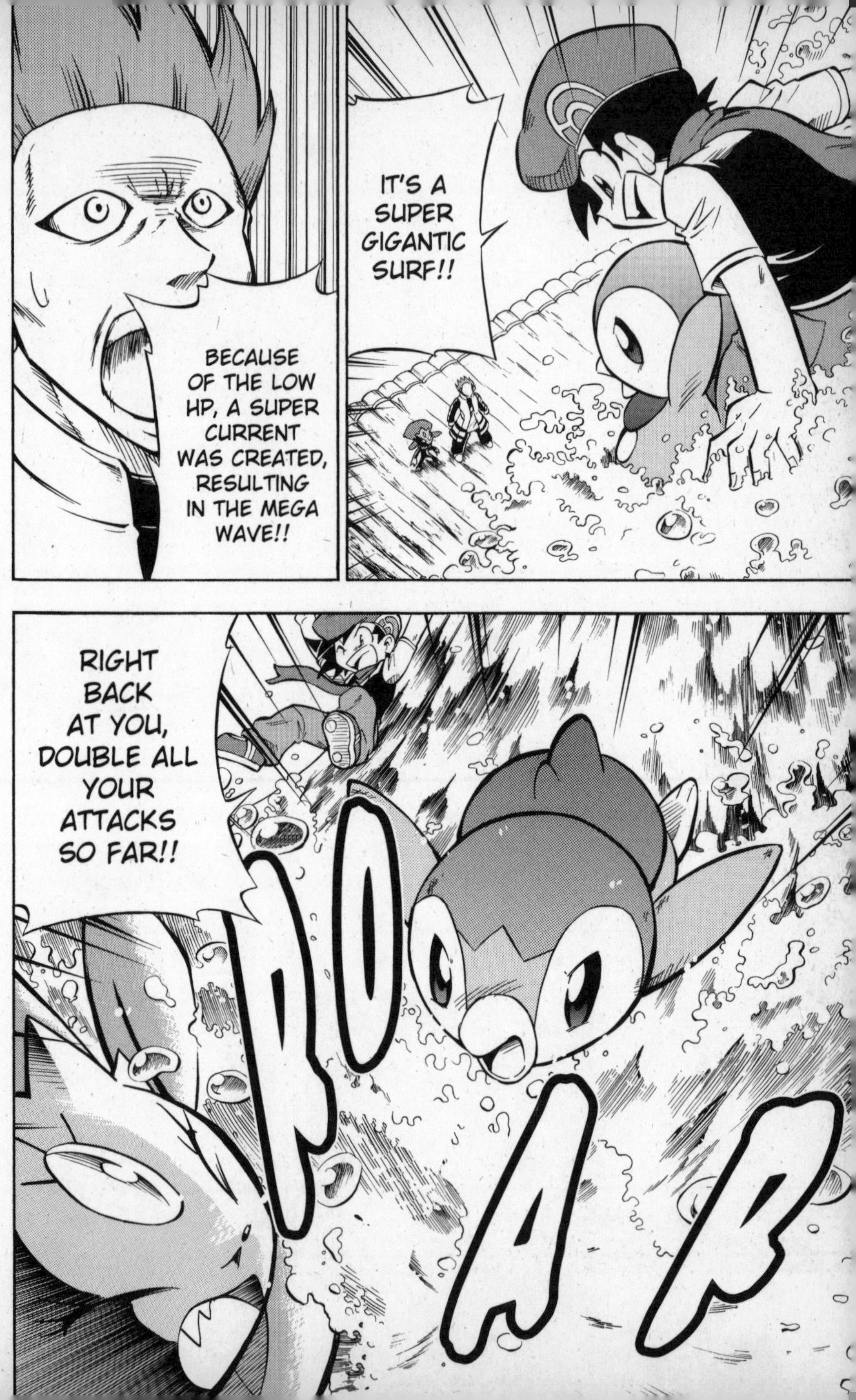
IT'S A SUPER GIGANTIC SURF!!
BECAUSE OF THE LOW HP, A SUPER CURRENT WAS CREATED, RESULTING IN THE MEGA WAVE!!
RIGHT BACK AT YOU, DOUBLE ALL YOUR ATTACKS SO FAR!!
ROAR

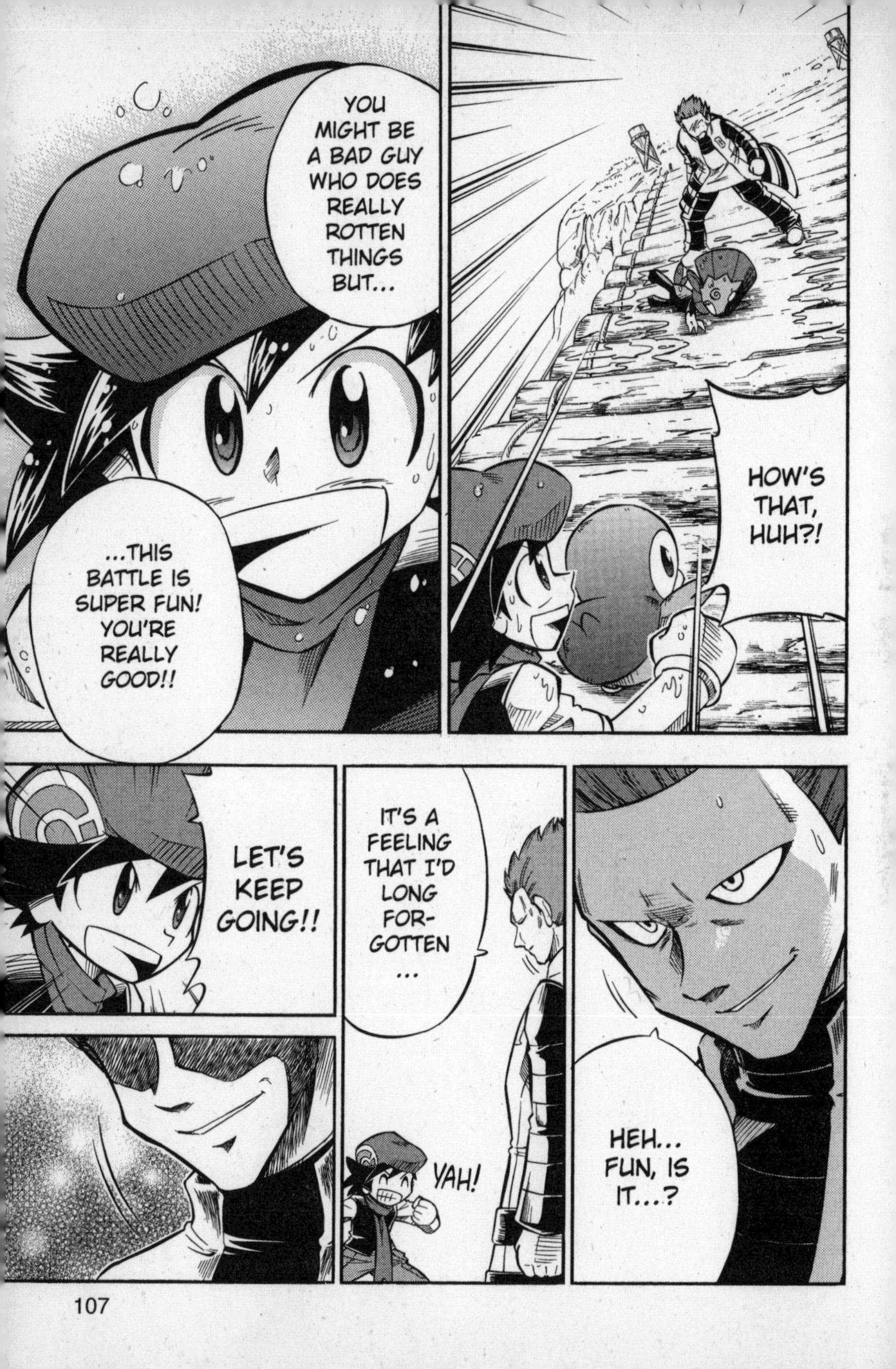
HOW'S THAT, HUH?!
YOU MIGHT BE A BAD GUY WHO DOES REALLY ROTTEN THINGS BUT...
...THIS BATTLE IS SUPER FUN! YOU'RE REALLY GOOD!!
HEH... FUN, IS IT...?
IT'S A FEELING THAT I'D LONG FOR-GOTTEN ...
YAH!
LET'S KEEP GOING!!

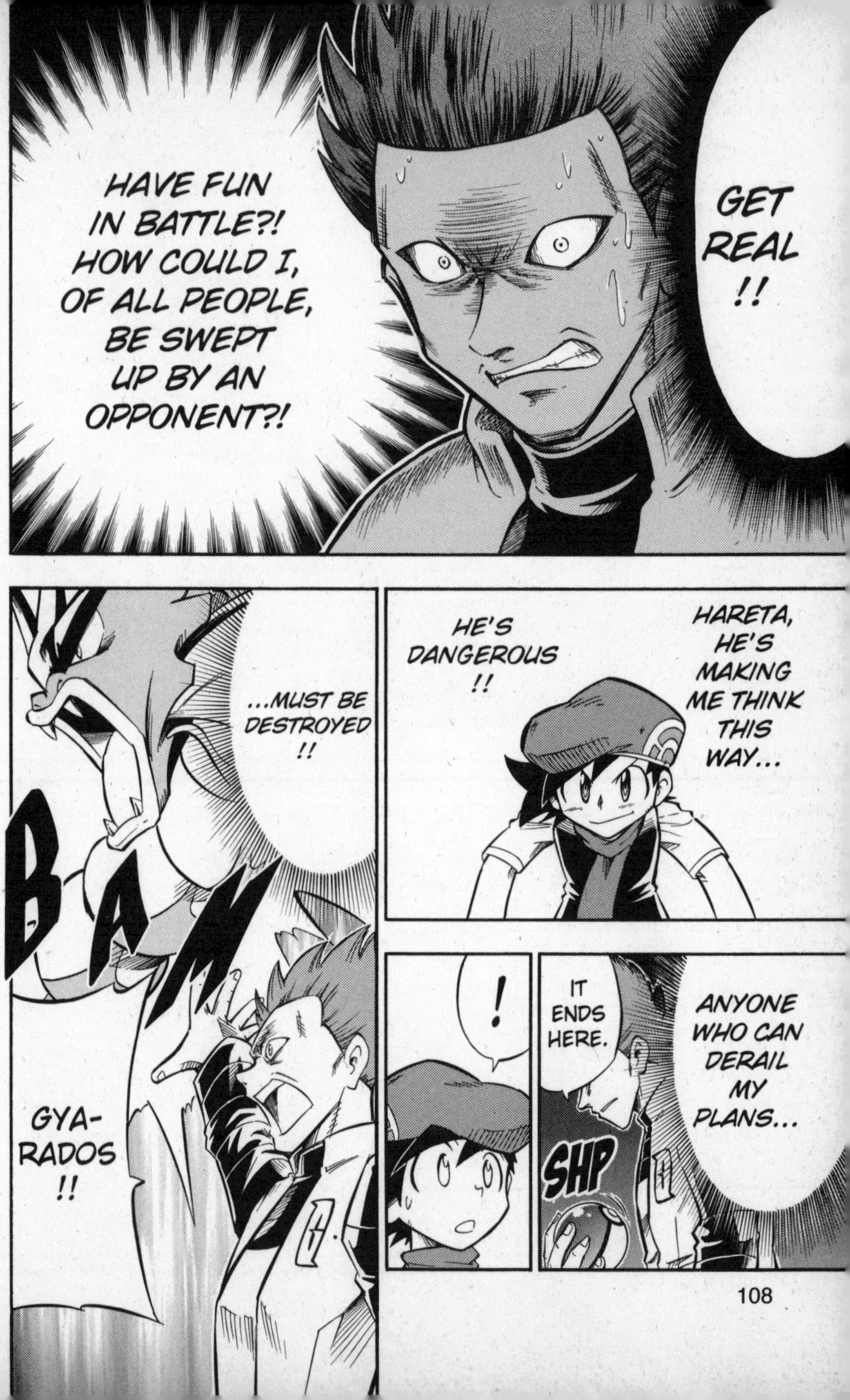
HAVE FUN IN BATTLE?! HOW COULD I, OF ALL PEOPLE, BE SWEPT UP BY AN OPPONENT?!
GET REAL !!
HARETA, HE'S MAKING ME THINK THIS WAY...
HE'S DANGEROUS !!
ANYONE WHO CAN DERAIL MY PLANS...
IT ENDS HERE.
SHP
!
...MUST BE DESTROYED !!
BAM
GYA-RADOS !!

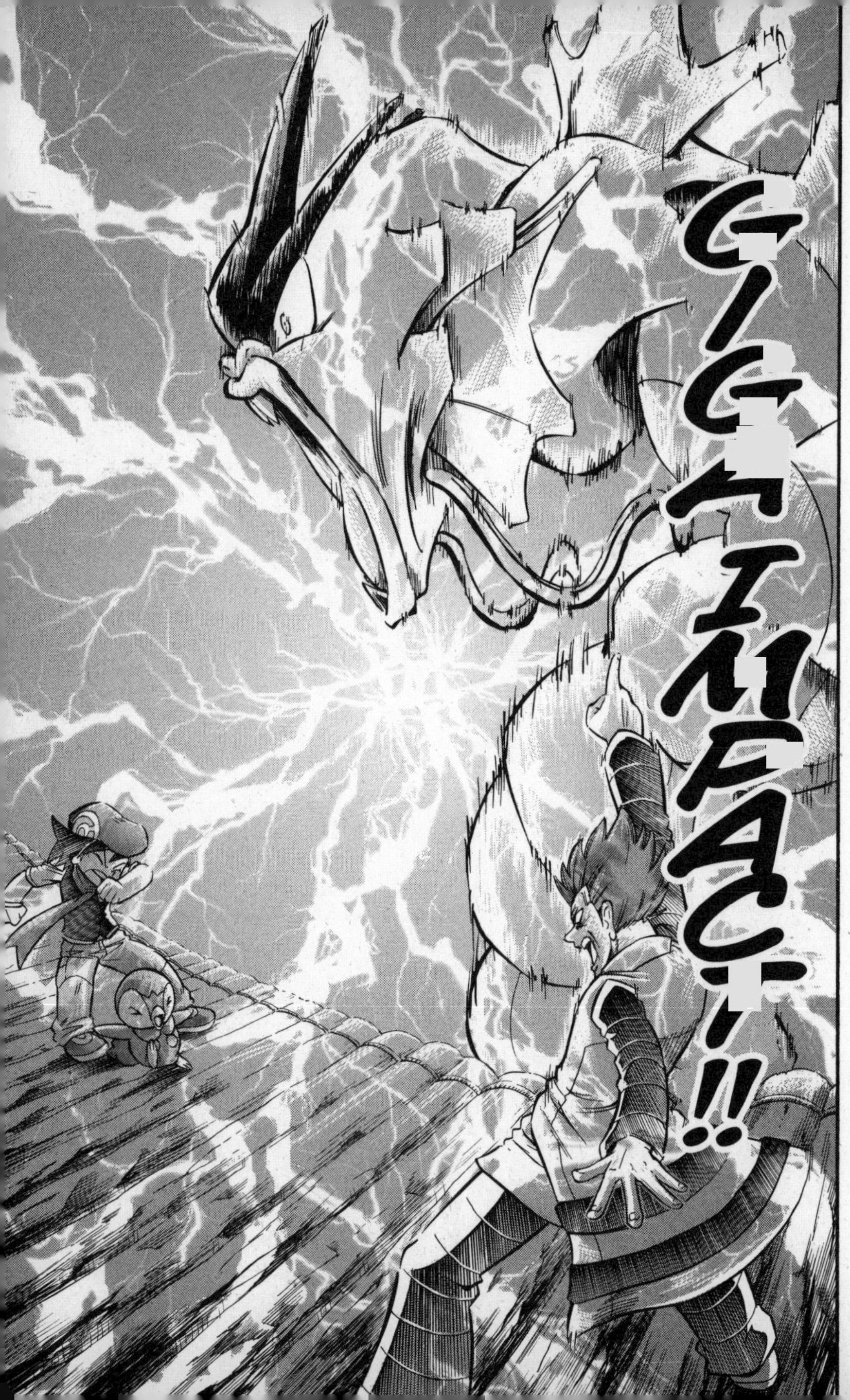
GIGA IMPACT!!

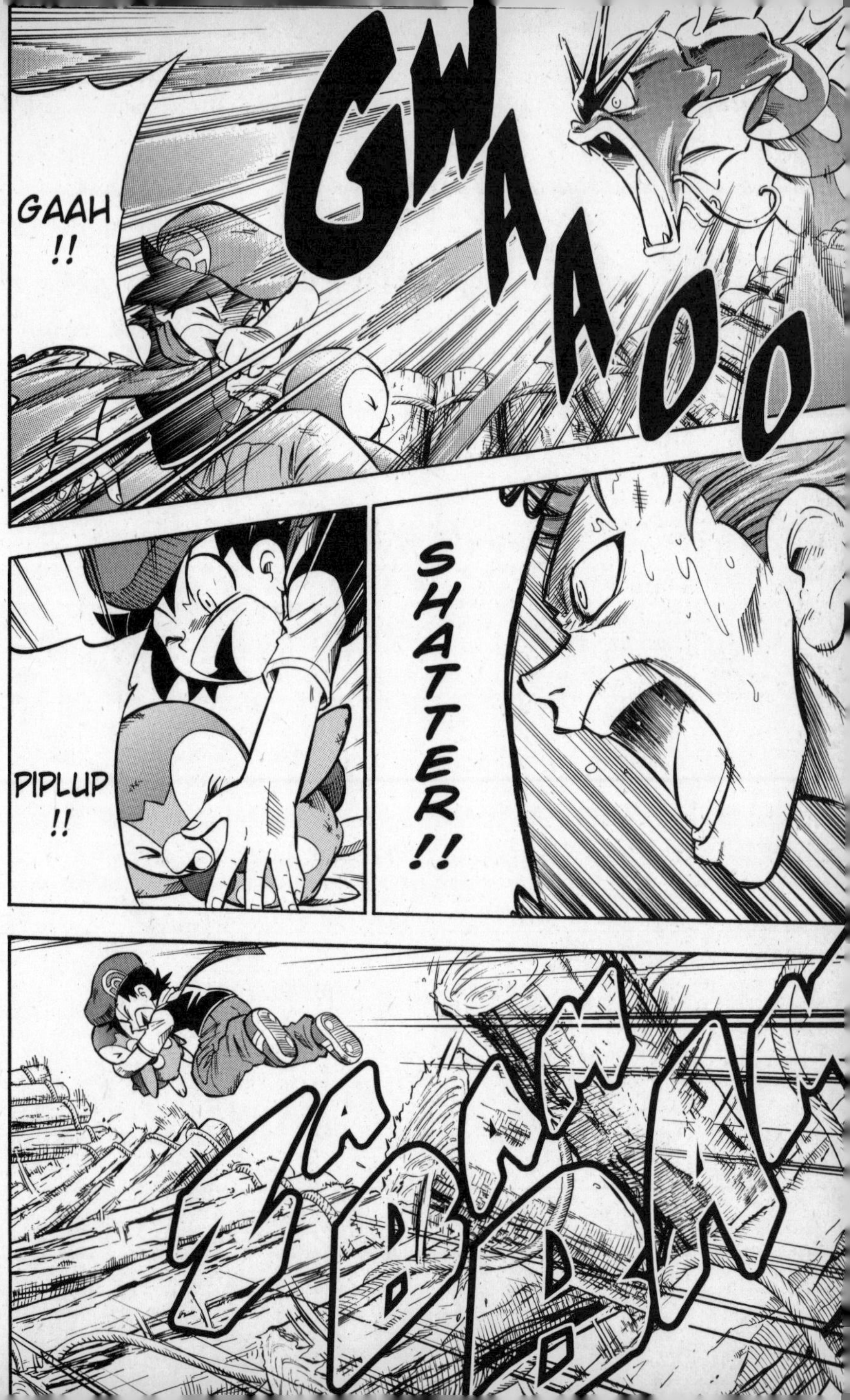
GWAAOO
GAAH!!
SHATTER!!
PIPLUP!!
ZABOOM

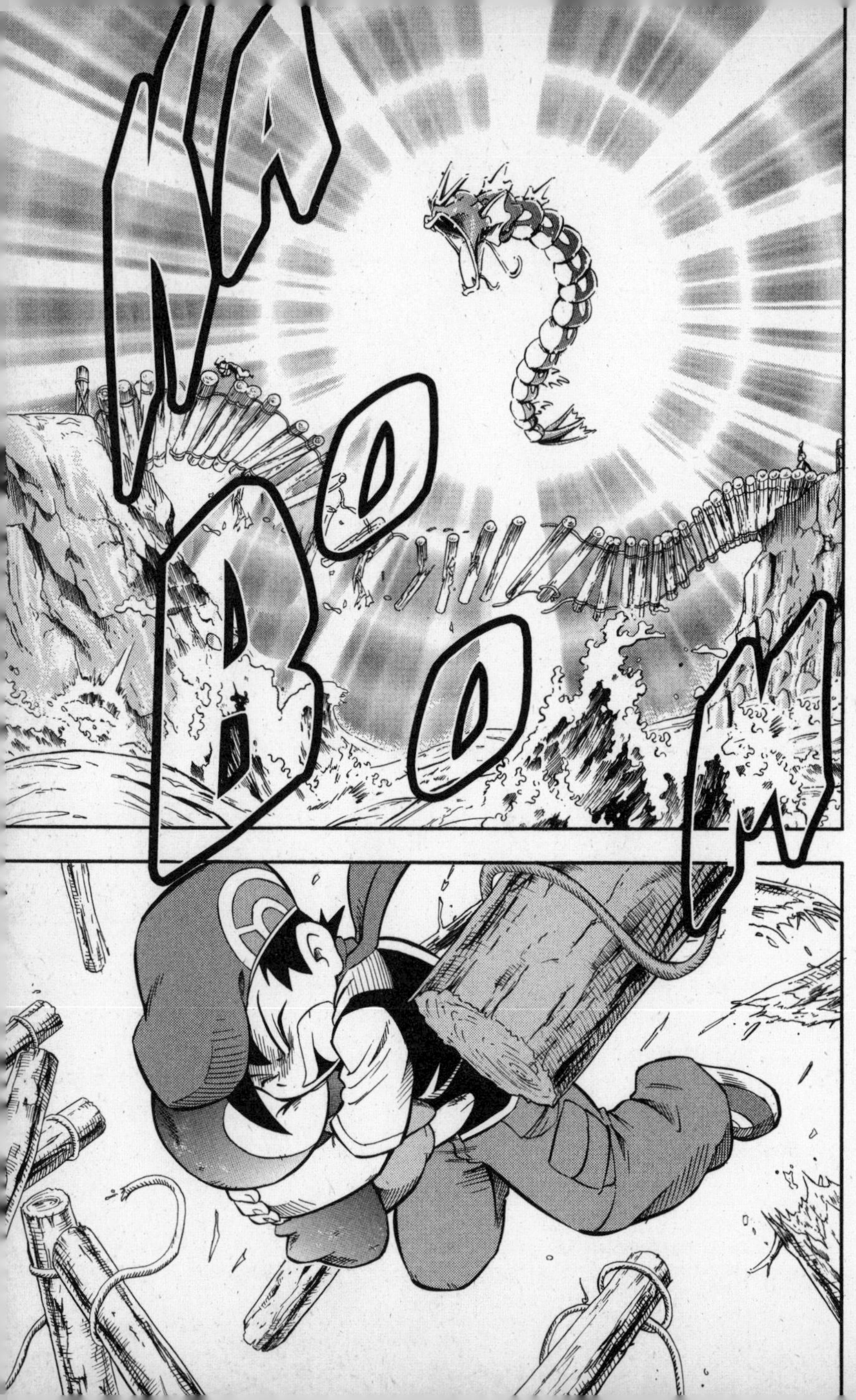
KABOOM

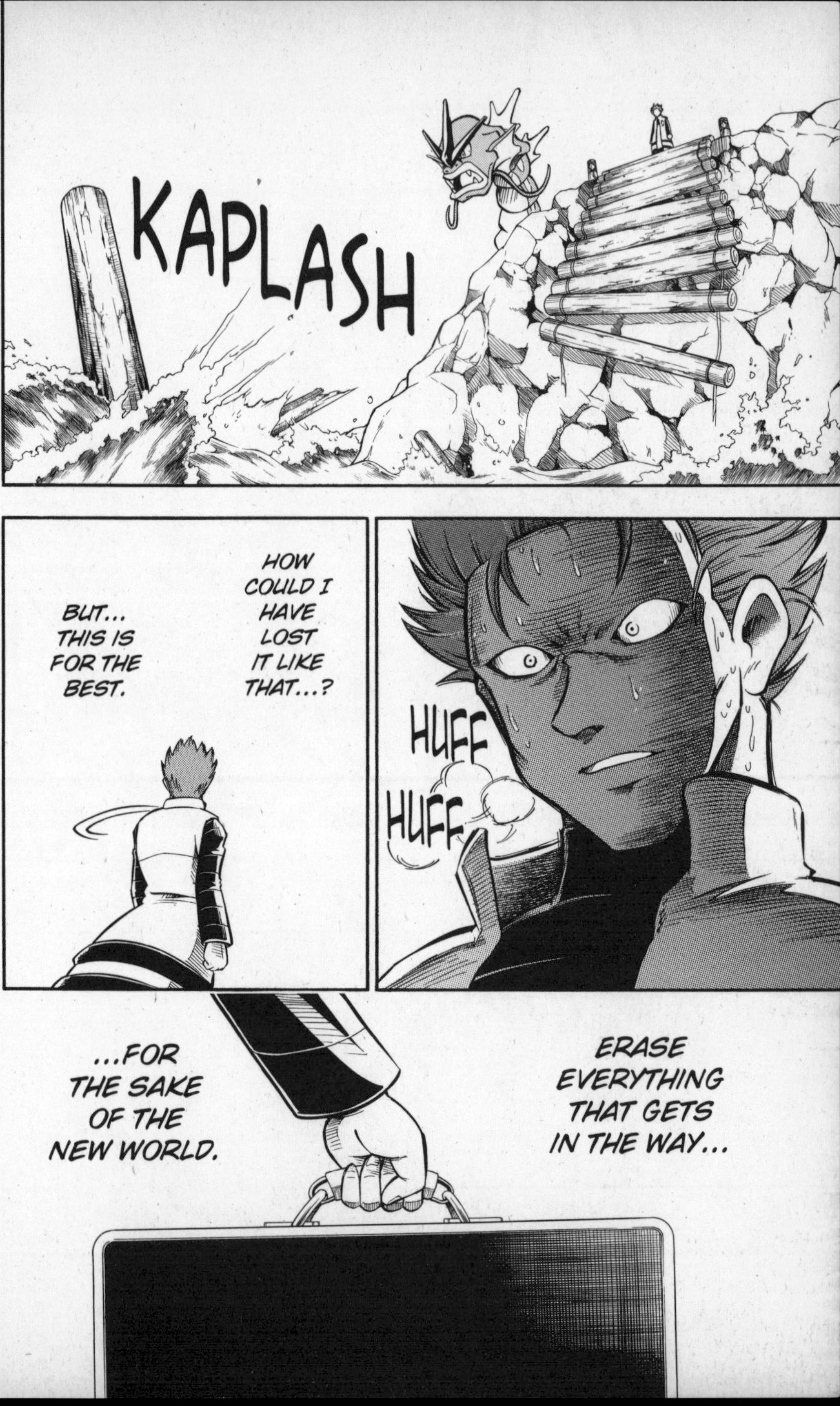
KAPLASH
HUFF HUFF
HOW COULD I HAVE LOST IT LIKE THAT...?
BUT... THIS IS FOR THE BEST.
ERASE EVERYTHING THAT GETS IN THE WAY...
...FOR THE SAKE OF THE NEW WORLD.

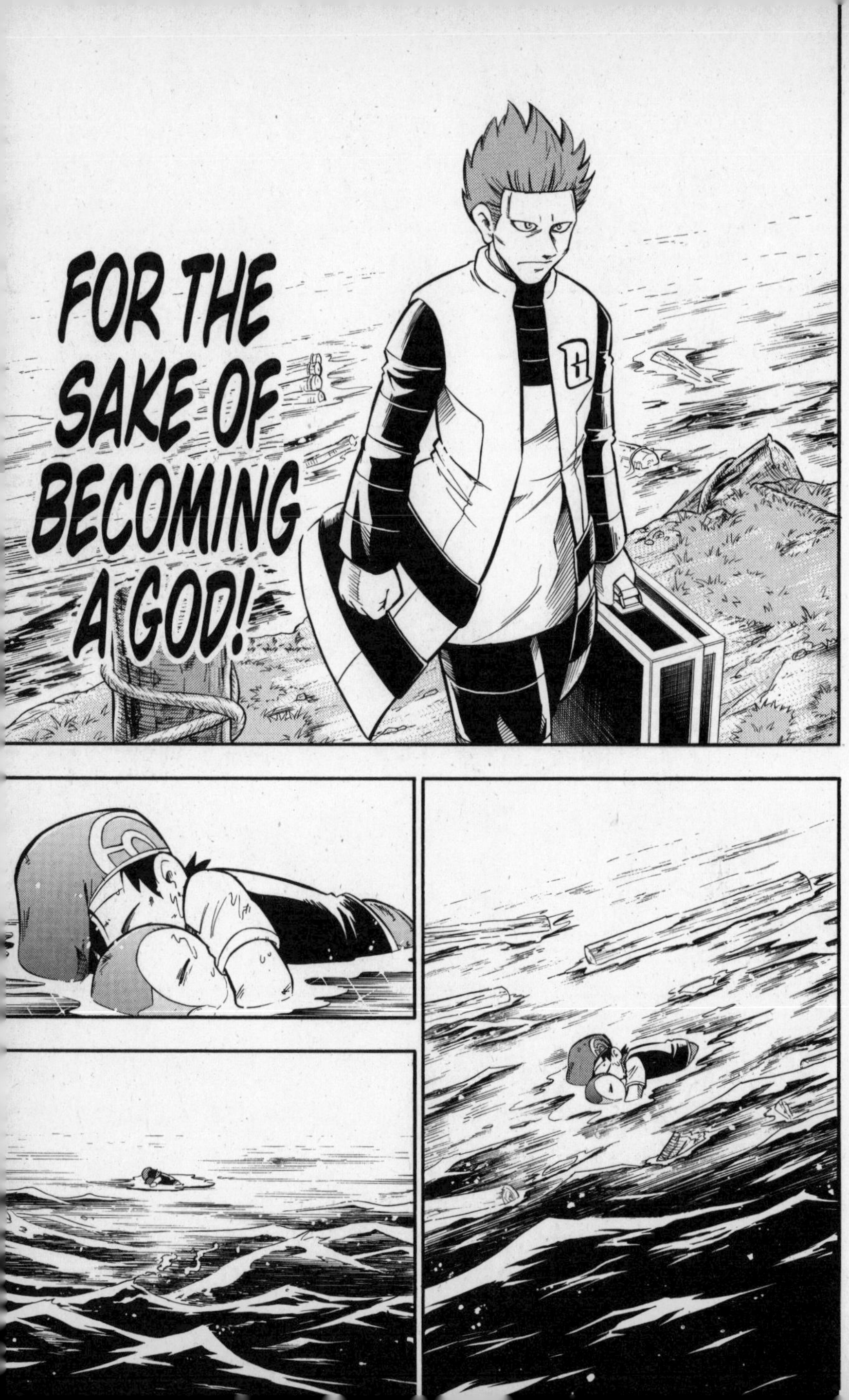
FOR THE SAKE OF BECOMING A GOD!

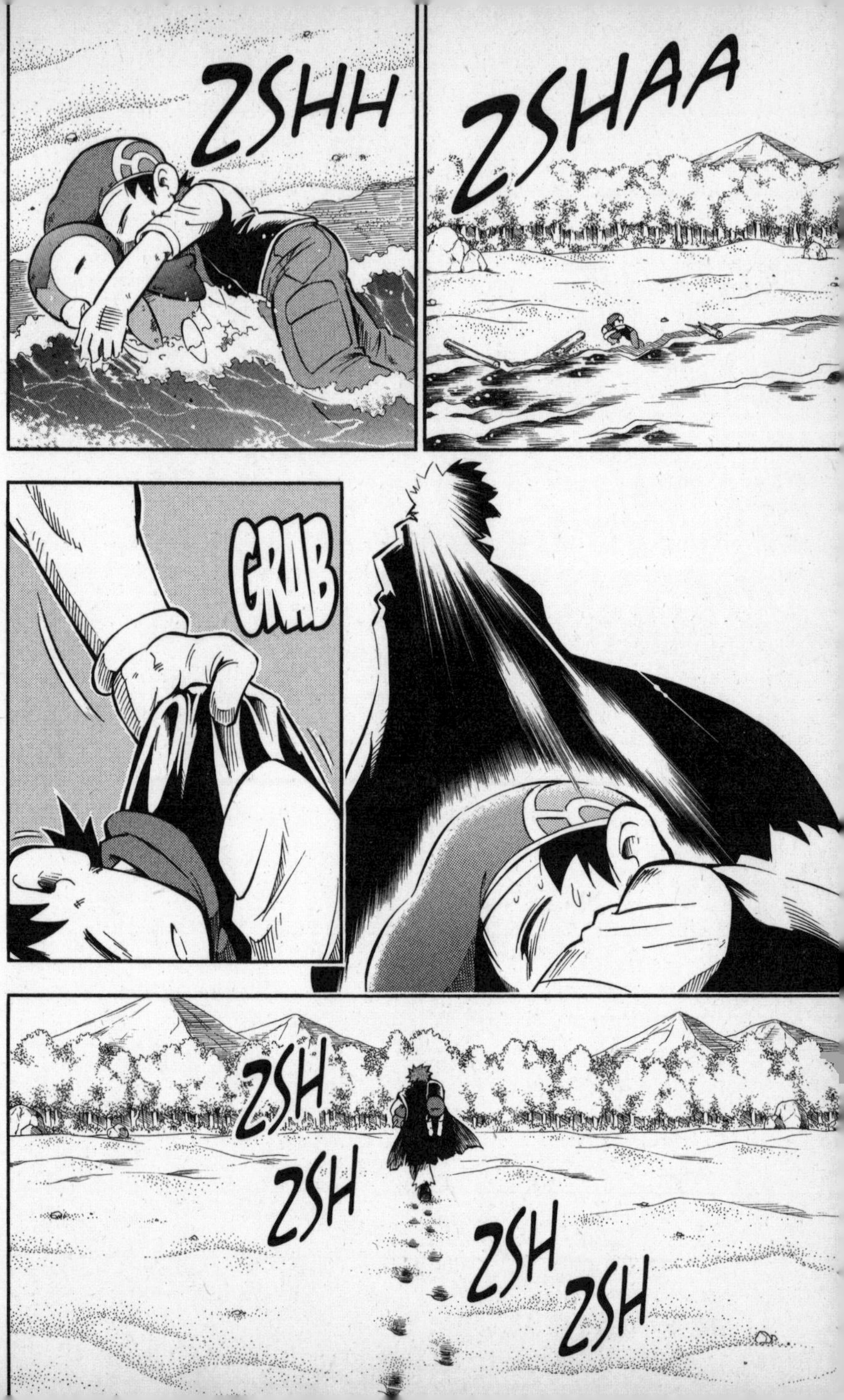
ZSHAA
ZSHH
GRAB
ZSH
ZSH
ZSH
ZSH

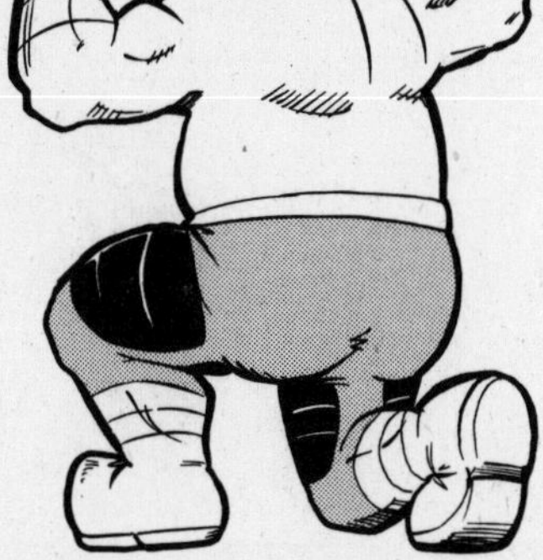
FLEX

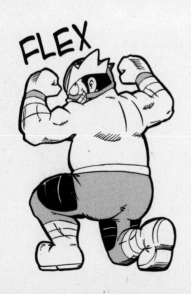

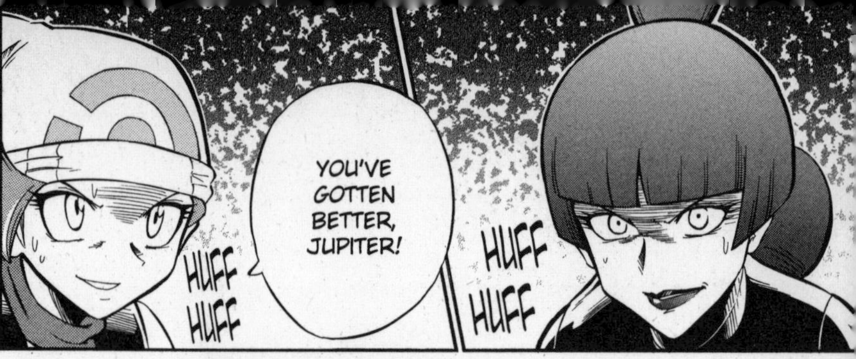
HUFF HUFF
YOU'VE GOTTEN BETTER, JUPITER!
HUFF HUFF

CHAPTER 4

CHALLENGE! THE FORTRESS OF STEEL!!

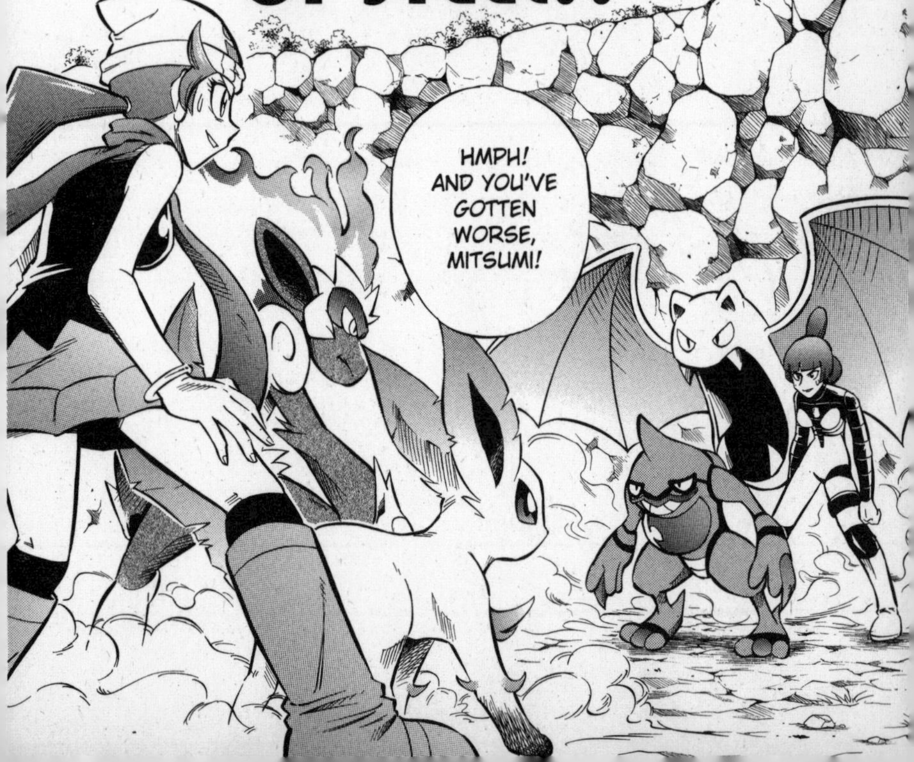
HMPH! AND YOU'VE GOTTEN WORSE, MITSUMI!

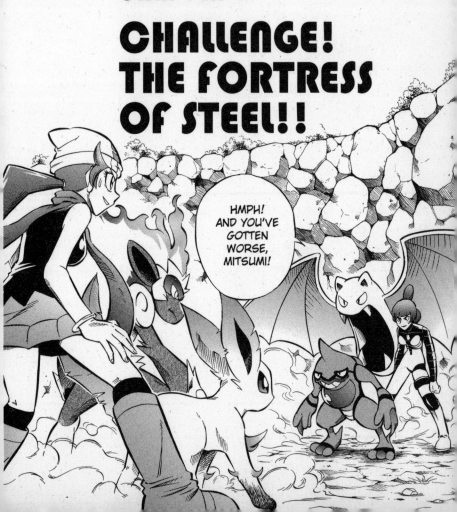

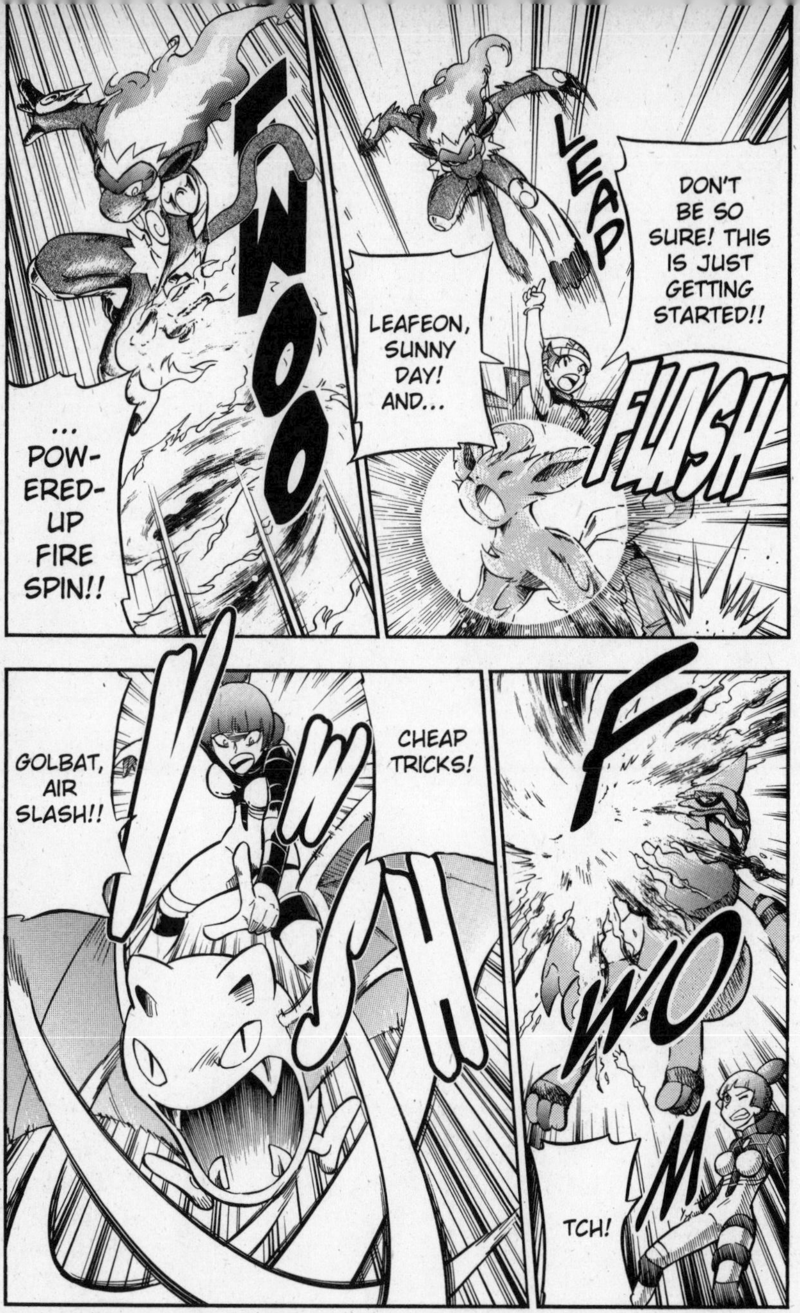
LEAP
DON'T BE SO SURE! THIS IS JUST GETTING STARTED!!
LEAFEON, SUNNY DAY! AND...
FLASH
FWOO
... POW-ERED-UP FIRE SPIN!!
FWOOM
TCH!
CHEAP TRICKS!
GOLBAT, AIR SLASH!!

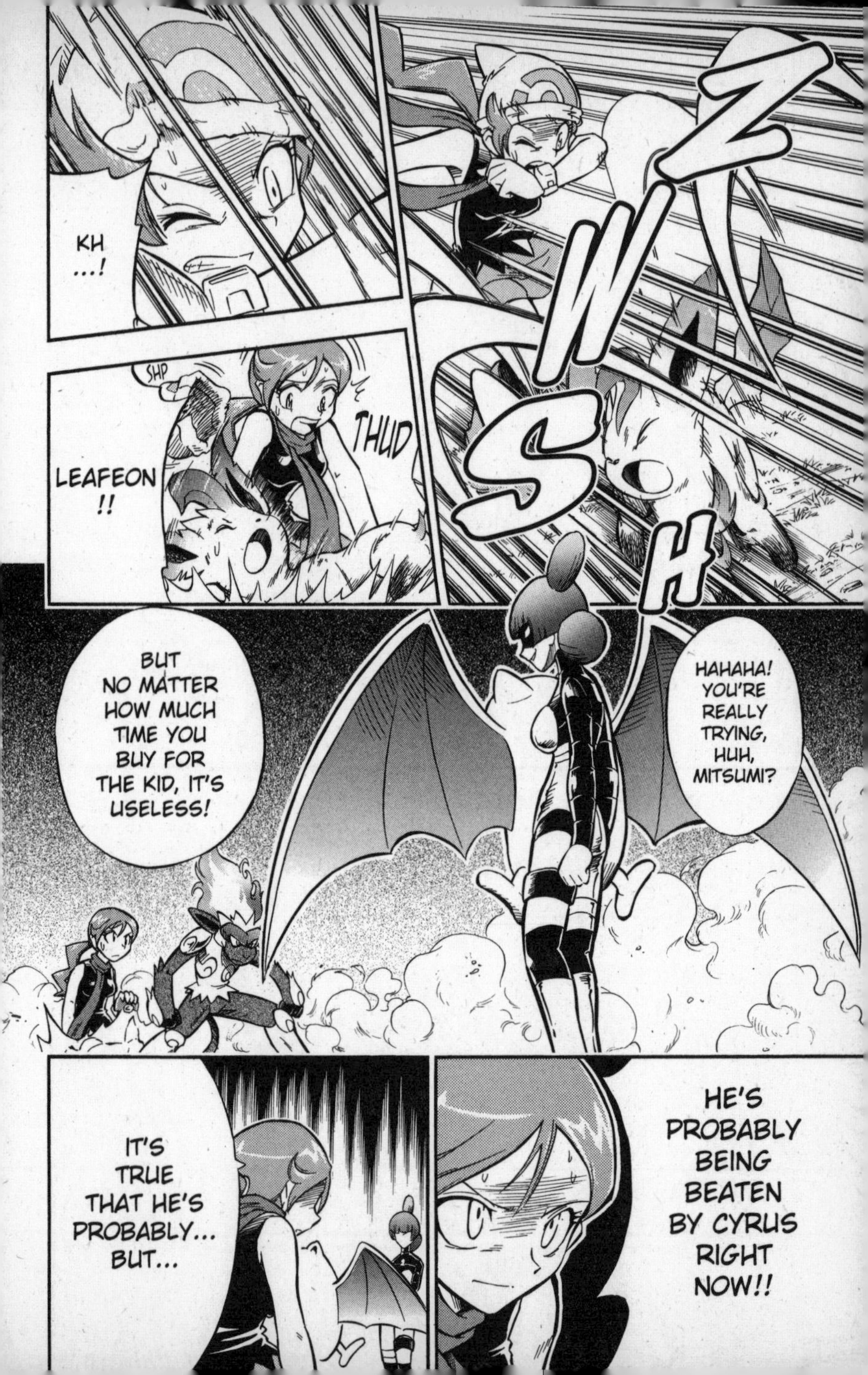
SWISH
KH ...!
SHP
THUD
LEAFEON!!
HAHAHA! YOU'RE REALLY TRYING, HUH, MITSUMI?
BUT NO MATTER HOW MUCH TIME YOU BUY FOR THE KID, IT'S USELESS!
HE'S PROBABLY BEING BEATEN BY CYRUS RIGHT NOW!!
IT'S TRUE THAT HE'S PROBABLY... BUT...

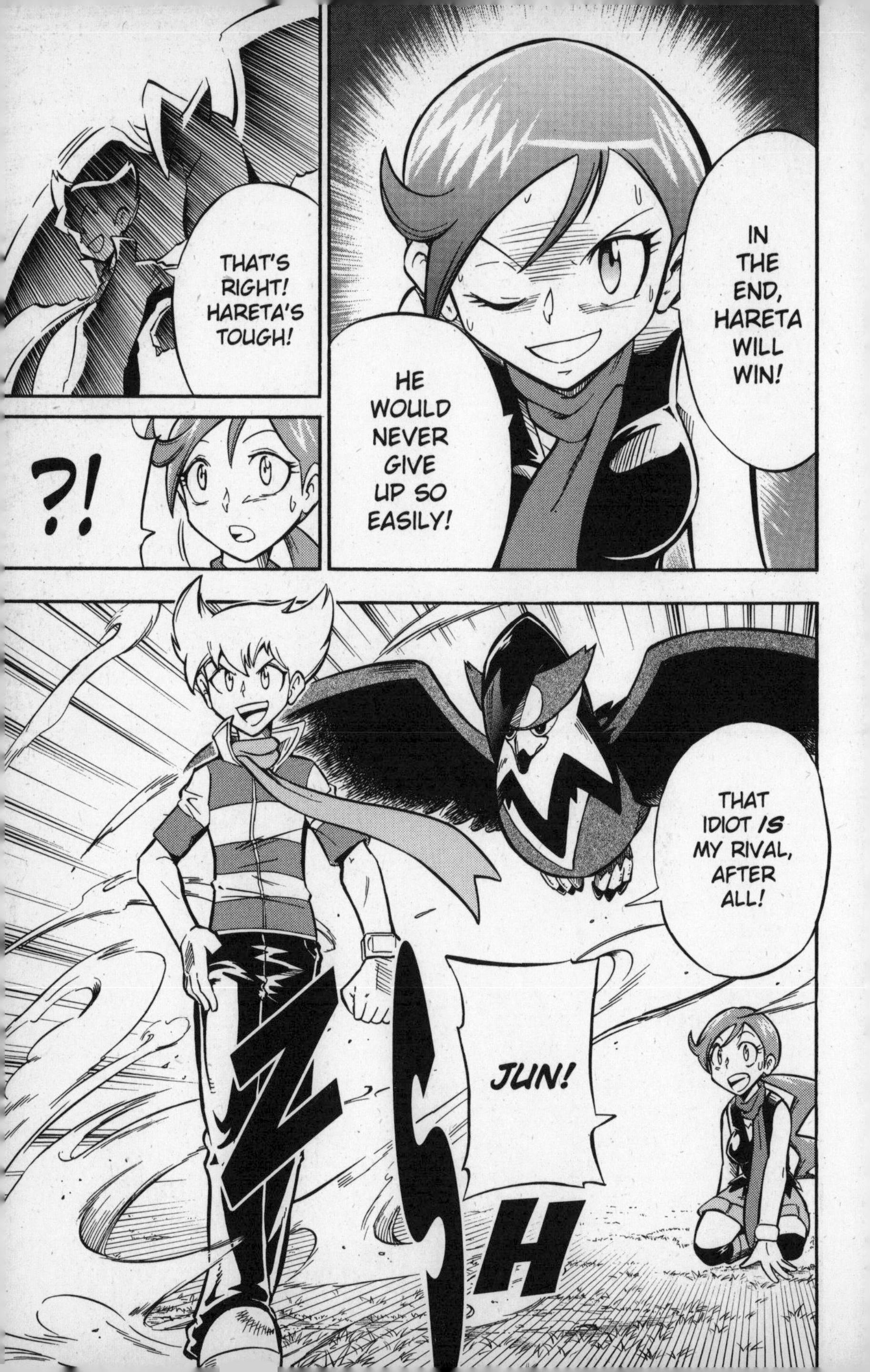
IN THE END, HARETA WILL WIN!
HE WOULD NEVER GIVE UP SO EASILY!
THAT'S RIGHT! HARETA'S TOUGH!
?!
THAT IDIOT *IS* MY RIVAL, AFTER ALL!
JUN!
ZSH

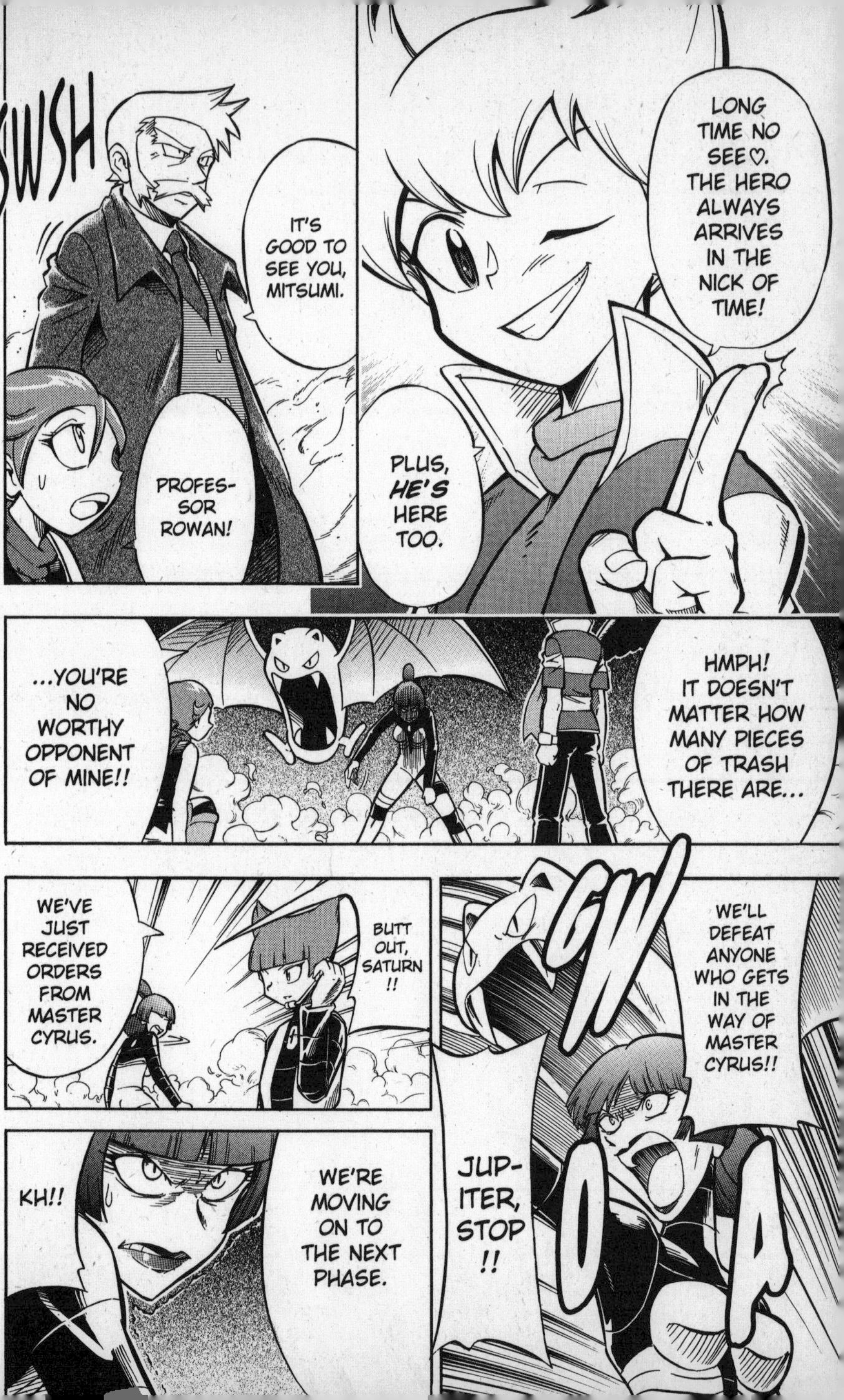
LONG TIME NO SEE♡. THE HERO ALWAYS ARRIVES IN THE NICK OF TIME!
PLUS, **HE'S** HERE TOO.
SWSH
IT'S GOOD TO SEE YOU, MITSUMI.
PROFES-SOR ROWAN!
HMPH! IT DOESN'T MATTER HOW MANY PIECES OF TRASH THERE ARE...
...YOU'RE NO WORTHY OPPONENT OF MINE!!
WE'LL DEFEAT ANYONE WHO GETS IN THE WAY OF MASTER CYRUS!!
JUP-ITER, STOP!!
BUTT OUT, SATURN!!
WE'VE JUST RECEIVED ORDERS FROM MASTER CYRUS.
WE'RE MOVING ON TO THE NEXT PHASE.
KH!!

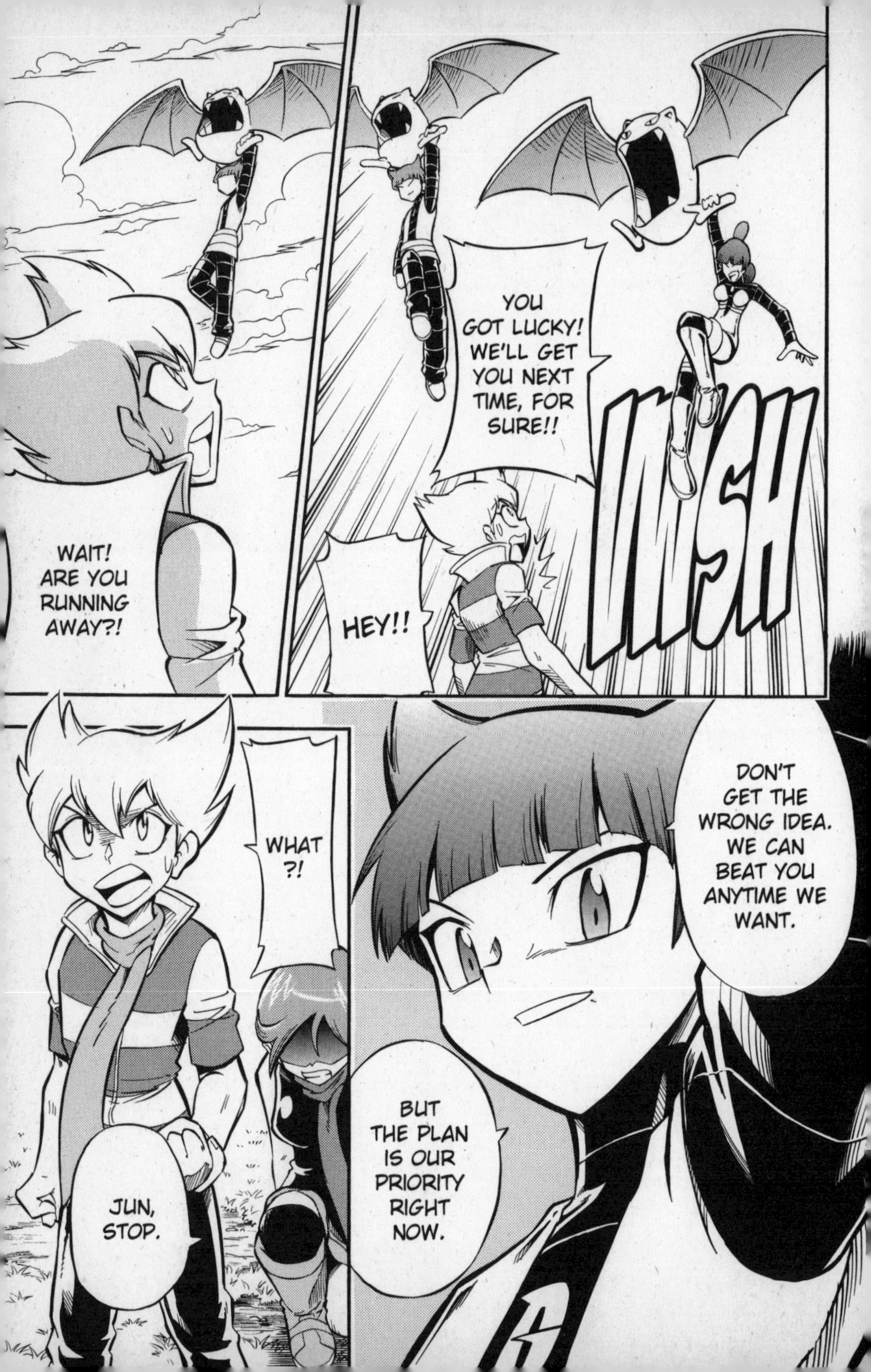
YOU GOT LUCKY! WE'LL GET YOU NEXT TIME, FOR SURE!!
HEY!!
WAIT! ARE YOU RUNNING AWAY?!
DON'T GET THE WRONG IDEA. WE CAN BEAT YOU ANYTIME WE WANT.
BUT THE PLAN IS OUR PRIORITY RIGHT NOW.
WHAT ?!
JUN, STOP.

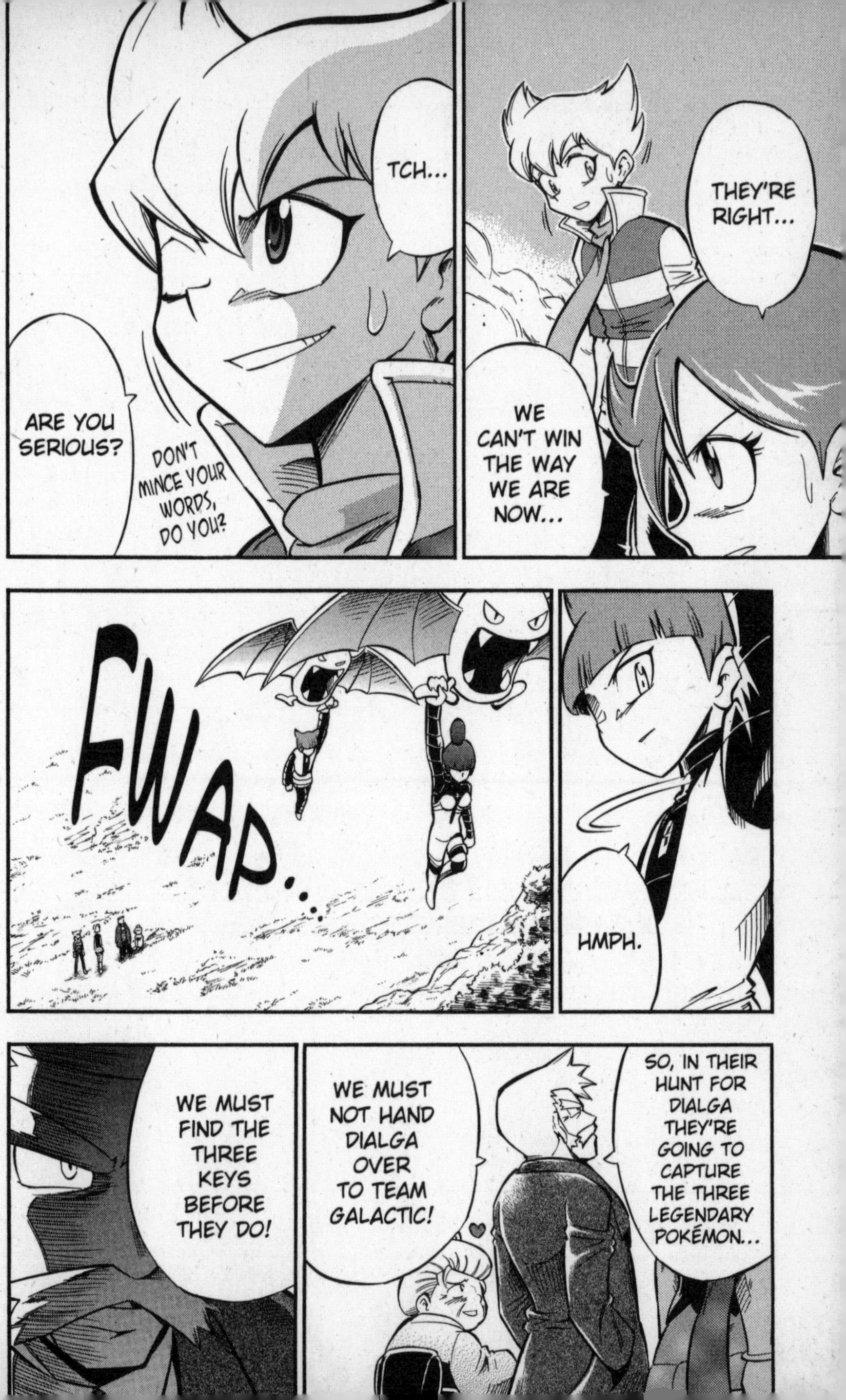
THEY'RE RIGHT...
WE CAN'T WIN THE WAY WE ARE NOW...
TCH...
DON'T MINCE YOUR WORDS, DO YOU?
ARE YOU SERIOUS?
HMPH.
FWAP...
SO, IN THEIR HUNT FOR DIALGA THEY'RE GOING TO CAPTURE THE THREE LEGENDARY POKÉMON...
WE MUST NOT HAND DIALGA OVER TO TEAM GALACTIC!
WE MUST FIND THE THREE KEYS BEFORE THEY DO!

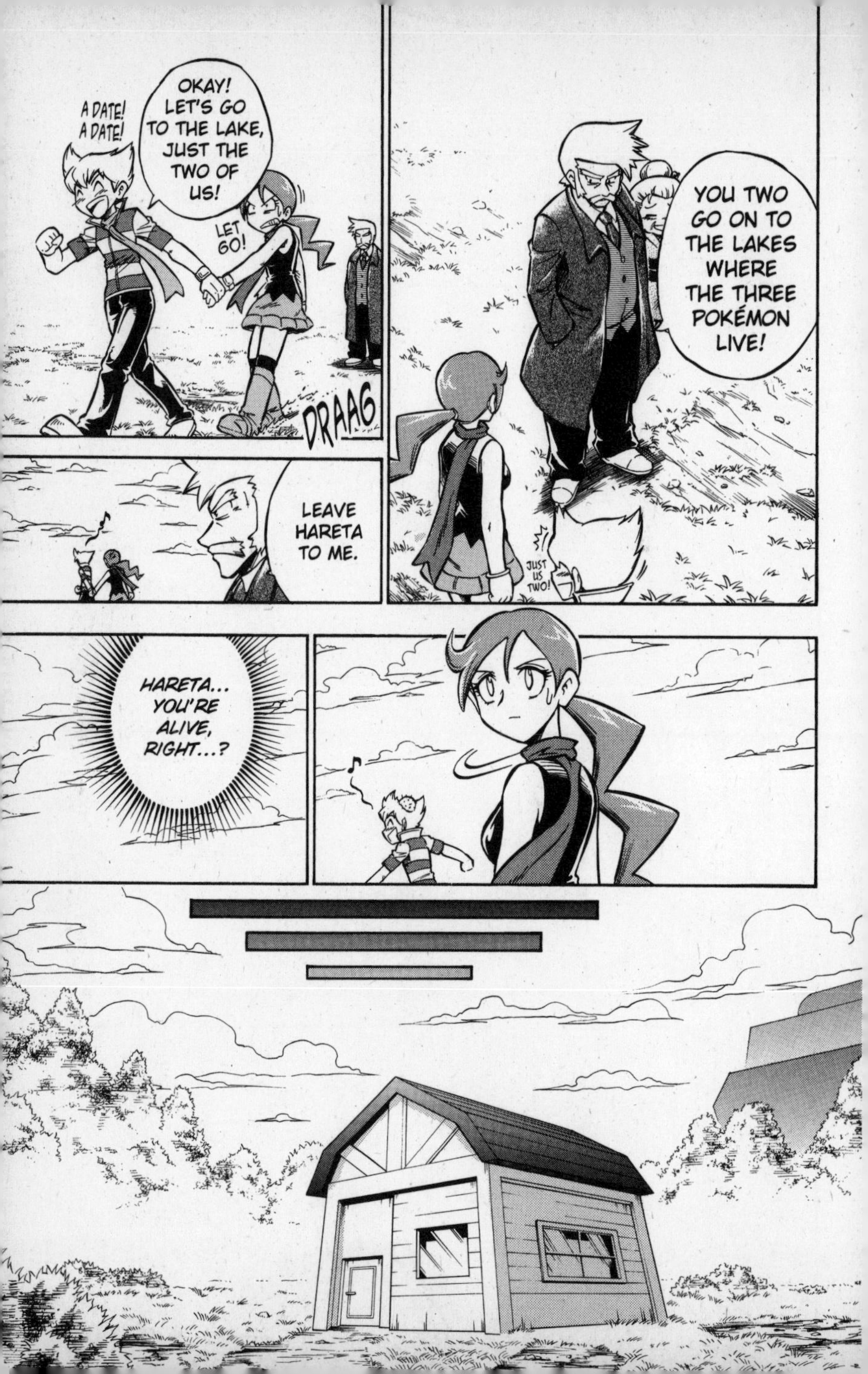
YOU TWO GO ON TO THE LAKES WHERE THE THREE POKÉMON LIVE!
JUST US TWO!
OKAY! LET'S GO TO THE LAKE, JUST THE TWO OF US!
A DATE! A DATE!
LET GO!
DRAAG
LEAVE HARETA TO ME.
HARETA... YOU'RE ALIVE, RIGHT...?

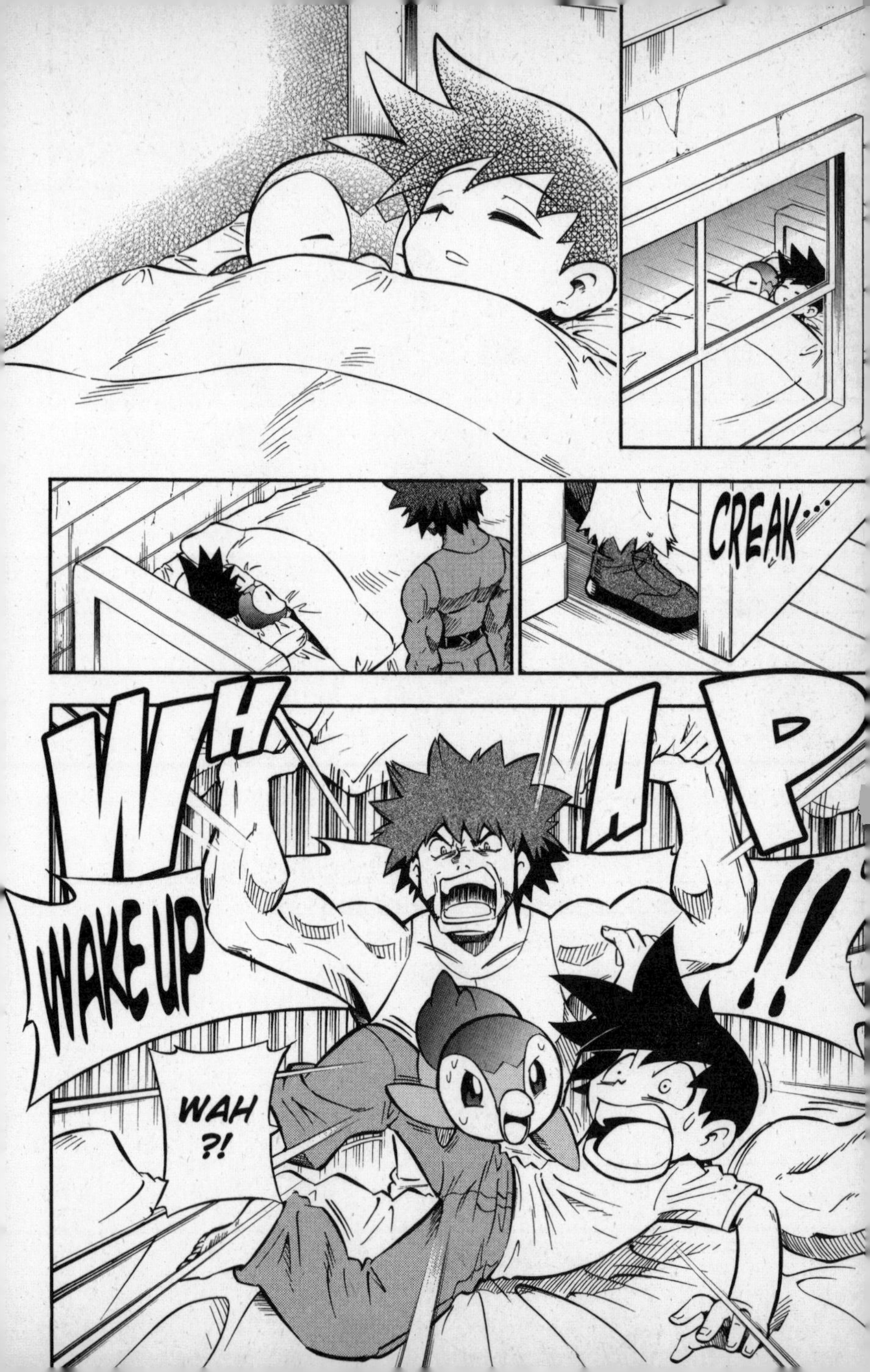
CREAK...
WHAP
WAKE UP!!
WAH?!

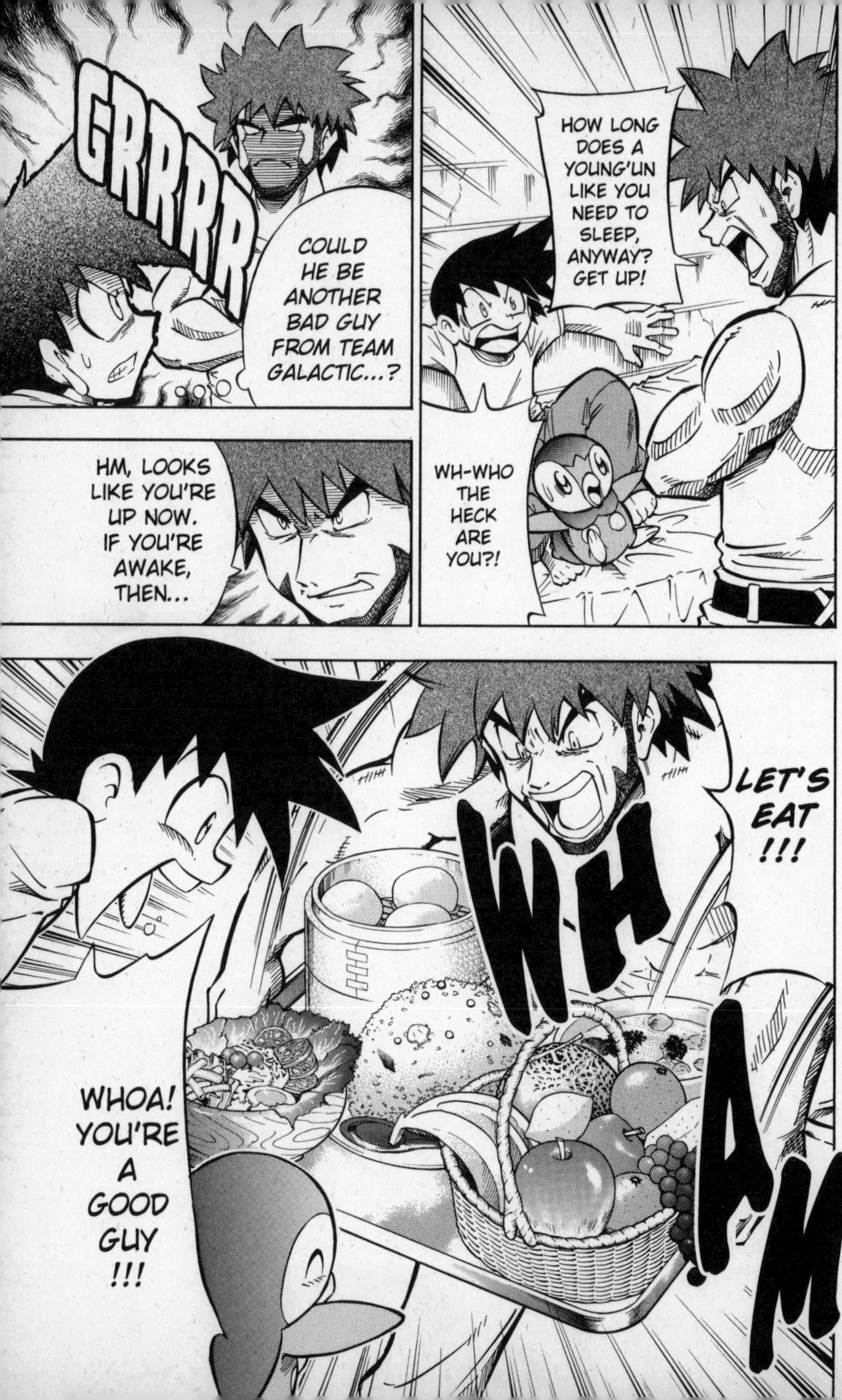
HOW LONG DOES A YOUNG'UN LIKE YOU NEED TO SLEEP, ANYWAY? GET UP!
WH-WHO THE HECK ARE YOU?!
GRRRR
COULD HE BE ANOTHER BAD GUY FROM TEAM GALACTIC...?
HM, LOOKS LIKE YOU'RE UP NOW. IF YOU'RE AWAKE, THEN...
LET'S EAT!!!
WHAM
WHOA! YOU'RE A GOOD GUY!!!

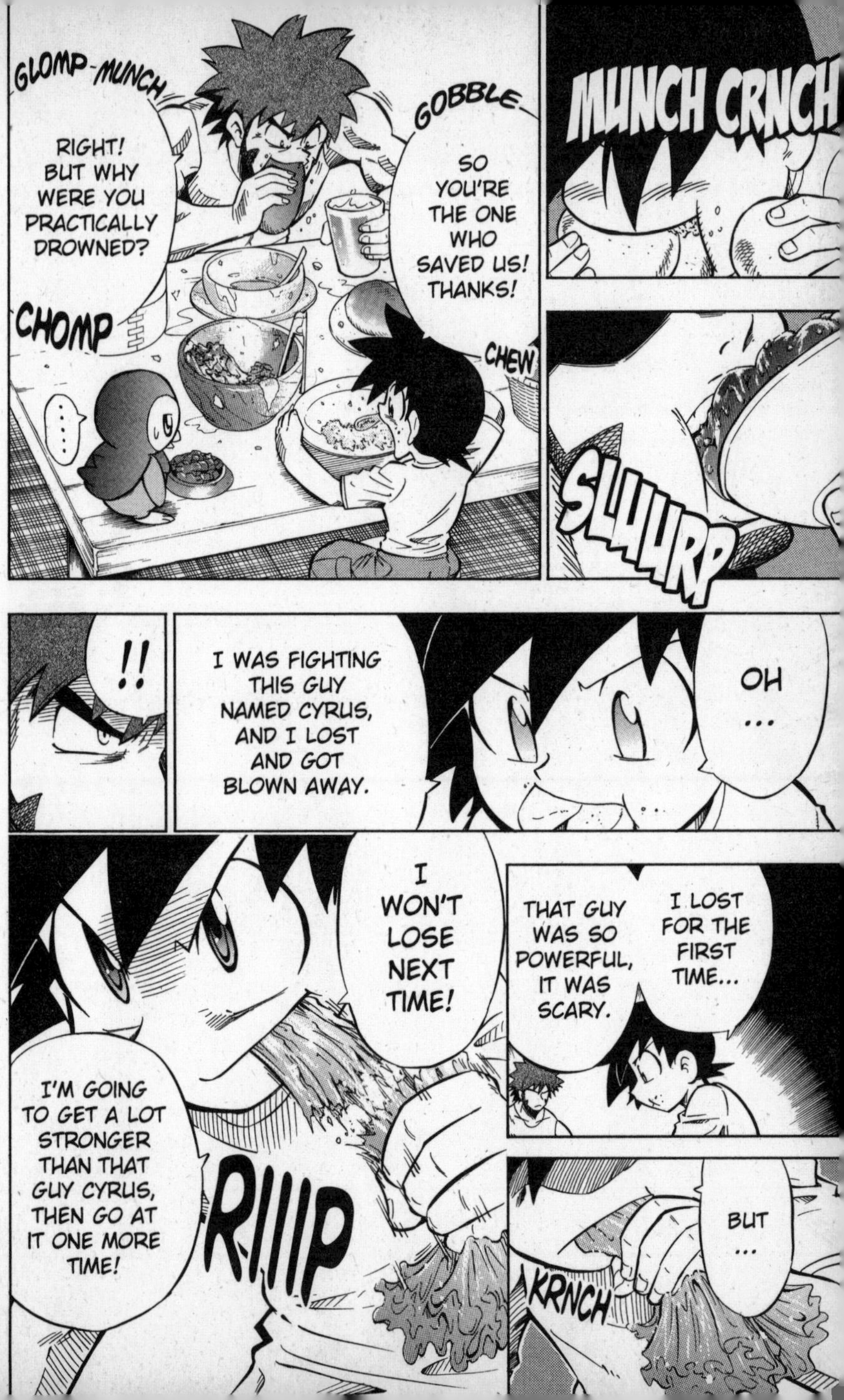
MUNCH CRNCH
SLUUURP
GOBBLE
SO YOU'RE THE ONE WHO SAVED US! THANKS!
GLOMP-MUNCH
RIGHT! BUT WHY WERE YOU PRACTICALLY DROWNED?
CHEW
CHOMP
......
OH ...
I WAS FIGHTING THIS GUY NAMED CYRUS, AND I LOST AND GOT BLOWN AWAY.
!!
I LOST FOR THE FIRST TIME...
THAT GUY WAS SO POWERFUL, IT WAS SCARY.
BUT ...
KRNCH
I WON'T LOSE NEXT TIME!
I'M GOING TO GET A LOT STRONGER THAN THAT GUY CYRUS, THEN GO AT IT ONE MORE TIME!
RIIIP

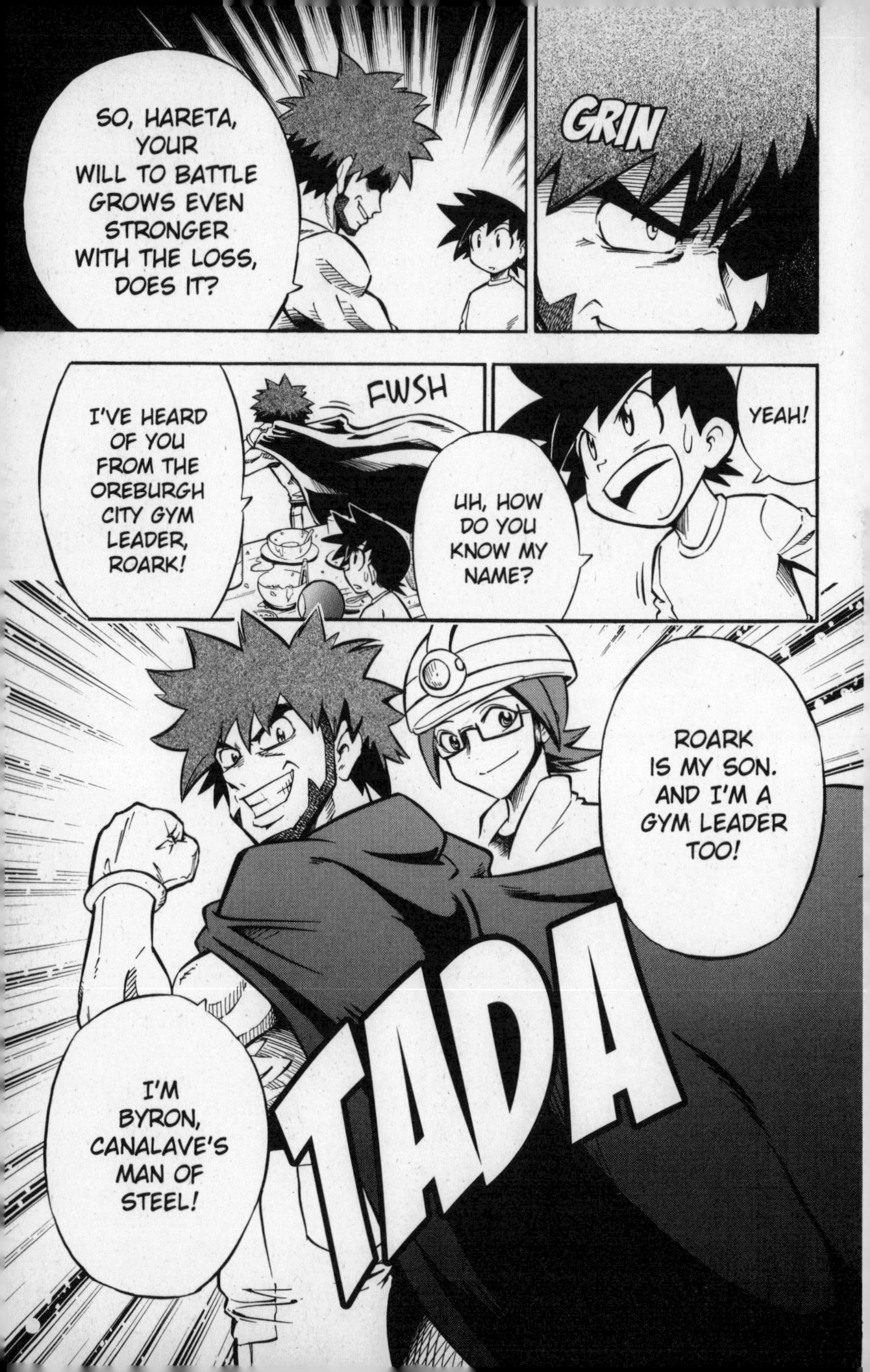
GRIN
SO, HARETA, YOUR WILL TO BATTLE GROWS EVEN STRONGER WITH THE LOSS, DOES IT?
YEAH!
UH, HOW DO YOU KNOW MY NAME?
FWSH
I'VE HEARD OF YOU FROM THE OREBURGH CITY GYM LEADER, ROARK!
ROARK IS MY SON. AND I'M A GYM LEADER TOO!
TADA
I'M BYRON, CANALAVE'S MAN OF STEEL!

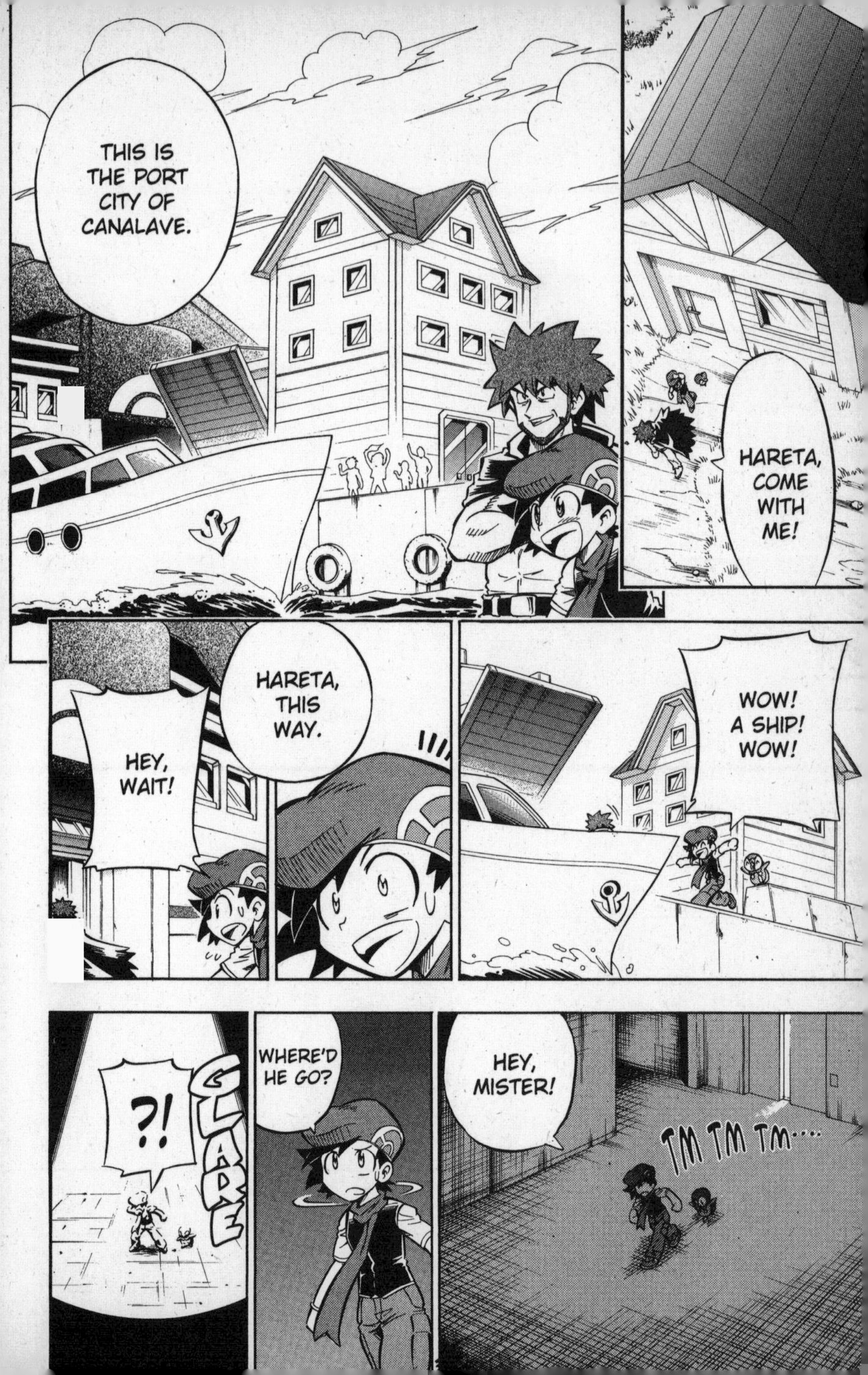
HARETA, COME WITH ME!
THIS IS THE PORT CITY OF CANALAVE.
WOW! A SHIP! WOW!
HARETA, THIS WAY.
HEY, WAIT!
HEY, MISTER!
TM TM TM...
WHERE'D HE GO?
?!
GLARE

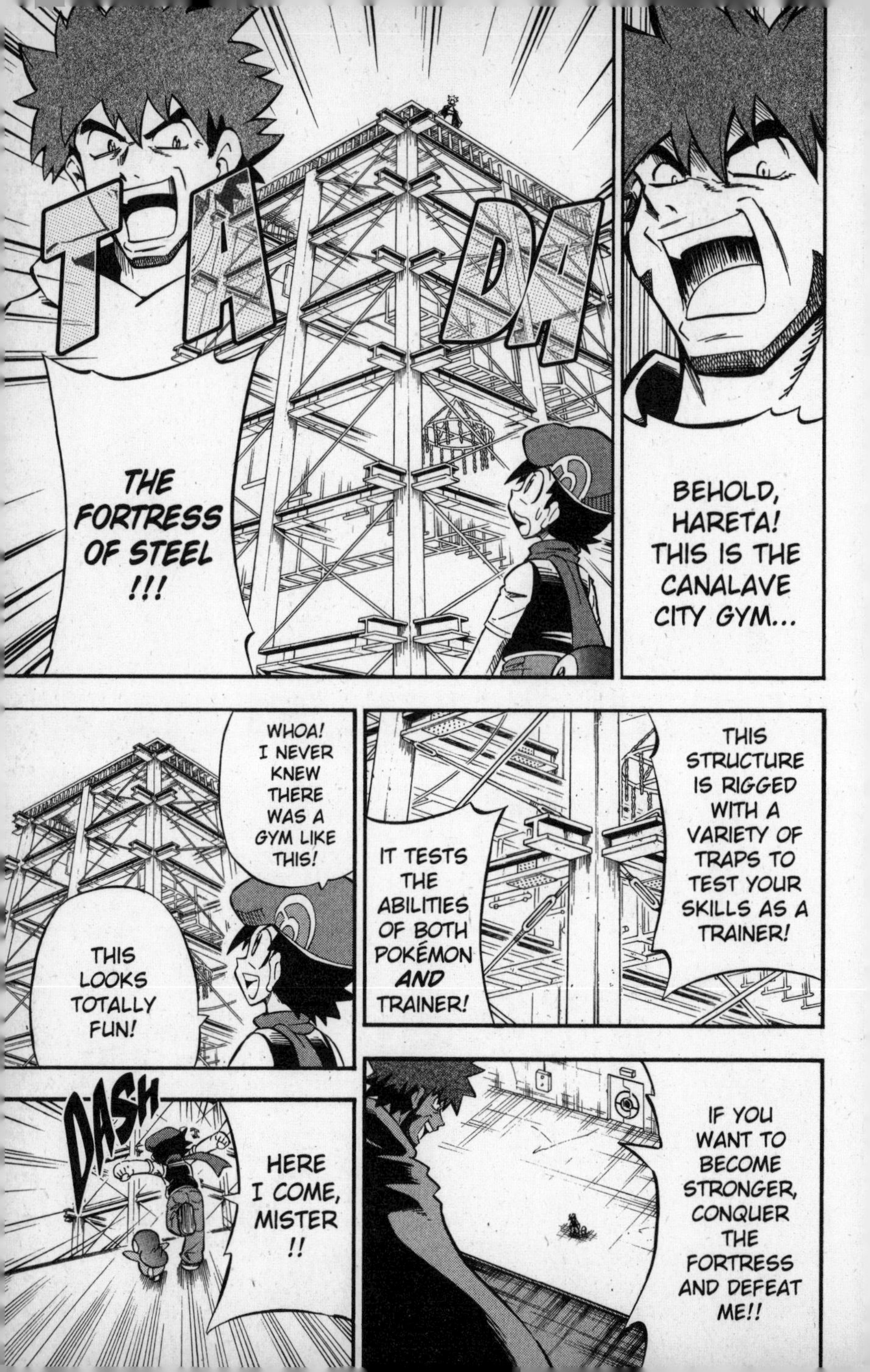
BEHOLD, HARETA! THIS IS THE CANALAVE CITY GYM...
TA DA
THE FORTRESS OF STEEL !!!
THIS STRUCTURE IS RIGGED WITH A VARIETY OF TRAPS TO TEST YOUR SKILLS AS A TRAINER!
IT TESTS THE ABILITIES OF BOTH POKÉMON *AND* TRAINER!
WHOA! I NEVER KNEW THERE WAS A GYM LIKE THIS!
THIS LOOKS TOTALLY FUN!
IF YOU WANT TO BECOME STRONGER, CONQUER THE FORTRESS AND DEFEAT ME!!
DASH
HERE I COME, MISTER !!

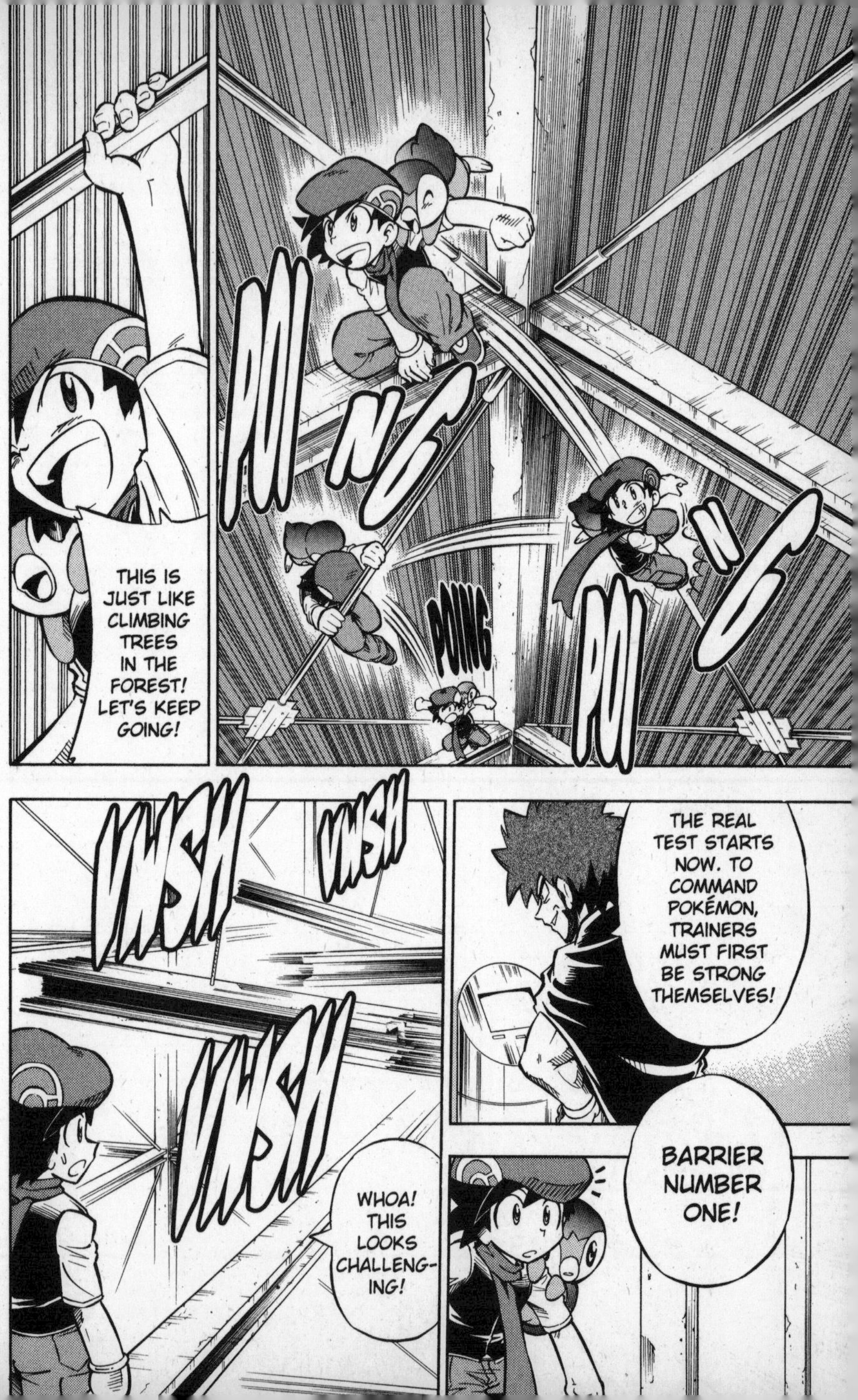
POING
POING
POING
THIS IS JUST LIKE CLIMBING TREES IN THE FOREST! LET'S KEEP GOING!
THE REAL TEST STARTS NOW. TO COMMAND POKÉMON, TRAINERS MUST FIRST BE STRONG THEMSELVES!
BARRIER NUMBER ONE!
VWSH
VWSH
VWSH
WHOA! THIS LOOKS CHALLENG-ING!

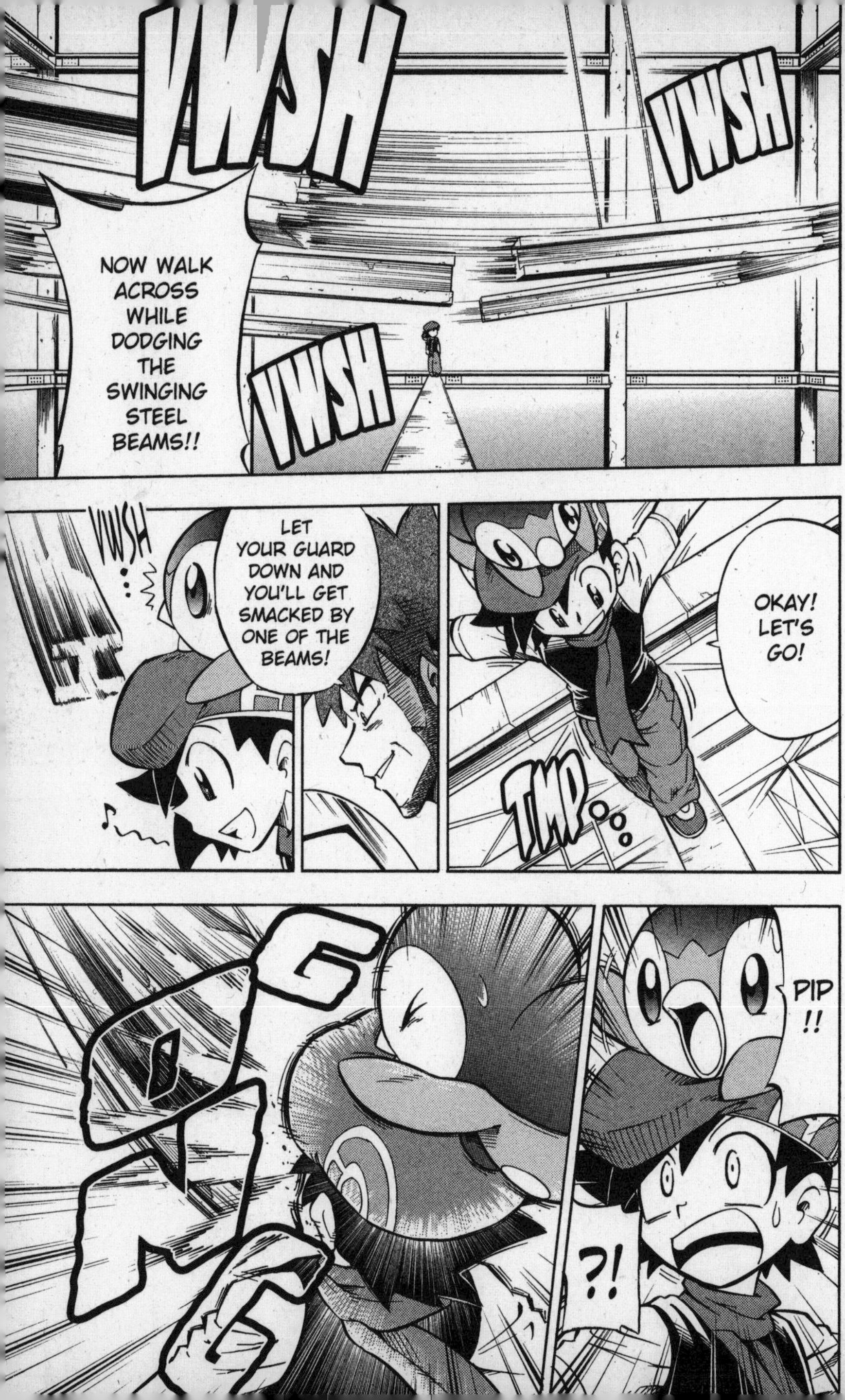
VWSH
VWSH
NOW WALK ACROSS WHILE DODGING THE SWINGING STEEL BEAMS!!
VWSH
OKAY! LET'S GO!
TMP
LET YOUR GUARD DOWN AND YOU'LL GET SMACKED BY ONE OF THE BEAMS!
VWSH
PIP !!
?!

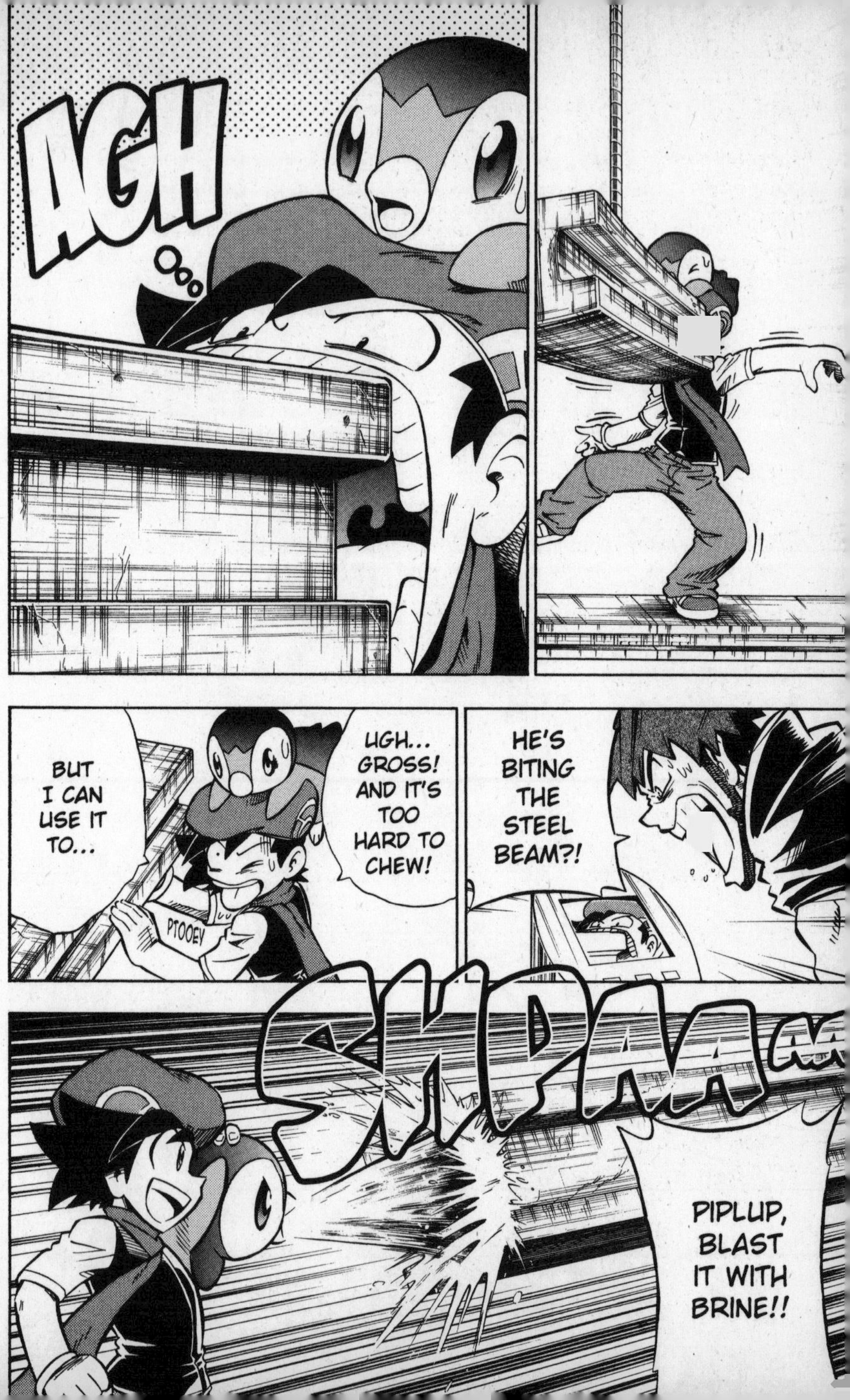
AGH
HE'S BITING THE STEEL BEAM?!
UGH... GROSS! AND IT'S TOO HARD TO CHEW!
BUT I CAN USE IT TO...
PTOOEY
SHPAA
PIPLUP, BLAST IT WITH BRINE!!

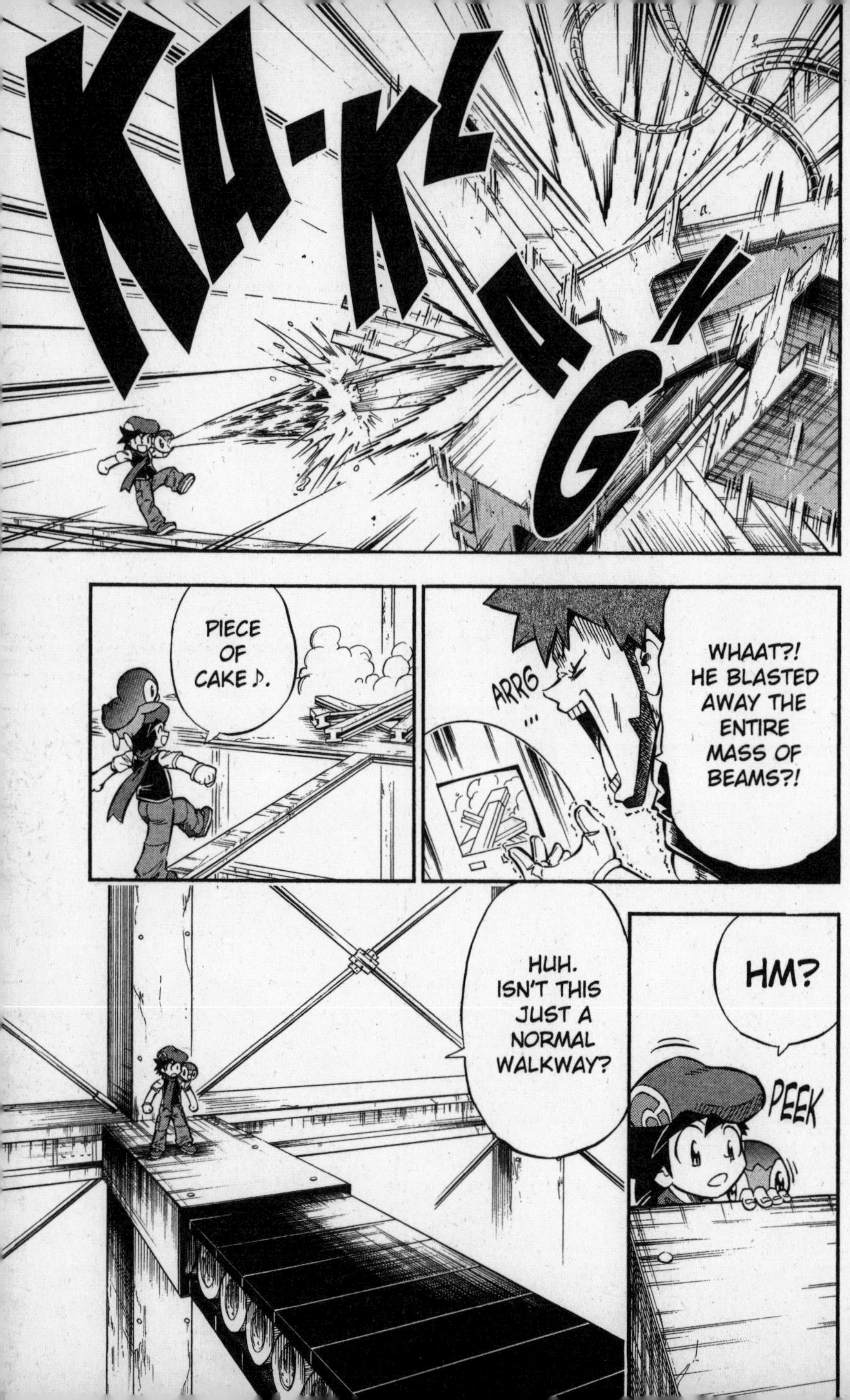
KA-KLANG
WHAAT?! HE BLASTED AWAY THE ENTIRE MASS OF BEAMS?!
ARRG...
PIECE OF CAKE♪.
HM?
PEEK
HUH. ISN'T THIS JUST A NORMAL WALKWAY?

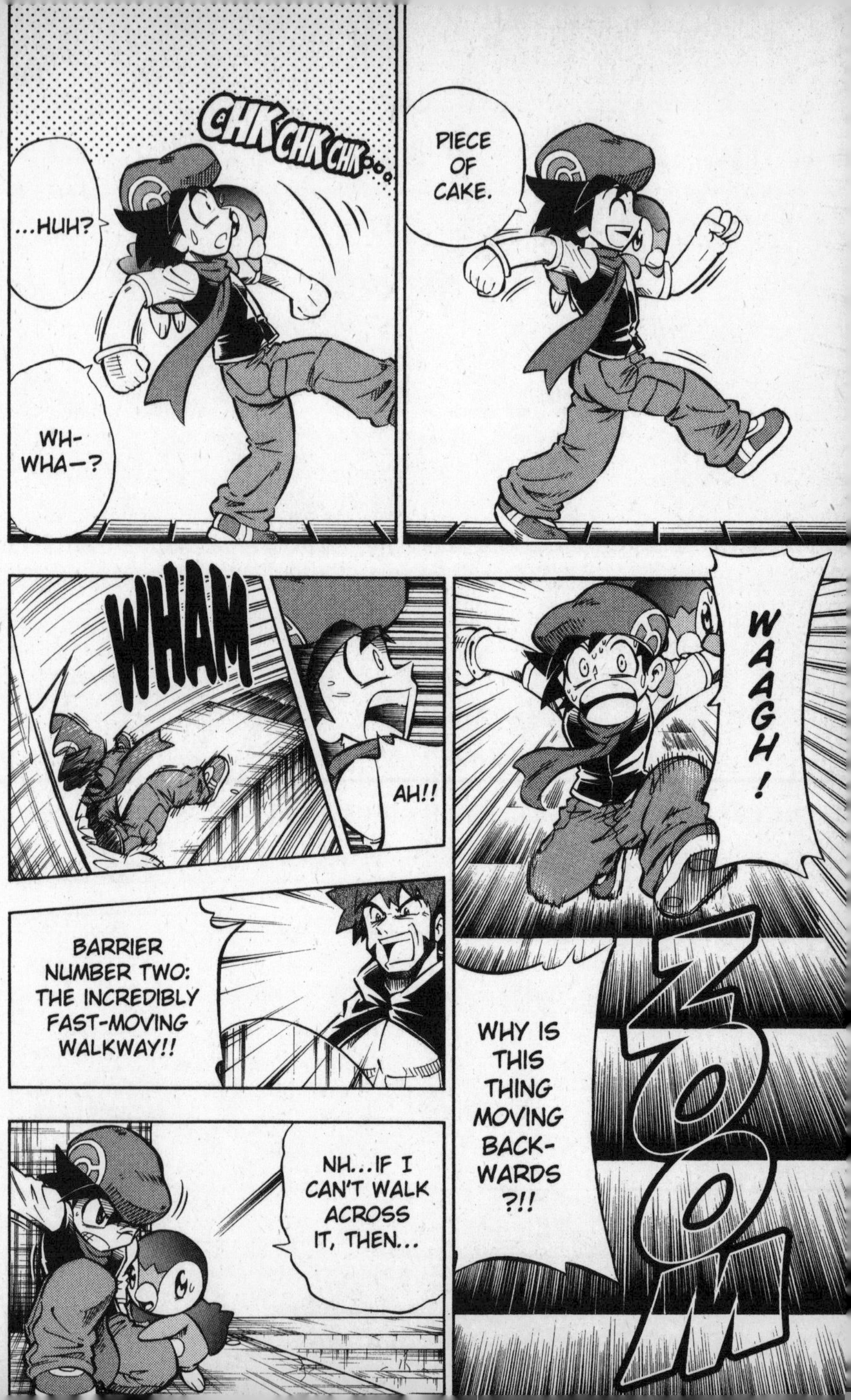
PIECE OF CAKE.
CHK CHK CHK
...HUH?
WH-WHA—?
WAAGH!
WHY IS THIS THING MOVING BACK-WARDS?!!
ZOOM
AH!!
WHAM
BARRIER NUMBER TWO: THE INCREDIBLY FAST-MOVING WALKWAY!!
NH...IF I CAN'T WALK ACROSS IT, THEN...

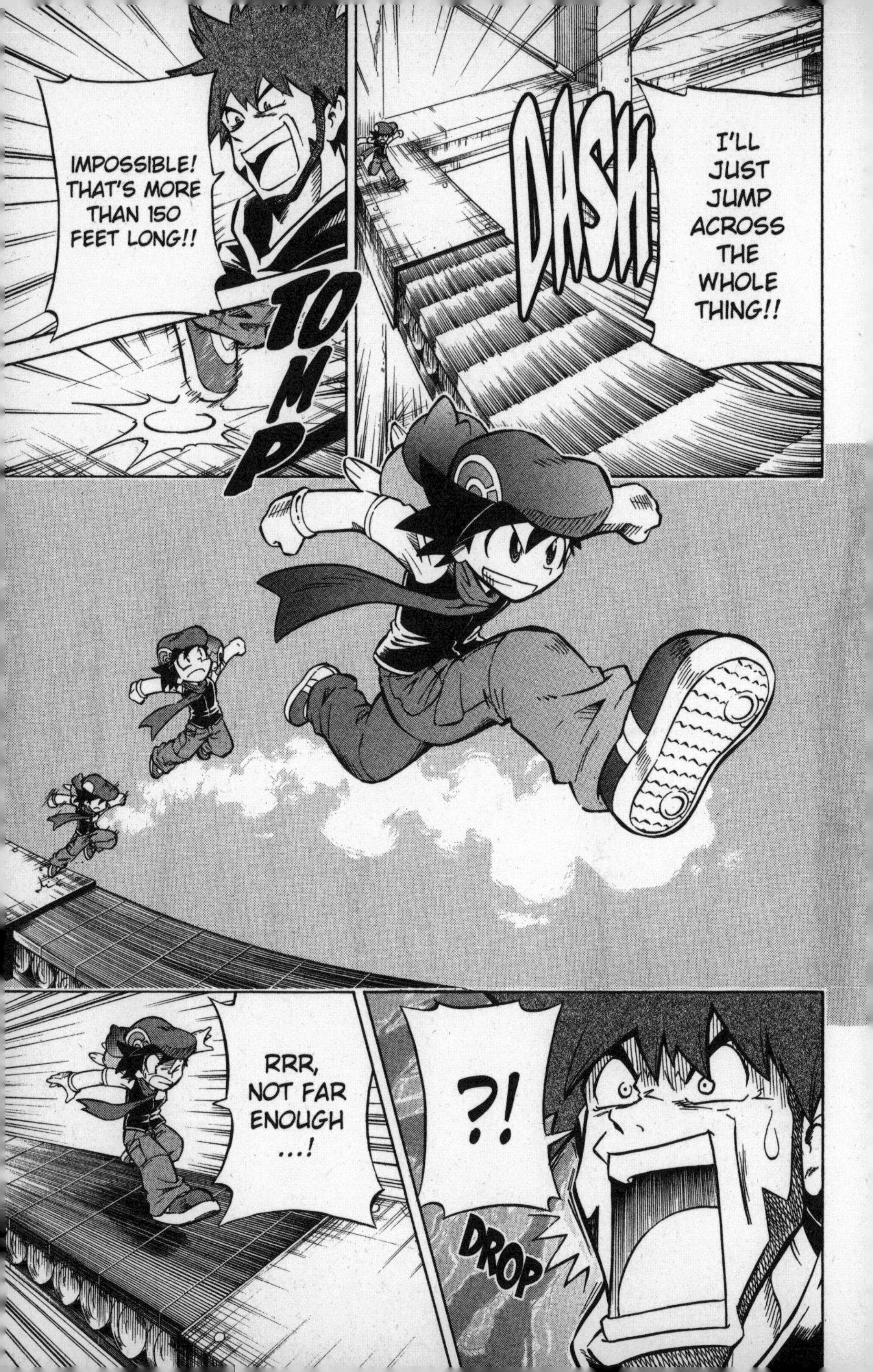
I'LL JUST JUMP ACROSS THE WHOLE THING!!
DASH
IMPOSSIBLE! THAT'S MORE THAN 150 FEET LONG!!
TOMP
?!
DROP
RRR, NOT FAR ENOUGH ...!

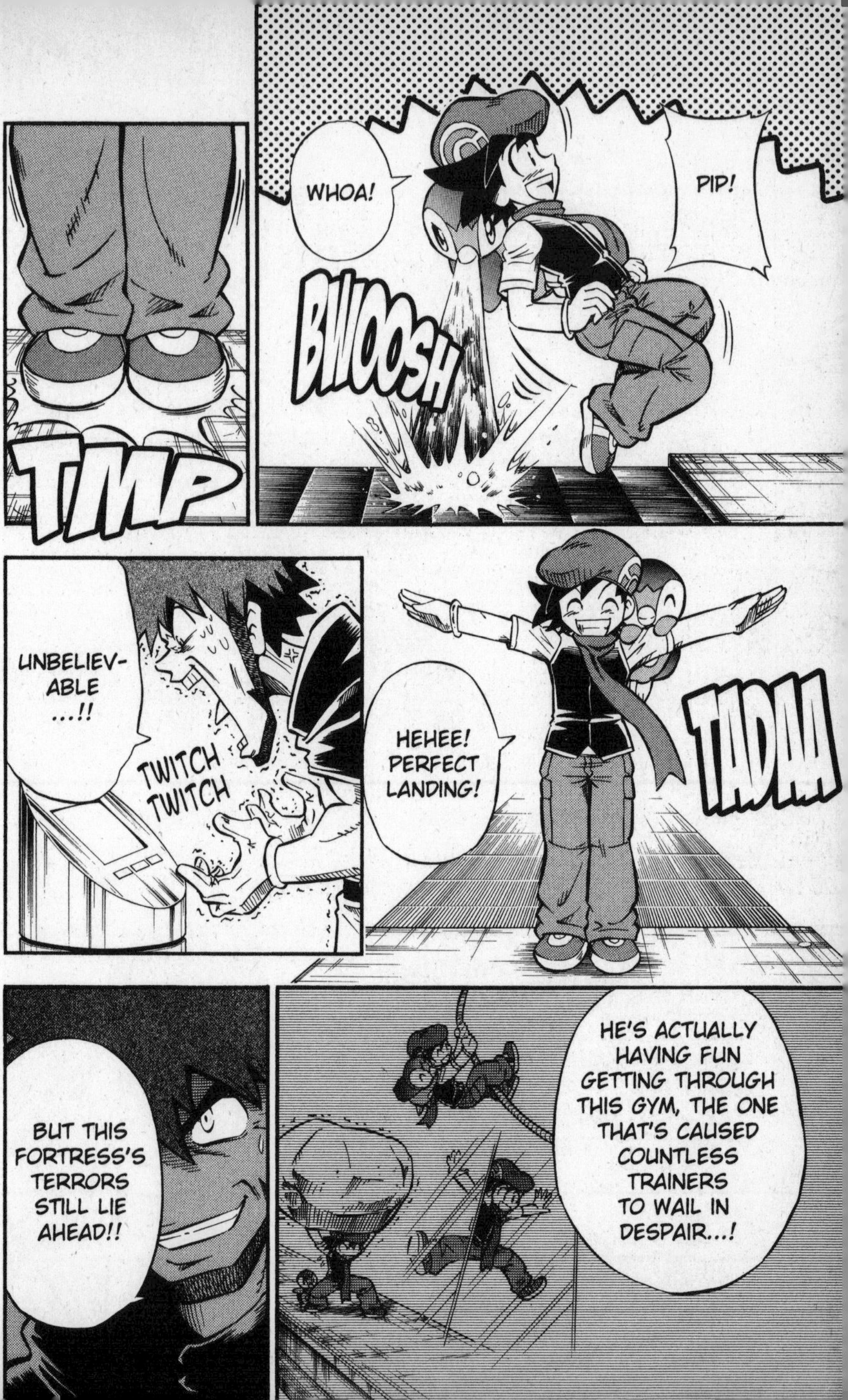
PIP!
WHOA!
BWOOSH
TMP
TADAA
HEHEE! PERFECT LANDING!
UNBELIEV-ABLE ...!!
TWITCH TWITCH
HE'S ACTUALLY HAVING FUN GETTING THROUGH THIS GYM, THE ONE THAT'S CAUSED COUNTLESS TRAINERS TO WAIL IN DESPAIR...!
BUT THIS FORTRESS'S TERRORS STILL LIE AHEAD!!

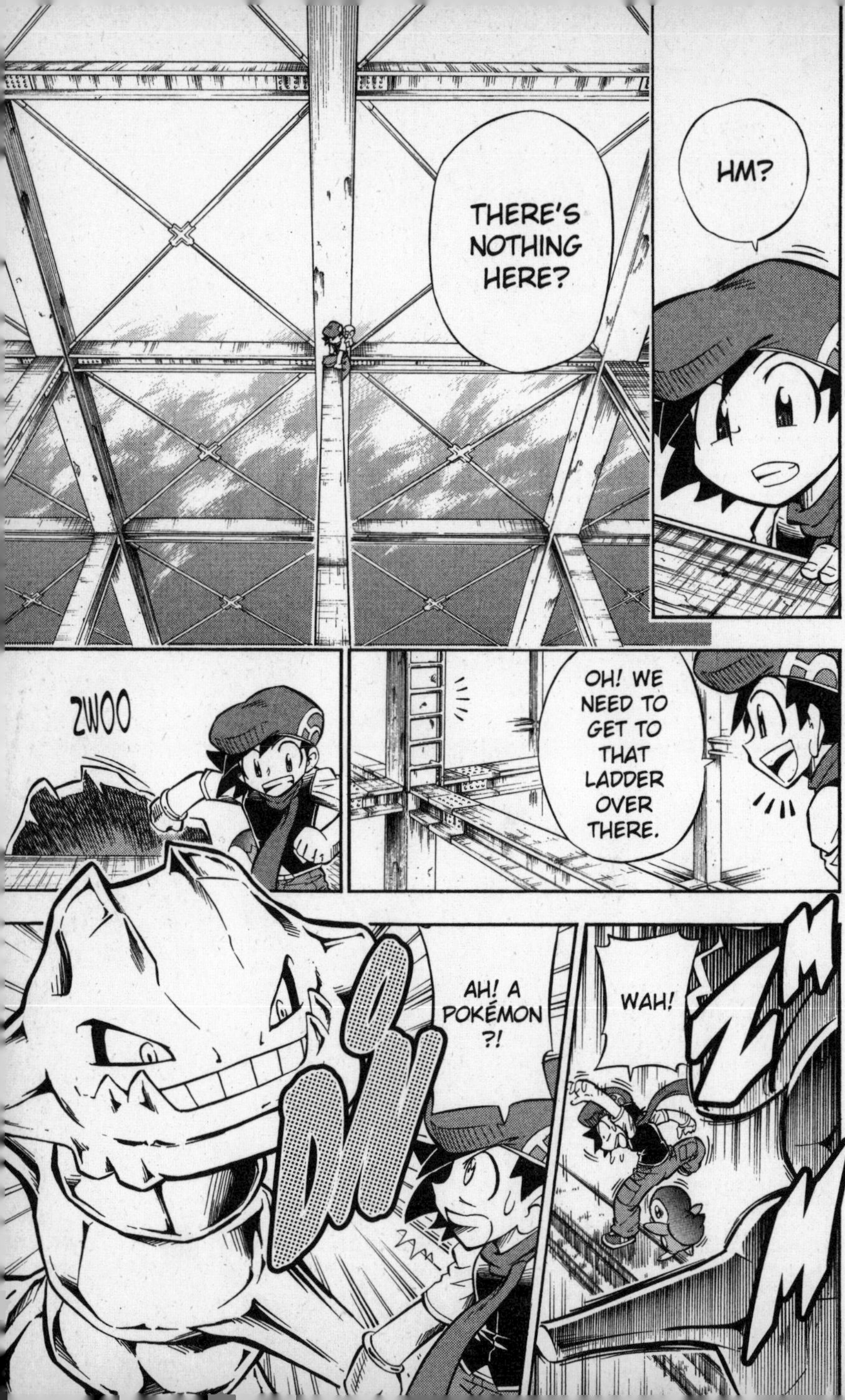
HM?
THERE'S NOTHING HERE?
OH! WE NEED TO GET TO THAT LADDER OVER THERE.
ZWOO
WAH!
AH! A POKÉMON ?!

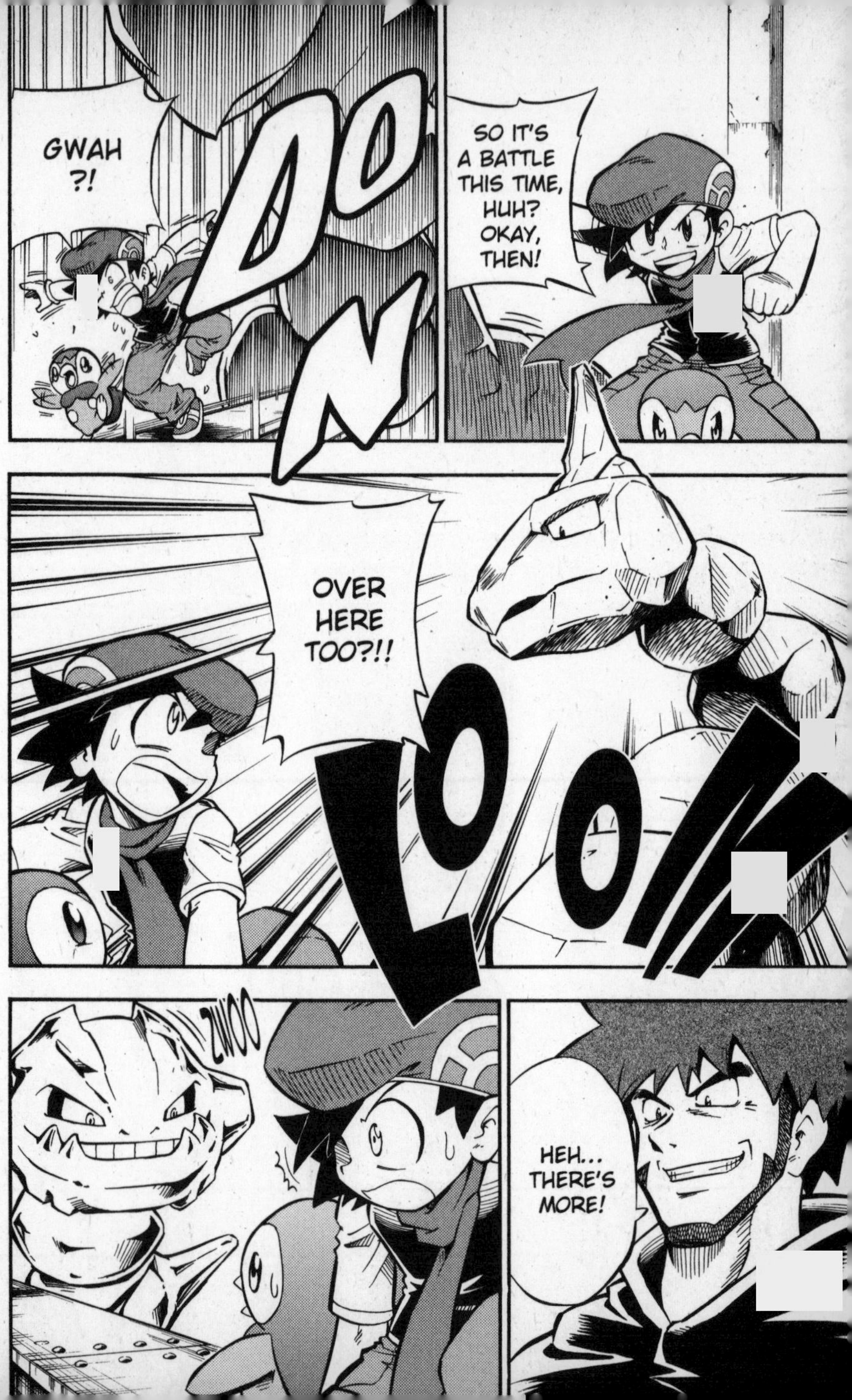
SO IT'S A BATTLE THIS TIME, HUH? OKAY, THEN!
GWAH ?!
DOON
OVER HERE TOO?!!
LOOM
HEH... THERE'S MORE!
ZWOO

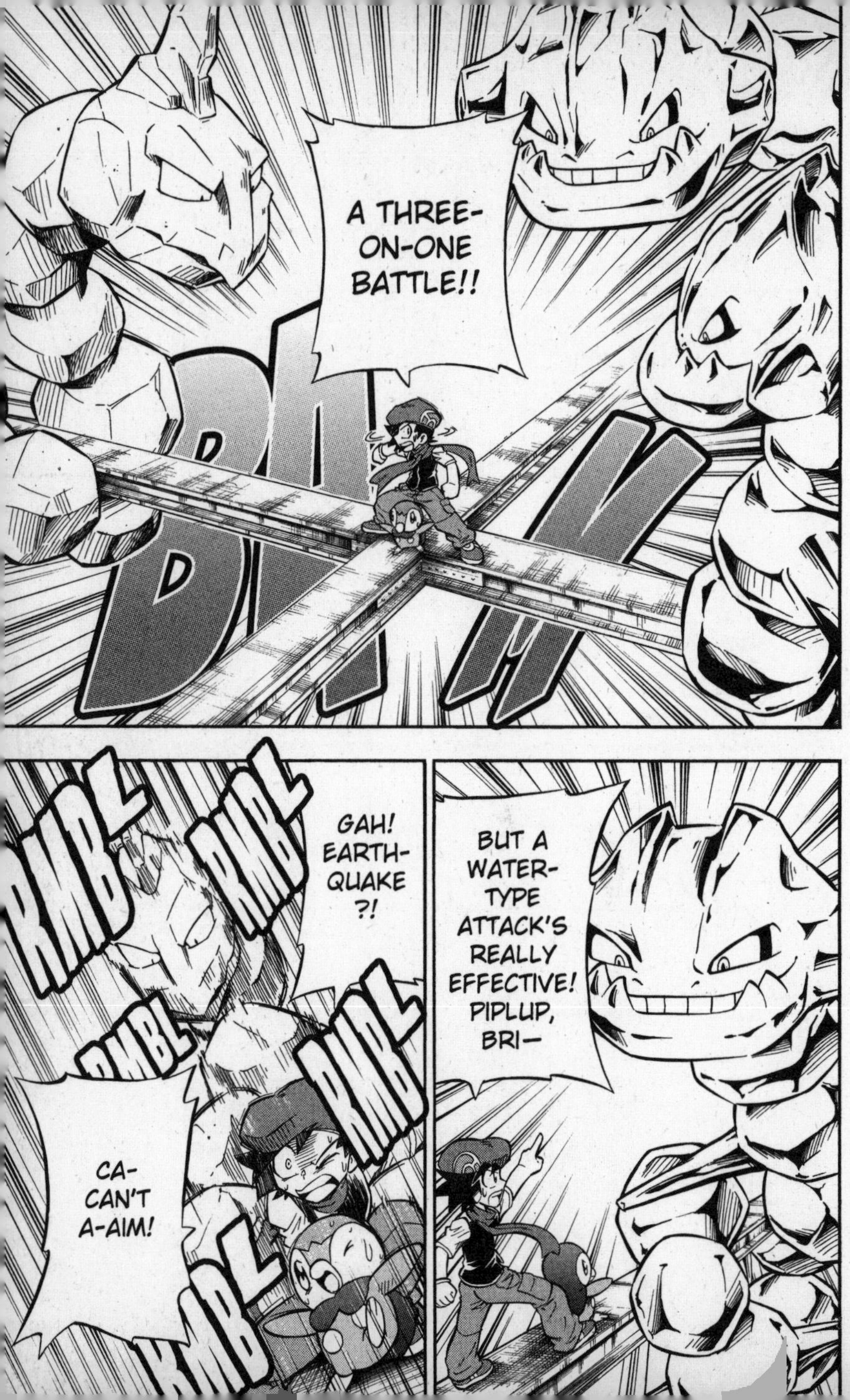
A THREE-ON-ONE BATTLE!!
BUT A WATER-TYPE ATTACK'S REALLY EFFECTIVE! PIPLUP, BRI—
GAH! EARTHQUAKE?!
CA-CAN'T A-AIM!

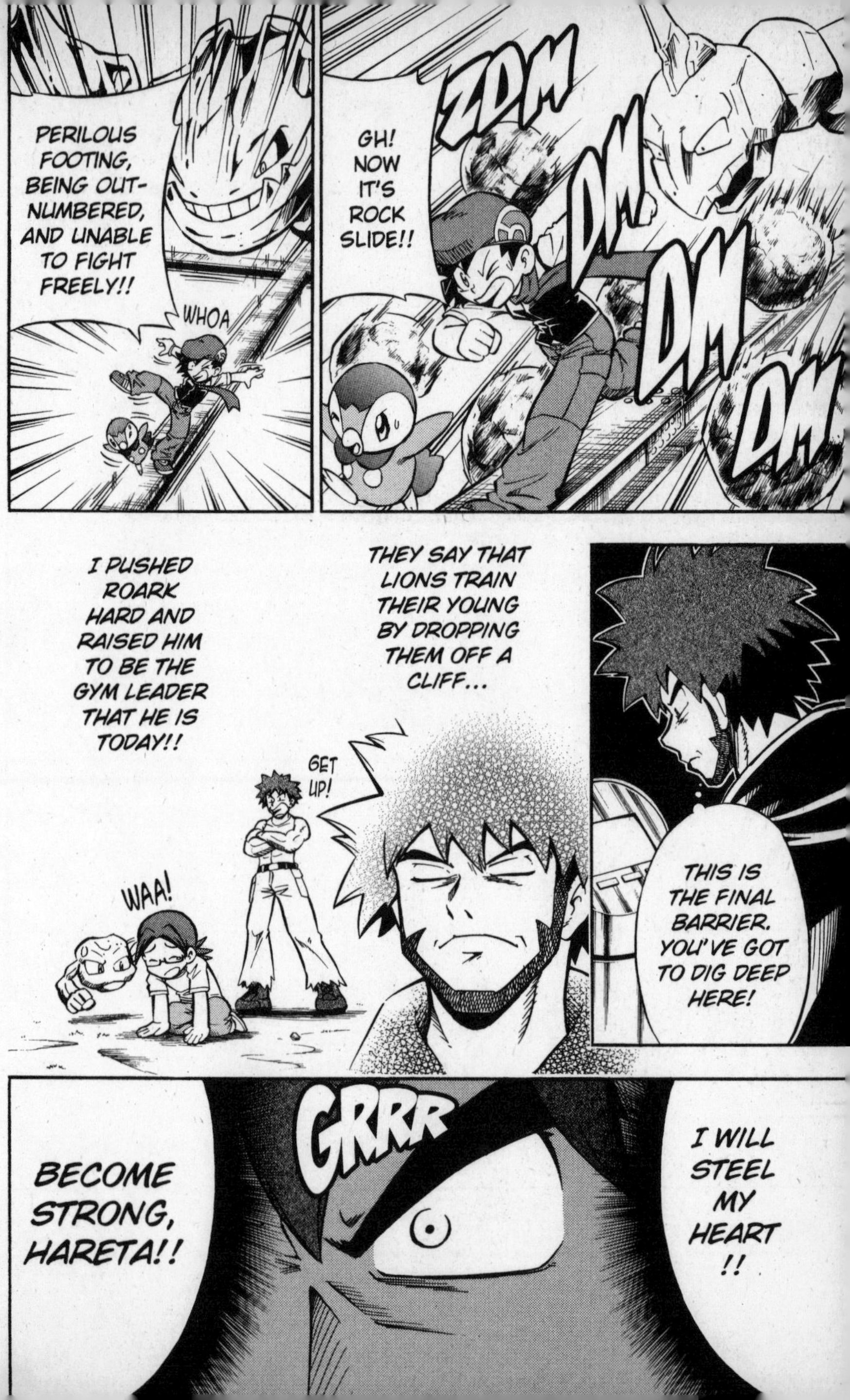
ZDM
GH! NOW IT'S ROCK SLIDE!!
DM DM DM DM
PERILOUS FOOTING, BEING OUT-NUMBERED, AND UNABLE TO FIGHT FREELY!!
WHOA
THIS IS THE FINAL BARRIER. YOU'VE GOT TO DIG DEEP HERE!
THEY SAY THAT LIONS TRAIN THEIR YOUNG BY DROPPING THEM OFF A CLIFF...
I PUSHED ROARK HARD AND RAISED HIM TO BE THE GYM LEADER THAT HE IS TODAY!!
GET UP!
WAA!
I WILL STEEL MY HEART!!
GRRR
BECOME STRONG, HARETA!!

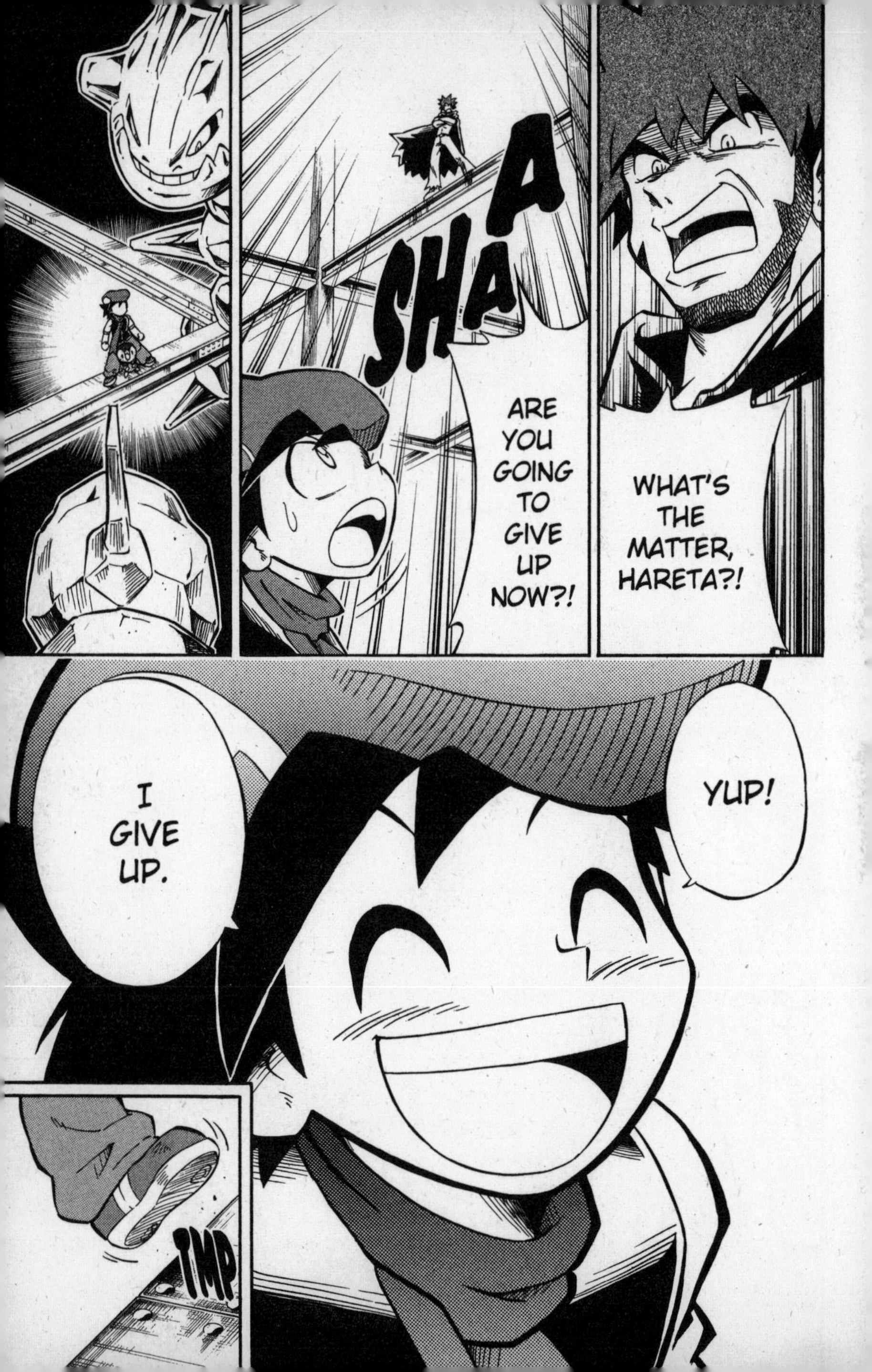
WHAT'S THE MATTER, HARETA?!
SHA A
ARE YOU GOING TO GIVE UP NOW?!
YUP!
I GIVE UP.
TMP

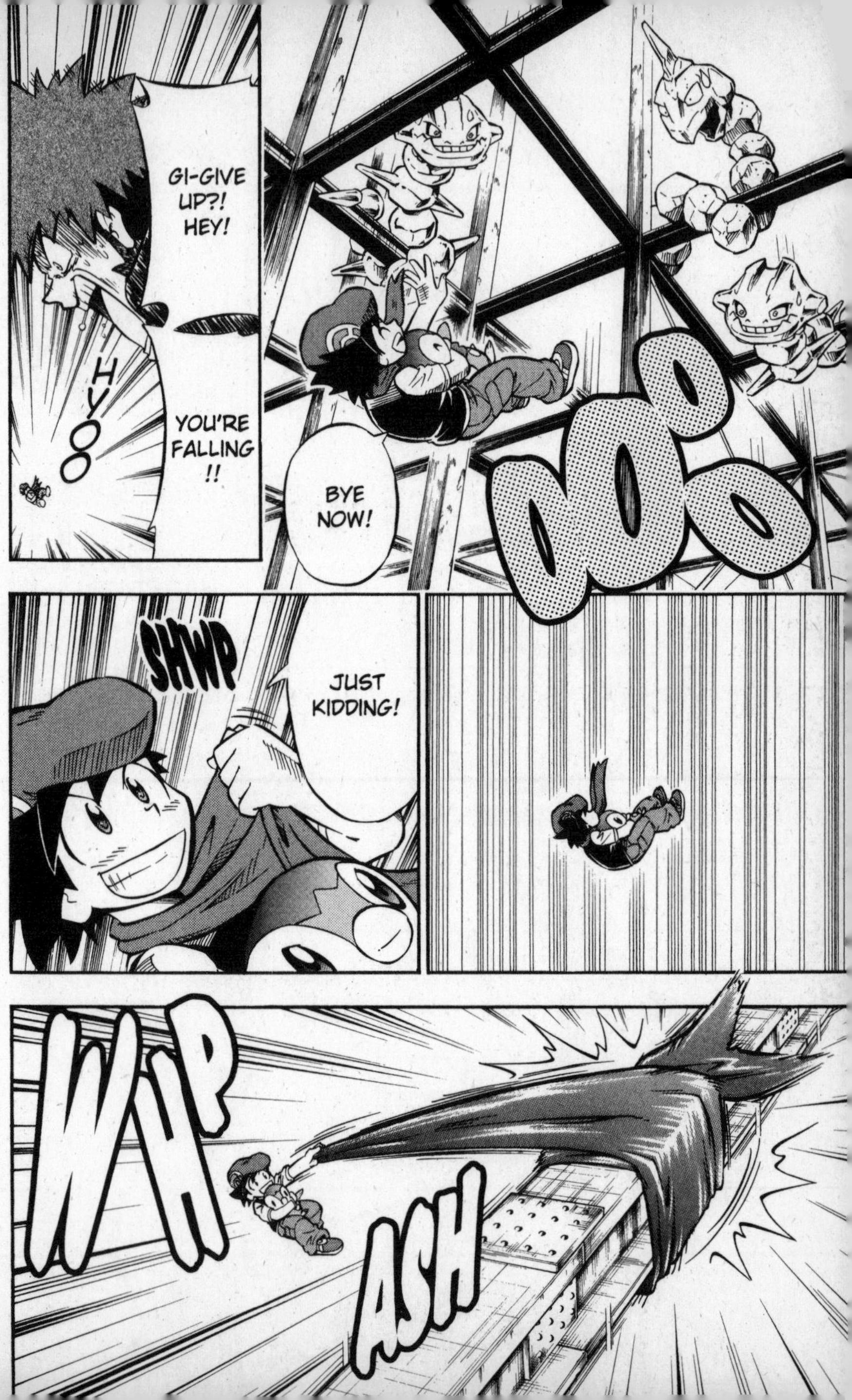
BYE NOW!
DOOO
GI-GIVE UP?! HEY!
HYOO
YOU'RE FALLING !!
SHWP
JUST KIDDING!
WHIP
ASH

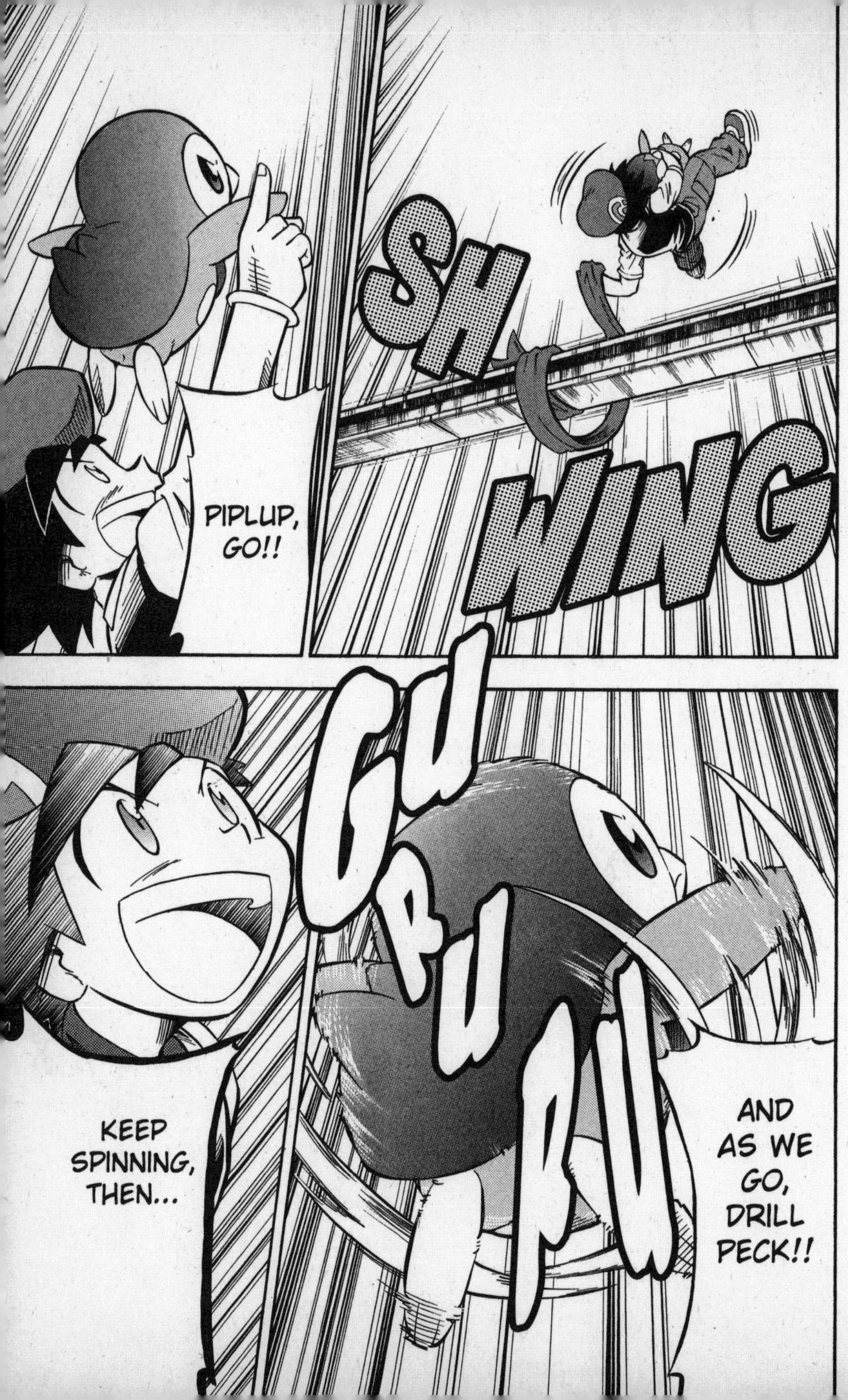
SH
WING
PIPLUP, GO!!
GUPUPU
AND AS WE GO, DRILL PECK!!
KEEP SPINNING, THEN...

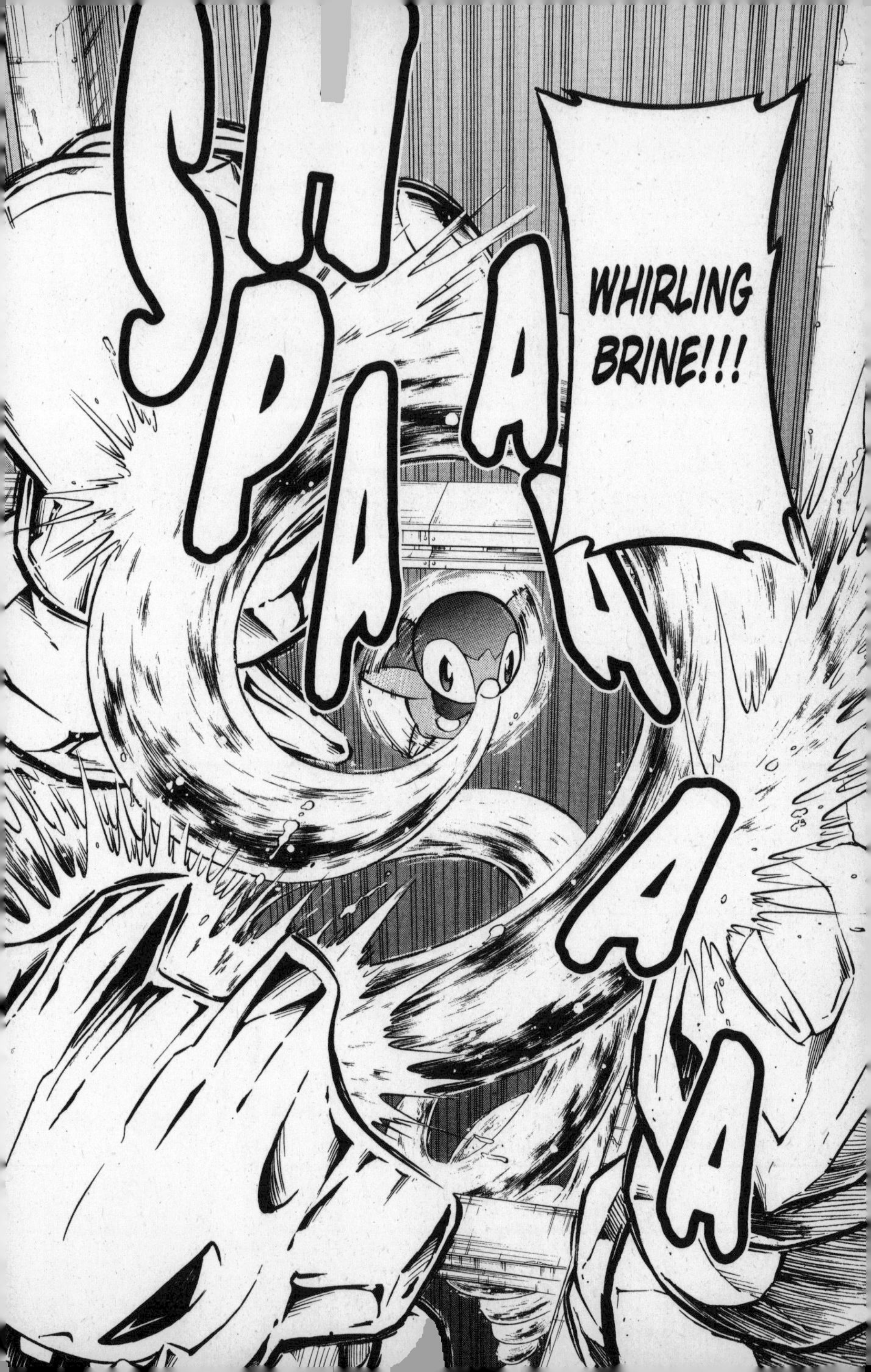
WHIRLING BRINE!!!

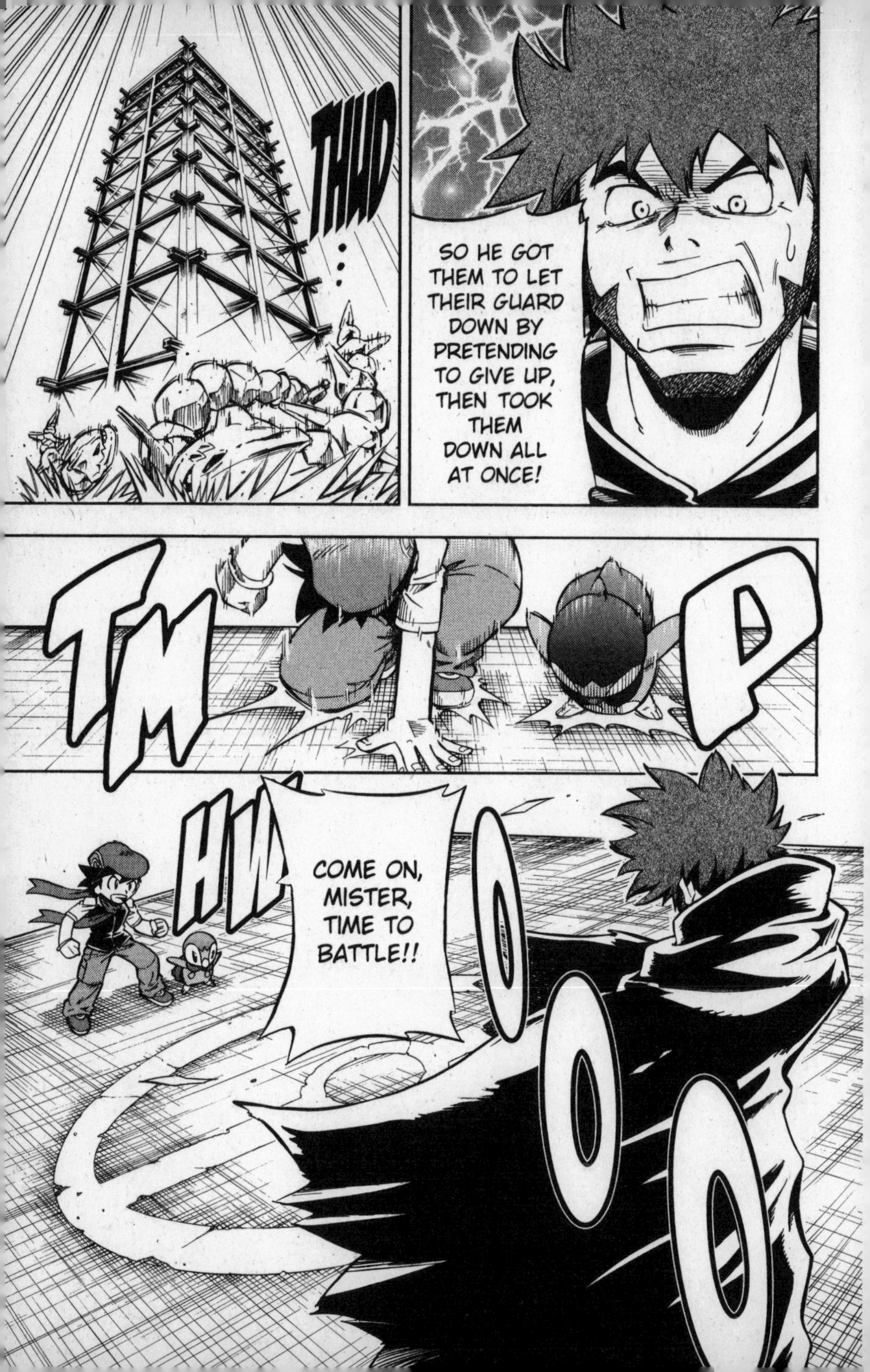
SO HE GOT THEM TO LET THEIR GUARD DOWN BY PRETENDING TO GIVE UP, THEN TOOK THEM DOWN ALL AT ONCE!
THUD
...
TMP
HWOOO
COME ON, MISTER, TIME TO BATTLE!!

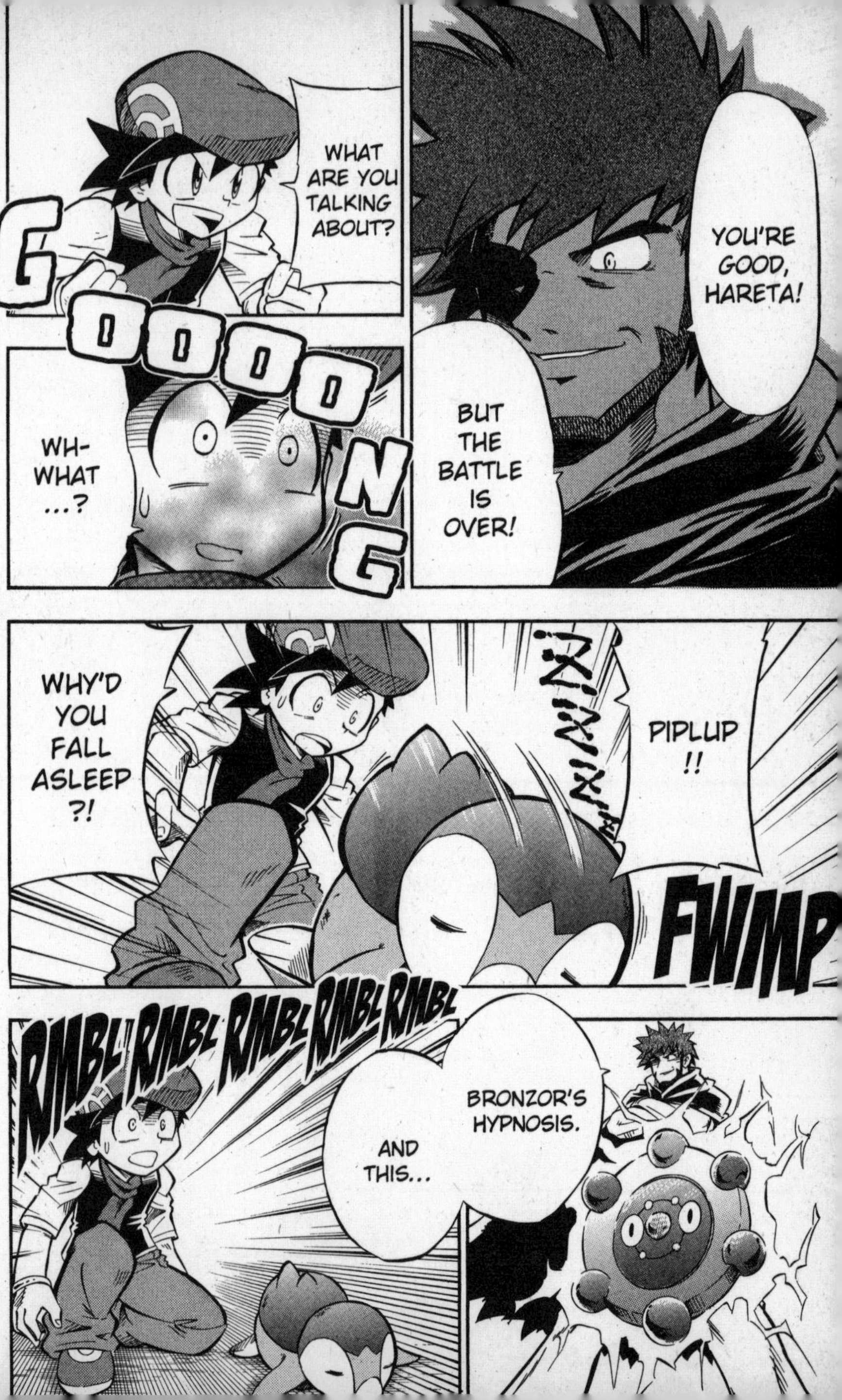
YOU'RE GOOD, HARETA!
BUT THE BATTLE IS OVER!
WHAT ARE YOU TALKING ABOUT?
GOOOOONG
WH-WHAT ...?
PIPLUP !!
FWMP
WHY'D YOU FALL ASLEEP ?!
BRONZOR'S HYPNOSIS.
AND THIS...
RMBL RMBL RMBL RMBL RMBL

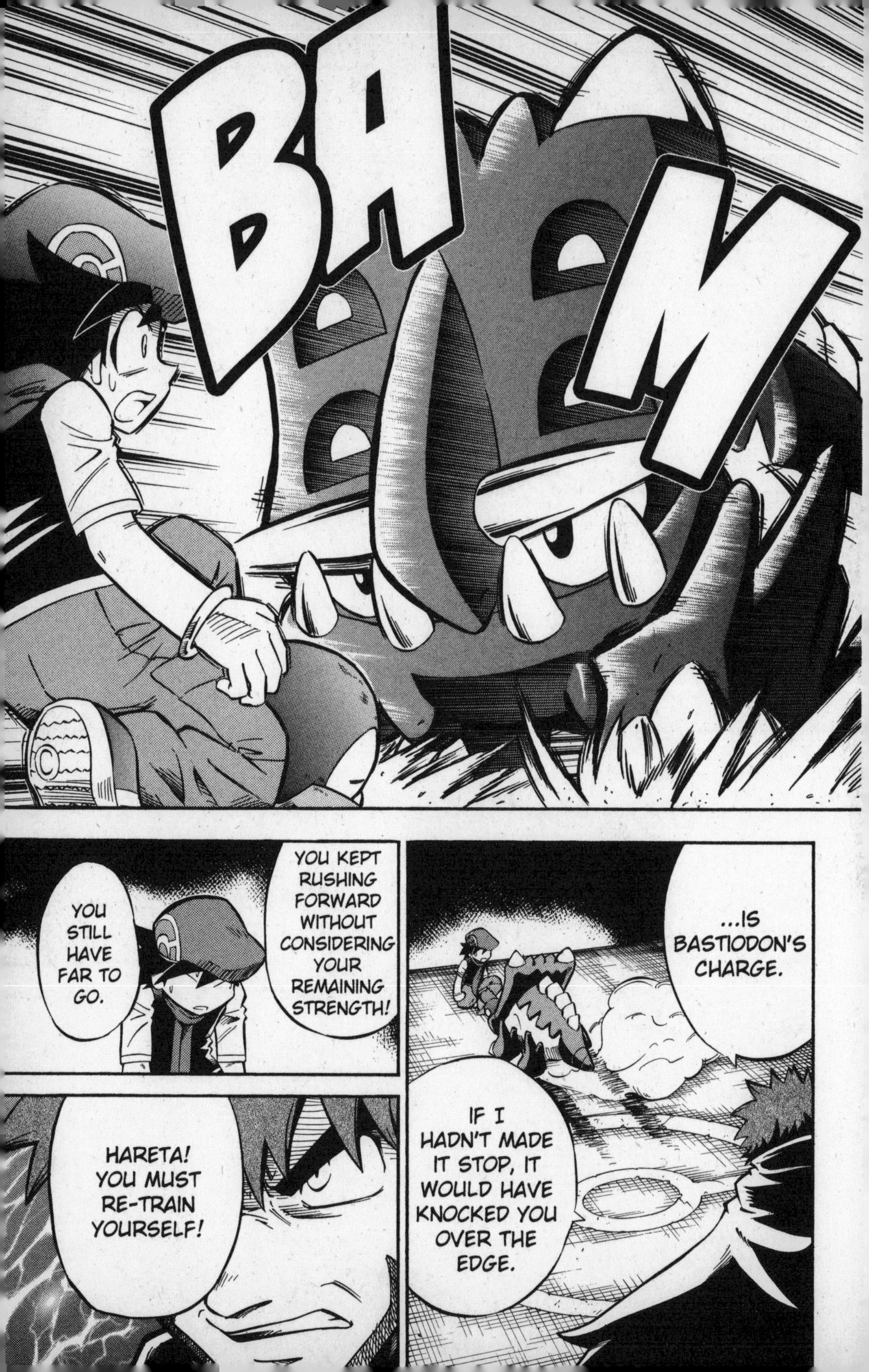
BAM
...IS BASTIODON'S CHARGE.
IF I HADN'T MADE IT STOP, IT WOULD HAVE KNOCKED YOU OVER THE EDGE.
YOU KEPT RUSHING FORWARD WITHOUT CONSIDERING YOUR REMAINING STRENGTH!
YOU STILL HAVE FAR TO GO.
HARETA! YOU MUST RE-TRAIN YOURSELF!

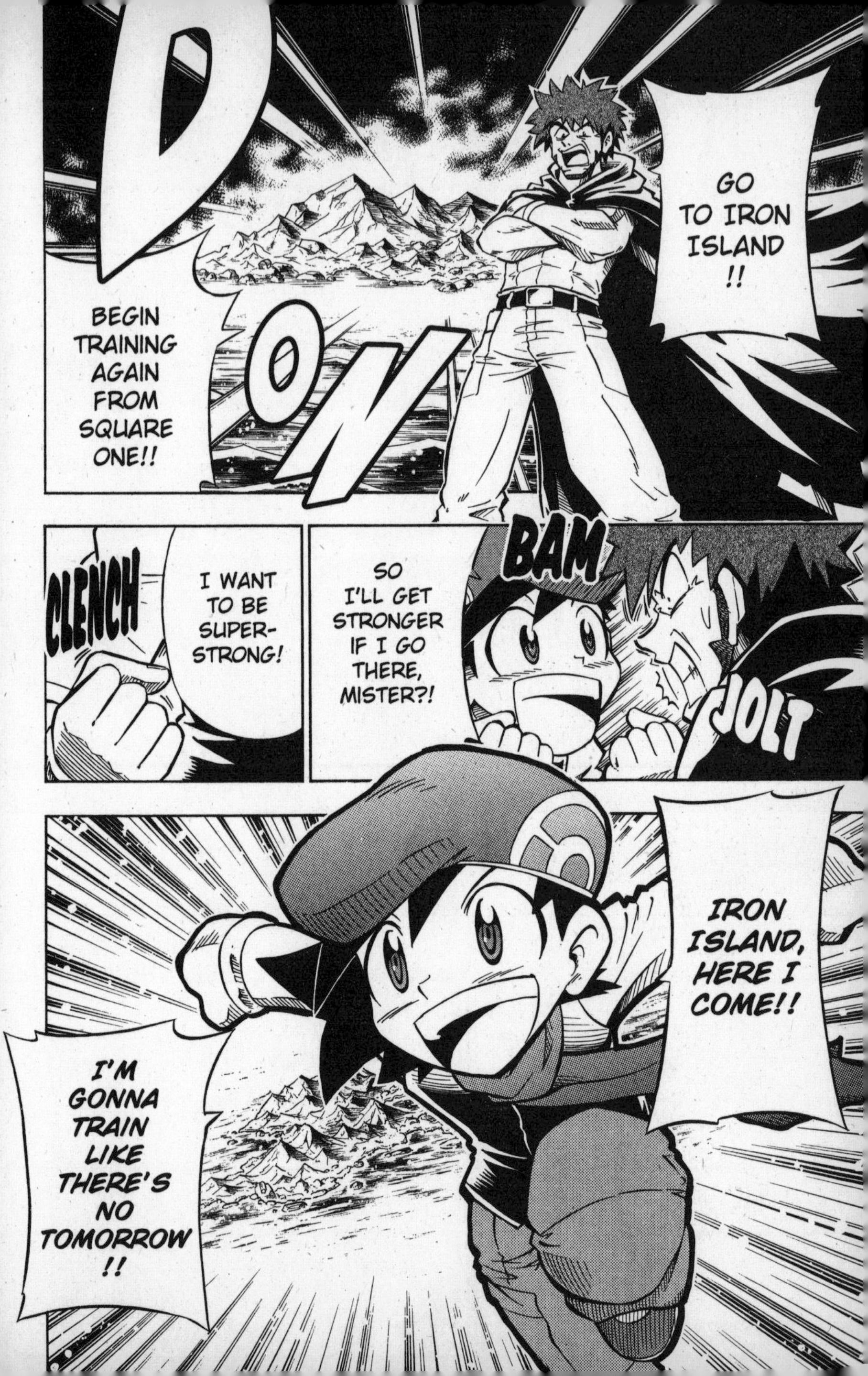
GO TO IRON ISLAND!!
DON
BEGIN TRAINING AGAIN FROM SQUARE ONE!!
BAM
SO I'LL GET STRONGER IF I GO THERE, MISTER?!
JOLT
I WANT TO BE SUPER-STRONG!
CLENCH
IRON ISLAND, HERE I COME!!
I'M GONNA TRAIN LIKE THERE'S NO TOMORROW!!

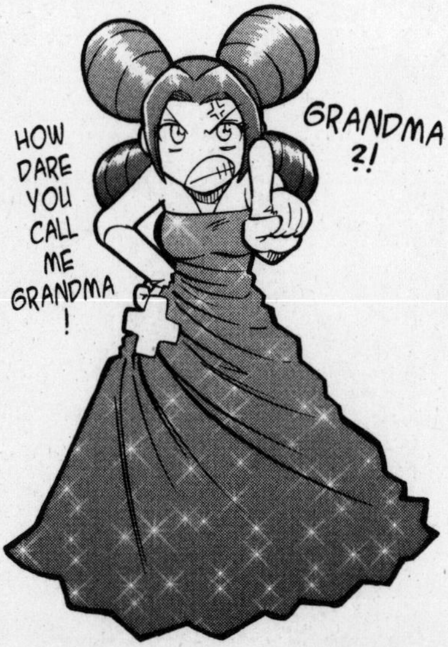
GRANDMA ?!
HOW DARE YOU CALL ME GRANDMA !

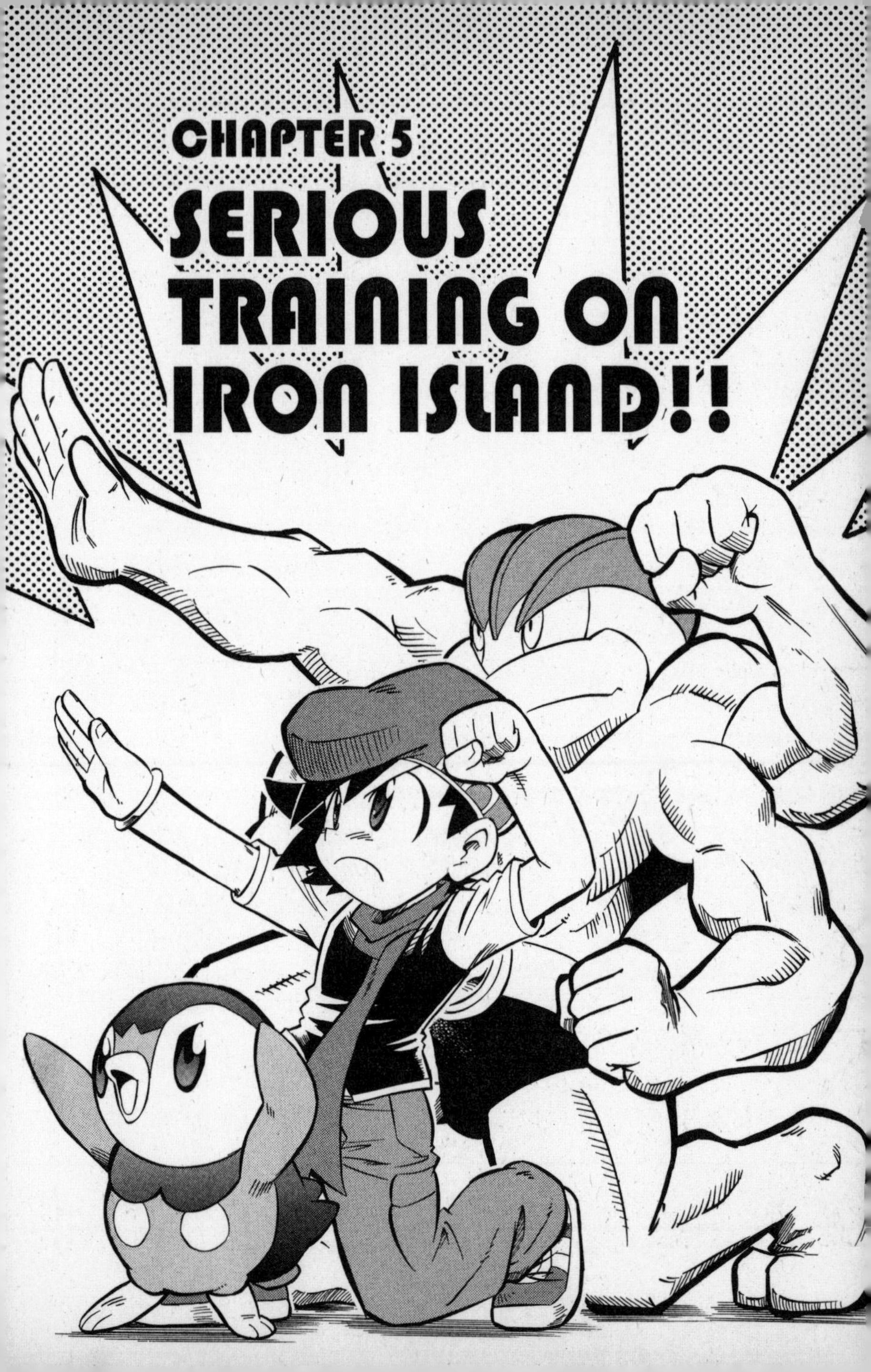
CHAPTER 5
SERIOUS TRAINING ON IRON ISLAND!!

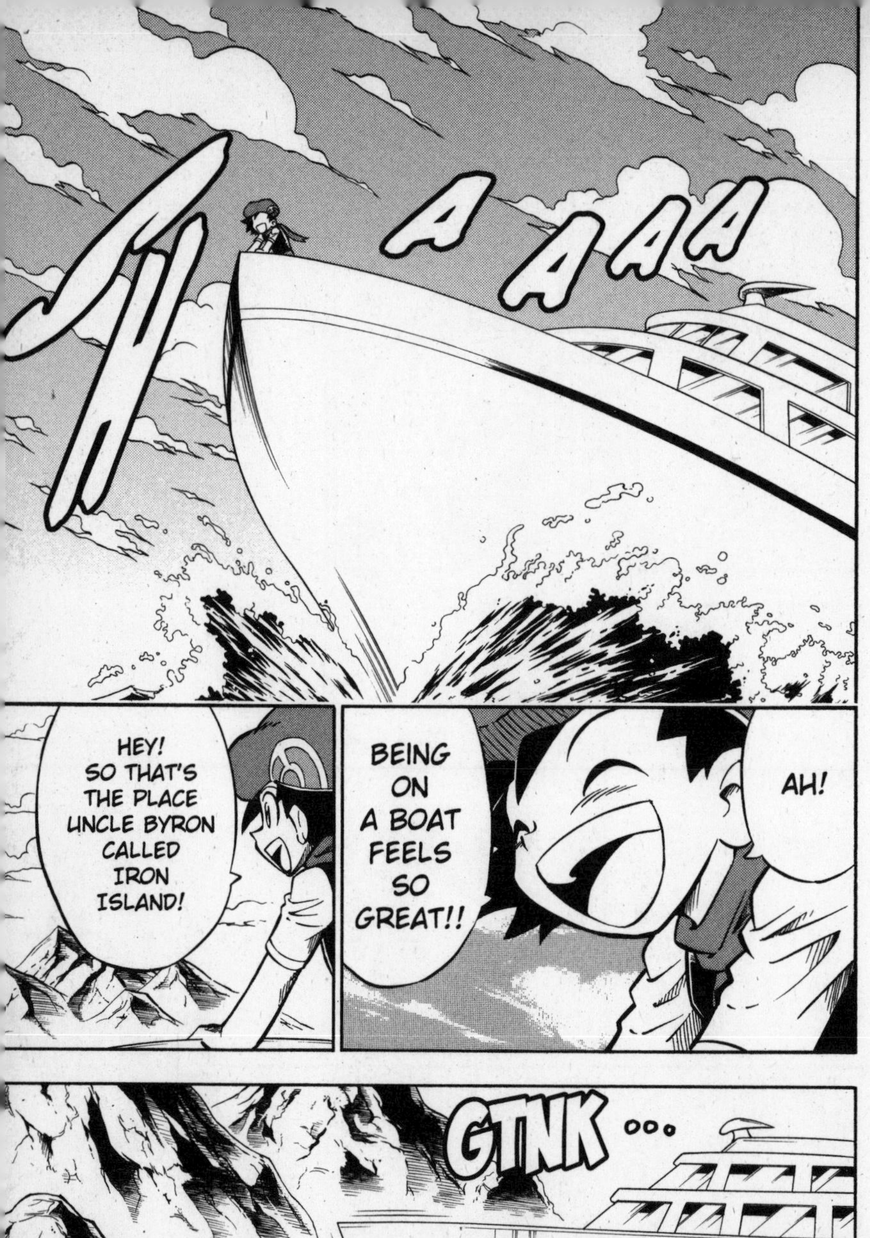
AAAAAH
AH!
BEING ON A BOAT FEELS SO GREAT!!
HEY! SO THAT'S THE PLACE UNCLE BYRON CALLED IRON ISLAND!
GTNK...

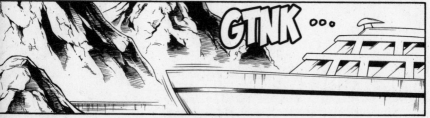

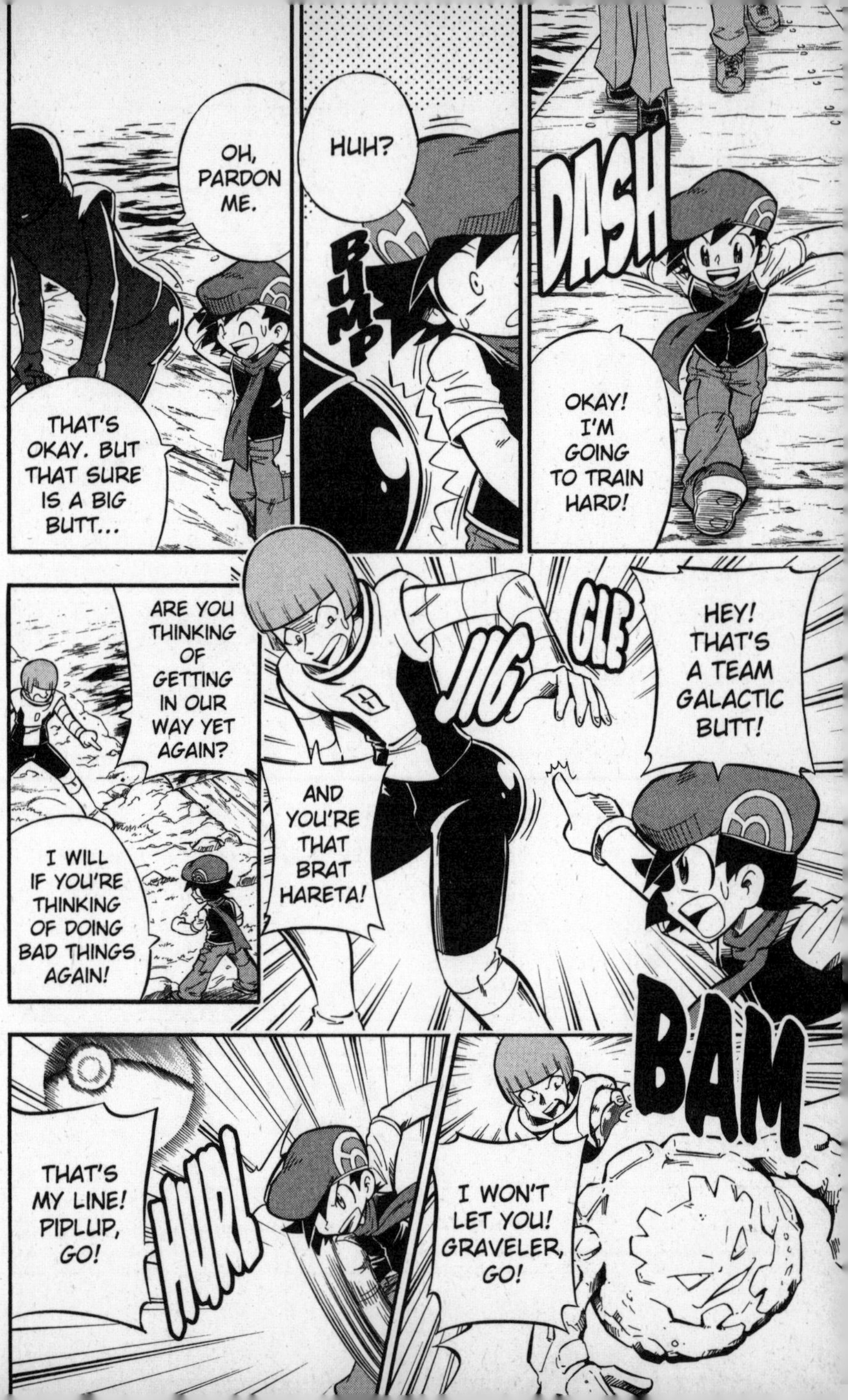
DASH
OKAY! I'M GOING TO TRAIN HARD!
HUH?
BUMP
OH, PARDON ME.
THAT'S OKAY. BUT THAT SURE IS A BIG BUTT...
HEY! THAT'S A TEAM GALACTIC BUTT!
JIG GLE
AND YOU'RE THAT BRAT HARETA!
ARE YOU THINKING OF GETTING IN OUR WAY YET AGAIN?
I WILL IF YOU'RE THINKING OF DOING BAD THINGS AGAIN!
BAM
I WON'T LET YOU! GRAVELER, GO!
HURL
THAT'S MY LINE! PIPLUP, GO!

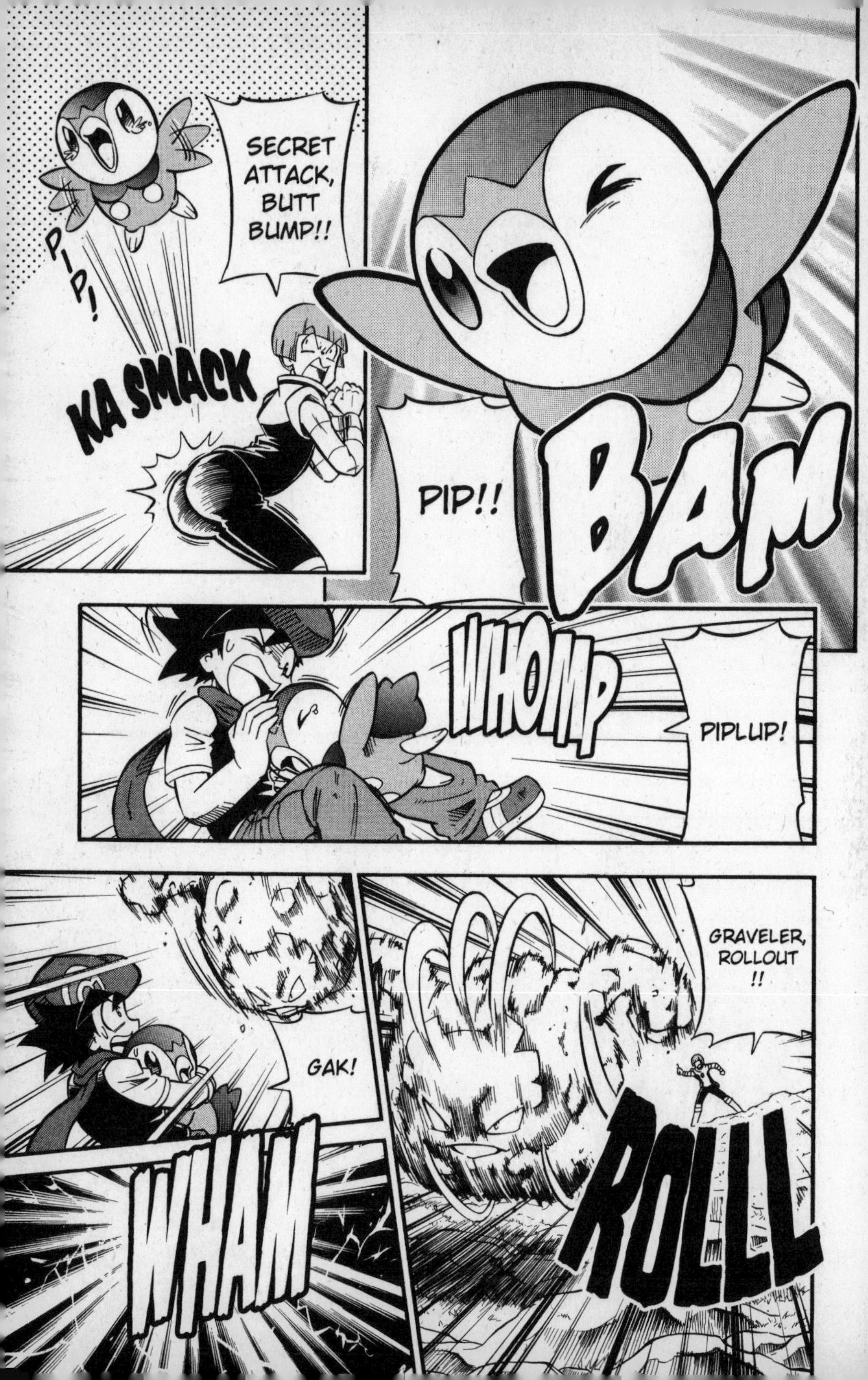
PIP!!
BAM
SECRET ATTACK, BUTT BUMP!!
PIP!
KA SMACK
WHOMP
PIPLUP!
GRAVELER, ROLLOUT !!
ROLL
GAK!
WHAM

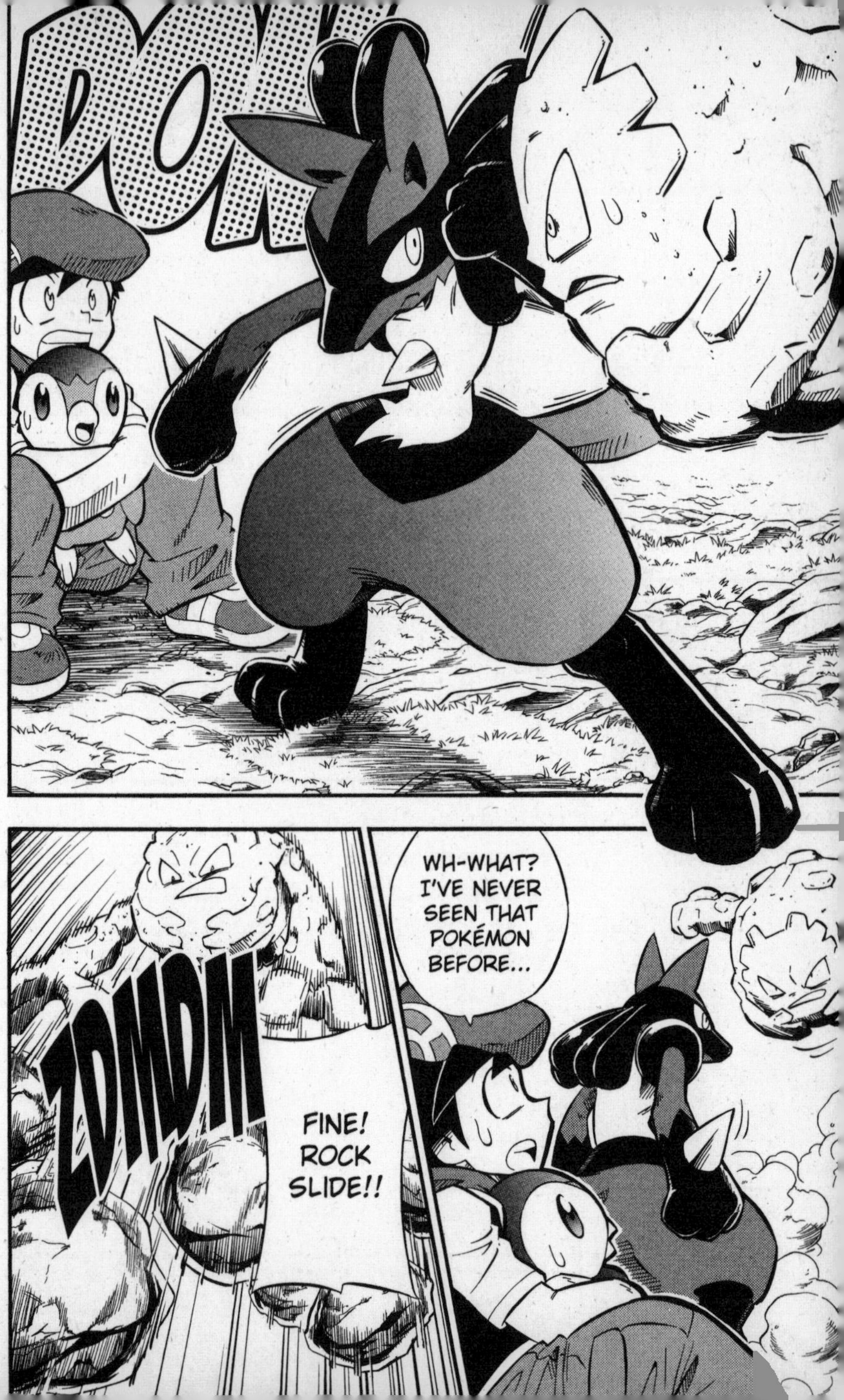
WH-WHAT? I'VE NEVER SEEN THAT POKÉMON BEFORE...
FINE! ROCK SLIDE!!

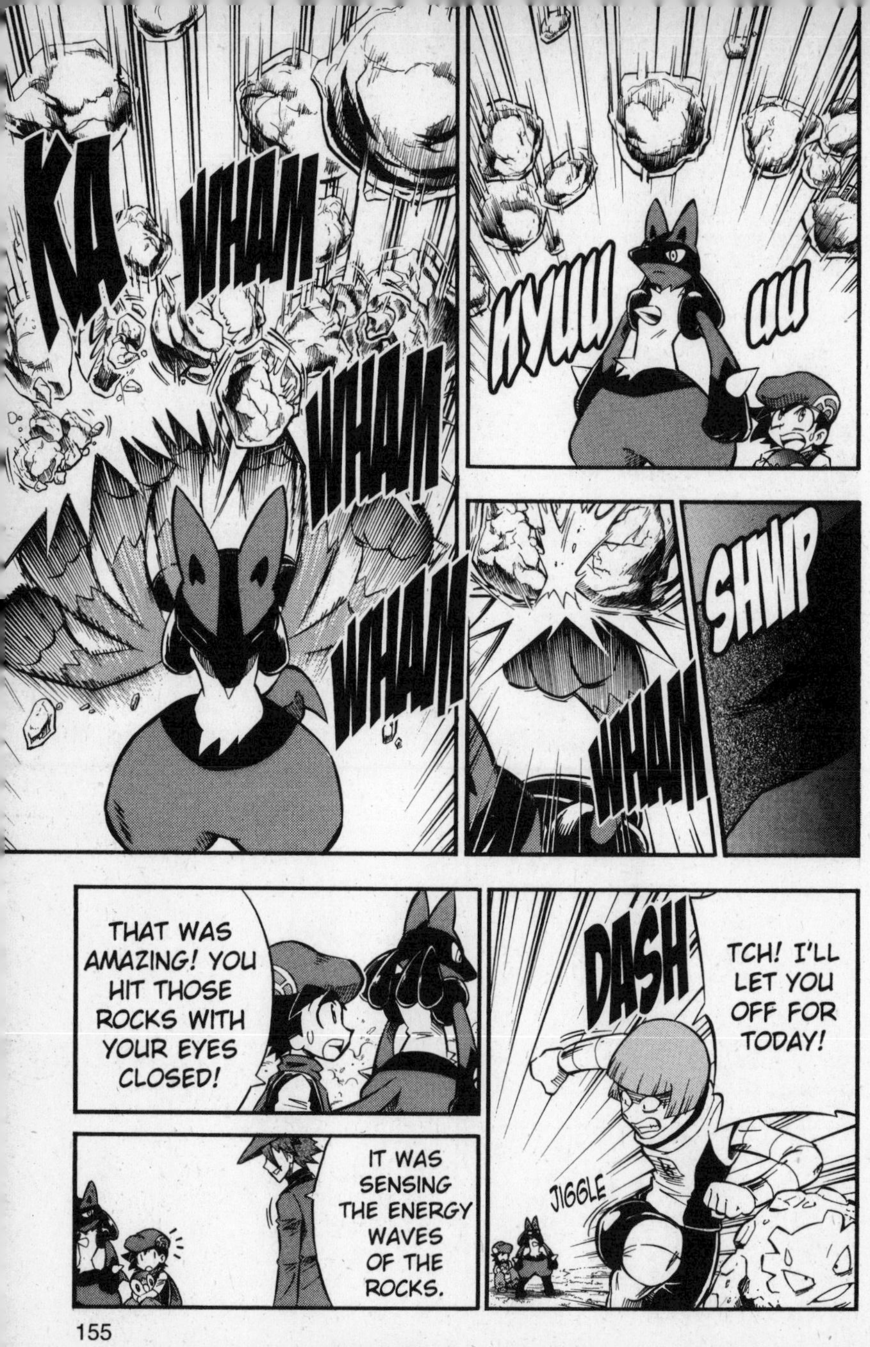
HYUUU
UU
SHWP
WHAM
KA WHAM
WHAM
WHAM
DASH
TCH! I'LL LET YOU OFF FOR TODAY!
JIGGLE
THAT WAS AMAZING! YOU HIT THOSE ROCKS WITH YOUR EYES CLOSED!
IT WAS SENSING THE ENERGY WAVES OF THE ROCKS.

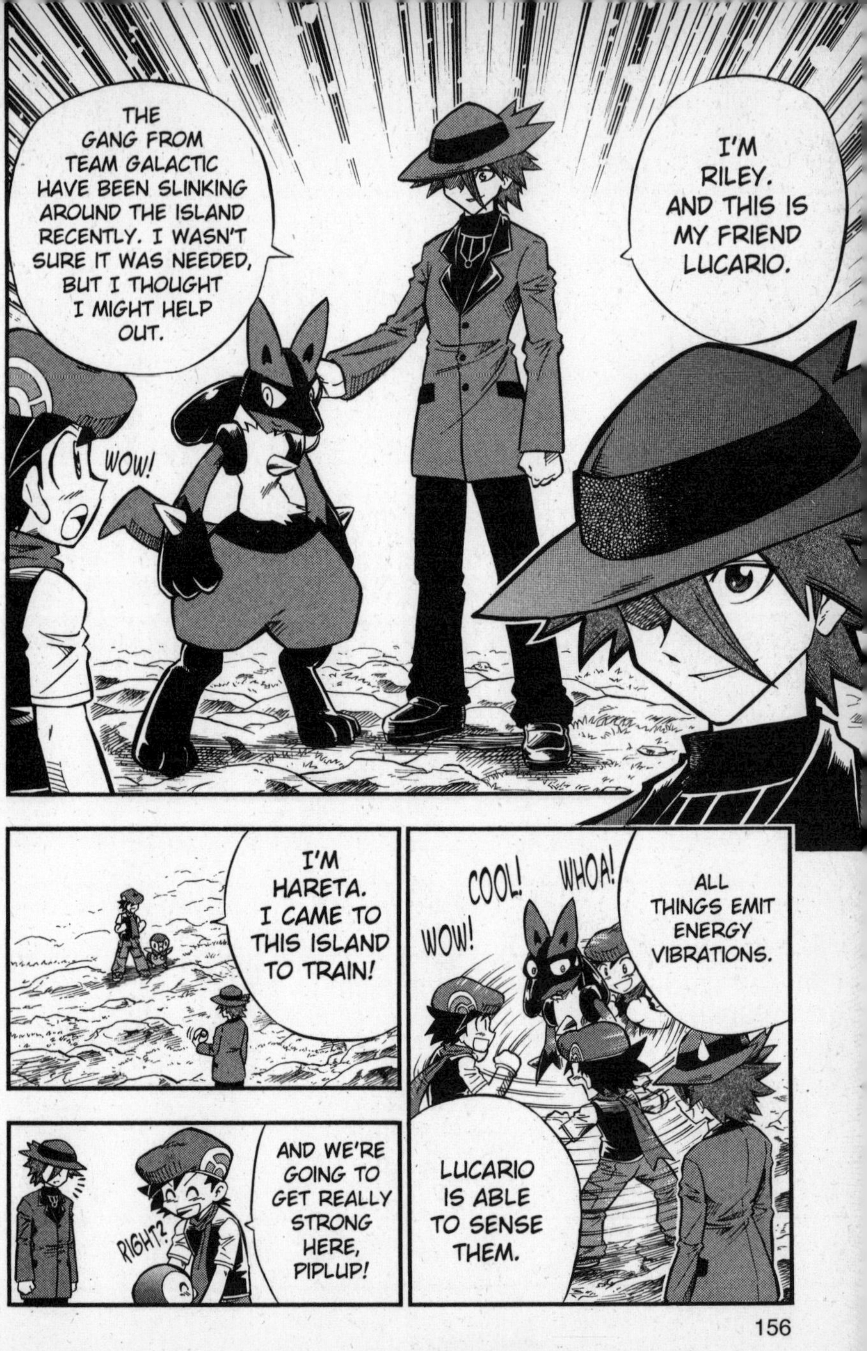
I'M RILEY. AND THIS IS MY FRIEND LUCARIO.
THE GANG FROM TEAM GALACTIC HAVE BEEN SLINKING AROUND THE ISLAND RECENTLY. I WASN'T SURE IT WAS NEEDED, BUT I THOUGHT I MIGHT HELP OUT.
WOW!
ALL THINGS EMIT ENERGY VIBRATIONS.
WHOA!
COOL!
WOW!
LUCARIO IS ABLE TO SENSE THEM.
I'M HARETA. I CAME TO THIS ISLAND TO TRAIN!
AND WE'RE GOING TO GET REALLY STRONG HERE, PIPLUP!
RIGHT?

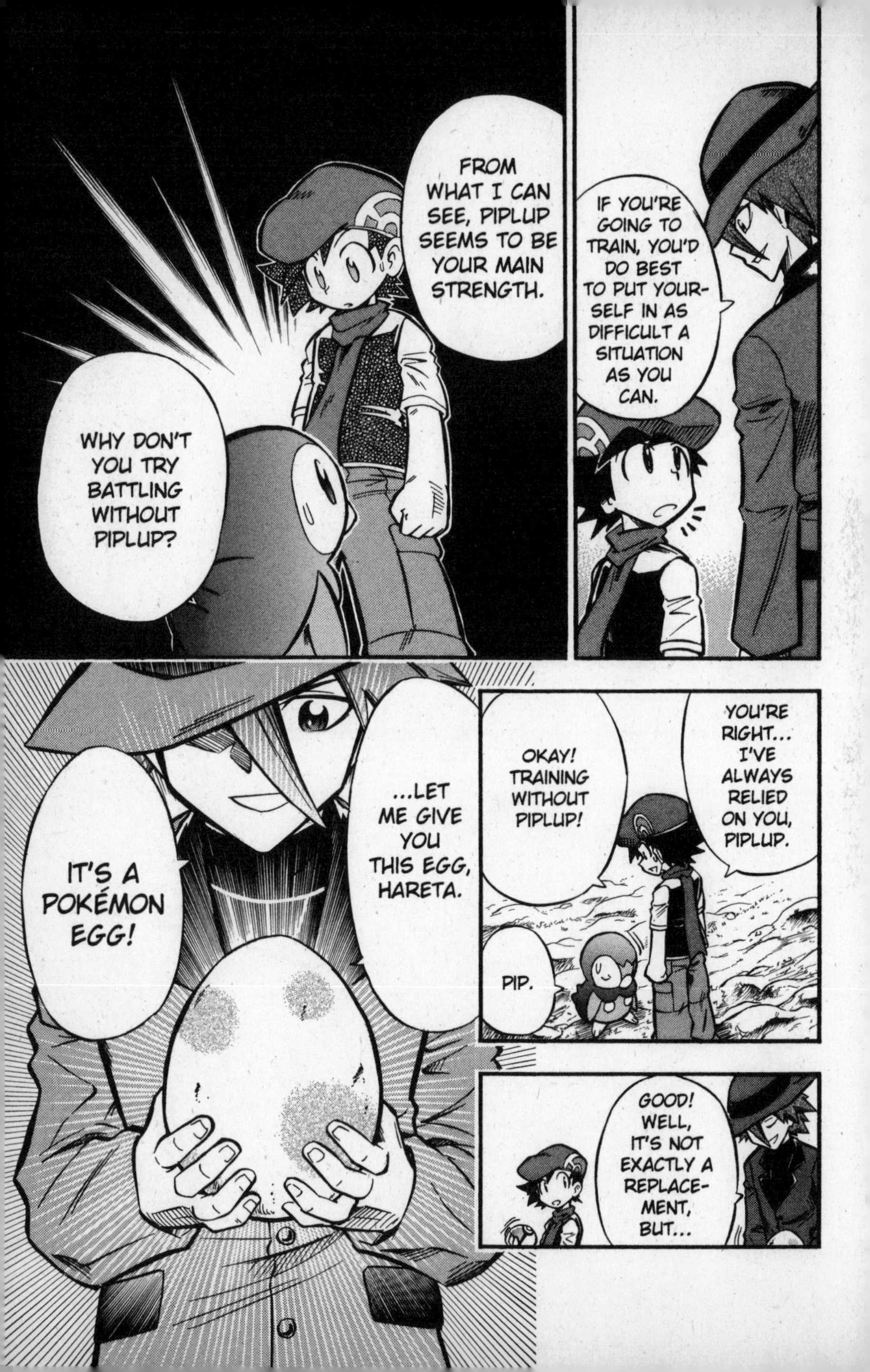
IF YOU'RE GOING TO TRAIN, YOU'D DO BEST TO PUT YOURSELF IN AS DIFFICULT A SITUATION AS YOU CAN.
FROM WHAT I CAN SEE, PIPLUP SEEMS TO BE YOUR MAIN STRENGTH.
WHY DON'T YOU TRY BATTLING WITHOUT PIPLUP?
YOU'RE RIGHT... I'VE ALWAYS RELIED ON YOU, PIPLUP.
OKAY! TRAINING WITHOUT PIPLUP!
PIP.
GOOD! WELL, IT'S NOT EXACTLY A REPLACEMENT, BUT...
...LET ME GIVE YOU THIS EGG, HARETA.
IT'S A POKÉMON EGG!

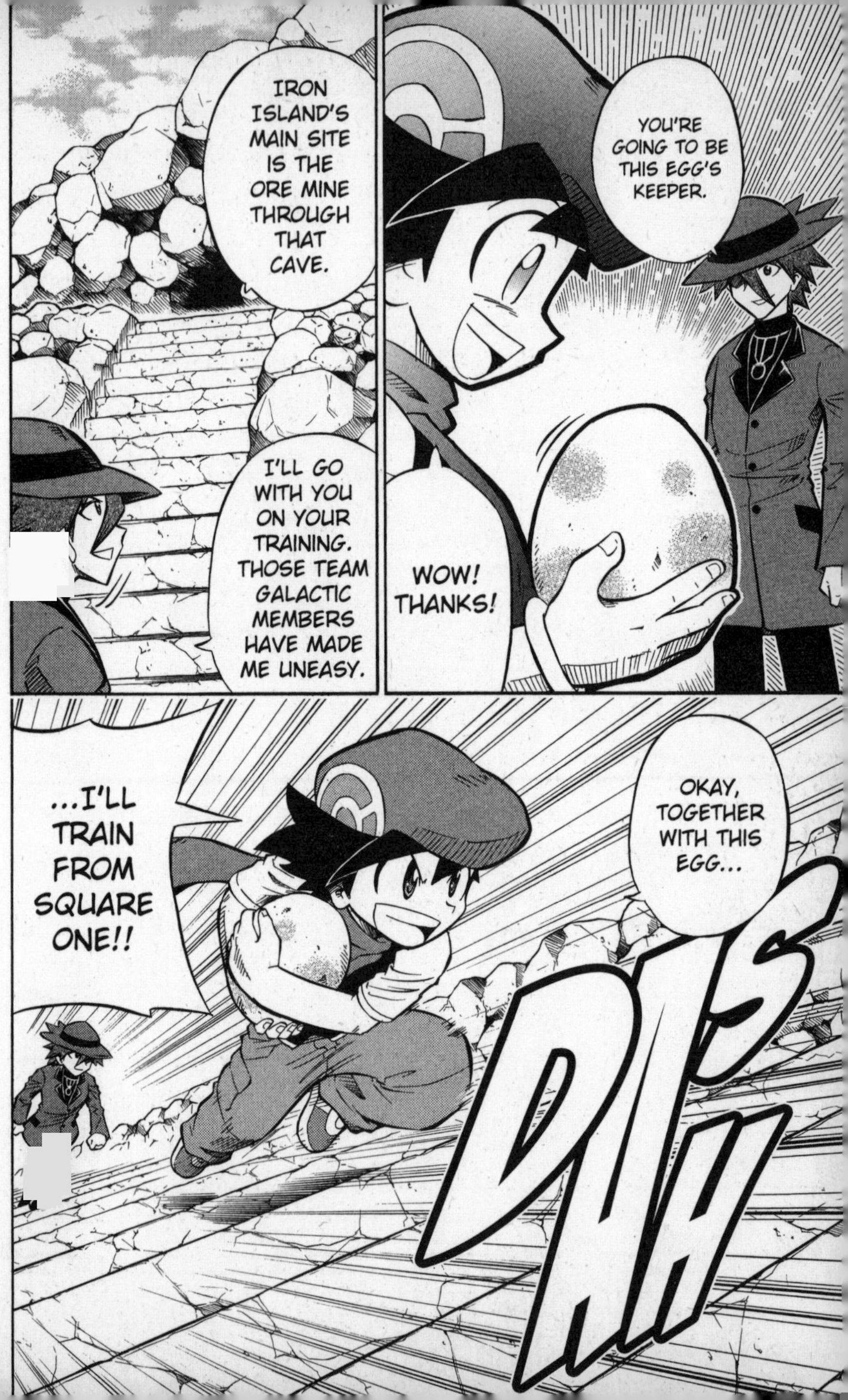
YOU'RE GOING TO BE THIS EGG'S KEEPER.
WOW! THANKS!
IRON ISLAND'S MAIN SITE IS THE ORE MINE THROUGH THAT CAVE.
I'LL GO WITH YOU ON YOUR TRAINING. THOSE TEAM GALACTIC MEMBERS HAVE MADE ME UNEASY.
OKAY, TOGETHER WITH THIS EGG...
...I'LL TRAIN FROM SQUARE ONE!!
DASH

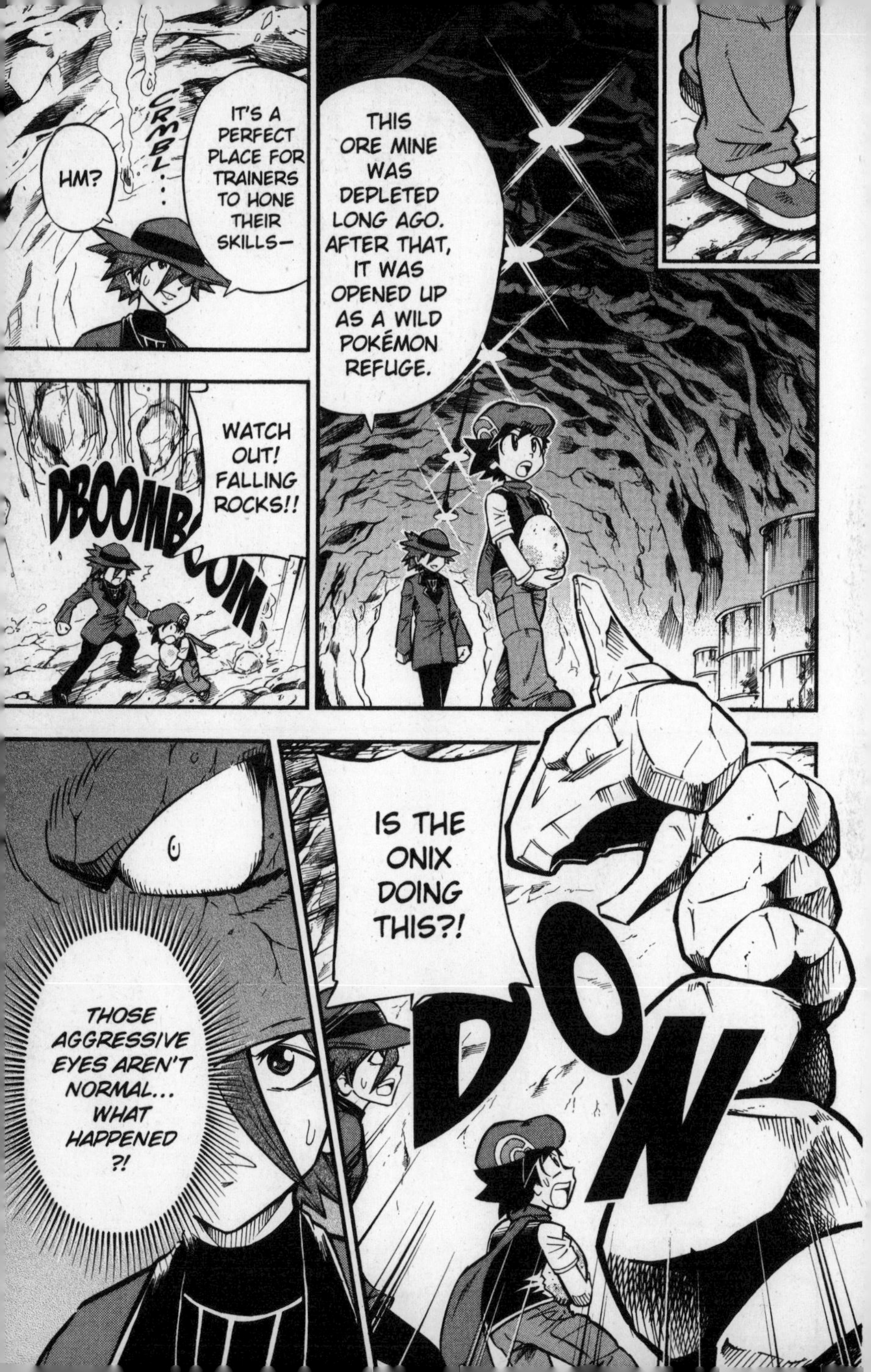
THIS ORE MINE WAS DEPLETED LONG AGO. AFTER THAT, IT WAS OPENED UP AS A WILD POKÉMON REFUGE.
IT'S A PERFECT PLACE FOR TRAINERS TO HONE THEIR SKILLS—
CRMBL...
HM?
WATCH OUT! FALLING ROCKS!!
DBOOMBOOM
IS THE ONIX DOING THIS?!
DON
THOSE AGGRESSIVE EYES AREN'T NORMAL... WHAT HAPPENED ?!

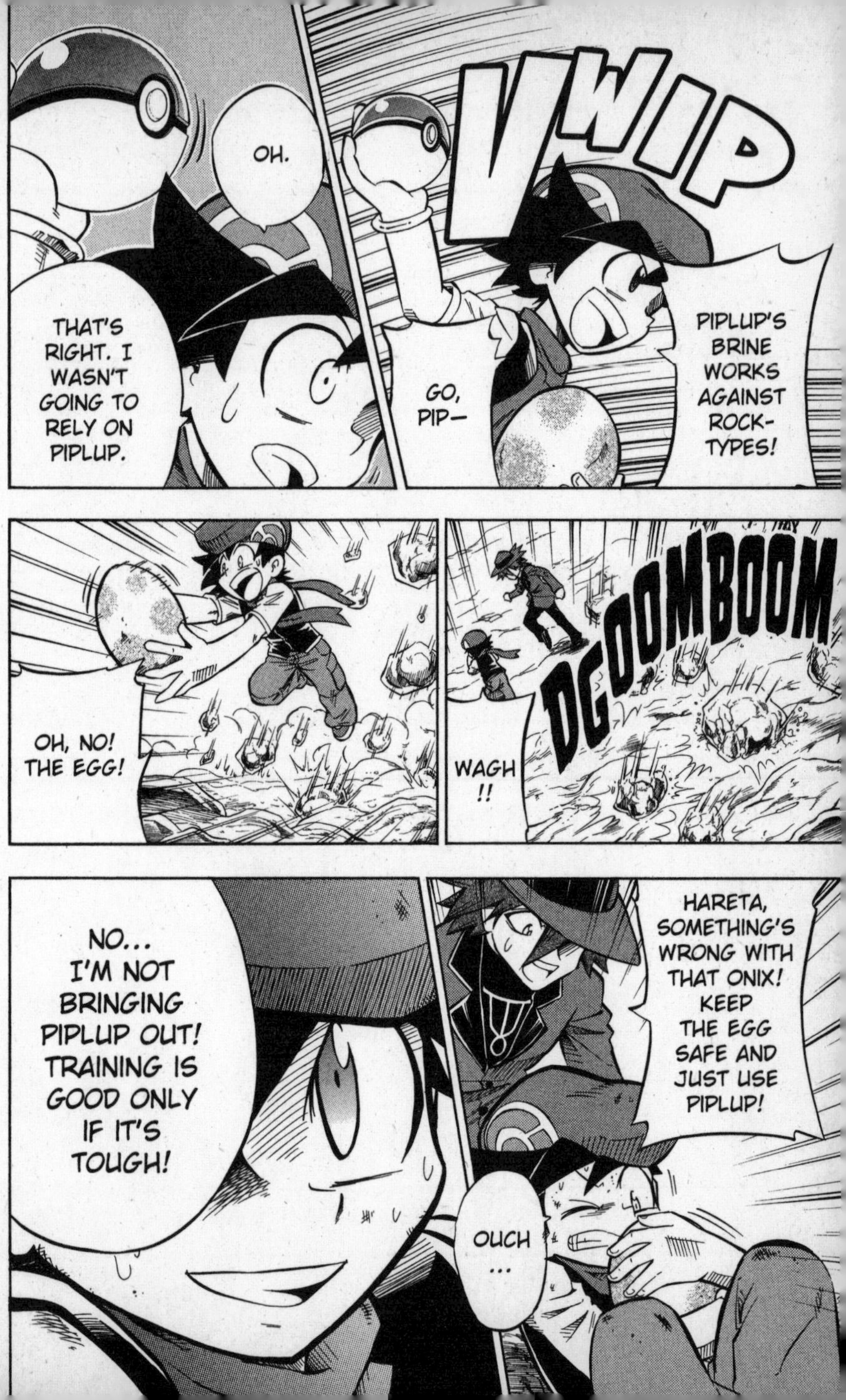
VWIP
PIPLUP'S BRINE WORKS AGAINST ROCK-TYPES!
GO, PIP—
OH.
THAT'S RIGHT. I WASN'T GOING TO RELY ON PIPLUP.
DGOOMBOOM
WAGH !!
OH, NO! THE EGG!
HARETA, SOMETHING'S WRONG WITH THAT ONIX! KEEP THE EGG SAFE AND JUST USE PIPLUP!
OUCH ...
NO... I'M NOT BRINGING PIPLUP OUT! TRAINING IS GOOD ONLY IF IT'S TOUGH!

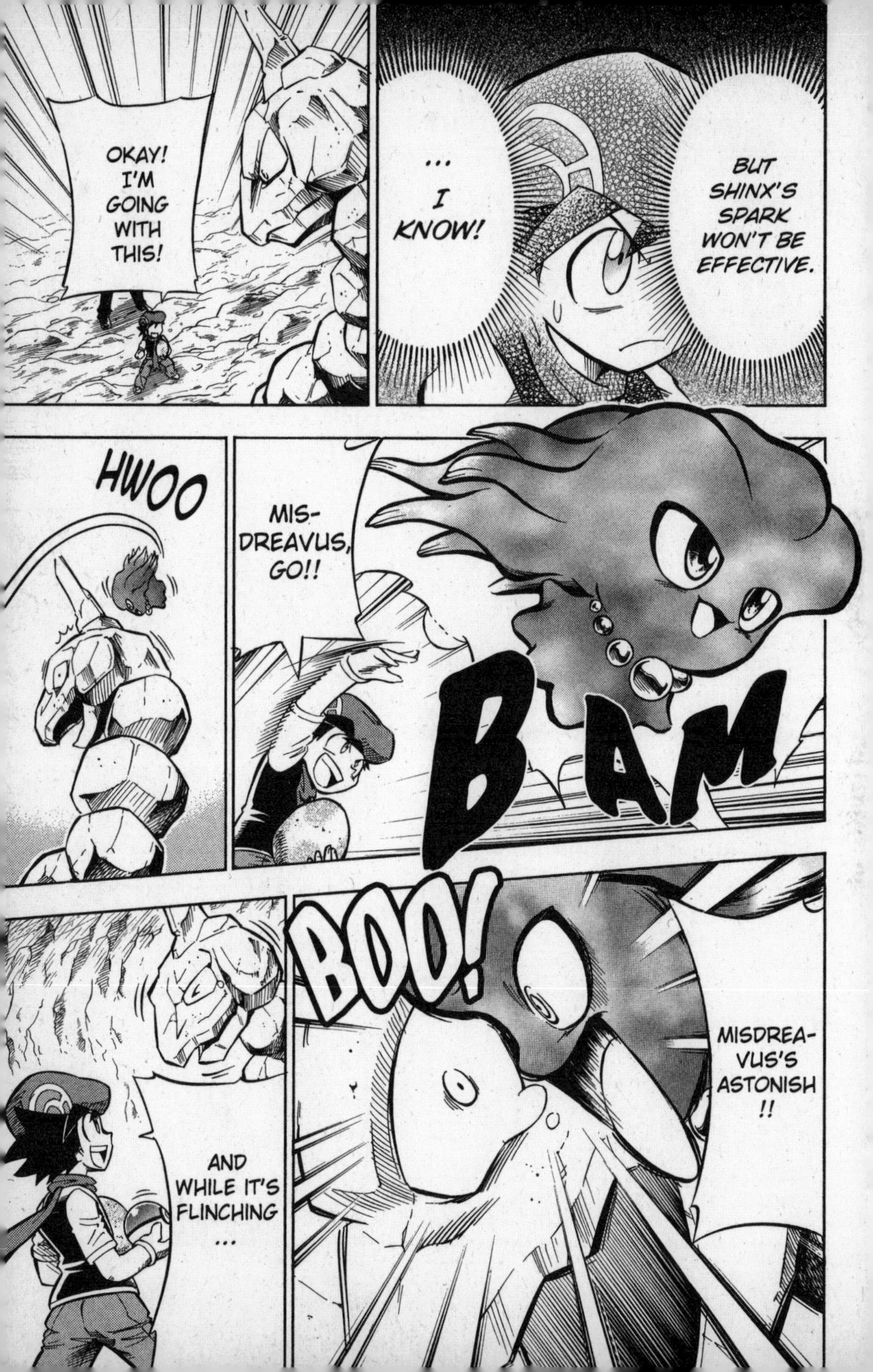
BUT SHINX'S SPARK WON'T BE EFFECTIVE.
... I KNOW!
OKAY! I'M GOING WITH THIS!
MIS-DREAVUS, GO!!
BAM
HWOO
BOO!
MISDREAVUS'S ASTONISH !!
AND WHILE IT'S FLINCHING ...

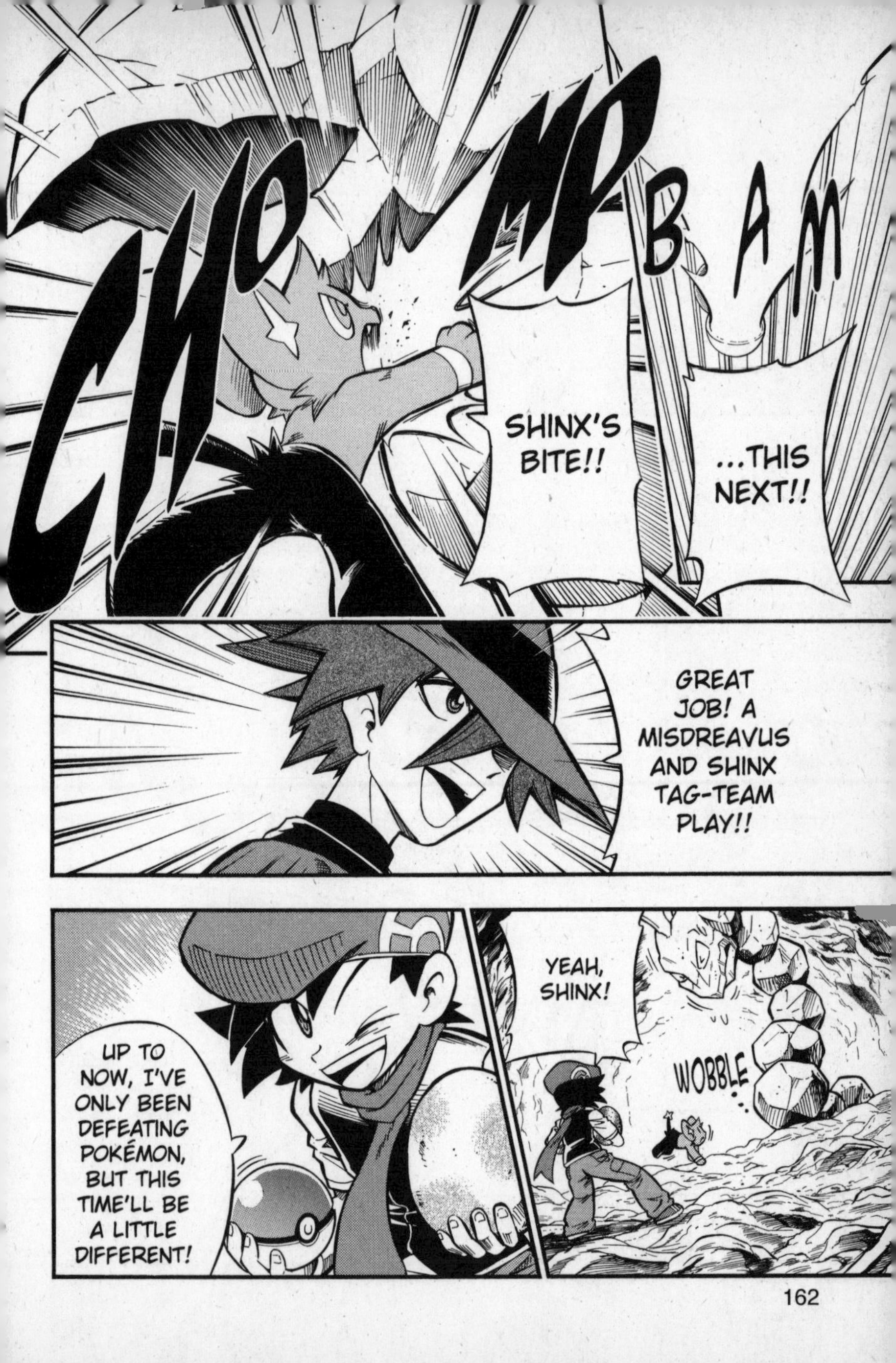
CHOMP
BAM
SHINX'S BITE!!
...THIS NEXT!!
GREAT JOB! A MISDREAVUS AND SHINX TAG-TEAM PLAY!!
YEAH, SHINX!
WOBBLE
UP TO NOW, I'VE ONLY BEEN DEFEATING POKÉMON, BUT THIS TIME'LL BE A LITTLE DIFFERENT!

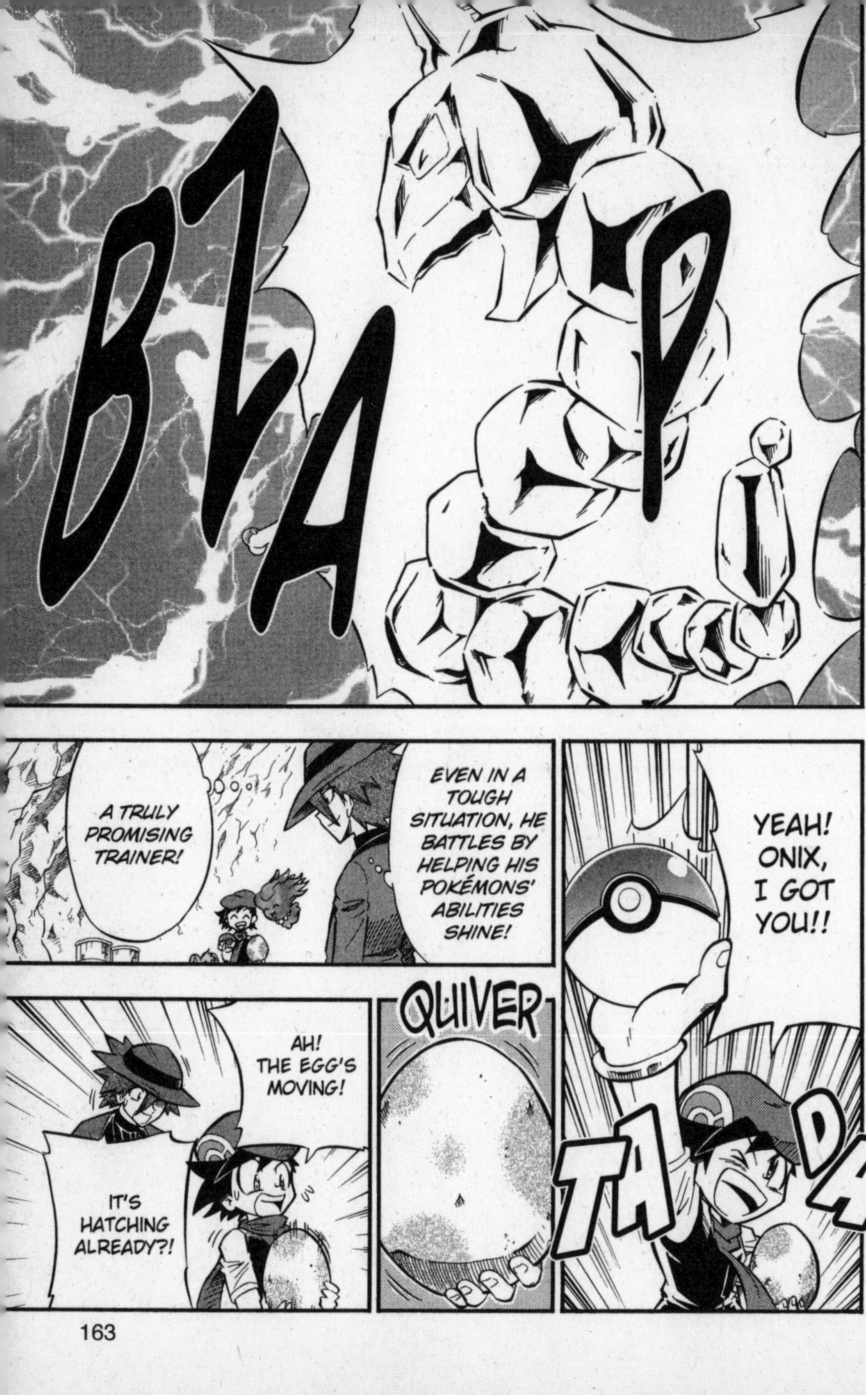
BZAP
YEAH! ONIX, I GOT YOU!!
TA DA
EVEN IN A TOUGH SITUATION, HE BATTLES BY HELPING HIS POKÉMONS' ABILITIES SHINE!
A TRULY PROMISING TRAINER!
QUIVER
AH! THE EGG'S MOVING!
IT'S HATCHING ALREADY?!

FLASH

RIO
!!

BAAM

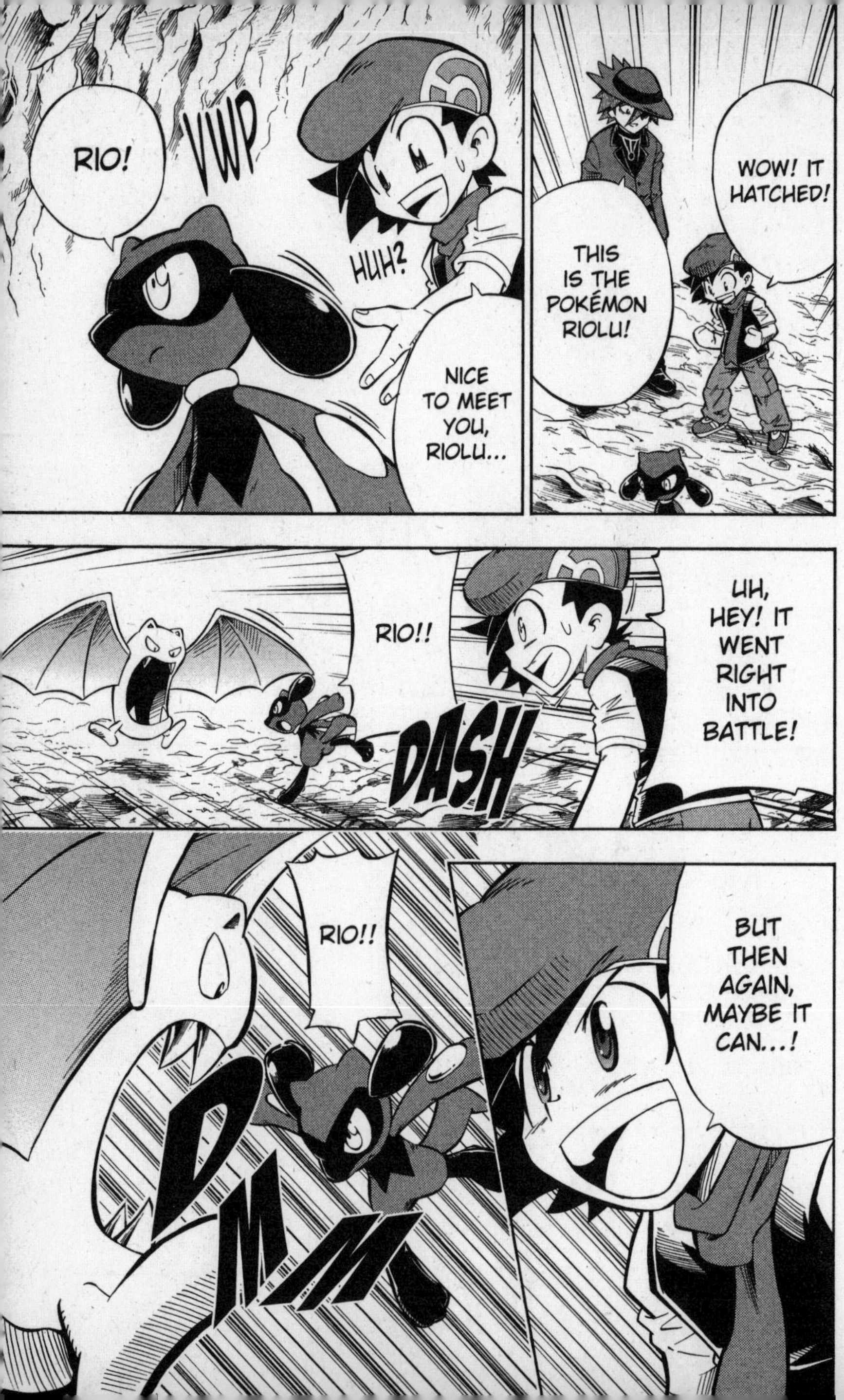
WOW! IT HATCHED!
THIS IS THE POKÉMON RIOLU!
NICE TO MEET YOU, RIOLU...
VWP
RIO!
HUH?
UH, HEY! IT WENT RIGHT INTO BATTLE!
RIO!!
DASH
BUT THEN AGAIN, MAYBE IT CAN...!
RIO!!
DMM

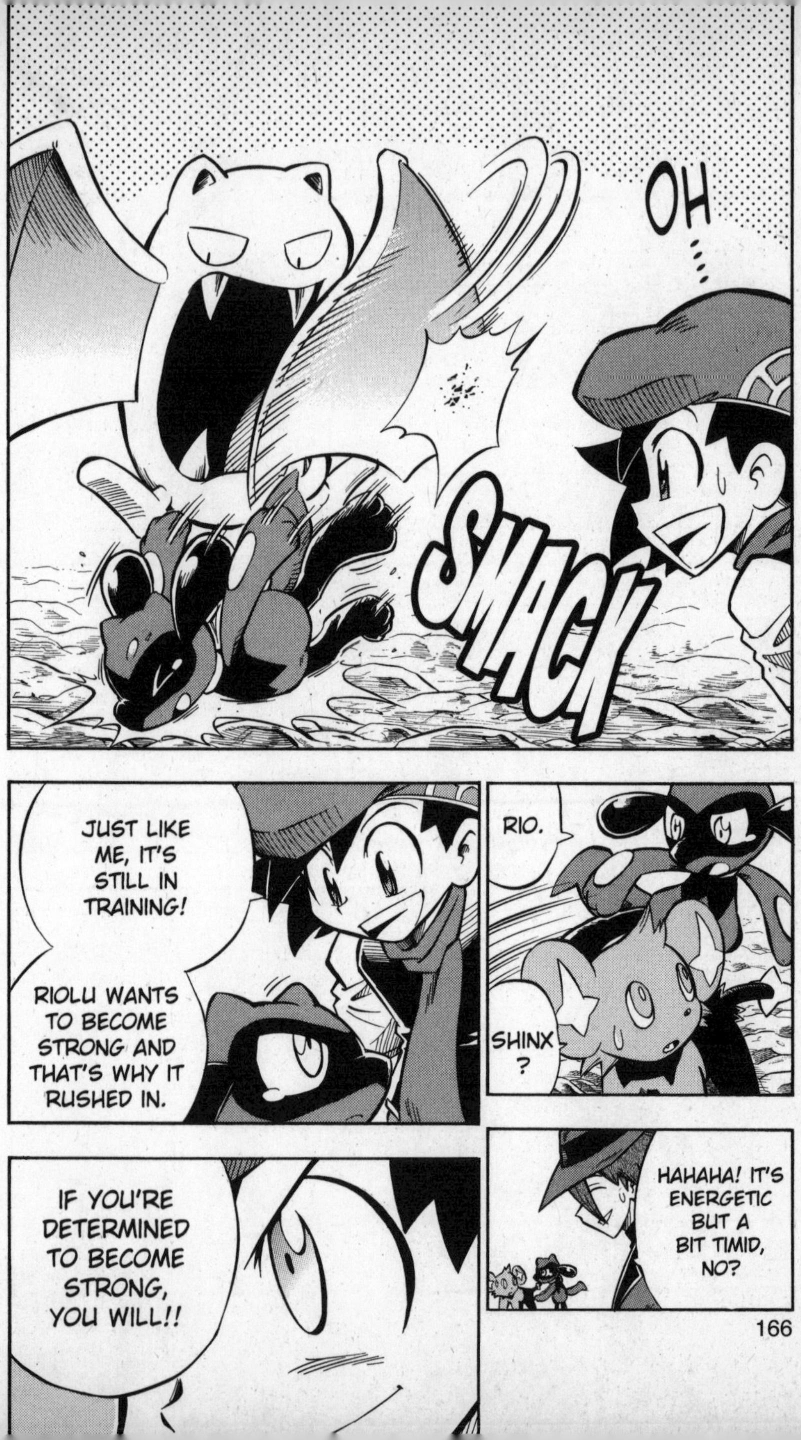
OH...
SMACK
RIO.
SHINX ?
JUST LIKE ME, IT'S STILL IN TRAINING!
RIOLU WANTS TO BECOME STRONG AND THAT'S WHY IT RUSHED IN.
HAHAHA! IT'S ENERGETIC BUT A BIT TIMID, NO?
IF YOU'RE DETERMINED TO BECOME STRONG, YOU WILL!!

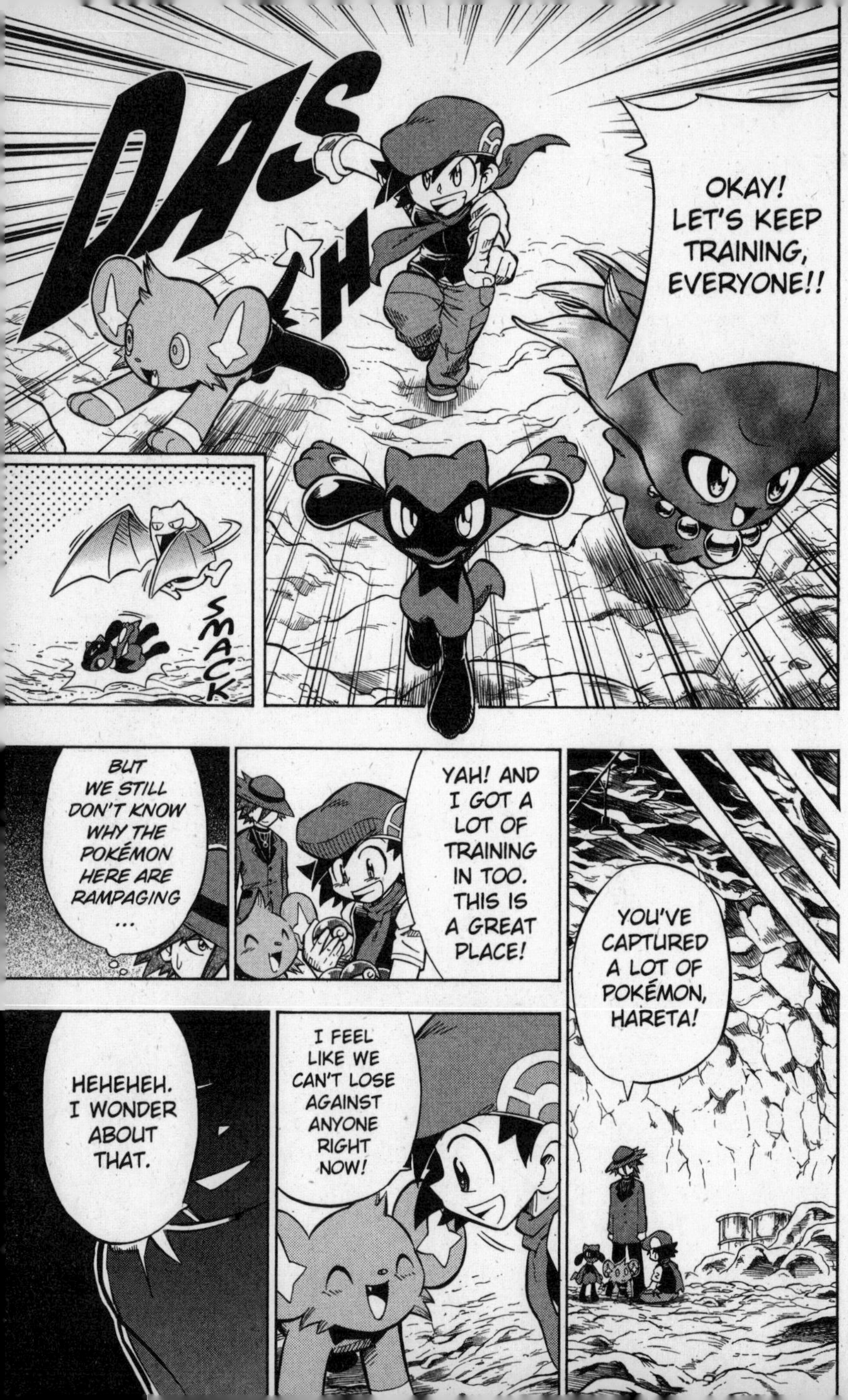
OKAY! LET'S KEEP TRAINING, EVERYONE!!
DASH
SMACK
YOU'VE CAPTURED A LOT OF POKÉMON, HARETA!
YAH! AND I GOT A LOT OF TRAINING IN TOO. THIS IS A GREAT PLACE!
BUT WE STILL DON'T KNOW WHY THE POKÉMON HERE ARE RAMPAGING ...
I FEEL LIKE WE CAN'T LOSE AGAINST ANYONE RIGHT NOW!
HEHEHEH. I WONDER ABOUT THAT.

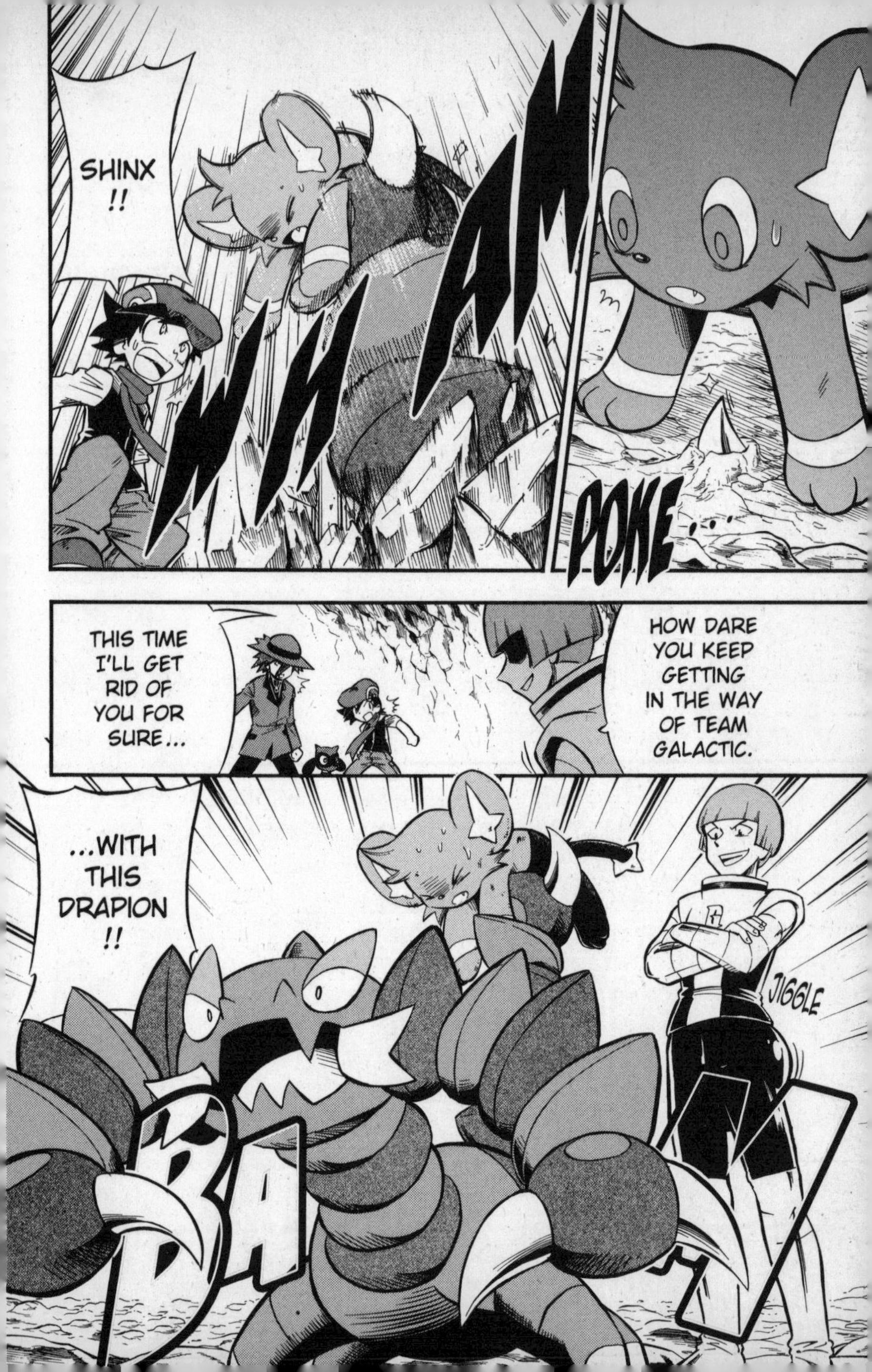

POKE
SHINX !!
WHAM
HOW DARE YOU KEEP GETTING IN THE WAY OF TEAM GALACTIC.
THIS TIME I'LL GET RID OF YOU FOR SURE...
JIGGLE
...WITH THIS DRAPION !!
BA

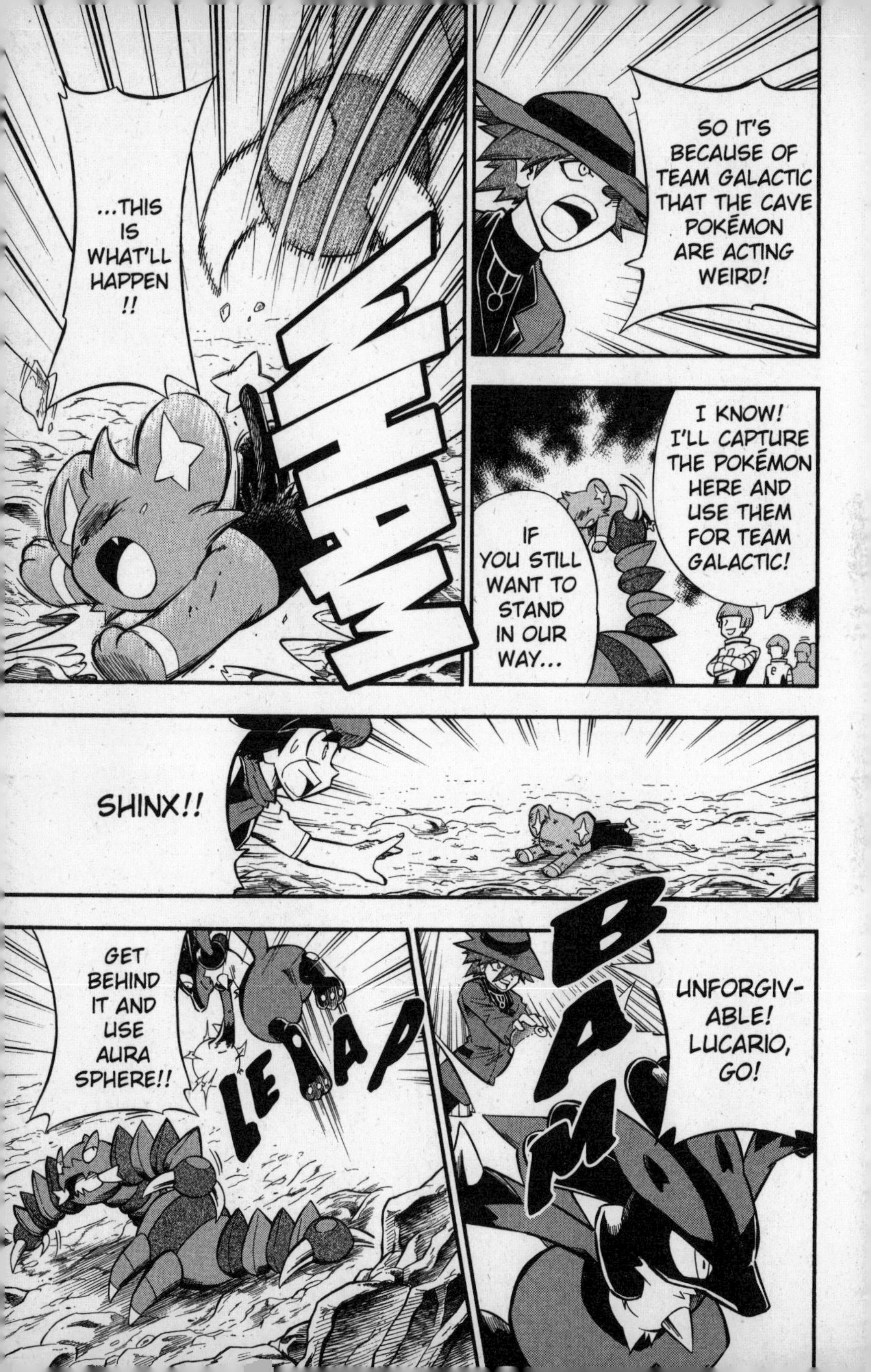
SO IT'S BECAUSE OF TEAM GALACTIC THAT THE CAVE POKÉMON ARE ACTING WEIRD!
I KNOW! I'LL CAPTURE THE POKÉMON HERE AND USE THEM FOR TEAM GALACTIC!
IF YOU STILL WANT TO STAND IN OUR WAY...
...THIS IS WHAT'LL HAPPEN!!
WHAM
SHINX!!
UNFORGIV-ABLE! LUCARIO, GO!
BAM
GET BEHIND IT AND USE AURA SPHERE!!
LEAP

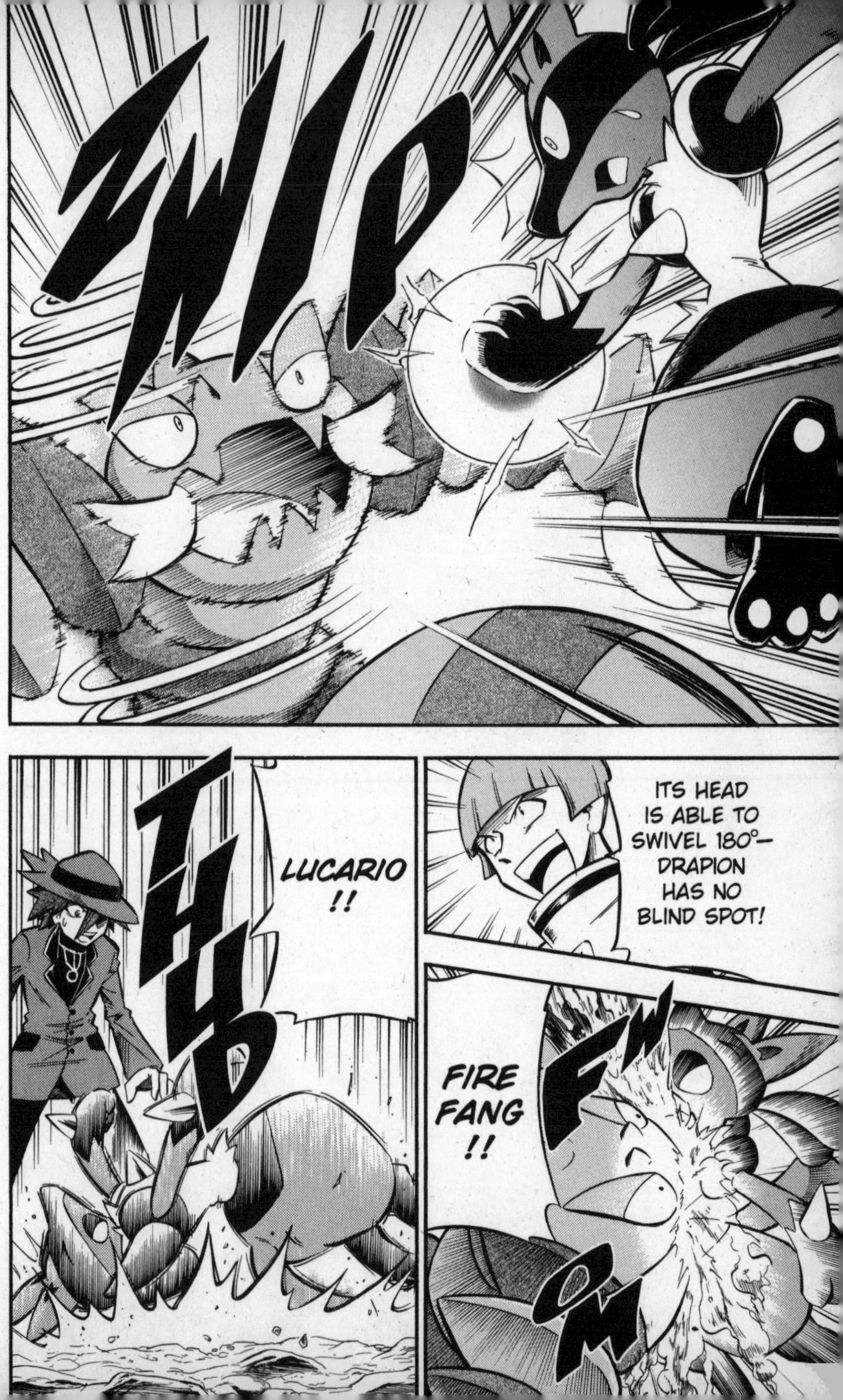
ZWIP
ITS HEAD IS ABLE TO SWIVEL 180°—DRAPION HAS NO BLIND SPOT!
FIRE FANG !!
FWOM
THUD
LUCARIO !!

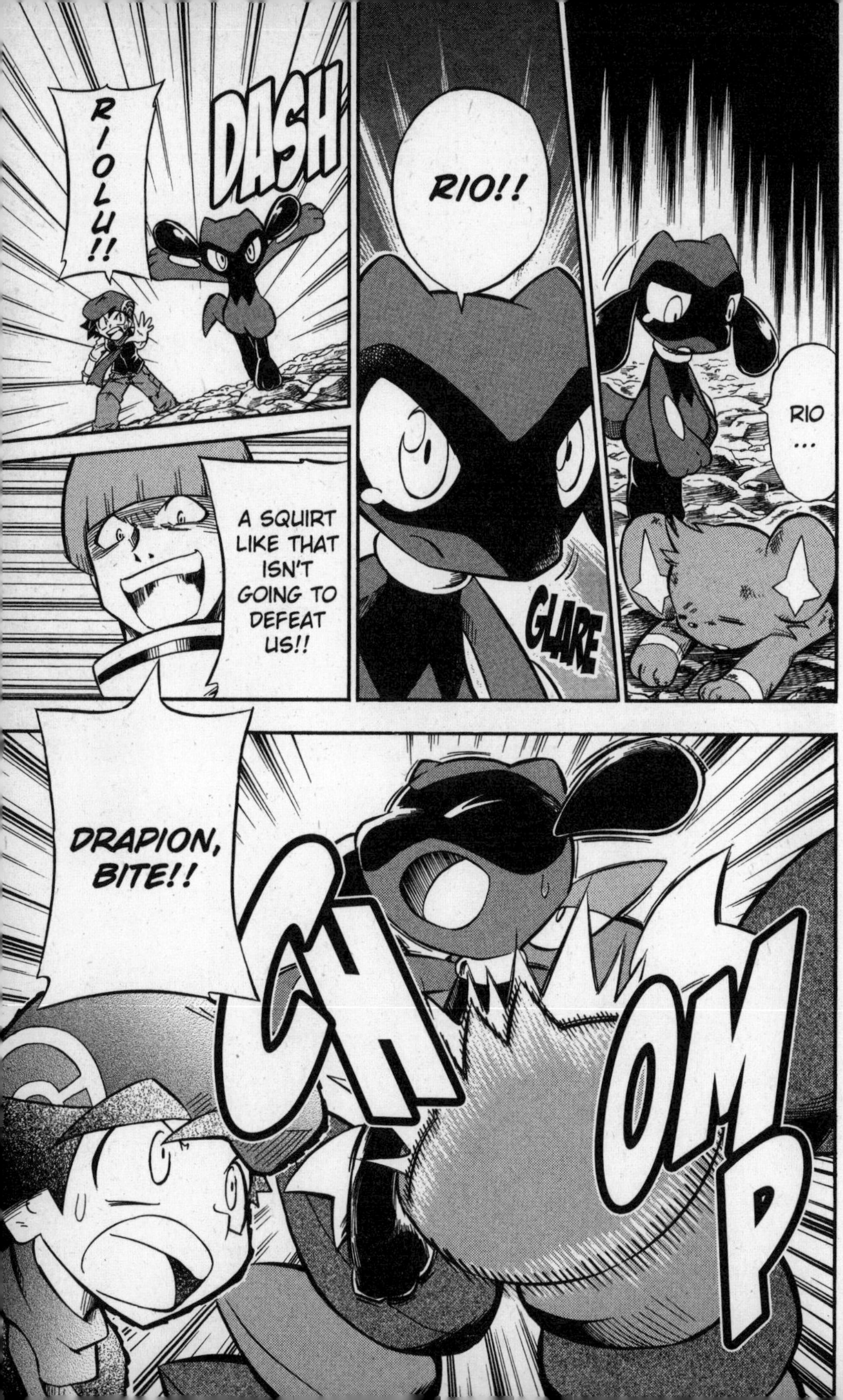
RIO ...
RIO!!
GLARE
RIOLU!!
DASH
A SQUIRT LIKE THAT ISN'T GOING TO DEFEAT US!!
DRAPION, BITE!!
CHOMP

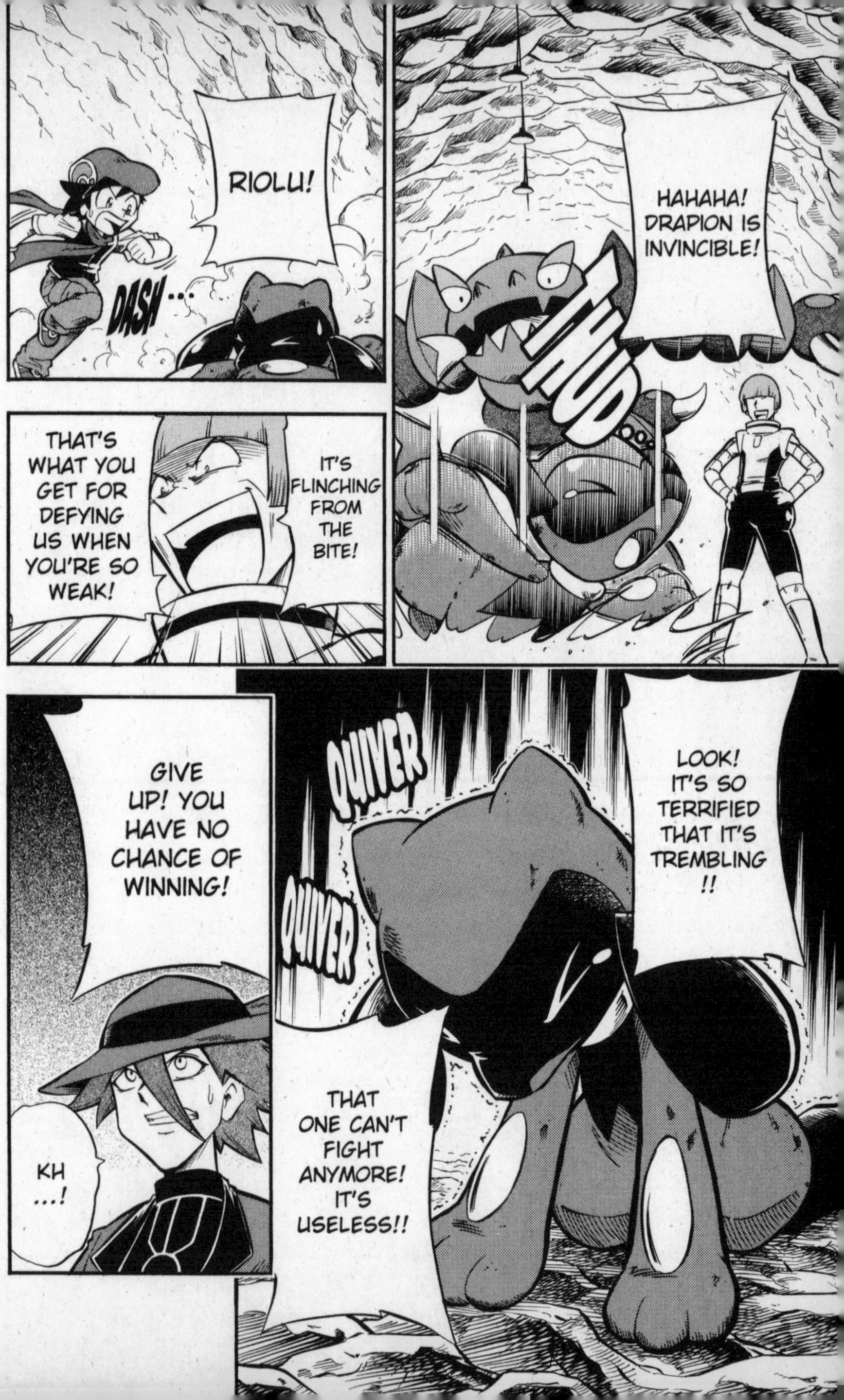
HAHAHA! DRAPION IS INVINCIBLE!
THUD
RIOLU!
DASH...
IT'S FLINCHING FROM THE BITE!
THAT'S WHAT YOU GET FOR DEFYING US WHEN YOU'RE SO WEAK!
LOOK! IT'S SO TERRIFIED THAT IT'S TREMBLING!!
QUIVER
QUIVER
THAT ONE CAN'T FIGHT ANYMORE! IT'S USELESS!!
GIVE UP! YOU HAVE NO CHANCE OF WINNING!
KH...!

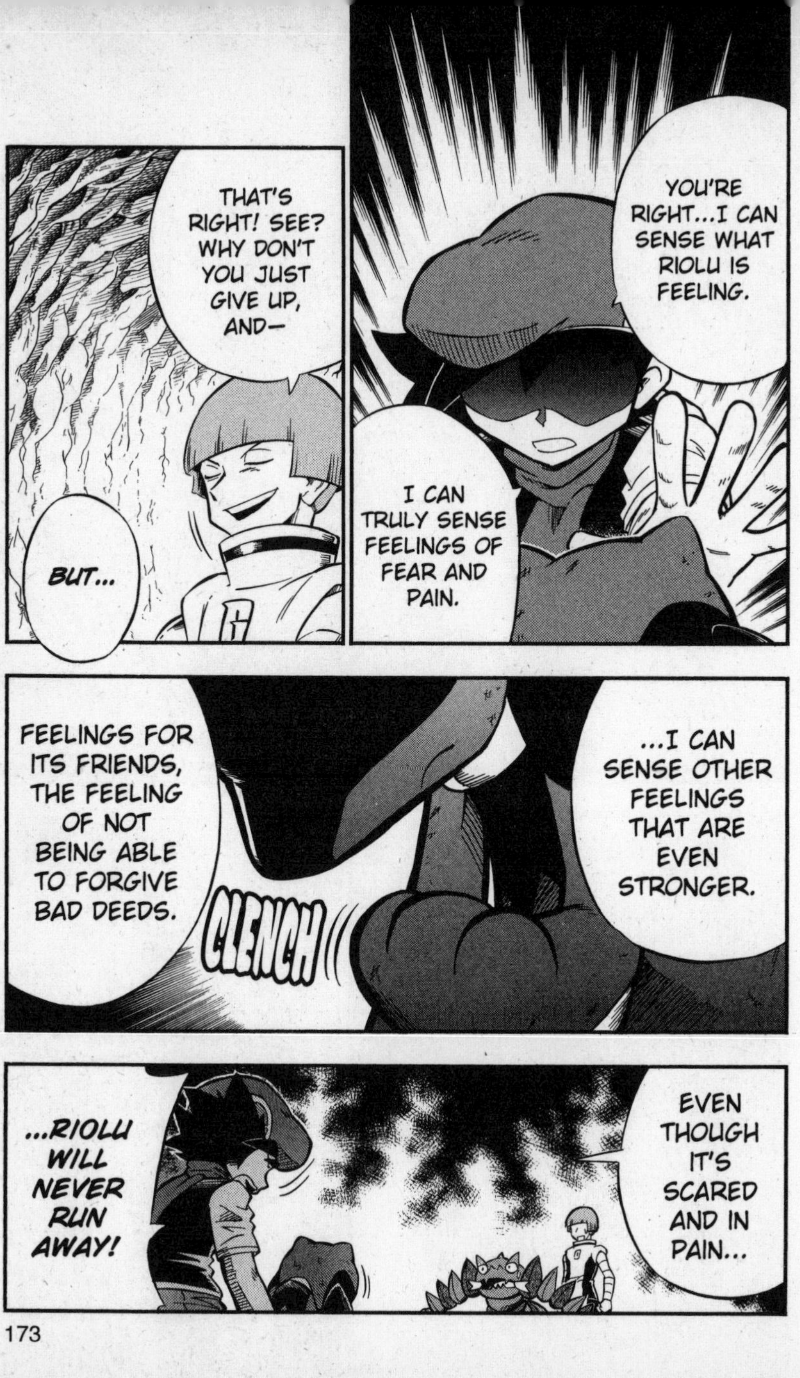
YOU'RE RIGHT...I CAN SENSE WHAT RIOLU IS FEELING.
I CAN TRULY SENSE FEELINGS OF FEAR AND PAIN.
THAT'S RIGHT! SEE? WHY DON'T YOU JUST GIVE UP, AND—
BUT...
...I CAN SENSE OTHER FEELINGS THAT ARE EVEN STRONGER.
CLENCH
FEELINGS FOR ITS FRIENDS, THE FEELING OF NOT BEING ABLE TO FORGIVE BAD DEEDS.
EVEN THOUGH IT'S SCARED AND IN PAIN...
...RIOLU WILL NEVER RUN AWAY!

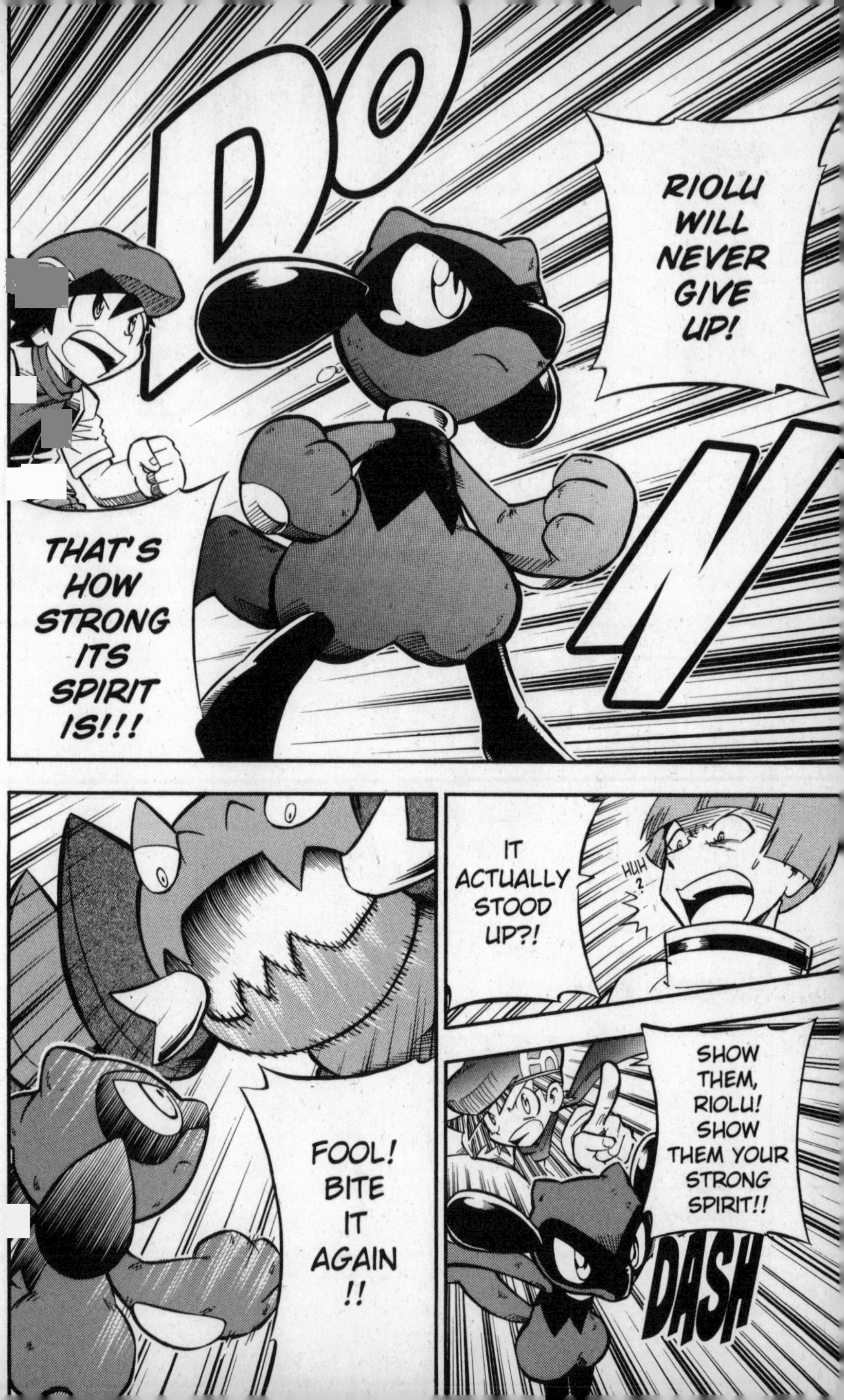
DO
N
RIOLU WILL NEVER GIVE UP!
THAT'S HOW STRONG ITS SPIRIT IS!!!
IT ACTUALLY STOOD UP?!
HUH?
SHOW THEM, RIOLU! SHOW THEM YOUR STRONG SPIRIT!!
DASH
FOOL! BITE IT AGAIN!!

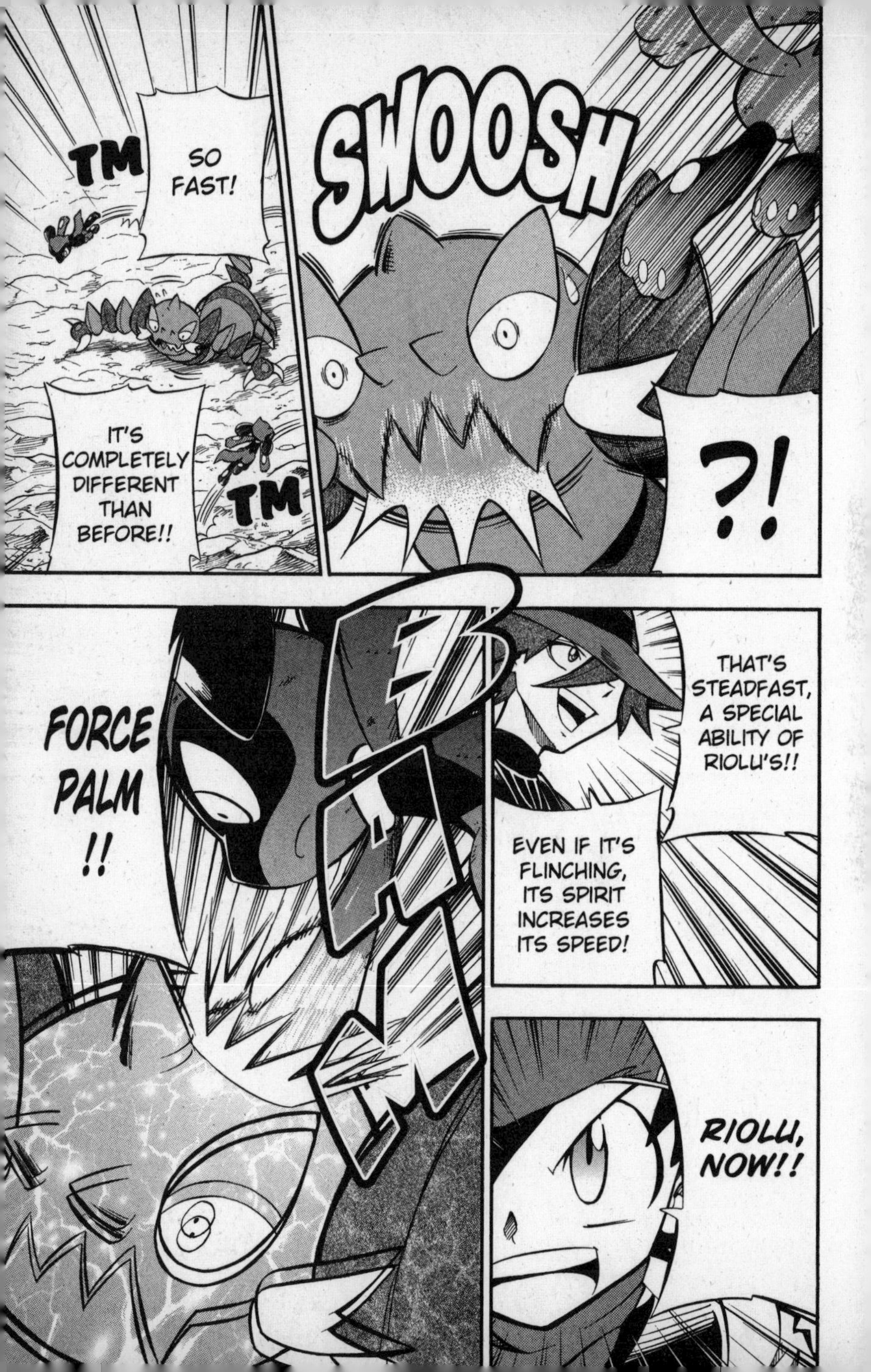
SWOOSH
?!
SO FAST!
TM
IT'S COMPLETELY DIFFERENT THAN BEFORE!!
TM
THAT'S STEADFAST, A SPECIAL ABILITY OF RIOLU'S!!
EVEN IF IT'S FLINCHING, ITS SPIRIT INCREASES ITS SPEED!
RIOLU, NOW!!
FORCE PALM!!

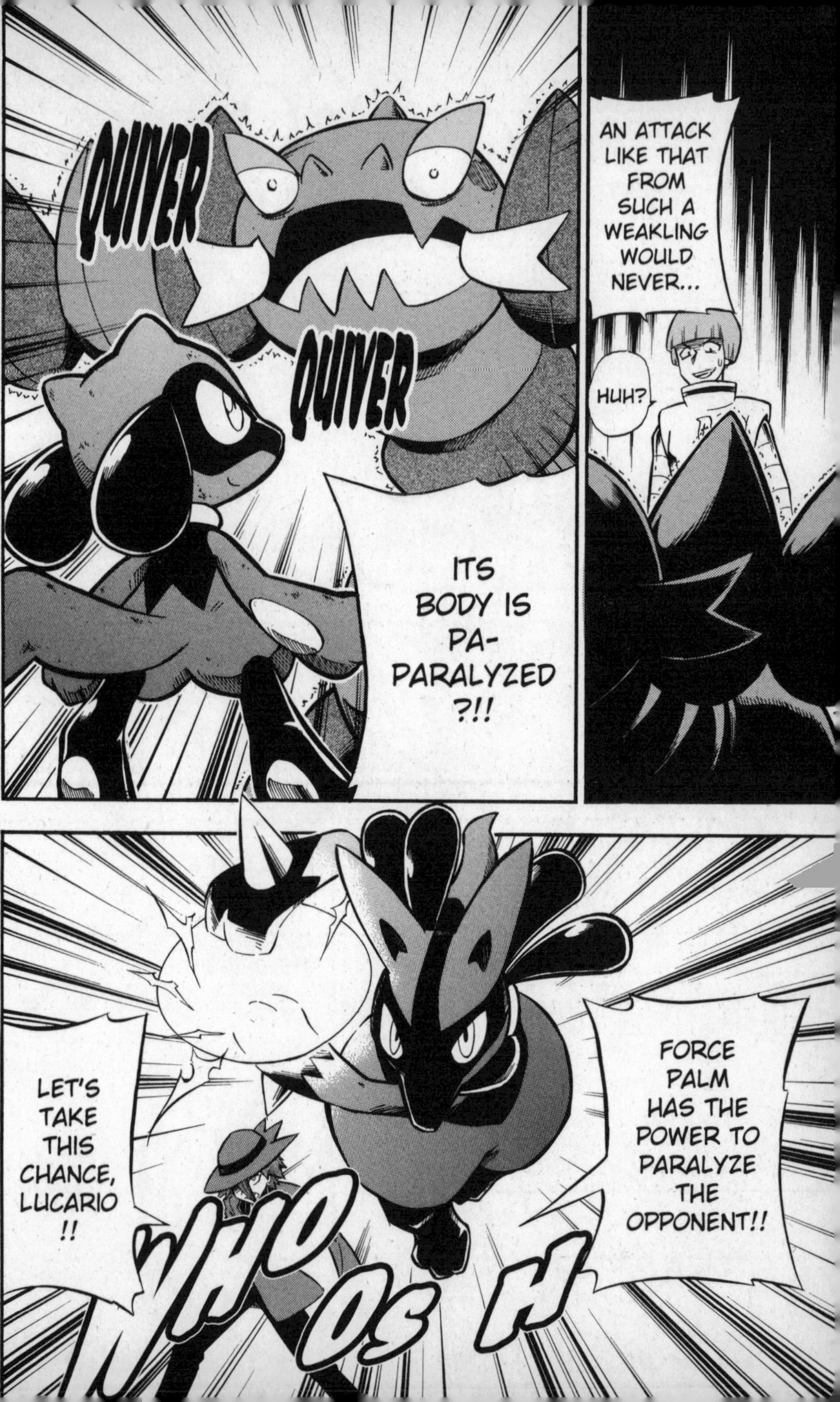
AN ATTACK LIKE THAT FROM SUCH A WEAKLING WOULD NEVER...
HUH?
QUIVER
QUIVER
ITS BODY IS PA- PARALYZED ?!!
FORCE PALM HAS THE POWER TO PARALYZE THE OPPONENT!!
LET'S TAKE THIS CHANCE, LUCARIO !!
WHOOSH

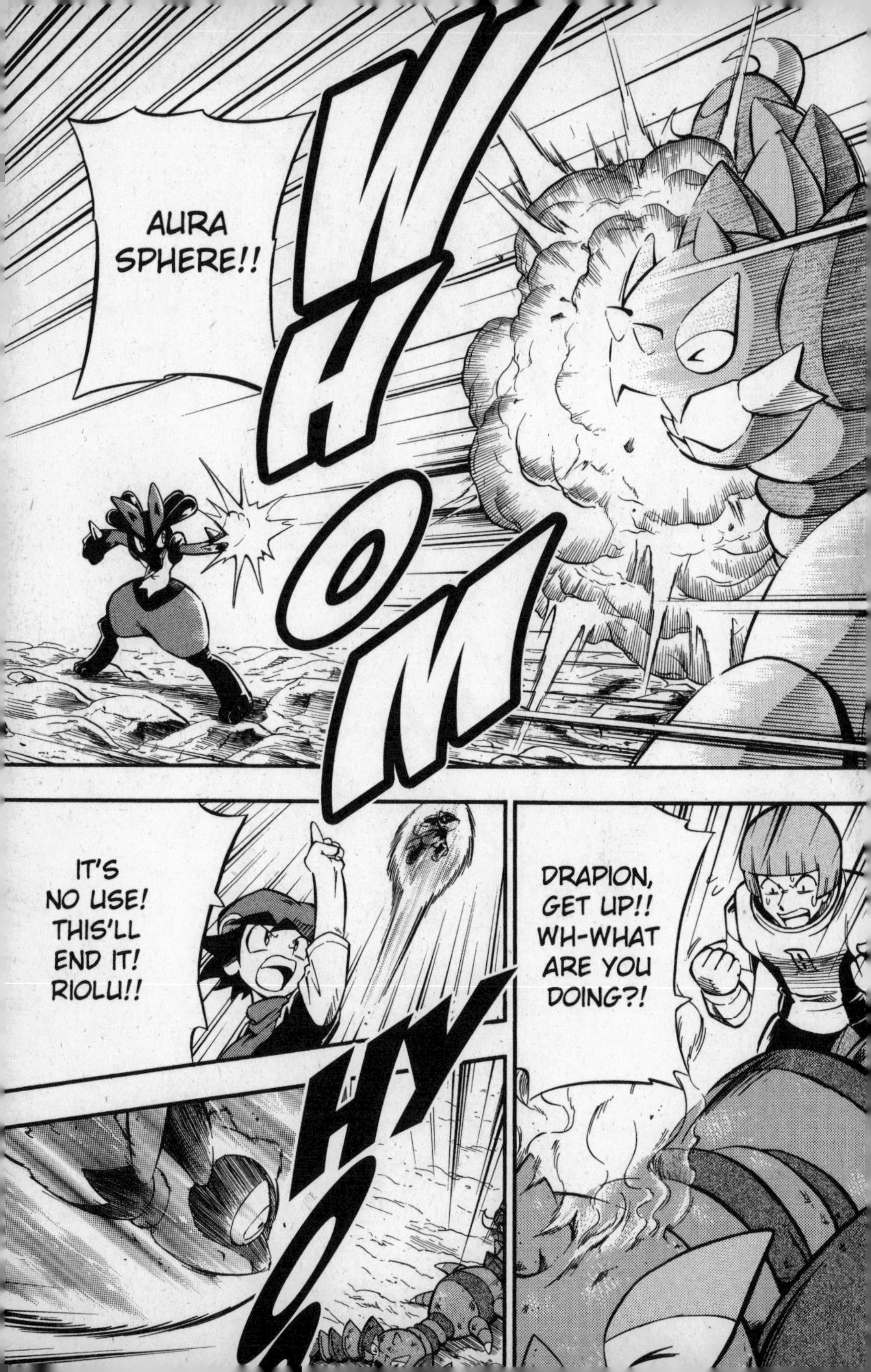
AURA SPHERE!!
DRAPION, GET UP!! WH-WHAT ARE YOU DOING?!
IT'S NO USE! THIS'LL END IT! RIOLU!!

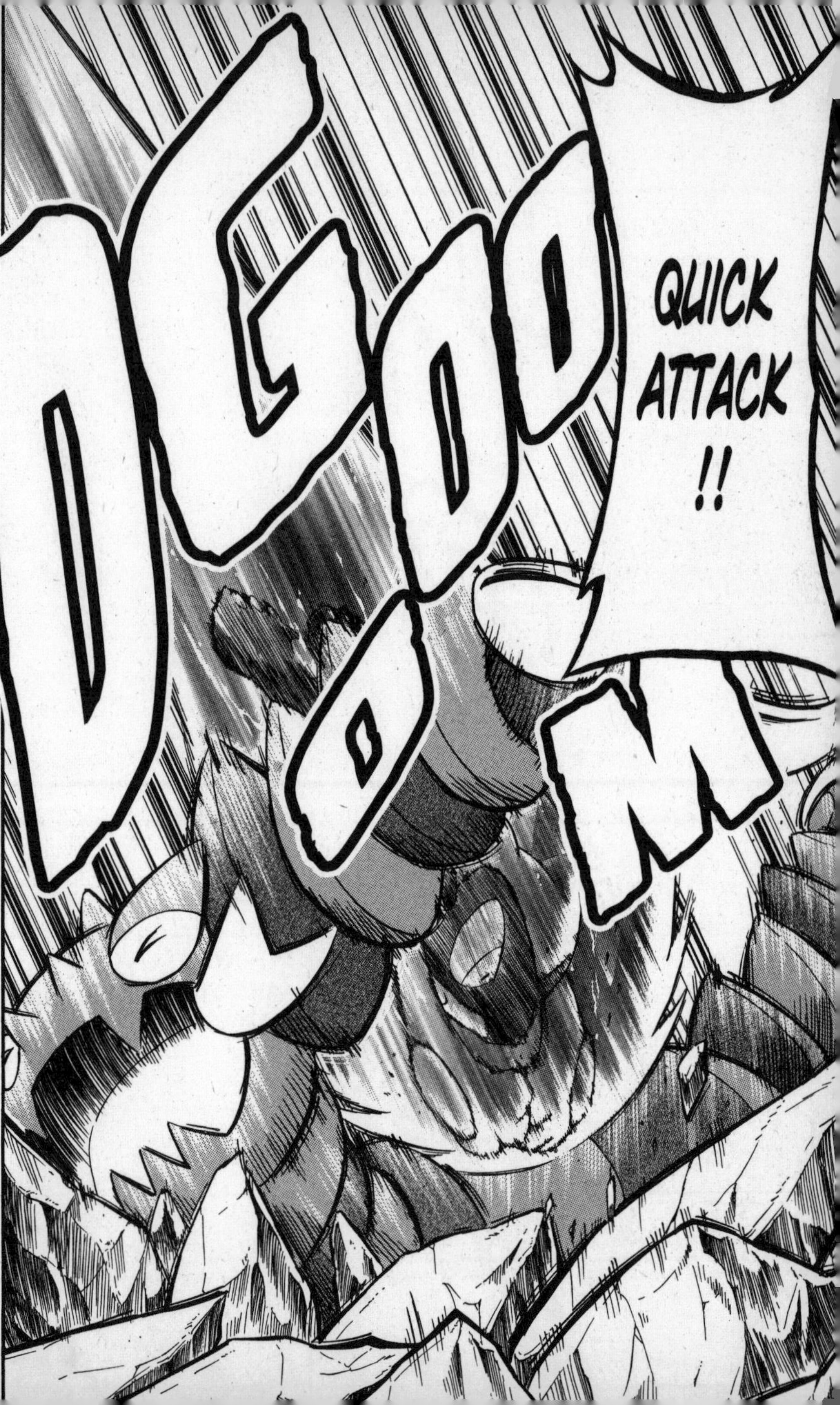
QUICK ATTACK!!

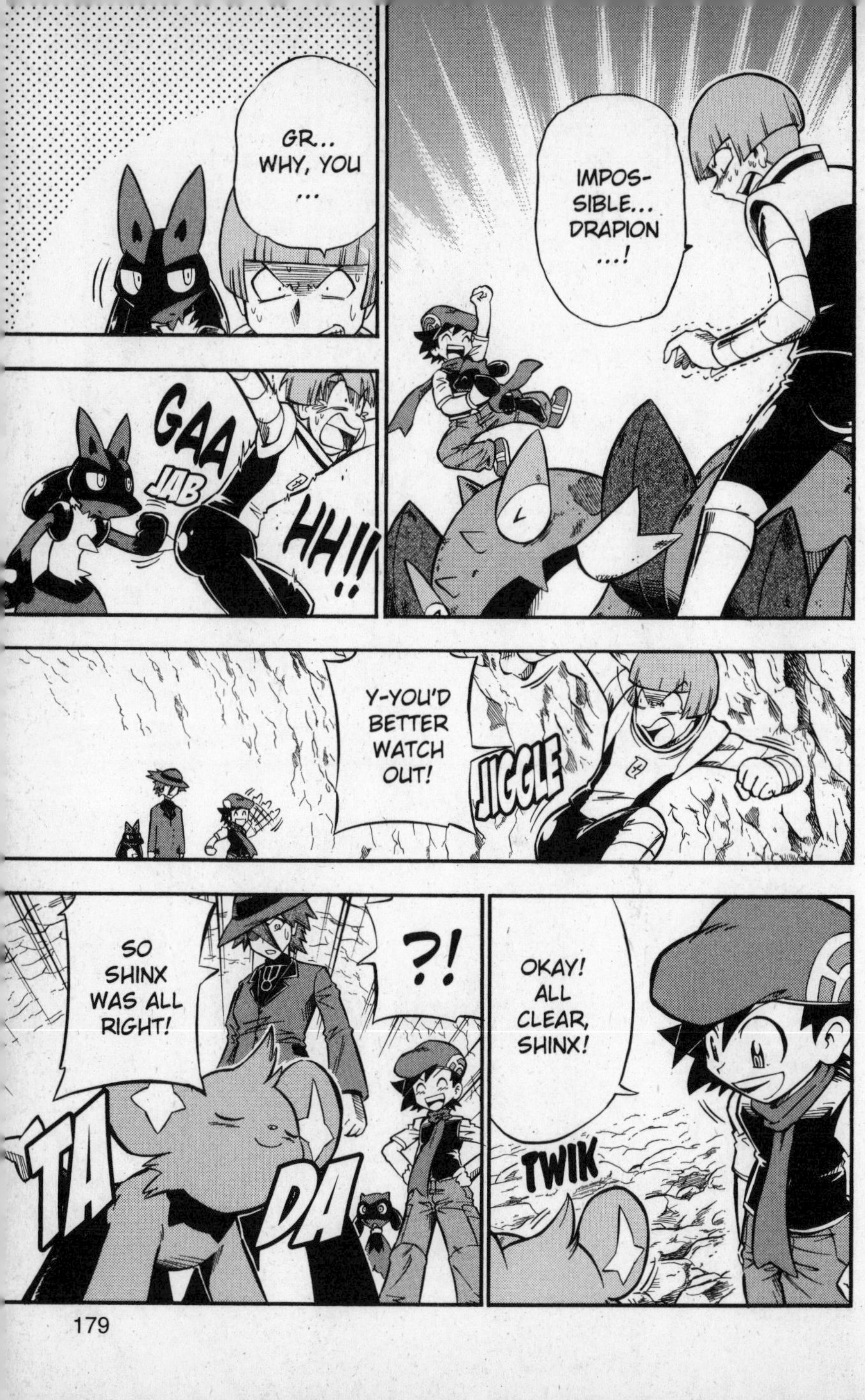
IMPOS-SIBLE... DRAPION ...!
GR... WHY, YOU ...
GAAHH!!
JAB
Y-YOU'D BETTER WATCH OUT!
JIGGLE
OKAY! ALL CLEAR, SHINX!
TWIK
?!
SO SHINX WAS ALL RIGHT!
TA
DA

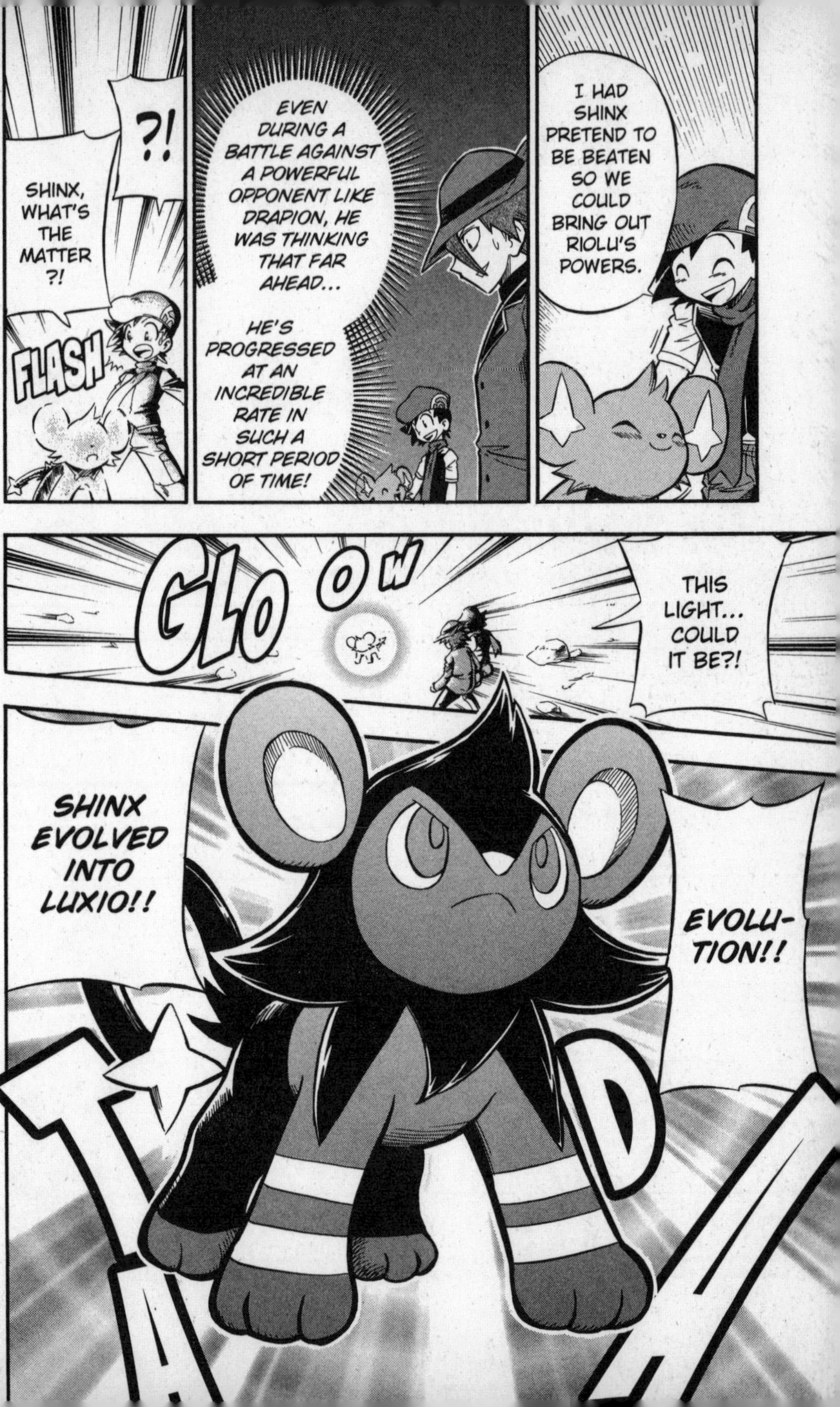
I HAD SHINX PRETEND TO BE BEATEN SO WE COULD BRING OUT RIOLU'S POWERS.
EVEN DURING A BATTLE AGAINST A POWERFUL OPPONENT LIKE DRAPION, HE WAS THINKING THAT FAR AHEAD...
HE'S PROGRESSED AT AN INCREDIBLE RATE IN SUCH A SHORT PERIOD OF TIME!
?!
SHINX, WHAT'S THE MATTER ?!
FLASH
THIS LIGHT... COULD IT BE?!
GLOOW
EVOLUTION!!
SHINX EVOLVED INTO LUXIO!!

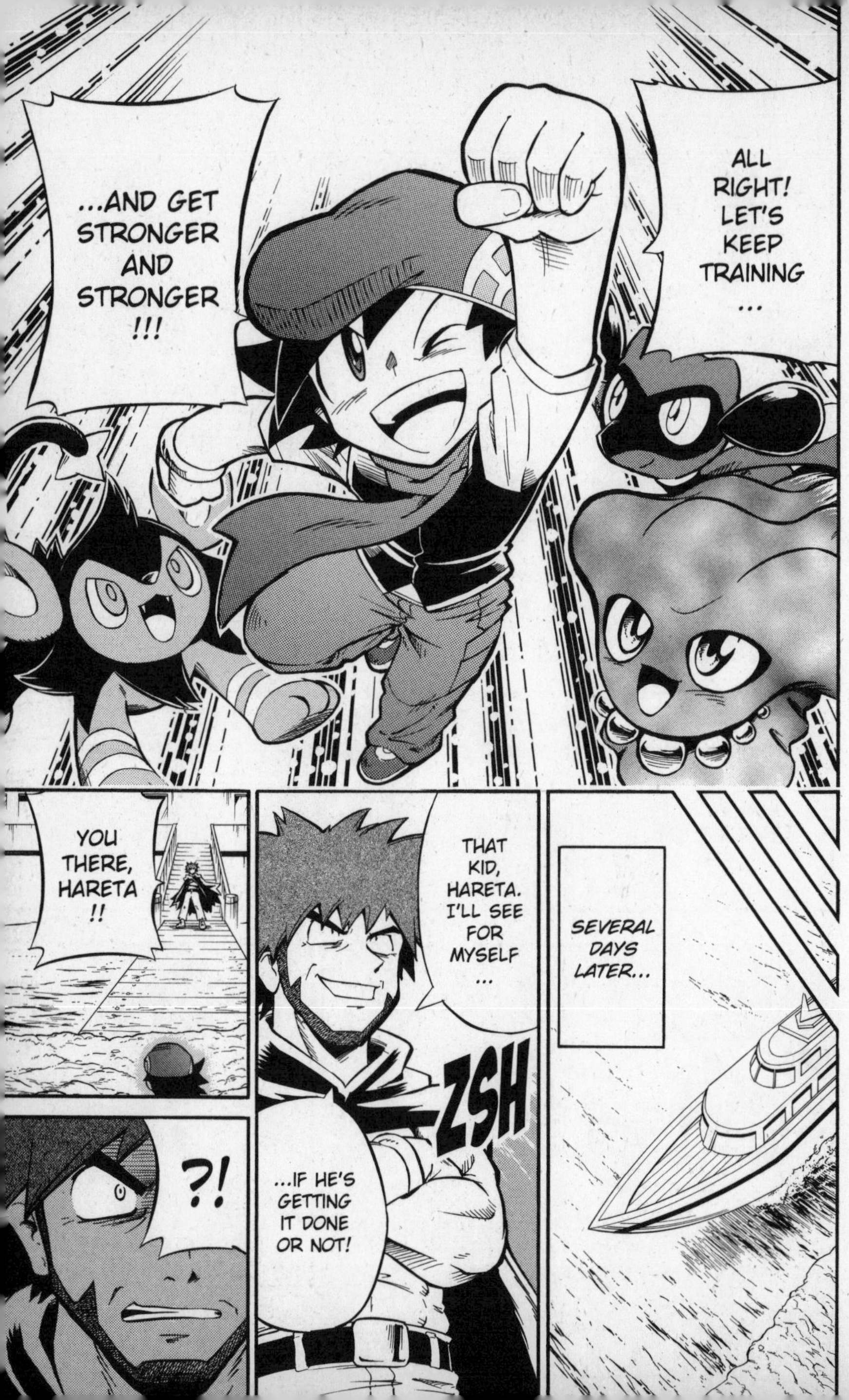
ALL RIGHT! LET'S KEEP TRAINING ...
...AND GET STRONGER AND STRONGER !!!
SEVERAL DAYS LATER...
THAT KID, HARETA. I'LL SEE FOR MYSELF ...
ZSH
...IF HE'S GETTING IT DONE OR NOT!
YOU THERE, HARETA !!
?!

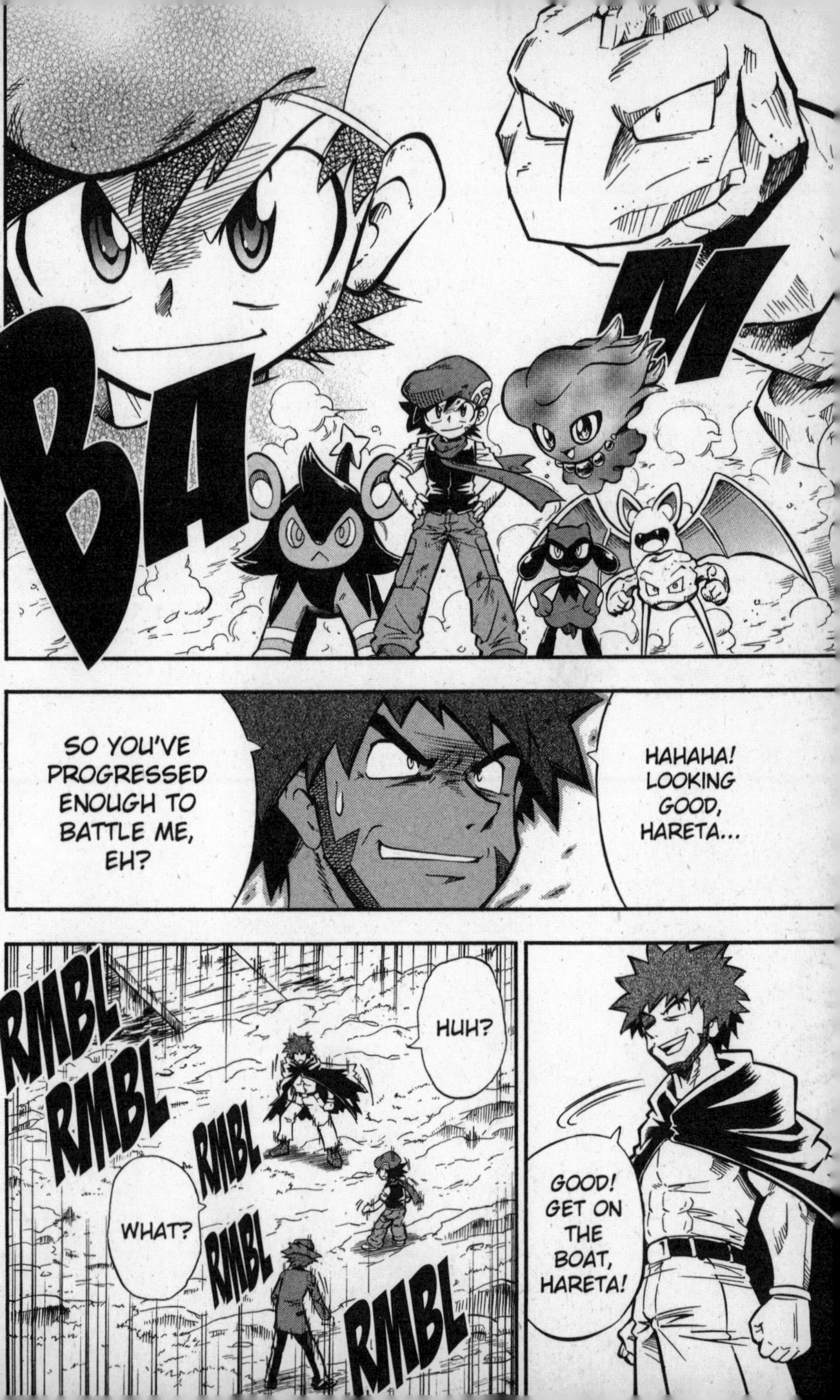
BAM
HAHAHA! LOOKING GOOD, HARETA...
SO YOU'VE PROGRESSED ENOUGH TO BATTLE ME, EH?
GOOD! GET ON THE BOAT, HARETA!
HUH?
RMBL RMBL
RMBL RMBL
WHAT?
RMBL

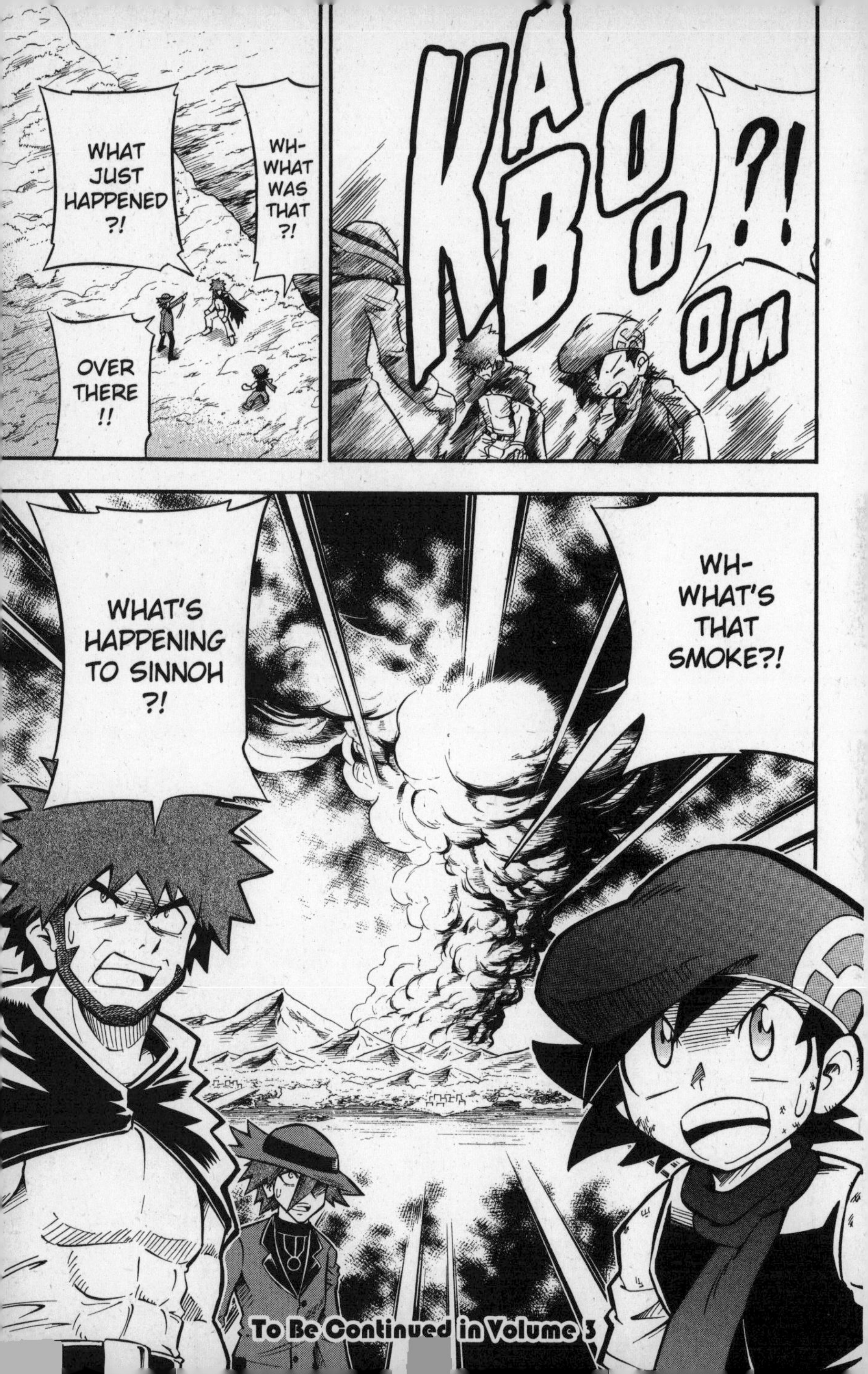
KABOOM
?!
WH-WHAT WAS THAT?!
WHAT JUST HAPPENED?!
OVER THERE!!
WH-WHAT'S THAT SMOKE?!
WHAT'S HAPPENING TO SINNOH?!
To Be Continued in Volume 3

WHEN
IS IT
MY
TURN
AGAIN
?

D·P SNAPSHOTS

PLEASE STOP CRYING!

PLANTING SEEDS

MITSUMI SOWS.

PIPLUP REAPS.

NAP TIME

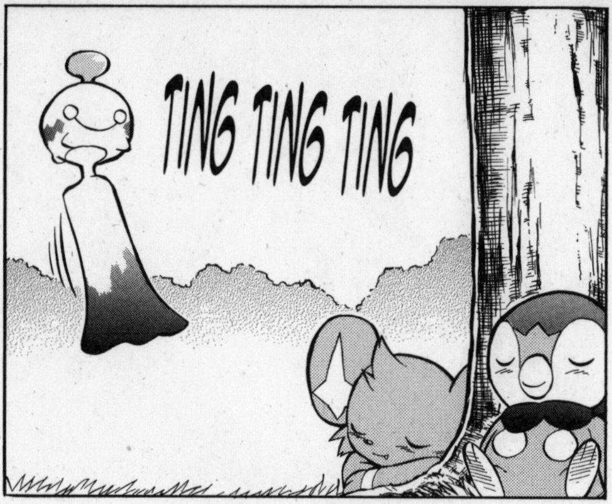
TING TING TING

SLEEP TIGHT.

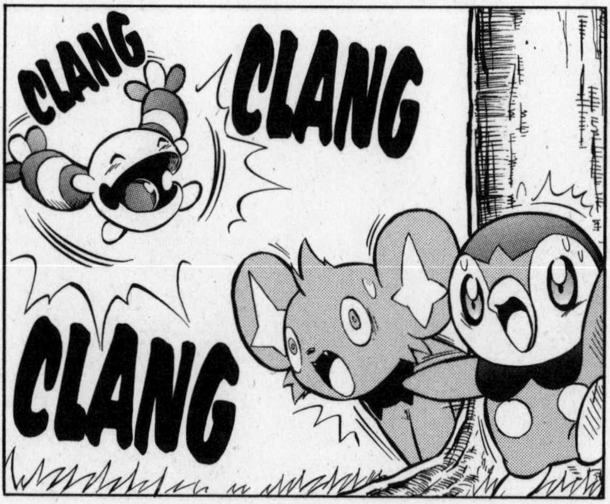
CLANG
CLANG
CLANG

WAKE UP!

SKYWARDS!

PIPLUP IN FLIGHT!

ACTUALLY...

In-the-Next-Volume

Cyrus, the brilliant and ruthless leader of Team Galactic, has set in motion his grand scheme to capture Dialga. Will his nefarious plans succeed? Not if Hareta has anything to say about it! And in his battle against Team Galactic he gains a major ally when he befriends a mysterious and amazing new Pokémon.

Available February 2009!